REUNION CRUISE

MARIA A. PALACE

This is a work of fiction. Names, characters, places, and incidents are products of the author's imagination or are used fictitiously and are not to be construed as real. Any resemblance to actual events, locations, organizations, or persons, living or dead, is entirely coincidental.

World Castle Publishing, LLC
Pensacola, Florida
Copyright © 2025 Maria A. Palace
Hardback ISBN: 9798265262974
Paperback ISBN: 9798891264717
eBook ISBN: 9798891264724
First Edition World Castle Publishing, LLC, December 9, 2025
http://www.worldcastlepublishing.com
Licensing Notes
Cover: Cover Designs by Karen
Editor: Karen Fuller

As the body catapulted over the ship's rail, the horn blew two resounding blasts, muffling any scream that might otherwise have been heard, before fading away into the abyss.

CHAPTER 1

On Sunday, August 30, 2015, after a whole day at sea, the *Dream Voyager* was nearing the end of a seven-day cruise to the island of Bermuda. In just a few hours, the ship would be making its final dock in the New York City Harbor.

It was in that darkness before the dawn that Agnes Haggerby woke up to a parched throat. The full moon shot a silvery ray through the porthole of the tiny economy cabin located on the ship's lower level. The beam was just enough to illuminate her path from the double bed to the mini-fridge on the opposite wall. Perhaps it was the power of the moon's gravitational pull, but the waves felt particularly rough tonight, causing the 78-year-old's feeble legs to become unsteady. Using her arms to guide her, she maneuvered her way to the icebox and pulled out a bottle of water. Carefully, she poured the cold liquid into an empty glass that was sitting on the adjacent credenza and set the open bottle down next to it. As she lifted the tumbler to her lips, the vibration of the waves crashing against the hull caused the plastic container to wobble and fall, streaming most of its contents onto the carpeted floor. *I hope we make it back all right,* she muttered to herself, making the sign of the cross. Fearing they could be in the middle of a storm, she set her glass back down to take a look outside. Using the cabinet for support, she inched her way toward the tiny encased window facing the ship's starboard side.

Measuring barely 5'2" in stature, she had to stand on her tiptoes in order to see out. Leaning up against the bulkhead, she pressed her nose up against the pane. She couldn't see all the way down to the ocean's surface, but she could see the horizon and what was the biggest, brightest moon she had ever laid eyes on. Little did she know that this was a full sturgeon moon or "supermoon," which happens only a few times a year. For a moment, she stood there transfixed by its striking luminescence, when all of a sudden, she spotted something out of the corner of her eye. As she jerked her head to the left, she observed what appeared to be an object falling from the sky, or more likely, from the upper part of the ship. Her pupils dilated to their maximum fullness when she realized this was not an object at all—but a human body.

In that instant, as the body disappeared from her view, the *Dream Voyager* sounded two thundering blasts from its powerful horn. The sound reverberated throughout the cabin, startling Agnes to her knees. Grabbing the edge of the credenza, she managed to pull herself back up. Her husband, Harvey, swaddled deep within the comfort of his bed, was apparently unfazed by the sound of her stumbling or even the horn's blast. All it did was cause him to flinch and whinny out a snort.

His wife plowed over to his side of the bed, grabbing him by the shoulders, and frantically began to shake him back and forth.

"Wake up, Harvey, wake up!" she yelled.

"Whaaat?" moaned Harvey, his eyes squeezed shut.

"I just saw a body falling from the sky!"

"Huh?"

"I mean, I think someone fell off our ship."

"You probably dreamt it, Agnes—all that worrying about your first time being on a cruise and all. Go back to sleep," he mumbled, scrunching up his pillow and rolling over to his opposite side.

"No, Harvey," persisted Agnes, her voice growing louder. "I had a parched throat, so I got out of bed to pour myself a glass of water, but the boat was rocking so much..." She pointed to the near-empty bottle rolling back and forth on the counter. "Look!" she shouted. "My water spilled all over the floor. I went over to look out the window to see if we were in the middle of a storm or something. That's when I saw it—a person, dropping straight down into the water!"

Harvey angled back around to face his wife, cracking open his lids. "Are you sure, Agnes?"

"Of course, I'm sure! It happened right when that deafening horn went off. How did you not hear it? It scared the bejesus out of me! That's when I fell."

Harvey rubbed his eyes. "You actually saw someone hit the water?"

"Well, no, not exactly, I couldn't see that far down. That little window is too high for me."

"Did you have your glasses on?"

"No, but it was really bright out. You know, on account of the full moon."

"It might have been a seagull or something."

"I think I know a human body when I see one, Harvey. I have to report it!"

Harvey lifted his torso up on his elbows and squinted. "What time is it?"

Agnes, whose vision had now adjusted to the darkness, located the light switch on the wall and flipped it on, temporarily blinding her husband. Then she walked over to her side of the bed to retrieve her bifocals, which were resting on the nightstand. Putting them on, she peered over at the alarm clock positioned next to the room phone. "It's 3:00 a.m., Harvey. Who should I call at this hour?"

"I don't know. Try calling the 24-hour help desk."

"How do I do that?"

"I'm pretty sure you just dial '1.'"

Holding the receiver close to her mouth, Agnes pressed the first white button on the square black telephone and let it ring until someone answered.

"Uh...hello, this is Agnes Haggerby from Room 103...Yes, guest level one. I want to report someone falling off the boat."

Harvey listened closely while his wife attempted to respond to a string of questions.

"A few minutes ago...From my window...I'm pretty sure it was a person...No, I couldn't tell if it was a man or a woman...I didn't actually see them go overboard...I couldn't tell how far above me it was, just that they were falling from mid-air...I couldn't hear anything except for that loud horn!"

A few minutes of discourse went by before Agnes hung up the receiver and said, "Harvey, put your robe on, someone is coming down to write up a report. She then scurried over to the bathroom. "I'd better get a towel to soak up some of that water on the carpet."

Ten minutes later, there was a knock on their door from one of the ship's officers. Another hour went by with an additional series of inquiries before the official had completed his written report. He thanked the couple and assured Mrs. Haggerby that their investigating personnel would begin a probe into the matter immediately.

"What are you going to do?" asked Agnes.

"Well, first we need to search for other possible eyewitnesses..."

"Are you going to wake everybody up?"

"No," said the officer. "Not the passengers. It's already four in the morning and we're preparing to dock in two hours, so there's no need to wake everyone up now."

"What happens after that?"

"I'll be conferring with the captain for his initial recommendations, and we'll proceed from there."

"What do you mean, *'proceed from there?'*"

"I don't think they need your step-by-step approval, Agnes," interrupted Harvey.

The officer cracked a smile and continued. "We'll be gathering statements from onboard personnel and anyone else who might have seen or heard something, as well as reviewing on-deck camera footage and collecting all viable evidence."

"Aren't you going to send out search boats?"

"If we have reason to believe someone actually went overboard — then yes."

"But I just told you, I saw someone fall off the ship!"

The officer glanced over at Harvey, who was grimacing, then back at Agnes. "During the disembarkation process, all passengers and ship personnel must be accounted for. If there is anyone who is unaccounted for, we will then take the appropriate measures."

"For God's sake, Agnes!" exclaimed Harvey. "I think they know what they're doing!"

Agnes gave the officer an unsettled look. "Does this happen often? I mean, people falling off cruise ships?"

"No, ma'am."

"So, what happens if you don't find the body?"

"Any further investigation of the matter will be referred to the FBI."

CHAPTER 2

Lithuanian women are considered to be among the most beautiful women in the world, and Margarita Kazlauskas was no exception. From the time she recognized herself in the mirror, it was evident that she liked what she saw. Her parents found her beauty to be both a blessing and a curse. While her father did his best to shelter his daughter from exploitation, her mother strove to bestow humility upon her only child by impressing upon her that beauty is only skin deep. As a result, Margarita's battle with her inner ego compelled her to solicit reassurance wherever she could find it. She discovered early on that with a little clever manipulation, she could extract the validation she so craved.

When Margarita was thirteen, her parents immigrated from Lithuania to the United States in search of a better life. With their meager savings, they moved to a small suburb on the outskirts of Cleveland, where they opened up a small fruit and vegetable market.

Even during that awkward teenage adolescence, Margarita was blessed with perfectly straight teeth and unblemished skin. In addition, she was mature beyond her years, both physically and mentally. Physically, because she had the proper measure of curves forming in all the right places, and mentally, because her innate Machiavellian instinct had just about reached its peak.

Any trepidation Margarita might have had on her first day of orientation at Ellison Junior High School was held at bay. She strutted into the packed gymnasium in her little plaid miniskirt with a crooked smile lingering over her delicate jaw, fully aware of the whooping young hounds trailing behind her.

Taking a quick inventory of the seating situation, she began to climb up over the bleacher seats, bypassing the cliques of girls enviously scrutinizing her every move. She scoped out a single space between two plain, non-threatening-looking females in one of the middle rows, and plopped down between them — much to the disappointment of the boys that had been following her, who were forced to scatter and find seats elsewhere.

Margarita, who lacked any reason for inhibition, promptly turned to each girl beside her and introduced herself. "Hi, I'm Margarita," she said, exuding a big, confident smile.

The scrawny, petite girl in a pixie cut to her left, nodded her head and let out a faint, "Hey. I'm Dana."

The other girl on her right, with a red headband holding her shoulder-length brown hair in place, reciprocated with a huge grin of her own. "Hi! I'm Rachel," she said exuberantly, sticking out her hand to offer up a hearty handshake. "I've never seen you before. Are you new around here?"

"Yes. I moved to the United States with my parents this summer."

"Where are you from? You've got like a Russian accent or something. Like those girls in the James Bond movies."

"I am from Lithuania."

Dana eyeballed the new girl suspiciously. "How did you learn to speak English so good?"

"Back in Lithuania, in school, we are required to learn English as a second language."

"So, how is living in America different from living in Lithuania?" asked Rachel. Margarita cocked her head, glancing up at the boys in the upper bleachers still trying to get her attention, and flashed them a teasing smile. "Other than the language, it is pretty much the same."

"Well, if you want to fit in, you're going to have to shorten your name," remarked Dana. "Margarita is *way* too hard to say.

Maybe, Margaret or something."

"Or *Margot*," exclaimed Rachel, excitedly. "That makes you sound like a movie star."

Margarita tilted her head and thought for a moment. "Hmm....I like the sound of that. Yes. From now on, I am Margot!"

From that day forward, the three *draugas* (which is the Lithuanian word for friends) were inseparable, forming a bond that continued throughout high school.

Dana admired Margot's confidence, and Margot, who overflowed with volcanic emotion, was drawn to Dana's aloofness and sarcastic wit.

Rachel, on the other hand, was an ingénue who could see no evil, hear no evil, and speak no evil. She felt she could learn a lot from someone as worldly as Margot, and Margot appreciated Rachel's innocence (mostly because she could easily be taken advantage of).

Between Rachel's naiveté, Dana's cynicism, and Margot's moxie, they made a good team.

Most of the other girls did not like Margot, either because they were jealous of her good looks or because of her unabashed conceit. So, the three draugas would carve their path through the crowded halls of Ellison Junior High as if no one else mattered. By design, Margot was always in the center, whipping her waist-length, raven black hair from side to side, like the shining star that she was, leaving her trail of light.

On her right, Dana would sidle alongside her with the moxie of a bodyguard. What she lacked in height, she made up for in attitude. The fact of the matter being that Dana was content merely to be allowed in Margot's perimeter.

And to Margot's left was Rachel, who scampered along trying to keep up, while secretly enjoying the convoy of pubescent male admirers following behind.

CHAPTER 3

Behind the tiny storefront sandwiched between a row of dingy brick buildings, Margot found a minor source of reprieve in the rear corner of her father's market. It was mid-June, and Cleveland was experiencing record-breaking heat. Overwhelmed by the smell of fermenting produce, she slouched with her hands resting over her bloated abdomen, trying to overcome her nausea, before an unsteady fan that she had erected atop a spindly wooden chair. The sweltering, recycled air did little to soothe her, compounded by the rickety blades that rattled unrelentingly as though she were being reprimanded.

Summer vacation had only just begun. She should be hanging out with friends, escaping to the beach, or air-conditioned movie theaters. But no. Not her. She was going to be thermally sequestered in the confines of her parents' fruit and vegetable market all summer long, working each and every day, from eight in the morning until five in the evening. As if that weren't bad enough, afterwards she would have to go upstairs to their cramped, two-bedroom apartment above the storefront and get dinner started. Her mom and dad would stay late to wrap things up and shut down the store, and never came up before 6:30 p.m.

Margot moved in closer to the fan, allowing the undulating waves to ripple through her pleated cotton skirt, exposing the peaks of her thighs. As she bent forward, the breeze hit her face, causing a cool sweat to trickle down her forehead. She began to feel a little sense of relief. But this would not last long, for she knew she had to get back to work soon, lest her parents become suspicious.

Slowly, she backed away from the ventilation and grabbed the handle of the paint-blistered broom resting against the wall. Carefully, she bent down to pick up the dust pan laying on the cracked cement floor and proceeded to scoop up the dirt that she had previously swept into a mound. Then she carried it over to the metal garbage can, which was holding open the back door, and dumped the debris in.

Margot sluggishly resumed her sweeping, but had a hard time concentrating on the task at hand. She would have preferred to be in school rather than working here. At least, school provided a social outlet. Though she hated studying and did only the bare minimum to get by—except for math. She excelled in math. Working with numbers seemed to come naturally to her.

Her mind wandered back to the last semester of her sophomore year. Her thoughts took her to a homework assignment she had turned in for her social studies class. The students had been instructed to pick any major city in the United States and write an informative article about it. Not wanting to put too much thought into it, she arbitrarily chose New York because it was the only city she could think of outside of Cleveland. It took only one trip to the local library to find a plethora of information about the city, which was good, because she hadn't intended to spend too much time on the subject. The funny thing was, by the time she had finished doing her research, she had made up her mind that one way or another, she would find her way to "The Big Apple." *It's where people go to find their fortunes. It's where people go to become somebody,* she thought, while visions of Times Square with its flashing neon lights and giant billboards clouded her brain.

That fog was harshly lifted when the sound of her father's voice resonated from the front of the store.

"Margarita! Come take these empty boxes out to the garbage!"

She couldn't bear to abandon her daydream of strolling through Central Park, attending Broadway plays, and shopping along Fifth Avenue, and tried to ignore his call. Her name rose from the rafters once again, ricocheting into her ears.

"Margarita!" he shouted.

"Coming, Papa!" she yelled back, leaning the worn-out broom against the cinder-block wall. Wiping the sweat off her forehead, she dried her hands on her knit shirt, then stretched it out in the front as far as possible. While making her way toward the entrance, she stopped at the counter where her mother was working. "Why can't I work the cash register?" she asked, knowing it would save her from constantly bending and lifting. "You know I'm good at counting money."

"I told you — next year," answered her mother. "You are still too young."

"What do you mean, 'too young?' I'm sixteen!"

"Do not question me. Right now, your job is to clean up. Go help your father. He is calling you."

Margot made it to the front of the store where her father was busy unloading produce from cardboard crates and laying it out on the display table.

"It is about time, Margarita. Where have you been?"

"I was in the back."

"I think you were hiding again — to get out of doing your duties."

"If I was hiding, Papa, it was in plain sight. All you had to do is look. And I told you to call me *Margot* from now on!"

"Margot, Shmargo. You will always be Margarita to me. Now take those empty boxes out to the bins."

Margot wrinkled her nose at the pile of large, heavy boxes stacked next to him and grumbled, "You said America was the land of opportunity. You and Mama work so hard day in and day out. And for what? We have no more here than we did in

Lithuania."

"Not everything is handed to you on a silver platter — even in America. You must work hard to create your opportunity."

"Yeah, well, I don't want to work that hard. How did we end up in Ohio anyway? Why didn't we move to New York? Now, that's the place of opportunity. I know, because I read all about it."

"Dear daughter, do not be seduced by the inflated dreams that a big city like New York promises. There is always a price to pay. No one receives anything for free."

"Well, we'll see about that," retorted Margot, stooping over to pick up as many of the corrugated containers she could carry. With an armful of cardboard obstructing her view, she channeled her way to the back entrance, kicked open the dented screen, and blindly crossed the alleyway to the tall green bin. After launching the boxes in, one by one, she turned her hands over to examine her sooty palms and wiped them clean against the sides of her skirt.

Just as she turned to go back inside, she was suddenly startled when a gaunt-looking juvenile in a white, short-sleeved T-shirt and oversized jeans jumped out from behind the bin and grabbed her by the waist.

"Dammit, Remy," she yelled, smacking him in the chest. "You scared the hell outta me!"

"I thought I'd surprise you," he laughed, sweeping his dark, oily bangs off to the side.

"I didn't expect you till I got off work. You know I'm stuck here till five."

"Yeah, but I couldn't wait that long to see you," he groaned, propelling her back against the garbage bin. And with one hand behind her neck, he leaned up against her and forced his tongue into her mouth while his other hand was reaching up under her skirt.

Instantly, she freed her arms and forcefully pushed him off.

"What's the matter?" he sneered cockily. "I thought you liked that."

"I'm not in the mood," said Margot, turning her head to look the other way.

Remy pulled her chin toward him and stared into her sunken eyes. "You don't look so good. Are you feelin' alright?"

"I'm fine," she asserted and held out her hand. "I just need a cigarette. Gimmee one."

Remy smirked. "You never give it up without somethin' in return, do ya, babe?"

He reached into the back pocket of his low-riding pants and pulled out a pack of Marlboro Menthols and a near-empty book of matches. After removing one of the cigarettes, he stuck it in his mouth to light it and threw the match to the ground. Then, he took one long drag of the cigarette before sliding it between his girlfriend's pale, pouty lips.

"There. All better?"

Margot bent her right knee and rested the bottom of her foot against the tall rusty container. Arching her neck back, she stared up into the sky while taking her first puff and proceeded to blow a perfectly round smoke ring into the air. She paused for a minute before taking a second drag, only to say, "Two more years of school and then I can get outta this hell hole."

"Oh yeah?" said Remy. "And where d'ya think you're going?"

Margot blew another smoke ring before answering and watched as it rose up into the atmosphere until it slowly evaporated, leaving a faint trail behind.

"I'll tell you where I'm going," she responded. "Someplace where I don't have to spend the rest of my life taking out trash and sweeping floors. A place where I can afford to have other people do it for me."

"And where you gonna find that fairy tale land, Princess?"

"...New York."

CHAPTER 4

The Graduating Class of 2000 led Margot and her friends to go their separate ways, although they promised to always stay in touch.

Dana earned a scholarship and went on to attend Ohio State University to study computer science. The enormity of the campus overwhelmed her, and being the loner that she was, she disappeared into the herd, never forming any meaningful relationships throughout her college life.

Rachel's ambition from childhood was to get married immediately after graduation and raise a family. Her dream arrived earlier than expected when her naivety landed her pregnant, and she was forced to quit school before the end of her senior year. As happy as she was to be carrying her high school sweetheart's baby, her prospect of becoming a mom was soon extinguished when, in her second trimester, she suffered a miscarriage.

If there was a silver lining to the story, it was that she was able to return to school right away and get her GED. Still aggrieved over her miscarriage and intent on learning everything she could to improve her health so as to ensure it would never happen again, she applied for a nutritional and home healthcare course at her local community college. That's when she made the decision to become a nurse. As she continued to pursue her nursing degree, she also found part-time employment at the local drug store. All the while, her equally dedicated teen spouse (who loved her as much as she loved him) worked seven days a week, from sunup till sundown, as a gas station mechanic in order to make ends meet. Money was scarce, so the two of them lived with her parents until they were able to afford a tiny, two-bedroom bungalow in the same neighborhood. Rachel had insisted on two bedrooms, with the idea of dedicating one as a nursery, because it was her intention to get pregnant again as soon as possible.

Margot never wavered from her dream of going to New York. Unfortunately, it took a little longer than she had hoped. Another year went by working in her parents' store before she had earned enough money for a one-way train ticket, as well as a little extra to tide her over until she could find a place to live.

And then, the unfathomable happened. On September 11, 2001, terrorists flew two planes into the famed World Trade Center, causing the Twin Towers to collapse. New York was in a state of catastrophe.

Her parents, who never wanted her to go in the first place, begged her to wait another year for the city to regain some sense of normalcy. By that time, Margot was 20 years old and itching to leave.

Through the advice of a former school counselor, she pre-arranged to stay at the YWCA in Manhattan's Upper West Side for a while. The accommodations were decent, except for the communal bathroom and having to share a room with three other women. Her consolation was in knowing that it was only temporary. The YWCA had a career staff to help her find work, and almost immediately, they paired her up with a temp agency that provided her with short-term clerical job assignments.

Things had undoubtedly changed since the September 11 attack, but she still loved to stroll along Fifth Avenue, just as she had envisioned, stopping in front of exclusive clothing boutiques to study the mannequins in the window. She'd picture herself wearing the same Burberry dress wrapped in silk Gucci scarves and carrying a Hermes alligator-skin bag. She remained stringent in her belief that the day would come when she could afford to shop in those stores. For the time being, however, she would have to wander off the beaten path to find bargains at the local thrift shops and second-hand clothing stores that were scattered throughout the city. To her advantage, she had a model figure and an eye for style, so no matter what she put on, she always looked as though she had just stepped off the runway.

In her final year of high school, Margot's parents had finally allowed her the opportunity to man the cash register at their market. It was the one aspect of the job that she didn't mind doing. It gave her a sense of empowerment. She especially loved the feel of crisp new bills between her fingers. She had a head for numbers, and counting money came easily to her. Because of that experience, she was able to land a month-long assignment as a teller for a credit union in Brooklyn.

That's when she met Doris Mulvaney. Doris was working in the loan department of the same credit union. Spurred on by Margot's bubbly personality, the two soon became friends. Every day, they sat in the back lunchroom together, eating their bagged lunches. Margot, because she could not afford to go out, and Doris, because she was too cheap to buy lunch. Except for Fridays. That's when they'd both splurge and go out for fast food.

Doris was living in a two-bedroom apartment in Brooklyn. Her roommate had just moved out, so she was looking for a replacement to help with the rent. Margot could not stay at the YWCA much longer, and the subway ride from Manhattan's Upper West Side to Brooklyn took a good thirty-five minutes, so she jumped at the chance. "As long as you're not allergic to cats," warned Doris. "That's why my last roommate had to leave."

It didn't take long for Margot to learn that you really don't know someone until you've lived with them. She knew that Doris's personality leaned toward the side of pessimism, but until then, she had no idea just how much. It turned out that they were as different as night and day. Margot always tended to see the glass as half-full while Doris invariably viewed it as near-empty. Whether acquired or inborn, even the cat which Doris had adopted from the pound had the same disposition as its owner. It was a disagreeable creature that wanted nothing to do with people. It had accepted its fate for two reasons: (1) shelter, and (2) food. When anyone new walked in the door, it would hiss and bat at their ankles with its needle-sharp claws until Doris scolded it. Eventually, it backed away, but not without one last fang-exposed snarl.

Nonetheless, the two women got along just enough to use each other to their own personal advantage. Margot would drag Doris to the clubs on weekends, and Doris would begrudgingly tag along in the hopes that she might fulfill her one goal in life. That was to find a husband. The problem was that Doris's cynical demeanor alienated most of the men she'd meet. Outwardly, Doris was reasonably attractive. She was 5'5" with auburn brown hair that curved naturally below her jawbone. And though slightly overweight, she had a pleasing womanly figure.

The thing that bothered Margot the most, though, was the way in which Doris looked at her — as if she hated her, yet wanted to be her. Doris sometimes tried to screen it with a smile, but Margot could still see the daggers shooting from her pupils.

So Margot put up with it because she could not afford to live on her own, and she did not want to go back home.

Likewise, Doris tolerated Margot. She'd grow extremely jealous whenever the two of them went out because Margot's good looks and flirtatious banter always landed her the guy. Many a night, Margot would exit an establishment arm-in-arm with a newfound lover, leaving Doris to fend for herself. There was the off-occasion when Doris benefited from her friend's alliance, when Margot's leftovers fell into her lap, resulting in a date or two.

So Doris put up with it—because she liked the extra rent money and she didn't mind the leftovers.

CHAPTER 5

Margot was slowly becoming disillusioned. New York was not panning out as she had expected. She and Doris had been living together for almost four years now, and she had yet to see a way out. She wanted to move but didn't make enough money to afford her own place. The good news was that there was no shortage of men to keep her occupied. When she grew tired of them, she'd throw them out like a worn slipper and move on to the next. She wasn't looking for commitment, just someone to help pay the rent. The only problem was that she had yet to meet someone who could fulfill her high expectations.

That's when the Temp-Right Staffing Agency, with whom Margot was contracted with, gave her a call. They told her that the architectural firm of Dillon, McCain & Dermot was looking for someone to fill in for their receptionist who was going on maternity leave, and asked if she would be interested in interviewing for the position. The agency coordinator impressed upon the fact that it was one of the most prestigious architectural firms in New York, and had already interviewed several candidates, so she'd have to put her best foot forward if she expected to have a chance at landing the job. Margot wasn't thrilled with the fact that it was merely a receptionist position, but it did pay well. Plus, it might give her an opportunity to rub elbows with the class of people she was seeking out. So she said yes.

Since she still could not afford a computer of her own, she went to the local library to access their computer system to prepare for the interview. She wanted to find out all she could about this "prestigious" company. What she learned was that they were one of the oldest architectural firms in New York City and that they employed over one hundred local architects and ninety-five worldwide architects. They even housed their own legal team. Margot was not easily intimidated, but the more she read, the more anxious she became. In addition to the credit union, her former assignments had included a non-profit agency, a copy center, two real estate offices, and a couple of small manufacturing companies. Nothing of this magnitude.

She decided she had better take the Agency's advice and dress as professionally as possible for the interview. She left the library and jumped on the subway train that would take her to Herald Square. When she arrived, she headed straight over to Macy's and took the escalator up to the women's suits and separates department, making a beeline for the clearance rack. After an hour of skimming through multiple racks, she found the perfect suit ensemble in a light gray. It was simple, yet sophisticated, and included a satiny rose blouse with a sash that tied around the neckline, which softened its formality.

The evening before her appointment, she made sure to set her alarm so she'd have plenty of time to get ready and arrive fifteen minutes early.

The next morning, she hustled out of the subway and hiked for three excruciating blocks in her too-tight pumps along an endless avenue of prominent office buildings until she finally reached her destination. Pushing her way through the massive revolving glass door, she found herself in a marble-lined lobby surrounded by cloned stiffs sprinting about in dark suits with briefcases locked in their grasp. Margot navigated her way toward the monumental column in the center of the lobby that displayed a bronze plaque engraved with a directory of all the businesses located in the building. As she approached the plate, she slowly ran her finger down the list until it landed on the name she was looking for:

Dillon, McCain & Dermot, LLP architects — Floors 15-20

After a quick survey of her surroundings, she spotted a hallway up ahead with a row of antique gold-plated elevators facing one another. There, she waited patiently until one of the arrows flashed red and parted its opulent doors to grant access to its illustrious portal. The moment she stepped into the golden mirrored chamber, she was transfixed by her glimmering reflection, and as it began its ascent, she was struck with a fleeting sensation. This was not an ordinary ride. This was the vehicle that would transport her to her ultimate destination.

When the 15th floor button illuminated, Margot exited the elevator and crossed the hall to a pair of oversized beveled-glass doors. As she entered the gleaming white reception area, her heart gave a flutter. The ceilings soared higher than she had ever seen, and off to the right, there was a grand circular stairway leading to a second floor with three additional golden-hued elevators overlooking the atrium.

What really gave her pause was the massive reception desk in the center of the room. It was elevated at least two feet from the floor, requiring a set of steps to get up there. Behind its sparkling, black marble counter was a curved, maybe ten-foot-high, mahogany wall with the firm's name inscribed in big gold letters. The corners of Margot's lips couldn't help but crease upward. *Is that where I'm going to be sitting if I get the job?*

As she approached the desk to announce her arrival, she noticed that hidden behind the mahogany barrier was a long hallway of offices separated by rows of Plexiglas walls.

"May I help you?" asked the attractive young woman seated on the pedestal.

"My name is Margarita Kazlauskas. I've been sent by the Temp-Right Agency. I'm here for an interview."

The receptionist looked Margot up and down and landed her a decided smile. "Yes. Have a seat. I'll let Ms. Simmons know you're here."

Margot made her way to the smooth, white cowhide sofa with large black and brown splotches facing the desk and sat down. While she waited for Ms. Simmons to appear, she envisioned herself sitting up there on her "throne," bestowed with the authority to allow or deny entry to those sacred corridors or high above those hallowed stairs to the anxious patrons awaiting their fate. *They would first, however, have to prove their merit,* Margot snickered to herself, *either in looks or net worth.*

No sooner did her daydream deflate when a forty-something woman in a brown tweed suit came over to greet her. The woman in the tightly-wound bun and dark-rimmed glasses formally stuck out her hand and introduced herself.

"Hello, Ms. Kazlauskas, is it? I'm Rhea Simmons, the office manager. I'll be conducting your interview."

Margot followed Ms. Simmons around the mahogany partition through the hallway of transparent suites until they reached her office.

During the interview, Margot put her best self forward, inflating her skills, just as she had practiced, then she waited for ten minutes while Ms. Simmons left the room. When the office manager returned, she had some papers in her hand. "I'd like to offer you the position of head receptionist if you're still interested, Ms. Kazlauskas."

Margot kept her cool. "Yes, I'm still interested."

"I normally don't hire applicants on the spot," said Ms. Simmons. "But when the right candidate comes in, I can sense it immediately. I've worked here long enough to know what the partners want. Ability is important, but presence and demeanor are equally essential. The receptionist position is representative of the company and what it stands for: style and integrity. You are the first person people come into contact with when they walk through those doors. Do you have any questions?"

"No," said Margot, undaunted. *You think I don't know I got this job because of my looks?* After signing all the appropriate documents, Ms. Simmons walked her new employee through the hallway, pointing out the different offices and who they belonged to, as well as the entirety of the main floor, including conference rooms, break rooms, copy rooms, etc., acquainting her with the layout of the company.

From there, Margot followed her up the curved staircase leading to the second level, which was fronted by the three elevators. The office manager explained that the next five floors were part of the architectural firm and were inaccessible from the main lobby elevators. "This first elevator takes you to floors 16, 17, and 18, which contain our engineering and design offices. The middle elevator takes you to the 19th floor, where the legal department is staffed, and finally, the third elevator takes you to the highest floor—the 20th floor. That's where the partners, Dillon, McCain & Dermot's offices are located, as well as the boardroom. We'll go there last."

Ms. Simmons retrieved the first elevator, which carried them up to the architecture and engineering floors. While there, Margot was given a hurried tour of the offices situated behind Plexiglas walls, similar to those on the main level, intermittently stopping for a quick introduction. She met so many people, she wondered how on earth she would ever remember their names, particularly since they all tended to look alike: short-haired males in stiff white shirts and skinny ties.

At long last, they approached an office where there was a woman in a burgundy suit sitting at the desk. She was an attractive blond, maybe in her late 30s. She was staring into her computer, and standing over her shoulder was an equally attractive and similar in age, dark-haired male in a navy blue suit. Before opening the door, Ms. Simmons gave a short knock on the glass partition, causing them to both look up. "Charles,

Bethany, I want to introduce you to Margarita Kazlauskas. She'll be taking over the reception desk while Jennifer is on maternity leave."

Margot flashed a confident smile and gave a short wave. "Um, you can call me Margot."

"This is Bethany and Charles Langford," continued Ms. Simmons. "Bethany is an architect and a rising star here at Dillon, McCain. And this is her husband, Charles. He's one of our in-house counselors."

Mrs. Langford smiled and said, "Hello," while her husband barely acknowledged her, quickly lowering his head back to the computer screen. Margot figured they must have been pretty preoccupied with the task at hand because neither of them made any further attempt at dialogue.

From there, Margot followed Ms. Simmons up another staircase, a floor above the architectural and engineering offices, which displayed a panorama of to-scale model replicas of completed works and works-in-progress, including towering office buildings, apartments, malls, and even a stadium.

After exhausting all three floors of the design and planning division, they headed up to the legal department, which occupied the entire 19th floor. Unlike the engineering quarters, these offices were privatized behind engraved, solid oak doors. At that point, it became clear that Ms. Simmons was in a hurry to get the tour over with because she rushed Margot through the halls, introducing her to a small handful of attorneys and legal assistants they happened to run into along the way.

Their final stop was, of course, the 20th floor. Or as Margot viewed it, *the floor where the Gods resided*. Each partner had a corner office with floor-to-ceiling glass walls overlooking the New York cityscape. Margot had the opportunity to meet just one of the partners, Alan Dermot, since he was the only one in at the time. She had no idea how old Dillon and McCain were, but Mr.

Dermot was much younger than she had expected a partner to be. He presented himself in a formal yet genial manner, standing up and stretching his hand over his desk to welcome her to the firm, before sitting back down and returning to his business.

When the tour was over, Margot spent the next few hours with the very pregnant, current receptionist, Jennifer, who explained the phone system and the preferred nuances of the partners and various other employees of the firm.

By the time Margot's orientation was over, it was almost three in the afternoon. Walking out of the building, her mind was in such a whirl that it took her a while to realize how much her feet were hurting. *I've got to wear more comfortable shoes next time.* She was excited to have gotten the job, but overwhelmed by the pompousness of the enterprise. Everyone was "dressed for success" and walked around with their noses in the air as though they were in competition with one another. *I can play that game too,* she thought. Unfortunately, her current wardrobe wasn't up to par for that kind of competition. The conventional two-piece gray suit she purchased at Macy's had served her well for the interview, but she was going to be on that pedestal "representing" the company, so she was going to have to up her game.

Instead of hopping on the subway headed for Brooklyn, she changed her course and began making her way (albeit reluctantly) to her favorite boutique. It was a second-hand store that specialized in gently-used clothes by only the top designers. Even though they were half the cost, they were still over her budget. She had been trying to save her money for a laptop computer, but since she was going to be making a good salary (much more than she ever had before), she made the decision to go ahead and splurge.

After filtering through row upon row of exclusive labels, her arms had accumulated a stack of interchangeable separates and blouses to try on. As she was heading to the changing room, one more thing caught her eye, something that had been left fanned over one of the racks. The price tag was pricier than the other outfits she had picked out, but it looked as though it had never been worn before. It was so stunning, she had to try it on.

It was a two-piece beige suit spun from raw silk and came with an embroidered satin camisole. When she slipped it on, it fit like a glove, as if it had been made especially for her. It made her feel so sexy that she felt compelled to find a purse and shoes to go along with it. She found a matching pair of pointy-toed, spike heels and a sleek, oversized patent-leather bag that was big enough to hold an extra set of shoes and even an extra set of clothes (if needed). It was more of a fancy valise than a purse — perfect for the office. This outfit, she thought, would have to be saved for a special occasion.

Margot left the shop both nervous and euphoric, overflowing with tote bags and maxed out in credit.

When Monday morning came, Margot showed up half an hour early, looking smart in one of her new outfits. People started arriving around 8:30 a.m. and continued to trickle in until about 9:00 a.m., which was when the power couple, Bethany and Charles, strolled in, side-by-side.

"Hi, Mr. and Mrs. Langford," greeted Margot. She specifically recalled their names because of the fact that they were the only married couple in the firm.

Once again, Bethany was the only one to respond. "Hi Margot. Ready for your first day?"

"I guess so. I just hope I can remember everyone's name. This company is so huge."

"Don't worry, you'll catch on, and you can begin by calling me Bethany."

"Thanks, Bethany."

Charles Langford had already begun making his way up the staircase. *What a pompous ass*, thought Margot. *He couldn't even say 'hi.'*

The day flew by and was fast coming to a close. Margot was wrapping things up when Mr. and Mrs. Langford stopped by her desk with their briefcases in hand.

"Any messages?" asked Bethany.

"Only one for Mr. Langford," said Margot, sticking her arm out to hand him a pink 'While you were away' slip.

He grabbed the note from her hand. Again, without as much as a word.

"We have to leave a little early today — dinner reservations," said Bethany. "In this town, it's hard to get reservations in the good restaurants, so you'd better show up on time or they'll give your table away. By the way, how was your first day?"

"Good," said Margot. "A few minor issues with the computer, but nothing that couldn't be rectified."

Charles Langford remained stone-faced while pretending to still be reading his message.

I wonder if all lawyers are like that, thought Margot. *Or if it's just him.*

The next morning, the dynamic duo walked in together again. Bethany went up to her office, but Mr. Langford lingered behind, flipping through an Architectural Digest magazine he picked up off the table in the waiting room. He threw it back down and glanced up at Margot for a brief moment. "I've got a ten o'clock appointment with Jordan Hughes. He's been here before, so when he arrives, just send him up to my office," he said, as he headed toward the circular stairway.

"Yes, Mr. Langford," Margot acknowledged respectfully. *Jerk.*

At noon, Bethany stopped by Margot's desk to let her know she wouldn't be back to the office for the remainder of the day. "Before you go," said Margot, "I have one more message-it's from a Mr. Burton Magnuson. He said he'd like you to call him first thing tomorrow morning."

Bethany stared at the pink, handwritten note and blurted out, "When did he call?"

"Just a few minutes ago. I tried buzzing you, but you must have been on your way down to the lobby."

"You should have put him on hold and tried to find me," Bethany said sternly. Then she lifted her eyes back up to Margot. "We should have lunch soon. I need to fill you in on who's who and why some people take precedence over others."

CHAPTER 6

At the end of the day, Margot gathered up her things and exited the heavy glass doors of Dillon, McCain & Dermot to join the group of people waiting for the elevator. Once it arrived, everyone filed in, and just as the door was about to close, someone ran up to stop it. As the door opened back up, the person standing there was none other than Charles Langford. His eyes immediately caught Margot's, yet he remained tight-lipped while he inched his way into the crowd, parking his backside directly in front of her.

As the elevator was descending, Margot's temperature was rising. Two weeks had passed since she started working there, and he still hadn't had the decency to even acknowledge her. When they reached the first floor, the door opened and he scampered out as fast as he could, lest he'd be forced to say "hello." He was halfway through the lobby when Margot couldn't stand it any longer. This was personal. She'd never been ignored like this before. She had to say something, even though it could potentially cost her her job.

Sprinting as fast as she could in her high heels, she soon surpassed him, then stopped abruptly and turned around, halting him in his tracks and causing him to come face-to-face with her. Then, she looked him straight in the eyes and said, "Do you have a problem with me?"

Startled, all he could come up to say was, "What?"

"The least you could do is say, 'hello' when you come in in the morning. Even the partners, Dillon, McCain & Dermot, say 'hello.' You can't even bear to crack a smile."

Langford turned three shades of red and squeezed his lips together so tightly that Margot couldn't tell if he was going to try to get around her or hit her, but she was not about to budge until he apologized.

He did in fact attempt to steer around her, while countering with, "Who do you think you are talking to me like that? I don't have to answer to you."

The audacity! Margot jumped back in front of him, shouting, "You may be a big-time lawyer, but that doesn't make you better than me!"

An embarrassed Langford's neck muscles tensed up while he twisted his head around to see if anyone had witnessed the exchange. "I just don't want to give rise to any suspicion of..."

"Of what?" interrupted Margot.

Again, Langford glanced from left to right to make sure no one he knew was in earshot, and in a hushed voice, mumbled, "My wife and I both work in the same building, for the same company. You know how gossip can run rampant if there's even a hint of impropriety."

"Impropriety! What impropriety?" asked Margot, raising her voice indignantly.

Langford took hold of her elbow, moving in closer to whisper in her ear. "As I'm sure you are well aware, you are a very beautiful woman. If I were to merely smile at you, someone might read something into it. I just don't want to give my wife any reason to be jealous."

Margot swatted his hand off her elbow and churned out a laugh. "Trust me, she has no reason to be jealous," and pointedly looking him in the eyes, added, "You're not my type anyway."

Charles appeared shocked at her response. "Oh really? And what is your type?"

"Someone who's not afraid to be themselves, for one thing."

An uncomfortable pause followed before Charles lifted his fist to loosen the knot in his tie.

Margot felt adequately vindicated, but had to add one more comment for good measure, "Rest assured, Mr. Langford, I won't be bothering you again."

As she turned to leave, he suddenly grabbed her arm once more. "Look, Miss Kauzlaskas..." The creases in his forehead began to diminish as two words spilled out of his mouth, "I'm sorry."

Margot raised her eyebrows, almost shocked by his apology. "Are you *really*, Mr. Langford?"

"Yes. Let me make it up to you. Would you like to share a cab ride home? Oh...and you can call me Charles."

CHAPTER 7

The following week, Bethany Langford invited Margot to have lunch with her. She suggested a popular eatery that catered to young professionals and was within walking distance of work. "The service is fast and efficient, *and* they have a liquor license," she touted.

No sooner had the ladies sat down than a waitress, who addressed Bethany as "Mrs. Langford," came by to take their drink orders. Bethany immediately ordered a glass of Chardonnay. When the waitress asked her guest, who was still eying the drink selections, what she'd like, Margot was reluctant to order. She felt like she was still on "probation" with the firm and wanted to maintain a certain amount of professionalism—until Bethany broke in, flaunting her superior rank. "Feel free to have a cocktail. They won't fire you, you're with me."

Hmm, thought Margot. *Maybe she and her husband aren't so different after all.* Margot plopped the menu down on the table. "Alright then, I'll have the same."

"If you don't mind my asking, Margot, how old are you?"

"I'm 25."

Bethany looked surprised. "Really? I would have guessed you were older. You're very mature for your age."

Margot released a pleased smile.

"So tell me about yourself. I seem to detect a slight accent. Where are you from?"

Margot went on to reveal some of her history until the waitress returned with their beverages. "Are you ladies ready to order?"

Bethany took a sip of her wine and looked up at the server. "How's the tuna today? Is it fresh?"

"Delivered this morning."

"Good. Then I'll have the tuna club, light on the mayo."

The attendant once again turned to Margot. "Have you decided?"

She was still busy assessing the menu, unable to make up her mind. This place was not cheap, and she was on a tight budget.

"Order what you want," broke in Bethany. "Lunch is on me."

That was all Margot needed to hear. She was more than happy to take advantage of the offer. "I'll have the same," she said, handing the menu back to the attendant.

"So, Bethany, what about you? Tell me about yourself."

Bethany started out a bit restrained, as though she didn't want to expose too much of herself to an underling, but after a couple of sips of wine, she began to open up. She went on to explain how she grew up in a small town in Maine and that Charles was from Massachusetts. "We met while we were both going to school in Boston. He was going to Boston College for his law degree, and I was attending Boston Architectural College. We actually met in a coffee shop. It was really crowded, as usual. I was on my laptop sipping a latte when he asked if I wouldn't mind sharing a table. And that's where it all began. After graduation, we got married and decided to move to New York to further our careers.

"How long have you and Mr. Langford been with Dillon, McCain & Dermot?" asked Margot.

"We've been with them four years now—which brings me to one of the reasons I wanted us to have lunch together—besides getting to know you better." Bethany took another swig from her wine glass. "There are a few clients who are *very* important to the firm. They bring in an enormous amount of revenue, and you need to make sure you are especially nice to them. One such person is *Burton Magnuson*. He's been a client of the firm long before Charles and I came on board. He's commissioned a number of apartment/retail towers in and around New York City. His latest endeavor is a multi-million dollar project to be aptly named, *Magnuson Towers*."

Margot made sure to make a mental note of the name: *Burton Magnuson...multi-million dollar project...*

After their food arrived, Bethany changed her tone. "You know, Margot, I've never really had anyone in the firm I could relate to. It's nice to have another female in the company that I'm not competing with. As you've undoubtedly ascertained by now, Dillon, McCain & Dermot is a long-established company comprised of 'good 'ol boys.' The only other woman architect in the firm is Adrienne, and she can't be trusted. She pretends to be my friend, but I know she views me as her adversary. She's always sucking up to the partners. The only time she talks to me is to find out what I'm working on so that she can copy it or try to improve upon it."

As Bethany rambled on, Margot continued eating, while paying close attention to every detail.

"And then there's Rhea Simmons, the office manager. For the four years I've worked there, I still don't know anything about her. She's as transparent as a cinder block wall and just as warm. She makes the bare minimum effort at small talk. The partners like her because she's strictly business. She's straightforward and doesn't pull any punches. She comes in on time and stays an extra fifteen minutes each and every day before going home; and since I've been there, she has never taken a sick day."

Margot swallowed another bite of her sandwich. "What about Jennifer?"

"Who?"

"You know, the receptionist I'm filling in for?"

"Oh, I never even considered her. She's got a five-year-old at home. I don't have any children, and all she ever talked about was babies, crafts, and cooking. I just couldn't relate. I think she's been biding her time until her second one is born. I've got a feeling she's not coming back."

Margot smiled and lifted her glass to her lips. "It sounds like you're a good judge of character."

"I like to think I am, but then again, I grew up in a bubble, so my sights were limited. I was an only child, and my parents were both professors at the local college. They were never around much, and I wasn't into sports or outdoor activities, so I used to spend all my time reading and drawing as opposed to socializing."

"That explains why you got into architecture."

Bethany sighed, "I guess things have a way of working out, don't they?"

When they were finished with their meal, Bethany turned to Margot and said, "You know, Margot, since moving to New York, it's always been Charles and I, or work. I never had the opportunity to form any close friendships with other women. This was fun. Let's do this again real soon. I've got an off-site inspection on Friday, but I'll be back in the office on Monday. Let's have lunch then."

That Friday, most of the staff had left early, except for Ms. Simmons, of course. Margot stalled around, preoccupying herself until the office manager walked out the door, not because she had anything more to do, but in an attempt to garner points. Just as Margot was about to grab her purse and leave, her desk phone buzzed. If it were an outside call, she would have let it go to voicemail, but the light was flashing red, which meant that it was an in-house call, so she thought she had better pick it up. Much to her surprise, it was Charles Langford.

"Oh...good...you're still here. Would you mind stopping by my office before you leave?"

Margot hesitated. "Umm, sure. Is everything alright?"

"Yeah...I just need to run something by you, that's all."

The last time she had had a conversation with him was when they shared the cab ride home after she had confronted him in the lobby. When the cab stopped in front of her apartment to drop her off, he insisted on paying the fare. Then, just as she was about to step out, he had grabbed her arm, locking eyes with her for a few fleeting seconds, as if he were about to say something. Instead, he let go of her arm and simply said, "See you on Monday."

Since then, he had reverted back to his usual, stiff-lipped demeanor whenever he walked past her desk, barely acknowledging her when she said, "Good morning, Mr. Langford" or "Have a good evening, Mr. Langford." So when he called her up to his office, she wasn't sure what to make of it. The only thing that came to mind was that *maybe after the cab ride, he changed his mind about being sorry when I confronted him the way I did and decided to report me to the office manager. Maybe he wants to tell me that I'm going to be fired.*

If that was the case, then she had to be prepared to fight fire with fire. Before descending from her platform, she pulled out a small compact mirror from her purse and reapplied her lipstick. Then she straightened out her pencil skirt and tiptoed up the circular staircase, fearful that anyone remaining in the building could hear the clicking of her heels against the marble tile. When she reached the landing, she rode the middle elevator up to the nineteenth floor of the legal department and proceeded cautiously through the uncompromising corridor of solid oak doors.

She couldn't remember which office was his, noting the names on every door she passed, until she came to 1907 with the golden nameplate: Charles Langford, Esq.

Before entering, she unbuttoned the top three buttons of her blouse and tousled her silky black tresses. Then, she took a deep breath before turning the brass knob as quietly as possible. She crept in to find a posh reception area filled with ornate oak furniture, leather couches, and fine artwork, but there was no one in sight. "Hello...hello," she called out. "Is anybody here?"

A few minutes passed before Charles Langford stepped out from one of the back offices. There was something about the way he looked that caught her off guard. She had never seen him without his suit coat on or his tie knotted stringently in place. His white fitted shirt was relaxed over his beltline and unbuttoned at the collar, leaving his cobalt blue tie to hang loosely around his neck, and his normally moused hair was dangling loosely over his forehead. Damned if he didn't look sexy.

"Sorry," he said, rather nervously. "My receptionist has already left."

"So...what did you need to see me about?" asked Margot, hesitantly.

Charles rested his backside against the edge of the secretarial desk and folded his arms in front of him. "I just wanted to make sure everything is going well with you."

"Um, yes," said Margot. "Everything's fine. How about you? Is everything okay?"

"Yes, yes," Charles answered, clearing his throat. "I just wondered, um...whether you had any questions or concerns regarding any company matters..."

"Look, if this is about what I said to you before the cab ride, I really didn't..."

"No, no. It was fine. You were right to say that to me. I just wanted to fill you in on some other company protocols you may not yet be aware of. Perhaps we could discuss them while we grab a bite to eat."

"But, I thought Beth..."

"Bethany won't be home tonight—and I don't like to eat alone. I was hoping you could join me. If that's alright with you?"

"I appreciate the gesture," said Margot. "But I wouldn't want to give rise to any hint of impropriety."

Charles' cheeks flushed, and he grinned back at her meekly. "I'm sure we can work around that."

"Then, yes. I'm famished."

CHAPTER 8

Perched upon her pedestal, staring down at her computer, Margot became distracted by the pinging of the elevator landing across the hall. A few seconds later, a distinguished-looking gentleman strolled through the entryway of Dillon, McCain & Dermot. She guessed him to be in his late 60s. He was not very tall, but carried himself as though he were. He sort of reminded her of Aristotle Onassis, the Greek shipping tycoon, from photographs she had seen of him in magazines.

As he approached her desk, he took a moment to check the time on his gold watch tethered to the vest of his three-piece suit. Instead of announcing himself, the first words that came out of his mouth were, "I haven't seen you here before."

"My name is Margot, and you are?"

"What happened to Jennifer?"

"I'm filling in for her while she's on maternity leave."

"Ahh...yes. You'll have to excuse me, I've been out of the country for a while."

"May I ask who you're here to see, Mister...uh...?"

Before he could answer, Bethany scurried out from the rear hallway toward the front desk. "Burt!" she exclaimed, reaching out to give him a warm, double-fisted handshake. "Margot, I'd like you to meet a very important client of ours, Mr. Burton Magnuson."

So we meet at last, thought Margot, leaning over just enough to expose just the right amount of cleavage from her V-neck chiffon blouse, and extending her arm out for a handshake as well.

Instead of shaking her hand, Mr. Magnuson bent over to kiss the top of it, and with a gracious smugness, raised his head until his eyes met hers. "You may call me Burt."

Bethany couldn't help but raise an eye at her receptionist as their glances met in the crossfire. An awkward moment of silence followed, after which Bethany cleared her throat and turned to her client, "I was just coming out to tell Margot here that we were expecting you. We're all ready for you in the conference room, if you'll follow me. Can I get you anything?"

"No thank you," said Burt, turning his head to impart one last glance upon the new receptionist before following the architect into the conference room.

An hour later, Bethany and her client strolled out of the meeting engaged in brisk conversation. As they neared the lobby, Margot could hear Mr. Magnuson expressing his satisfaction. "Mrs. Langford, the presentation for your vision of *Magnuson Towers* was excellent, and I look forward to seeing this project to its ultimate completion under your guidance."

"Well, it helps when you have a client who knows what he wants."

"I think it's important to convey my intentions as early as possible, so that the end result is satisfactory for everyone involved."

"I guarantee it will be everything you imagined and more," boasted Bethany. "In the meantime, I'll have Margot set up an appointment for you and Charles to meet right away so that you can unroll all the legal yarn."

When they arrived at the front desk, Bethany looked up at her receptionist and asked, "Margot, how soon can you get Mr. Magnuson in to see Charles?"

Margot scrolled through her computer screen. "Next Tuesday?"

Bethany's eyes were on Burt while his were focused on

Margot. "Can you make that early?" he asked. "I like to get business out of the way early, so I'm left with enough time in the afternoon to take care of more personal matters."

Margot lifted her head back up. "Our first appointment is at eight-thirty."

"Perfect. I'll see you then," said Mr. Magnuson, turning to shake Bethany's hand once more before heading out. "It was a pleasure meeting you, Margot, and I look forward to seeing you again next Tuesday."

Margot could have sworn she heard him click his heels before walking out of the lobby and trailed him visually while he crossed the hall and waited for the elevator doors to open. As he entered and turned to face the entrance of the firm, she could feel his resolute gaze bore a hole through the glass and strike her directly in the heart. It literally rendered her breathless until the elevator doors closed.

Bethany was still standing next to the reception desk as the two of them watched the elevator shut. Margot lowered her head, shaking it back and forth. "Wow. So, that was the *legendary* Burton Magnuson."

"Yeah," said Bethany. "Looks like you made quite an impression on him, too."

CHAPTER 9

Dillon, McCain & Dermot officially opened at 8:30 a.m., but on this particular Tuesday morning, Margot made sure to get there half an hour early so she wouldn't miss Burton Magnuson's arrival.

The first thing she did when she climbed up on her pedestal was to re-check her make-up and reapply a fresh coat of pale pink lipstick. It was the color she had chosen to complement the beige raw silk suit she had purchased at the second-hand, high-end boutique. She had yet to wear it, saving it for a special occasion. That day had arrived.

As soon as the firm's most prominent client advanced through those doors, Margot flashed him her most enticing smile. "Have a seat, Mr. Magnuson. I'll let Mr. Langford know you're here."

"Please, call me Burt."

"Okay...Burt. Can I get you anything to drink? Coffee, tea...or something else?"

"No thank you," he responded, his smile lingering as he made his way to the sofa directly facing her.

He sat down and picked up a magazine from the coffee table, and casually began to skim through it while nonchalantly lifting his eyes to watch her. In spiked heels, she had carefully stepped down from her platform and was making her way toward the coffee table. Her jacket tapered tightly around her tiny waist with a ruffle that flared out, accentuating her perfectly rounded hips, and the front of her skirt had a slit on the left side that rose to her shapely mid-thigh.

He wasn't born yesterday. He knew what she was up to, purposely bending over in front of him, pretending to rearrange the architectural design magazines. Proffering himself a gentleman, he did his best not to be so overt as to gape at the front of her jacket, whose lapels fanned open to reveal a delicately embroidered, silky camisole underneath.

No words were exchanged throughout the ritual until they were both distracted by the sound of an upstairs elevator opening. There, at the top of the stairs, stood Burton's attorney, Charles Langford, emitting a pompous mobster vibe with his over-moused hair and dark-blue, pin-striped suit.

He had come down to personally accompany his wealthy client back up to his nineteenth-floor office. Margot started to make her way back to her desk and shot Charles a covert glance. In exchange, he casually looked her up and down, all the while maintaining his characteristic poker face, breaking it only to greet Burt.

Langford stretched out his hand to his client as an indication for him to lead the way. As they headed up the stairs, Charles turned his head toward Margot one more time, only to give her an irreverent look.

At the conclusion of their meeting, Attorney Langford walked Mr. Magnuson back down the steps, stopping in front of the reception desk to shake hands and bid each other goodbye. Margot was on the phone while the two men lingered for a moment as if each of them wanted to say something to her. After a minute or so, she put the call on hold and told Attorney Langford that the call was for him.

"Tell him I'll be with him shortly," said Charles, shifting back to Burt. "Sorry, I need to take this. I'll be in touch," he said, patting Burt on the shoulder just before rushing up the steps to his office.

Mr. Magnuson waited in front of the receptionist's desk

and watched Langford as he hurried up the stairs. As soon as the attorney jumped into the elevator, Burt turned his eyes toward Margot.

"Did you need something, Mr. Magnuson?" she asked.

"I hope I'm not being too forward, but are you busy for lunch, Margot?"

In her most demure voice, she responded, "I don't believe I am."

"Then, would you do me the honor of meeting me at *Chez Luis* at noon?"

"I'd love to. Is that the place on...?"

"I'll have a car pick you up in front of the building at 12:00 o'clock."

At quarter of twelve, Charles descended from his office and stopped in front of Margot's desk, purporting to check his messages. In a guarded fashion, he glanced up at her and commented, "You look nice." After which, he lowered his voice to a near whisper and added, "Do you want to meet for lunch? I know a place 'far from the maddening crowd,' if you know what I mean."

"What about Beth...I mean, Mrs. Langford?" she whispered back.

"She's tied up in a meeting."

"I'm sorry, but I already have plans for lunch."

Langford gave her a suspicious glare.

"In fact, I'm running late and I still have to go to the ladies' room. Margot looked at the clock on the wall. "Where's Kerry? She should be here by now." Kerry was basically a "girl Friday," a young intern who helped with a variety of miscellaneous administrative and clerical duties, including filling in for the receptionist during lunch.

After a few in-house calls, Margot eventually tracked her down in the mailroom. "It's almost noon, and I have to get going.

Can you come up here right away?" she blurted out nervously.

"Be right there," replied the intern.

"Where're you going?" asked Charles, just as Kerry was approaching the desk.

"You look nice," Kerry said to Margot, forcing Charles to end his interrogation.

"Thanks," said Margot, grabbing her new oversized purse and making a mad dash for the ladies' room. The first thing she did when she got there was to go into the stall and remove her camisole. She shoved it into her purse and buttoned up her jacket. When she came out, she stopped in front of the mirror, pulled out a tube of maroon red lipstick, and slathered it over her formerly pink-hued lips. A quick smack and a pucker, and she was out the door.

Margot was happy to see that Charles had left because when she walked outside, a shiny black sedan was parked directly in front of the building. The driver must have been given a precise description of her because as soon as he spotted her, he jumped out to open the rear passenger door for her.

Chez Luis was a three-star Michelin restaurant where the average person needed to reserve a table no less than six months in advance.

The minute Margot walked in, the Maître d' showed her to her table. Burt was already seated there with a bottle of Dom Perignon by his side, chilling in a silver bucket of ice. Like a gentleman, he immediately stood up to greet her when he saw her, taking her hand and laying a kiss upon it before she sat down.

"Thank you for coming," he said. "I was afraid you might change your mind."

"Why on earth would you think that?" she asked, smoothing her skirt while she positioned herself on the chair.

"For one thing, I never asked if you were married."

"I never asked if you were married," countered Margot.

"You are very clever. I like that in a woman. But, what about the age difference?"

"What does age or marital status have to do with anything? This is just lunch, isn't it?" Margot couldn't help but notice the direction of his eyes while she spoke.

It was obvious that Burt had observed she wasn't wearing the camisole she had previously had on at the office. Instead, the top of her jacket expanded to reveal a plunging, white, lacy demi-bra, exposing a lovely protrusion of supple ivory cleavage.

"Of course," said Burton, clearing his throat. "Just lunch... By the way, excuse me for not saying this before, but you look absolutely ravishing."

"Why, thank you," said Margot, lowering her head modestly, pretending to be embarrassed by the comment.

A waiter came by posthaste to uncork the bottle of expensive Champagne and poured a small amount into Burt's glass for his inspection. Only after Burt signaled his approval did he proceed to fill the two crystal flutes.

"I've never been treated so regally," proclaimed Margot, thinking she could get used to this.

"A woman such as yourself shouldn't be treated any other way."

Margot had been witness to this type of over-inflated rhetoric on TV and in the movies, but wallowed in it nonetheless.

Burt raised his glass in a toast, "To your beauty."

Margot lifted the bubbling beaker to her nose and let out a giggle, "I probably shouldn't be drinking during lunch, I have to be back to work in an hour."

"I'm sure Dillon, McCain & Dermot will forgive you if you're a bit late. Although I would prefer you didn't mention you were with me. I like to keep my personal life private."

"Of course," answered Margot. "As do I." She then turned her attention toward the menu, which was written in fancy French cursive. As she tried to decipher the translations, Burt continued to stare at her from across the white linen-covered table.

"You have the most translucent hazel eyes I've ever seen. You're not from here. Where did you come from, Ms. Margot?

"Well, my birth name is Margarita Kazlauskas. I was born in Lithuania."

"Aahh—Lithuanian. I thought I detected a slight accent."

"I was thirteen when my parents came to the United States."

"Did they come straight to New York?"

"Actually, no. We settled just outside of Cleveland, Ohio. "I came to New York on my own in 2002."

"What were you expecting to find in New York?"

"Opportunity, I guess."

"And have you found that opportunity?"

"That remains to be seen."

"I sense that you are an ambitious woman, Margot."

"I am—very ambitious," she continued with a giggle. "The only problem is, I don't like to work that hard."

"A woman like you does not have to work that hard."

Margot lifted her glass for another swig of bubbly. "So, how did you become so successful, Mr. Magnuson?"

"I am of Scandinavian heritage and a product of humble beginnings, such as yourself."

"But you have no accent."

"I was merely an infant when we settled in New York."

"So, if you weren't born rich, how did you acquire...your status?"

Before answering, Burton took a moment to polish off the rest of his Dom, then he looked her straight in the eye and said, "Success has everything to do with the relationships you form, Margot. You might want to keep that in mind."

Margot pondered the statement for a moment before

replying, "I'll be sure to remember that."

The waiter returned to take their orders. Margot picked up her menu again after barely having had a chance to review it. "I have no idea what any of these dishes are. What do you recommend?"

Burt laid down his menu and looked up at the waiter. "We'll start with the escargot, followed by two Caesar salads. For me, I'd like the *Coq au Vin*, and for the lady, the *Sole Amandine*. And for dessert, the *L'ile Flottante*, which we will share." He turned to Margot, "You'll love that. It's a luscious meringue floating on an island of custard, and finished off with a light drizzle of caramel sauce." He looked back at the attendant. "Oh, and a bottle of your best *Alsatian white*."

Margot was not ignorant of the fact that he was doing all he could to impress her, and she intended to take full advantage of it. "I like a man who knows what he wants."

"I know exactly what I want," said Burt, maintaining a steady gaze on his date.

Margot didn't respond. She, too, knew exactly what he wanted.

"So...Margot, are you an only child?"

"Yes. Why do you ask?"

"'*Only* children are very self-assured."

"What makes you think I'm so self-assured?"

"I can tell by the way you carry yourself. For instance, when you walked into the restaurant, you acted like you deserved to be here."

"Don't I?"

"Of course, you do," said Burt, refilling her flute. "Have you ever wished you had siblings?"

"No. I've always liked being the center of attention. Although I never liked the responsibilities that come with being an only child."

Burton appeared to be in deep concentration. He stretched his hands across the table and took hold of hers. "I'd like to make *you* the center of my attention; that is, if you're up for the *responsibility*."

Well played, thought Margot, lifting her glass to put forth a toast of her own. "I'm up for the responsibility if you're up for the challenge."

Burt raised his beaker, striking it gently against hers. "To the beginning of a long-lasting relationship," he proposed with an angled smile. "Of course, a man in my position has to remain discreet about these things — both personally and professionally."

"Of course," responded Margot, firmly locking her eyes on his. Beneath the table, she kicked off her heels and started to inch her foot toward his leg, but immediately retracted it when someone approached the table. A young man in a tweed jacket and button-down oxford shirt came up behind Burt and placed his hands on his shoulders. "Hey, Dad!" exclaimed the young man, obviously taking Burt completely by surprise.

Magnuson turned a shade of red before twisting around to observe the familiar unshaven face with dark-rimmed glasses, whose point of focus wasn't on his father, but his date.

"What are you doing here?" asked a befuddled Burton.

"I was just leaving. I had a business lunch with someone who I'm hoping to partner with for that venture I was talking to you about. Remember?" The young man shot another glance at Margot before oscillating back to his father. "Are you also here for *business*?"

Burt cleared his throat. "Um, Margot, I'd like you to meet my son, Robert. Robert, this is Margot. She's...uh...she just joined the firm of Dillon, McCain, and I thought I'd acquaint her with my architectural strategies."

"I'm sure she'll catch on fairly quickly," said Robert, cracking a wicked grin. "Well, I've gotta get going. Tell Mom I promise to call her *real soon*. Nice meeting you, Miss...uh...?"

"Kazlauskas," spoke up Margot.

"Margot Kazlauskas," repeated Robert, as he went on his merry way.

Burton was quiet as he watched his son disappear from the room until Margot broke the awkward silence. "So, how many 'children' do you have, Burt?"

Before answering, Burt took an extra big gulp from his glass and raised his napkin to dab the corners of his lips. "Two. Robert is twenty-four and Kathryn is nineteen."

"I see a big resemblance to you in Robert."

"Yes, well, in physical appearance only. Kathryn is the spitting image of her mother, both inwardly and outwardly."

"I hope to meet her one day — Kathryn."

"That might not be for a while. She's attending the University of Cambridge at present."

"And your son, Robert?"

"He's in his second year of law school here in New York."

"That would be a wonderful asset for you, wouldn't it?"

"Yes, it would be convenient to keep my business ventures 'all in the family,' so to speak. Unfortunately, he's thinking of dropping out in favor of some get-rich-quick scheme."

"Didn't you say that success has everything to do with the relationships you form?"

"Okay, maybe he's more like me than I care to admit," chuckled Burt. "You're a quick learner, Miss Kazlauskas. You and I will get along just fine."

CHAPTER 10

Rubberneckers stopped to observe who was about to get out of the limo when it pulled up to the curb on Madison Avenue. Aware of her audience, Margot wriggled out of the rear passenger seat in a way as to allow a fair amount of exposed thigh from the slit in her skirt, but punctilious enough to prevent it from sliding all the way up to her crotch. The last person she wanted to see when she was stepping out of the car was Charles Langford. But as luck would have it, he happened to be exiting the building through the revolving door that very moment. Instantly, he caught sight of her and rushed over to confront her.

"You're half an hour late," he said indignantly, while looking at his watch.

"Sorry," blurted out Margot, avoiding eye contact and hurrying toward the entrance.

Charles skimmed alongside her, trying to keep up. "They must be paying you pretty well to be able to afford a chauffeur-driven vehicle," he said sarcastically. "Where were you?"

"That's none of your business," she answered, trying to get around him as he attempted to block her.

"Where are *you* going?" Margot retorted back. "I don't recall you having any appointments this afternoon."

"I'm taking a late lunch."

"Why isn't Bethany with you?"

"She's still not out of her meeting. I didn't want to wait any longer."

Margot pushed his arm out of the way. "Look, I've gotta go."

As she pushed open the revolving door, he shouted out to her in a more subdued tone, "I'll call you later."

Margot arrived at the office to find her fill-in, Kerry, sitting behind the reception desk, leafing through a Vogue Magazine with an open pack of Doublemint on the counter.

"Sorry, I'm late, Kerry. I just need to go to the ladies' room. I'll be right back."

"It's okay," said Kerry, snapping a wad of gum between her teeth. "It's always quiet during lunch. We've only had like three calls while you were out."

Margot got to the ladies' room, removed her jacket, and slipped her camisole back on. Then she took out a makeup removal pad from her purse, wiped off the red lipstick from her lips, and re-applied the lighter shade of pink.

Kerry watched Margot as she was approaching the desk. "So, how'd your date go?" she asked.

"What makes you think I had a date?"

"By the looks of what you're wearing, I'd guess it was more than just a 'date,'" she replied, shooting Margot a playful wink before prancing off the podium.

Margot was on the subway heading home when she heard her cell phone buzzing inside her handbag. Reaching in, she pulled it out to find that it was a call from Doris.

"Mind if we get Chinese carry-out tonight?" asked Doris. "It's been a long day, and I don't feel like cooking."

"Okay, but I'm not that hungry," said Margot. "I had a pretty big lunch. Just order me a vegetable eggroll."

When she walked into the apartment, Doris was in the small kitchenette removing the Chinese take-out containers from their bag and laying out some plates and utensils. As quietly as she could, Margot made a mad dash to her bedroom in order to avoid the likelihood of her roommate critiquing her outfit. After throwing on some sweats, she then wandered over to the kitchen table to join Doris.

"Did you just get home? I didn't even hear you come in."

"Oh...uh, yeah. I needed to get out of those stiff work clothes and get comfortable. You know what I mean?"

"Yeah. I had the worst day. The computers were down, and I had all these appointments I had to cancel."

"That sucks," said Margot, pulling a spring roll out from one of the cartons.

"You're lucky you're just a receptionist. You don't have to deal with shit like that."

"Just a receptionist? I'll have you know, there's plenty of crap I have to deal with too."

"Like what?"

"Besides answering the phones, I also have to keep track of everybody's calendars. Not to mention having to put up with difficult clients and all the office politics surrounding them."

Doris rolled her eyes. "Yeah, whatever. So, where'd you go for lunch?"

"What?" garbled Margot, through her mouthful of vegetables.

"You said earlier that you were still full from lunch. Where'd you go?"

Margot didn't want to mention she went to the well-known *Chez Luis* because that would lead to a barrage of questions, and she wasn't ready to divulge any information pertaining to Burton Magnuson at this time. "I don't remember the name," she said, taking the last bite of her eggroll.

"Did you go with Bethany again?"

"Um...yeah."

"So what'd you have?"

"Uh...fish. I had fish."

"Fish! That's not filling."

Margot was really starting to get irritated. Doris was so

obsessed with food. The fact was, she could stand to lose a few pounds. She gathered up her empty carton and leftover sweet 'n sour packet and got up to throw them in the trash, then she walked over to the sink to pour herself a glass of water. "As much as I'd like to continue this conversation, I've got some work I need to do. I'm going to my room," she said, grabbing her fortune cookie off the table.

Doris gave Margot a strange look before digging back into her Chow Mein. When she was done, she found her way to the couch and sat down to watch television. Just as she grabbed the remote, her cat, Shadow, jumped up on the backside of the sofa and sprawled itself right behind her head.

Margot perched herself on her bed with two pillows propped up against her back and her new laptop on her knees. Well, it wasn't exactly new. She had bought it after receiving her first paycheck at Dillon, McCain & Dermot, and got it for a fraction of the price because it was refurbished.

She was intent on learning as much about this Burton Magnuson as she could. When she typed his name into the Google search engine, a multitude of headlines popped up. There were all sorts of articles relating to his long list of superstructures. *This dude is freakin' rich,* she said to herself, as she filtered through them one by one.

She stumbled upon an article that was about ten years old. It had a picture of the wealthy entrepreneur cutting a ribbon for the christening of one of his office towers. He was standing in front of the building surrounded by his family, whose names were listed in the caption below it. Burt's hair hadn't gone completely white yet, and he looked a little thinner than he was now. His two middle school-aged children, "Robert and Kathryn," were dressed like a couple of spoiled Oxford brats with their black blazers and Argyle vests. And judging from his wife, "Meredith's," appearance, she looked like the proverbial, stiff-upper-lipped, boring, self-centered socialite that she probably was. She decided to delve further into Meredith Magnuson and found that she was indeed heavily involved with charity fundraisers and other philanthropic projects. Margot snickered to herself. *Of course, she is. Typical of all these high-browed women, so preoccupied with their own causes, they don't have time to spend with their poor, neglected husbands.*

Just then, Doris barged into Margot's room.

"Hey, don't you believe in knocking?" yelled Margot, instantly shutting her laptop.

"I just wanted to tell you your favorite show, 'The Bachelor,' is on."

"Oh, thanks."

"What were you doing on your computer?"

"Just some research for work. But I'm done."

"What kind of research would a *receptionist* possibly need to do?"

Margot let out a huff. "I'm trying to get ahead in the company, okay?"

Doris tightened her lips. "It just started."

Margot set her laptop aside, grabbed her fortune cookie, and followed Doris into the living room, where they made themselves comfortable on the couch.

"You didn't read your fortune yet?" asked Doris.

"No. Did you?"

"Yeah, it said something stupid like, 'jealousy is the root of all evil.' Who writes these? That's not a fortune! Open yours."

Margot ripped off the cellophane and broke her cookie in half. She pulled out the little typewritten strip of paper and read it out loud. "'Keep your friends close and your enemies closer.'"

"See what I mean?" said Doris. "Why doesn't it say something like 'a handsome stranger will come into your life?'"

Margot didn't respond. She was still mulling over her

fortune. *Hmm, 'Keep your friends close and your enemies closer.'*

While the bachelorettes were each uniquely vying for the bachelor's attention on the highly-rated television show, Doris stuck her finger up her throat and pretended to gag. "I can't believe how low these women are willing to go to get a man."

"You might want to pay attention," said Margot, "You might learn something."

"Maybe *you* should go on the show since you're such an expert."

"No need, I've already got my sights set on someone."

"Oh, really? Who?"

Margot snickered. "That's for me to know and for you to find out."

****

It had been eight weeks since Jennifer went on maternity leave. The former receptionist was scheduled to return next week. Friday had arrived, and this was to be Margot's last day at the architectural firm. As the end of the workday drew closer, she couldn't help but feel a little bittersweet. She had gained so much while working here — in more ways than one. She wondered how her leaving would affect her future. As she was counting the minutes on the clock, Ms. Simmons buzzed her to come into her office. Margot entered the office manager's office and sat down.

"It seems Jennifer has decided to become a 'stay-at-home mom,'" began Ms. Simmons. "You know the firm has been extremely satisfied with the way you've taken over for her during her absence. Rather than go through the whole process of trying to find a permanent replacement, we'd like to first offer the job to you — if you're interested."

CHAPTER 11

Little did Ms. Simmons know (nor anyone else at Dillon, McCain, for that matter) that prior to offering Margot the permanent position as receptionist, Burt had already set her up in a high-rise in Midtown. It was close to the architectural firm where she continued to work and far enough away from Burt's residence on Park Avenue, which he still shared with his wife, Meredith.

Almost a year had gone by, that Burt and Margot's relationship continued to carry on in secret. Burt was perfectly satisfied with the arrangement. As for Margot, she was growing ever more restless. She wanted more.

Another boring workweek had come to an end. Margot was tidying up her workspace and looking forward to a more stimulating evening when Bethany, who was on her way out, stopped by her desk. "Hey, Margot. Charles is working late again—on a Friday, nonetheless. Can you believe it? Do you wanna stop at Don Pablo's for a drink? I need someone to talk to."

"Um, I was planning on meeting a friend for dinner..." wavered Margot.

"Oh, that's alright," said Bethany. "I mean, if you have plans..."

"No, no, it's okay. You know me, I'm always up for a drink. Let me just send my friend...uh...Doris, a quick text before I go—see if she wouldn't mind eating a little later."

"Are you sure?"

"Sure. Just give me a second." Margot held her phone close to her face while she punched in a few words via text. "It's all good," she said to Bethany, tucking her phone back into her purse. "Let's go."

Don Pablo's was already crowded when they walked in. It was a popular after-work spot, especially on Thursdays and Fridays. Sports filled two big TV screens, and Latin music filtered in the background as they searched for a place to sit. They spotted an empty, lacerated high-boy in the corner next to the kitchen and were able to scam two unoccupied counter-high stools from a larger table nearby.

The decor was a little tacky, but the food was authentic, and the service was fast and friendly. As soon as they made themselves comfortable, a well-seasoned waitress came by with a basket of homemade tortilla chips and salsa. "What can I get you gals?"

"I'll have a Margarita on the rocks with salt," said Margot.

"Same here," said Bethany. "Except, make mine a double."

"Whoa!" said Margot, laughing. "I'm usually the one ordering a double."

Bethany didn't respond. Her eyes were focused on the television set over the bar where a boxing match was taking place. She was biting her upper lip, and her eyes were moist. It looked as though she were about to cry.

"Bethany, you okay?" said Margot, raising her voice slightly.

Bethany glanced back down at Margot and managed to summon a melancholy smile.

Margot folded her arms against the table and leaned in toward her friend. "So what's up, Bethany? Is everything alright at work?"

She waited patiently at the edge of her seat while Bethany mustered up the will to answer. "Margot, in the last year, you and I have become good friends. To the point where I feel like I can confide in you."

"Thanks, Bethany, I feel the same way," said Margot, anxious to see where this was going.

Before Bethany could continue, the waitress came by with their Margaritas. Margot watched silently while Bethany stirred the ice cubes around in her glass with her straw, before finally removing it to take a long, hard slug. She picked up her napkin and wiped the salty residue from her lips, and continued.

"As you know, I was born and raised in a small town near the University of Maine. My parents taught there. They were both college professors and incredibly smart. I idolized them, even though they were so absorbed in their academic life that there was little time left for me. As a result, I became intent on proving my self-worth to them. Maybe that comes with being an only child, I don't know. I held fast to that commitment even when I went away to college. My nose was always buried in books. I never took time to pursue a close relationship with anyone— male or female. Then I met Charles. He was as ambitious as I was. We became inseparable. Not only was he my first real boyfriend, but he was my best friend and confidant. I didn't need anybody else."

Bethany stopped to take another gulp of her Margarita. "This isn't something I normally tell people. To this day, it's still painful for me to talk about. It happened during my last year of college. It was a frigid day in February. My mother and father were on their way to an out-of-state lecture series when they were involved in a horrible automobile accident. A large semi-truck lost control of his vehicle when he skidded on the icy road and veered across the freeway, hitting my parents' small Honda Civic head-on. They both died instantly."

Margot stared into her drinking glass solemnly. "I'm sorry, Bethany."

"I know. Thank God I had Charles. He helped me through the most difficult time of my life. He forced me to stay focused on my studies. If it weren't for him, I don't think I could have finished that last year of college. The very next day after graduation, we went to City Hall and got married. Shortly after, we moved to New York. Charles was the catalyst that drove me to pour all my energy into my career. It didn't even matter that he told me he never wanted to have children. He was all I'd ever need." Bethany took a deep breath and exhaled. "Now, I fear I'm losing that."

"What do you mean?"

"I think my husband is having an affair."

"What?" Margot sounded off in a disquieting manner. "What makes you think that?" she added, taking a gulp of her cocktail and swallowing hard.

"I don't know. Just the way he's been acting. It's been going on for almost a year now. He's out of town more than he ever used to be. When he's not out of town, he often comes home late and is too tired to talk, let alone have sex. We used to have great talks and even greater sex. Now, it's all but evaporated."

Margot stayed busy swirling the lime around in her near-empty glass with her plastic straw, while avoiding Bethany's eyes. "Did you ask him about it?" she asked, lifting the straw out to take a lick from its dripping bottom.

"Yes. More than once. He says he's been consumed with the Magnuson Towers project and all the red tape that's involved."

"I hear stress can take its toll on a man's libido," said Margot. "I wouldn't worry about it. Once the project is completed, he'll probably get back to his old normal self."

Bethany took a moment to ponder Margot's assessment. "You're right," she said, taking one final gulp from her drink. "I'm probably making a mountain out of a molehill. I'm lucky to have a friend like you that I can confide in... So, tell me about this guy you've been seeing. Where did you meet him?"

When the bill came, Bethany grabbed it from the server's

hand and said, "This one's on me."

"Thank you."

"Don't mention it."

"I'm going to the restroom," said Bethany. "You coming?"

"No," said Margot. "I've gotta run. I still have to meet Doris for dinner. See you Monday." Margot waved off her friend and rushed out the front door to hail a cab. While on the curb waiting, she took out her phone to punch in another quick text:

On my way home — see you soon

As she rode the elevator up to her 15th-floor apartment, Margot leaned her head against the wall, exhausted from all the drama. The first thing she did when she walked into the room was kick off her heels and remove her jacket, tossing it on the nearest chair along with her purse. Next, she walked over to the wet bar to uncork a bottle of wine. That's when she heard her cell phone ringing from inside her clutch. *Now what?* she thought, running over to the chair. She pulled out her phone, answering it in the nick of time.

"I was about to hang up," said a familiar voice on the other end.

"Is this who I think it is?"

"Yeah, Dana. Remember me?" she replied sarcastically. "Your old friend from high school."

"I didn't pay attention to who was calling. I just grabbed the phone out of my purse and answered. I haven't talked to you since I moved out of Doris' place. How've you been?"

"I'm good. So hey, I'm gonna be in town for the weekend... uh...work-related, and I was thinking we could get together."

"That'd be great! Burt's away all weekend on business."

"Cool. I'm flying in tomorrow afternoon. Call you then."

Margot was still standing next to the chair when she heard a knock on the door. Thanks to the extra card key she had made for him, he didn't have to go through the concierge to come up.

Before opening it, she peered through the peephole — just in case. There he was in his custom-fitted suit with his briefcase at his side.

"How'd you get here so fast?" asked Margot, unlatching the door to let him in.

He dropped his attaché to the floor and wrapped his arms around her waist. "I couldn't get here fast enough. I missed you," he said with a heavy breath, going in for a kiss.

"You missed me?" exclaimed Margot. "It's only been three days."

"I know, but you know I can't get enough of you," he moaned, while pushing her toward the sofa.

"I hate to break this to you, but you're going to have to be out by noon tomorrow. I've got an old friend coming into town."

"It had better be a 'she.'"

Margot let out a chortle. "You could say that."

As his mouth made it to her breasts, clothes began to fly haphazardly as the two of them wrestled on the couch with brazen abandonment. Eventually, they found their way to the master suite, ending in an explosion of endorphins. "I need a cigarette," said Margot, as she lay in bed staring blankly at the ceiling.

"You know you can't smoke in here. You'll set off the smoke alarm."

"I know. I guess I'll have to settle for a drink instead." Margot rolled out of bed. "I'm getting a glass of wine. Want one?"

"Sure."

She straddled back into the bedroom naked, carrying two filled glasses of Chardonnay, and handed one to her lover before scooting down next to him.

"I had drinks with Bethany after work today," she said casually.

"Oh yeah, what did she have to say?"

"She told me she suspects her husband of having an affair."

Margot's bedfellow turned serious and took a slug of his wine. "Did she have any proof to back it up?"

"No. She just said that he's always working and they rarely have sex anymore."

"And what did you say?"

"I told her it's probably from all the stress associated with the Magnuson project."

He set his glass on the nightstand and leaned over and gently bit her lower lip. "That's just one more thing I love about you, you always know what to say."

"You're not the first person who's told me that," Margot said flippantly, before rolling over on top of him for another round of lovemaking.

Margot was on the verge of floating off into dreamland when her dark-eyed companion turned and lightly brushed his fingers across her smooth, sultry shoulder. "I've kept quiet about it all this time, but I don't know how much longer I can do this," he whispered.

"Do what?" asked Margot.

"Share you with this rich boyfriend of yours — what's his name?"

"I told you, *Omar*."

"Is 'Omar' some sort of sultan or something? Because he must be making a lot of money to keep you in this apartment."

"He's in the import-export trade."

"What do you mean, 'import-export?' Who is he, Margot? I want to know."

"That's none of your business! Besides, if I can share you, then you can surely share me."

CHAPTER 12

The sun shone brightly through the sheer bedroom curtains, alerting Margot that it was well past time to get up. Grabbing her cell phone off the nightstand, she saw she had two missed calls from Dana. Before she had a chance to call her back, the phone alerted her to a new text. It was Dana letting her know that she was in her hotel room and needed directions to her apartment. It was already eleven o'clock, so Margot shot Dana back a text with her address and told her to give her at least half an hour before heading out.

The naked man sprawled out on the bed with his face buried in his pillow, appeared unfazed by the light of day or by Margot's cajoling. "WAKE UP, WAKE UP!" she shouted, shaking his shoulders back and forth. "My friend is going to be here soon."

Gradually, he opened his eyes and, with a disarming smile, pulled her down on top of him. "Come on, baby, we have time for one more."

"No, we don't!" protested Margot, breaking away from his grip. As she ran into the bathroom to brush her teeth, he forced himself out of bed to make a futile attempt at getting dressed. While he bent over to put on his socks, he spotted her through the open archway, standing over the sink in her lacy bra and panties. With one sock on, he snuck up behind her and undid her bra, pulling it off and flinging it clear through the bathroom door.

Margot dropped her toothbrush in the sink and pushed him away again. "You have to go," she insisted, yanking her terry cloth robe off the wall hook. Quickly, she slipped it on and scrambled over to the couch to collect his shirt and tie, and whatever else she could find strewn along the floor. "Hurry up!" she commanded, throwing the ball of clothes at him.

He appeared to get the message and proceeded to get dressed, but as Margot was walking him to the door, he undid the sash on her robe and imposed one final lascivious kiss upon her lips in a last-ditch attempt to seduce her. In response, she lifted up his briefcase and suit jacket, which were lying by the entryway, and smacked them against his chest. "HERE—NOW GO!"

"When will I see you again?" he asked.

"I'll call you," she said.

No sooner had he left than she received a buzz from the downstairs lobby. "A Ms. Sherer is here to see you," formally announced the concierge.

"Send her up," said Margot, doing a quick scan of the room to make sure nothing looked out of place.

A few minutes later, there was a light rap on the door. Margot opened it to find Dana standing there with a dumbstruck look on her face. Not realizing that her robe was wide open in the front, she proceeded to give Dana a heartfelt squeeze followed by a hard, smacking kiss on the lips. "Look at you!" belted out Margot. "You haven't changed a bit."

Dana's pale complexion flushed into a ripple of crimson waves. "And you—you look...um...'bigger,'" she choked out, clearing her throat while gaping at Margot's enhanced bosom.

Margot glanced down at herself and realized that her robe was still open. "Oh, these," she said proudly, cupping her palms below each breast to prop them up. "Burt bought them for me. What do you think?"

Dana didn't answer and did her best to look away, but it was clear she didn't want to. As she glanced around the room, she couldn't help but take in the lingering aroma of men's cologne.

"Nice place you've got here. Looks like Burt's taking good care of you."

"Yeah. Sorry, I'm running late–overslept. Why don't you have a seat while I take a quick shower? Oh, and feel free to make yourself a cappuccino. The machine's over there on the counter, next to the fridge."

Dana strolled over to the open-concept kitchen with its white marble-top counters and built-in glass-encased wine cooler, until she came to the stainless steel espresso machine. She stared at the state-of-the-art appliance for a minute or so with a perplexed look on her face. "I don't know how to work these things," she shouted in the direction of the bathroom.

"There's juice in the fridge, if you prefer. Just help yourself," yelled back Margot. "I'm sorry, there's not much else I can offer you. The housekeeper, who does the shopping and cleaning, won't be in till Monday."

Dana walked over to the built-in refrigerator and opened one of the doors. Besides the juice, the only other items inside were a quart of low-fat milk, two individual fat-free yogurts, some gourmet cheese she'd never heard of, and a jar of martini olives. She pulled out the bottle, labeled "100% fresh-squeezed," and poured some into a glass from the cupboard.

With a juice glass in hand, she made her way from the kitchen to the white leather sofa while continuing to examine her surroundings. The whole apartment was light and bright with splashes of hot red and shadowy black undertones—just like Margot's personality.

As she sat down on the couch, she was temporarily transfixed by a single ray of sunlight streaming from the glass balcony door to the black lacquer bar against the wall. It created a surreal halo effect, causing the polished humidor and expensive whiskey bottles that sat on top to glisten like the crown jewels.

Dana leaned forward and set down her glass on the smoky-mirrored coffee table in front of her. In doing so, she repositioned her feet and felt something bump the heel of her Vans sneakers. Looking down, she noticed something sticking out from underneath the sofa. She bent over to see what it was and pulled up a man's wallet. She had never met Burt, so she was curious to see what he looked like. When she opened up the wallet, the picture on the driver's license wasn't that of a 60-something-year-old male with white hair, as Margot had described him. This was a picture of a much younger man with dark hair. Just as she was about to read the name on the license, Margot rushed back into the room wearing only her panties. Quickly, Dana shoved the billfold back under the couch.

"I can't find my bra," said Margot, glancing all around. "Maybe..." she started out, while making her way to the couch. "Maybe it's under here." She stooped down next to Dana and looked underneath. "Woops," she exclaimed, pulling out the billfold and clutching it tightly in her hand. "Looks like Burt forgot his wallet. I'd better text him and let him know it's here. But first, I need to find my bra." Margot remained standing in the limited space between a flustered Dana and the coffee table while she continued to scan the floor. "There it is!" she blurted out, scurrying towards the wall behind the bathroom door. "Sorry about that," she said, scooping it up from the floor. "I'll hurry," she promised as she scampered back into the bathroom.

Dana stayed seated nervously tapping her feet for a while, then got up to catch the spectacular view of the city through the glass door wall, which led out to a small balcony. On her way, she stopped to admire an assortment of framed photographs displayed along a bookshelf. Although taken in different settings and from different points of view, they were all pictures of Margot—one of them, an enlarged close-up of her face. Dana picked it up and gently stroked the beaming smile with her index finger. In that moment, Margot re-entered the room, applying lip gloss to her mouth, and Dana abruptly set the photo back down.

"This will have to do," said Margot, smacking her lips together.

"You don't need makeup," said Dana, her voice subdued.

Margot extended her hand and pinched Dana's cheek. "You're a doll."

"Margot, how come there aren't any pictures of Burt?"

"What?"

"I was looking at the pictures on the credenza, and there aren't any of Burt."

"Oh...you know. Given our situation, we have to keep things discreet—in case any 'unexpected' guests stop by. Come on! We have to get going if we want to get a seat at the restaurant I had in mind. They don't take reservations, and it fills up really fast. You'll love it. They've got a lot of vegetarian choices."

Dana followed Margot to the door. "Do you think he's ever going to leave his wife?"

"He won't have to because I have a feeling *she's* going to be leaving *him*."

Dana followed Margot to the door, and just before they walked out, Dana turned around to take one last eyeshot at the bottom of the sofa. "You might wanna make sure he doesn't leave *you* first."

CHAPTER 13

Burton Magnuson's limo driver drove to a gentrified section of New York's East Village and parked in front of a renovated six-story apartment building, where he waited patiently out front while his boss went inside. He made a note of the time on his control panel. It was already noon, but he knew it wouldn't take long. It never did.

Magnuson took the elevator to the fifth floor and walked along the dimly lit hallway until he reached Unit 511. It took a few hard knocks before an unshaven young man with disheveled hair peered through the peephole of his studio apartment. He unlatched the door chain, albeit reluctantly, and unlocked the door. "What are you doing here?" he asked, leaning against the entryway, slicking his hair back with the palms of his hands.

Burton raised his voice irately. "What do you mean, 'what am I doing here?' I'm your father, and I own this place. I don't need a special invitation."

Burt pushed his way through the doorway and looked around.

The curtains were drawn, and the sofa bed was pulled out. The sheets were knotted up in one corner, and there were clothes laying on the floor. Burt glanced over at the narrow counter separating the front room from the kitchenette and observed a half dozen or so empty beer cans as well as a completely drained bottle of *Absolute Vodka*. He walked over to the sofa bed, tossed the pillows aside, and sat down. On the coffee table in front of him was an open box of pizza with two uneaten slices still sitting there, and next to the pizza box, he noticed the residue of a white powdery substance. The scowl on Burton's face deepened.

"You look like hell, Robert. Did you just get up?"

Robert stared at the floor and pinched his nose. "No."

"Then what took you so long to answer the door?"

"I, uh...I was in the bathroom."

"Don't lie to me," shouted his father. "I know what you're up to!" He shoved the pizza box aside and swiped his hand across the smooth table top, then held his whitened fingers up to his son's face. "You told me you were going to quit the Cocaine!"

"I told you, I'm working on it. It's not that easy, man. Is that why you're here? To rub it in my face?"

"I'll tell you why I'm here," said Burt, pulling out an envelope from inside his suit coat and waving it before his son's eyes. "I just got a letter from Columbia informing me that you have officially dropped out! After all the money I endowed to that school to get you in. And you do this to me?"

"Look, Dad, I didn't do anything to you! You and Mom both knew how I felt about law school before you forced me into it. You know I'm not cut out for that shit. It's too bad I didn't inherit Mom's book smarts. But street smarts—I've got you to thank for that. You never went to college, and look where you're at now."

Burt calmed down a little and lowered his voice an octave. "Things were different back then. Nowadays, you need both— book smarts and street smarts."

"Yeah, well, not me. I'm a 'chip off the 'ol block.' You gotta trust me, Dad."

"Trust you? You couldn't even tell me you dropped out of school."

"Because I knew this was how you'd react. I was hoping you wouldn't find out until..."

"Until what? Until you ended up drugged out, dead in some ditch?"

"Don't worry, that's not going to happen. I've got a plan."

"A plan!" spewed Burt.

"I've got this deal going..."

Burt let out a cackle. "The only deals you've got going are your drug deals."

"That's not true! Remember that guy I met for lunch when I ran into you at *Chez Luis*? I'm working with him on this joint venture... I just need a little more cash."

"You're not getting any more cash from me. I've supported you long enough. I'm cutting you off until you've kicked your cocaine habit."

"You're cutting me off? Where will I live?"

"That's not my problem. I'll be damned if I'm going to keep funding your addiction."

Robert's nostrils flared, and his face erupted into an inferno of red blotches. "What about *your* addiction, Dad?"

"What do you mean?"

"I mean your addiction to prostitutes."

Burt's face took on a flush of its own, responding indignantly, "I don't know what you're talking about."

"Come on, Dad. I knew what was going on the moment I saw the two of you at the restaurant. I gotta hand it to you, you've got good taste."

"She's not a prostitute."

"Yeah, well, whatever you want to call her, we both know why she's with you. I kept my mouth shut this long. Just don't be surprised if Mom finds out." Robert paused for a moment. "Of course, if you help me out with the cash I need..."

"Don't you threaten me!" screamed Burt. "I can have you involuntarily committed to drug rehab for as long as I deem fit."

Silence befell the room until the senior Mr. Magnuson removed something else from his inner pocket. It was a checkbook.

"This is the last time I'm bailing you out, Robert. Now... How much do you need?"

CHAPTER 14

Margot had just entered her apartment and kicked off her heels. Work was getting to be a real drag. Things weren't exactly going as she had hoped. She shouldn't have to work this hard. At least she had a relaxing evening alone to look forward to. No needy men to satisfy tonight—just herself. She was about to uncork a nice bottle of Chardonnay when she thought she heard a knock on the door.

Both Burt and her lover were out of town, and the concierge hadn't called for permission to allow anyone entry to her apartment. Curious, she peeked through the peephole to see who was there. Cropped in the sphere of the fisheye lens, she could make out a well-dressed woman in a wide-brimmed hat standing in the hallway. The woman was looking downward, so Margot could not readily see her face. But she knew exactly who it was.

In the midst of deciding whether or not she should open the door, a series of flashbacks sped through her mind. All the subtle clues she had planted. Like the time she had sprayed one of his socks with her cologne. Or, the time she rubbed her ruby red lipstick into his gray silk pocket square before re-tucking it neatly back into his suit pocket. And then there was the time she pulled the note off the flowers he had sent her and folded it neatly into the back pocket of his trousers. She knew he would never notice it, because he always kept his oversized wallet in the inner compartment of his suit coats.

As Margot cautiously opened the door, a woman whose face she had seen before in newspapers and magazines raised her head to give her a death-piercing stare. "Are you Margarita Kazlauskas?" she asked.

"Yes," Margot answered tentatively.

"I'm Meredith Magnuson. May I come in?"

"Um, I'm expecting someone any minute..."

"It won't take long, I promise," said Mrs. Magnuson, pushing her way in.

Margot stood silently holding the door open as Meredith strode through the open foyer and looked around. "Nice place you've got here."

"Thank you," responded Margot, releasing her grip on the door and allowing it to close on its own.

"Tell me. How is it that you can afford a place like this on a receptionist's salary?"

Margot stayed quiet.

"Never mind, you don't have to answer. I already know. My husband is paying for it."

"If you already know, then why are you here?" asked Margot.

Mrs. Magnuson made her way to the glass door wall leading out to the balcony and gazed out at the burgeoning city lights that had begun to overtake the newly falling dusk. Then abruptly, she pivoted to confront her husband's mistress across the room. "Don't play coy with me, *Miss Kazlauskas*. You know exactly why I'm here." Slowly, she began walking toward Margot. "You think you're so cunning that you can plant your little tokens to alert me to my husband's infidelity? I knew about you long before you had to make it overtly obvious." At this point, Meredith was standing directly in front of Margot, raising the callousness in her voice. "Do you think you're the first mistress my husband has ever had? Don't kid yourself. You're not so special; there were plenty more before you came along. When he gets bored with you, he'll toss you aside just like all the rest."

"Then why do you stay with him?" punched back Margot.

"Burton and I were 30 years old when we got married. By that time, we both knew what we wanted. He wanted someone from a well-to-do family who could help him pursue his financial ambitions. And I wanted someone with the drive to achieve those goals. Without me, he would not be where he is today, and he knows it. Sure, there were bumps along the way, but I've stuck by him through thick and thin. Together, we made two beautiful children, strengthening our bond. He has no intention of ever leaving me, especially for the likes of you. And I have no intention of leaving him. I've grown accustomed to the lifestyle my husband has provided. I will not let you take that away from me. You of all people should appreciate that. I know where you came from and where you want to go."

"If you're asking me to break it off with him, I won't," asserted Margot.

"I'm not asking you—I'm *telling* you. I've achieved significant social status in this town, and I will not allow you to jeopardize that. I won't be humiliated by some cheap whore. Besides, I know a great deal when it comes to my husband's business affairs. Believe me, he knows what the cost of leaving me would be. He would have to pay me off substantially in order to keep me quiet."

"What if I don't?"

"I have plenty of connections, Miss Kazlauskas. I'd tread carefully if I were you."

As Mrs. Magnuson headed toward the door, she turned once more to face her nemesis. "You know, when Burton and I were married, we made an oath: '*till death do us part.*' Nowhere in that oath did it specify *whose* death."

Margot cracked the door hard behind her and deadbolted it shut while a whirlwind of conflicting thoughts spun through her brain, wondering what to do next. She refused to be intimidated by anyone, let alone this woman. She *would* win Burt if it were the last thing she did. She just needed to come up with a plan. And then she remembered the one-year anniversary of when she and Burt had their first date was coming up. This would provide the perfect opportunity to surprise him with something that would knock his socks off. Or better yet, that would knock Meredith's socks off.

CHAPTER 15

It hadn't rained this hard in months. The vibrations from the force of the wind against the panes felt as though they were going to shatter into pieces. This was how Margot felt. Vulnerable. Like her perfect world could come crashing down at any second. She had never felt like this before, and she didn't like it. She stared at her reflection in the vanity mirror, hoping to summon back the confidence she had lost, but beneath the intensive row of lighted globes, all she could see was Meredith's taught, pale face. She closed her eyes, concentrating on the sound of the pelting rain. *Stay the course, Margot. You can do it,* she told herself. When she opened her eyes, the eerie vision had disappeared.

Normally, she would have been indifferent as to his comings and goings, but on this particular night, she was looking forward to the sound she had grown accustomed to, and then she heard it, overriding the thunderous clatter. The creaking sound of his key boring into the metal keyhole suddenly became music to her ears.

Margot gave herself a quick once-over before spraying Chanel N°5 into the air and stepping into its lingering scent. As soon as the front door swung open, she swished out of the bathroom and into the front room to greet him.

A smile that could only spell delight wafted across Burt's face when he saw what his lovely mistress was wearing. It was the sheer white negligee he had bought for her before leaving for his last trip. He removed his wet hat and set his dripping valise on the floor. "A week is too long to go without seeing you, my dear."

"Here, let's get you out of that soaking, wet raincoat," said Margot, stepping in to unbutton it for him. She hung it on the coat rack next to his hat and immediately grabbed him by the hand to lead him straight into the bedroom, where she proceeded to remove his tie, and then his belt...

Margot went over and above her skill set to prove she was still worth his while, leaving Burt laying on the bed with his eyes wide shut and a beam across his face.

"How was it?" asked Margot.

Burt let out a deep breath. "You wear me out. I need a nap after that."

She began pulling on his arm. "C'mon, Burt, get up. You can't sleep now. It's too early. We haven't even had time to talk."

"What's there to talk about?"

"I don't know — stuff."

"Alright," said Burt, slowly bringing himself up into a sitting position. "I could really use a cigar right now, but since I don't want to have to stand out on the balcony in the rain, I guess I'll have to settle for a nice stiff drink instead."

Margot ran over to get his robe and helped him put it on. Then she led him into the living room and gently pushed him down on the sofa. "I'll be right back with your slippers," she said, hurrying off to get them. When she came back, she got down on her knees and rubbed his arches before carefully slipping them onto his feet. "Now, don't move," she ordered, hopping back up. "I'll get your drink."

"You're being very generous tonight," said Burt, suspicious of all the added attention he was receiving. "Is there something you aren't telling me?"

"No, honey. I've missed you, that's all," replied Margot, from the wet bar. "You've been gone an awful lot lately."

"You can only conduct so much business over the telephone. Sometimes things require personal attention."

"The usual?" asked Margot, reaching for a bottle of his favorite scotch.

"That would be grand."

She scooped some ice into a Waterford tumbler, then topped it with a generous amount of Glenlivet and delivered it to him.

"You know me pretty well," said Burt, taking the glass from her hand.

"I should by now," said Margot, going into the kitchen to pull out a bottle of Chardonnay from the wine fridge for herself. When she returned, she set her goblet down on the coffee table and cozied up next to her man. "Do you know, at the end of next month it will be one year since we met?"

"Has it been that long?"

"Yes."

"I guess time flies when you're having fun," chuckled Burt.

Margot picked up her glass to take a sip of her wine. "I want to do something special for our anniversary, Burt. Maybe we can go out somewhere."

"You know we have to be very careful about being seen together in public."

"I know," moaned Margot. "Are you going to be gone all of next week, too?"

"That remains to be seen. Some people need a little extra persuasion when it comes to finalizing a deal. But I don't want to bore you with the details of my business transactions. Tell me about your week. What did you do to keep yourself busy?"

"Besides work, nothing much. "Bethany keeps asking me when she's going to get to meet my 'new boyfriend.'"

"And what did you tell her?"

"I told her 'Omar' spends most of his time in Turkey and comes into town only a couple times a month, so when we do get together, we prefer to spend our quality time alone."

Burt belted out a laugh. "And what does this 'Omar' do?"

"Why he is in the oriental rug trade, of course."

"Of course!" hooted Burt. "Oh, you're good."

"I did have lunch with an old friend who I hadn't seen for a long time."

"Oh?" said Burt, with a slight hint of concern in his voice.

"Don't worry. Her name is Dana, and I've known her since junior high. She just happened to be in town on business."

"Does she know about *us*?"

"All she knows is your first name, that you're quite a bit older than me, and that we're living together. I told her I couldn't say anything more because of the confidentiality associated with your job."

"So, you didn't tell her that I was married?"

Margot took another gulp of wine. "That *might* have slipped out... But don't worry, she is the least gossipy person I know. If anyone can keep a secret, it's Dana."

Burt suddenly became quiet and took a swig of his scotch. "My wife confronted me and said she knew I was having an affair."

Margot did her best to sound shocked. "When? I mean, how could she have found out?"Burt reflected back on his last conversation with his son. "I don't know, but I have a good idea. In any case, she said she was going to be meeting with her lawyer if I didn't put an end to it immediately."

Margot set her glass on the table and got down on her knees, holding his cheeks between her palms. "You're not going to end our relationship, are you, Burt?" Crocodile tears welled up in her eyes. "Please tell me you're not going to leave me!"

Burt took her hands into his and kissed her firmly on the forehead. "Don't worry, my dear, she's threatened to leave me before. Besides, I could never give you up—not as long as you stay true to me."

Margot got up and walked around to the back of the couch and proceeded to rub his neck, circling her thumbs firmly along the grooves while working her way down. "Burt..." she began, then paused.

"What is it, Love?"

"Am I your first?"

Burt looked confused. "My first what?"

"Your first 'kept woman,'" said Margot, instituting her technique in and around his shoulders, then moving to his upper back.

"No...you're not my first," sighed Burt, shifting his neck from side to side. "But if you play your cards right, you'll be my last."

Margot slid her thumbs back up to the nape of his neck and pressing as hard as she could, answered, "Don't worry, Burt, I'll be your last—I'll make sure of it."

CHAPTER 16

By the time Margot woke up, Burt was already in the kitchen, dressed to go, and taking a final gulp from his coffee cup. "Can I at least make you breakfast?" she asked him.

"No thanks, I told Meredith my plane was landing this morning," said Burt, grabbing his overcoat.

Margot rushed over to help him with the sleeves. "But, it's Saturday. Can't you call her and tell her your flight was delayed, or something?"

Burt leaned over and kissed her on the cheek. "I have to go now."

"I'm going to miss you," frowned Margot, pouting her lips.

Burt picked his briefcase up off the floor and opened the door. "Didn't you have something planned for today?"

"I was thinking about checking out that new multi-level fitness center that just opened up. It's supposed to be state of the art with everything you could possibly need. But, I don't know...I hear it's pretty expensive."

"Don't worry your pretty little head about that. Just put it on my charge I gave you."

"You're too good to me," said Margot, planting a big kiss on his wrinkled lips and giving him a big hug. "Let me get that for you," she said, opening the door for him. Their weekly newspaper was lying on the floor outside the entryway, so she bent over and picked it up. "Don't forget your paper," said Margot, waving it in the air.

"You can throw it out. I don't have time to read it today."

"Okay," she said, shutting the door behind him. Margot had expected his leaving early. He usually spent his weekends with his wife, leaving her free to do whatever she wanted. In anticipation of that fact, she had already made an appointment with the sales representative at the new fitness center. Her appointment wasn't for another two hours, so she walked over to the espresso machine, made herself an Americano, and carried her steaming cup to the table and sat down.

Normally, she wasn't big on reading the newspaper, but since she had nothing better to do for the moment, she thought she'd give it a glance before tossing it in the trash. As she flipped through it, she came upon the society page, where one of the headlines caught her eye:

Jameson Art Gallery Hosting Fundraiser for the Arts

She had passed the Jameson Art Gallery many times while strolling along Fifth Avenue. Oftentimes, she would see signs outside the gallery promoting special events. She lifted the paper closer to her face and began to read the article.

On April 30th, the gallery was planning on holding a special event to raise money for starving artists. The featured artist was one, **Aleksander Orlov**, a so-called "rising star in contemporary photography." As Margot read on, the column stated that the individual hosting the soiree was none other than a well-known socialite by the name of *Meredith Magnuson*. Upon seeing that, the gears in Margot's brain began grinding at full speed. As she lowered the paper, she got a faraway look in her eyes. *This could be the opportunity I was looking for.*

It just so happened that April 30 was the exact date of her and Burt's one-year anniversary. Since March had just begun, she still had almost two months to come up with the perfect gift — one he'd never forget.

Margot showed up at the front desk of the exclusive health club with a designer duffel bag in tow and was immediately taken on an in-depth tour of the facilities. The club turned out to be all it was touted to be. The first floor was where the hardcore training took place with weights and barbells, etc. The second floor consisted mostly of workout machines, like spin cycles, treadmills, Stairmasters, and rowing machines. The third floor was where the dance fitness classes and yoga studio were, and finally, the fourth floor was the spa level, where one could opt for a massage or spa treatment or simply relax in the steam sauna. Now, this was the type of gym for her.

At the end of the tour, she happily handed over Burt's credit card and signed on. "I'll probably be working out mostly on weekends for a while, but that may change in the near future," she told the sales rep.

"Welcome aboard, Ms. Kazlauskas," said the fit young specimen in spandex pants and a wide smile.

"Please, call me Margot."

"You can start immediately, Margot. So if you'd like to try out any of our facilities, feel free.

Margot patted her gym bag. "As a matter of fact, I just happen to have my workout clothes with me."

She started out by doing a quick workout with one of the in-house instructors named Carl. He had rippling abs and a waist almost as small as hers. To her dismay, following a few failed attempts at flirty banter, she came to the realization that he was not into women.

The yoga class had already started, so she opted to run on the treadmill instead. After half an hour, she was ready for a hot, soothing sauna. The yoga class was just letting out, so she jogged up the staircase to the fourth floor in order to beat the crowd.

While she was in the locker room, an older woman approached her. She might have been in her 50s, or maybe even in her 60s, with a few facelifts behind her. "I haven't seen you here before," she said. "Are you new?"

"Yes, this is my first day."

The woman stuck out her hand. "I'm Gwendolyn."

Margot was unable to keep her eyes off the cluster of big rocks flashing on Gwendolyn's slim fingers. "Glad to meet you. I'm Margot."

As the two women got to talking, the subject turned to art, and it soon became clear that Gwendolyn was a wealthy art aficionado. In an effort to sound sophisticated and "in-the-know," Margot asked her if she had ever heard of an up-and-coming photographer by the name of "Aleksander Orlov."

"Of course! His work is going to be displayed at the Jameson Art Gallery next month," she exclaimed. "He's an amazing talent. He can turn an ordinary picture into an extraordinary work of art. And he's not bad on the eyes either," she added with a wink.

"Does he have his own studio?" asked Margot.

"Apparently, he does all his work where he resides — in one of those industrial lofts over on 44th."

Margot's mind was already churning.

"Were you planning on attending the exhibition?" asked Gwendolyn. "I'm definitely going to be there. Of course, it's by personal invitation only."

Margot arched her lips coyly. "Then, I guess I'm going to have to *make sure* I get an invitation..."

CHAPTER 17

Margot pacified herself with a cigarette while she paced in front of the partially restored warehouse in New York's SoHo District, waiting for someone to exit the gated entryway.

The opportunity came when a gray-bearded chap in a tweed beret, with a cell phone to his ear and clutching a leash led by a miniature bulldog, attempted to push the gate open with his shoulder. Immediately, Margot dropped her cigarette butt, crushing it with her forefoot, and ran to hold the iron gate open for him. Giving a nod of thanks, the elder gentleman and his furry companion capered out while she made a mad dash in before it locked again.

Lucky for her, the old gent who'd just exited the building apparently left the main door ajar, so she was able to get in without once again having to wait for someone to come out. Upon entering the ground floor, she found herself in a short, dark hallway with only one elevator. It wasn't your ordinary elevator either. It was one of those ancient freight elevators like you see in movies with visible concrete walls and an expanding lattice door that had to be manually opened and closed.

She pulled it open with all her force, then yanked it back shut until she heard the clicking sound of the latch. As she pushed the top button, the elevator rumbled and groaned before it began its ascent to the eighth floor. She couldn't help but cringe at each excruciating grinding noise it made while it rose ever-so-slowly until it reached the top floor, where it screeched to a wobbly halt. *I hope I won't have to do this too often*, she said to herself, exhaling a sigh of relief.

Stepping out of the elevator, she came into another hallway with a single window at the very end and only three other doors. One of them was the emergency exit by the window, one was a standard-size door next to the elevator, and directly across from it was a huge, heavy metal entryway with the unit #800 scrawled on its surface with black paint. This had to be the right place because it was at least twelve feet tall and had extra-wide double doors, suitable for moving large artwork in and out.

There was a button next to the door, which she assumed was a doorbell, and a tiny camera aimed at her in the top corner of the ceiling above it. She pushed the button several times, but when no one answered, she took her fists and banged on the echoing metal as hard as she could. Apparently, that worked better than the doorbell because someone finally answered. The door opened just enough to reveal the face of a man with mussed-up, jet-black hair partially covering one of his eyes. He was peaking over the side and peering at her without saying a word.

"Aleksander Orlov?" asked Margot.

"Yes," answered the man with a heavy Russian accent. "What do you want?"

"I'm sorry to bother you, but..."

"I do not see anyone without appointment," he said and started to close the door in her face.

Margot pushed it back open. "I want to hire you."

"Too busy," he said, attempting to nudge the door shut again.

"Wait!" said Margot. "You can name your price. Money is no object!"

Slowly, Mr. Orlov pulled the door open all the way to let her in.

The artist's studio was just as she imagined it to be. The whole space was almost completely open and probably took up most of the top floor. Exposed bricks surrounded the interior except for three oversized curtainless windows, while giant air ducts and propeller fans hung from the lofty ceiling. Easels displaying art canvases in all sizes and coloration, ranging from 8" x 10" black and whites to full-blown color posters, took up most of the floor area, which made up for the lack of furniture.

While Margot was checking out his interior, he was busy checking out her exterior—from top to bottom. "What is your name?" he asked, probingly.

"I'm sorry," she said, extending her hand. "I'm Margarita Kazlauskas."

"Kaz-lau-skas..." he repeated phonetically. "You are Lithuanian."

"Yes," she answered, pleased with his recognition of her heritage.

"It is true what they say, 'Lithuanian women are the most beautiful in the world.'"

A smooth talker, thought Margot. *I like that. And Gwendolyn was right, he looks pretty good himself in those tight jeans and dark-ribbed turtleneck. Plus, I've always been a sucker for dark hair and dark eyes.*

Margot retook control of the conversation. "I take it you're Russian?"

"And how can you tell?" he asked sarcastically.

"Several things. Your name, your accent. But most of all, the way you carry yourself, with a sense of superiority."

The artist released a crooked smile, notably taking pleasure in her assessment.

"When did you come to the United States?" asked Margot.

"When I learned that Russia does not appreciate modern photography. They prefer old paintings. So what can I do for you, Margarita Kazlauskas?"

Margot began to wander around the room, inspecting all

of the photographs positioned throughout the space, while he followed closely behind, paying attention to all of her backside. "Your work is amazing," she exclaimed. "The people and the scenes you capture look surreal, almost dreamlike."

"A good photographer has the ability to suspend time."

"I want to be suspended in time," said Margot, turning around abruptly, only to find him no more than six inches from her face. "I want to be captured on one of your canvases."

Orlov maintained his gaze with unflinching eyes.

"Don't you think I'm worthy?"

"I would not waste my time if I did not."

"Good. Because I need it by next month."

"That is impossible. I have an opening at the Jameson Art Gallery at the end of next month — of which I am still preparing for. I can do it the following month."

"No, you don't understand. Next month is my one-year anniversary. I want to give it to my husband as a surprise gift."

The artist looked at her ring finger. "Why do you not wear a wedding ring?"

"I lost it... That's not important." Margot moved in even closer to him. "I told you, I'm willing to pay *whatever* amount you deem appropriate."

Aleksander raised his eyebrows and tilted his head as he started walking toward the other side of the room. Margot was quick to follow until he came to a makeshift partition. Behind it was a vainglorious, king-size, round bed covered in rumpled satin sheets. He fell backwards onto the mattress with his arms spread out and stared up at her. "Given the short amount of time you are giving me, I may need an extra down payment..."

Five weeks later, Margot returned to Aleksander Orlov's studio to inspect the final print. The photograph that had been blown up to a grand scale was completely covered with a white cloth to protect it from sun exposure. Margot stood impatiently while Alek, with a large, boastful grin, removed the cloth. There she was in all her pulchritude, strategically covered in burgundy rose petals, while seductively sprawled atop a round bed swathed in silvery satin sheets.

Margot's face lit up with self-adoration.

"It turned out even better than I had imagined," said Alek. "You are so photogenic. Your face, your body! You were made for the camera. Why is it that you have not gone into modeling?"

"Maybe I'm just waiting to be *discovered*," Margot replied guilefully. "Perhaps at your showing at the Jameson Art Gallery this coming Friday?" She waved her hand over the print in a demonstrative fashion. "Don't you think this is worthy of being displayed?"

Alek pored over his masterpiece with discerning eyes. "You stated it was to be a gift for your husband."

"I said it was going to be a *surprise* gift. Wouldn't the surprise be that much better if he were to see it on the wall of an art gallery?"

Alek held his chin and nodded. "That would be a surprise, indeed. However, you *do* know that everything that is on display will be for sale."

"Trust me," said Margot. "He'll pay you handsomely for it. Besides," she added, grabbing him by the collar and pulling him in until his lips met hers. "Haven't I paid you handsomely for it, as well?"

Alek broke away for a moment. "The problem is that the artwork that will be displayed has already been pre-selected."

"You're the featured artist. I'm sure you can figure out a way to slip it in at the last minute."

"I cannot just 'slip it in.' It is too big."

Margot couldn't hold back her frustration. "Then replace that one over there," she said, pointing to an equally large portrait, marked, 'Exhibit B-7.' "A waterscape is not nearly as captivating as a *'bodyscape,'* wouldn't you agree?"

As Alek began to ponder the suggestion, Margot decided a little more convincing might be in order, so she took the opportunity to ravage him of all doubt, and sealed the deal.

CHAPTER 18

Burt stood before the vanity mirror, watching Margot secure his bow tie from behind. She was wearing a glittery cocktail dress with a V-shape neckline scooping down to her waistline. "We're awfully dressed up," he commented, a tinge of unease in his voice. "Why can't you tell me where we're going?"

"Because it's a surprise!" said Margot, pulling the knot tautly at each side. "There," she said, patting him on the shoulders. "Now you're ready."

It hadn't taken long for her to master the art of being a "kept woman." Especially when it came to spending money. Two months before her and Burt's one-year anniversary, she had made arrangements for the tiny but exclusive Italian restaurant, Antonio's, to close down to the public on a Friday evening, and cater only to them. At her behest, the chef was going to be preparing a seven-course meal, beginning with an appetizer of *Prociutto é Melone* and ending with an after-dinner *Espresso Creme Brulee*, while an Italian singer and two accordion players serenaded them.

"Seriously, Margot, I'm widely known in this town. You know we have to be discreet."

Margot slipped on her showy white fur coat and huffed in annoyance. "Alright, Burt. If you must know, I reserved a special table at a special restaurant, neatly tucked away in Brooklyn. I also made sure to have it closed off to the public while we're there, so you don't have to worry about being found out."

Burt let out a sigh of relief as she helped him on with his trench coat.

"You'd better bring this," she said, grabbing his favorite Churchillian Bowler hat from the top of the coat rack. Burt placed it on his head, trailing behind her as she led him to the front entrance of the building, where their limo was waiting.

The whole day had been overcast until the thick gray clouds reached their saturation point and began their purge the minute the couple stepped outside. As the chauffeur rushed out to open the door for them, Burt's trepidation resurfaced. "Come on, Burt," pressed Margot, lightly shoving him into the car. "We're getting wet!"

Once they were inside the vehicle, Margot began to give the driver directional instructions without specifically divulging the intended destination.

"Make a quick left at the light," she ordered from the back seat.

"But the Brooklyn Bridge is straight ahead," interrupted Burt. "You said the restaurant was in Brooklyn."

"It is," said Margot. "But there's one more surprise I didn't tell you about."

As they made their turn, the street lights bounced through the windshield, highlighting Burt's eyes. Margot witnessed his pupils expand with panic, so in an effort to reassure him, she took his hand in hers. "Don't worry, honey, we just have one quick stop to make before the restaurant. I promise, it won't take more than ten minutes."

Burt let out a controlled breath, trying to figure out where they were going, while the driver zigzagged per Margot's directions through narrow side streets and obscure alleyways. At long last, they ended up in the middle of a dark alley behind a row of similar brick-lined buildings.

"Pull up next to that dumpster," ordered Margot. The nearest entryway to the right of the dumpster was a heavy armored door with two security cameras overhead. There was no visible signage on or above the door except for the street number: **12385.**

"Are you sure this is where you want to be dropped off?" asked the puzzled driver.

"Yes," confirmed Margot, removing her bulky fur while waiting for the chauffeur to open his umbrella and help her out of the vehicle.

"Why are you taking off your coat?" asked Burt.

"Because...I'm hot," answered Margot, in reality, hoping to be more recognizable.

Burt was still sitting in the car when she ran over to his side. Frustrated, she grabbed him by his palms and tried to pull him out.

"What is this place, Margot?"

"Trust me, we'll be in and out before anyone has a chance to recognize you. Besides, you can hide beneath your hat," she smirked, tapping the rim until it was just above his lids. "Come on, Burt, I've been planning this for a long time. Get out of the car!"

An unenthusiastic Burt followed her up the two concrete steps to the back exit and waited silently while Margo pounded on the door several times. "Where is he?" she exclaimed loudly, squinting at the hands of her diamond-encrusted watch. "He knows I'm coming!"

"Who knows you're coming?" asked Burt. But before she could answer, the door swung open and an attendant in a white topcoat and white gloves appeared. "Margarita Kazlauskas?"

"Yes, that's me."

Maintaining his serious demeanor, the attendant held the door open and allowed them access. "Follow me," he said, leading them through a room filled with obscured hanging tarps and wooden crates until they came to another door which opened up into a dimly lit hall. They passed a men's and ladies' room and then continued down the hallway, which was lined with artwork illuminated beneath opaque sconces. Looking ahead, it appeared that the end of the hall opened up to a brightly lit gathering area. As they drew nearer, they observed the large open space to be abuzz with people.

At this point, Burt stopped in his tracks. "What are we doing here?"

Margot grabbed his hand, hoping to coax him further, but he would not have it. Just as he was about to turn around and head for the exit, a lanky, black-haired male, donned completely in black attire, rushed up to them. "There you are!" he exclaimed, landing a European kiss on each of Margot's cheeks. "You look ra-a-a-vishing." Then he turned to Burt. "You must be The husband," he articulated in a heavy Russian accent. "You are a very lucky man."

Burt appeared speechless. But before he could ask who he was, the man grabbed Margot by the arm. "Come. You must follow me."

Still apprehensive, but now curious, Burt followed the two through a dazzling maze of austere white dividers and partitions lined with contemporary art. The rooms were brimming with waiters in white coats and black bow ties circulating amidst a crowd of dressed-to-impress, schmoozing urban professionals, purporting to analyze the art while balancing their cocktails in one hand and hors d'oeuvres in the other.

Burt wasn't blind. This was obviously an art gallery. But which one? The photographic art that was on display was impressive. The prints came in all sizes. Some were small, while others took up a whole wall. Half were black and white, and half were in color. There were cityscapes, landscapes, and seascapes. There were portraits of people, alone and in groups. Some were candid, as if taken off guard, while others were posing like the Mona Lisa. But they all had one thing in common. They were all taken by the same photographer. Beneath each print was a white label identifying the piece by its title and the artist's name: *Aleksander Orlov.*

The name sounded very familiar. Where had he heard it before? His wife, Meredith, must have mentioned it. He seemed to recall her talking about some upcoming event she was going to be hosting at the Jameson Art Gallery, but he hadn't paid much attention to it at the time. He knew she was involved in a lot of fundraising events, but he was never interested in the details. He was merely content in knowing that it kept her busy while he got to spend time with his mistress. On rare occasions, he'd get roped into attending one of those "boorish gatherings," but for the most part, Meredith attended them alone, or rather, with her entourage in tow.

And then it occurred to him. *She* could be here. More importantly, so would her supporters and confidants—people who knew *him* as well. As his blood pressure began to rise, so did the redness in his face. He reached out to grab Margot's free hand. "Is this the Jameson Art Gallery?"

"Why, uh, yes. It is."

"Why did you bring me here? I demand we leave immediately!"

"I just have to show you one thing. It'll only take a minute, then we'll go," she shot back, as they entered a room where all the action seemed to be taking place.

Margot grasped Burt's clenched fist just as Alek pushed his way through the crowd that was clustered in front of one of the largest portraits in the room.

Burt stood before it with his mouth agape and his eyes like a deer in headlights. There, on the stark white wall, centered between two blazing spotlights, hung an enormous black and white portrait of a nude Margot sprawled out over shimmering sheets, in all her glory, except for the burgundy-colored rose petals strategically strewn over her milky-smooth skin.

Affixed below it was the label: *The Mistress*, by Aleksander Orlov.

And beneath it was the price tag: $137,000.

Upon seeing the expression on Burton's face, Alek felt a need to speak up. "The owner of the gallery, Mr. Jameson, loved it so much, he insisted I put it front and center and not to hide it in the back room like you asked me, Margot." Alek glanced proudly at Burt, whose face had assumed the same color as the rose petals in the picture (either from embarrassment or rage, or both). "What do you think?" he asked in his thick accent. "Your wife makes a stupendous model, does she not?"

Before Burt could say anything, a server came by offering complementary flutes of champagne. Instantly, Burt grabbed one by the stem and proceeded to chug the whole of it.

Margot squeezed his arm with both hands. "Happy Anniversary, Darling," she said unabashedly, planting a big, hard kiss against his pale, trembling lips.

While Burt stood stiff and motionless like a cadaver, glaring at the photograph, Margot's new acquaintance, Gwendolyn, from the gym, spotted Margot and strutted over to her. "Margot! I'm so glad you were able to get an invita..." Her words stopped dead in their tracks when she noticed the picture, turning to look at Margot, and then at the picture again.

At the same time, someone else came over and positioned herself directly between Burt and the photo. It was none other than the hostess herself, with what appeared to be fireworks shooting out of her nostrils.

Burt's jaw dropped as far as it could without breaking. "Meredith," he stuttered. "I didn't expect to see you here."

"What do you mean, you didn't expect to see me here? You knew I would be hosting this event. I can't believe you had the *gall* to bring that...that — *her* here. This abomination," she said, pointing to the portrait, "was put up at the last minute. If I had realized who the subject was, I would have made them take it down." With all eyes falling on Meredith, her voice dipped lower, but became tenser. "I can't believe you would do this to me, Burt. All I've ever asked of you is to keep your perverted indiscretions private and you not humiliate me in front of my peers. I've put up with a lot from you all these years, but this—this is the last straw. You'll be hearing from my lawyer." Meredith pivoted sharply and stormed off, with her entourage queued up behind her, following in single file.

Margot turned to Burt, with tears forming, and looked helplessly into his eyes. "It was supposed to be in the back room, Burt. And I didn't know your wife would be here, I swear. All I wanted was to give you something special—something that you'd always remember."

****

A year later, Burt sat in a conference room next to his attorney while his wife was seated across from him, her own lawyer at her side, while they finalized the terms of their divorce.

CHAPTER 19

Margot was in the parlor off the bedroom of Burt's palatial Miami mansion, getting ready for her big day. While her mother was busy fastening the overlaid satin buttons on the back of her wedding dress, Margot stared blankly into the full-length mirror reflecting back on the events that led up to this moment.

Burt's reaction to her luring him into the art gallery was one she had expected. He was so angered by her underhandedness that he threatened to leave her. Margot remained undeterred. She was ready to put the second part of her guileful plan into effect. She begged him not to leave, professing her undying love for him. She let him know that she was willing to give him all the time he needed to decide what he wanted to do. In the meantime, she would be staying with her parents back in Cleveland. (She had already informed her employer, Dillon, McCain & Dermot, that she was going to be taking a much-needed vacation.) So she packed her bags and left for Ohio.

While staying with her parents, they were none the wiser of what was going on in her personal life. Neither were her old high school friends, Dana and Rachel, whom she reconnected with while she was there. (Though Dana did have her suspicions.)

After just one week, Margot's assumptions were realized.

Burt called her. He told her he had not yet forgiven her, but he was ready to talk. Even though she had planned on staying in Cleveland another week, she booked a flight and flew back to New York the very next day.

Burt was in their apartment when she arrived. She dropped her bags at the door and flew into his arms. For the time being, their "talk" was put on the back burner.

Their discussion took place afterwards while they lay side-by-side in bed once again. Burt admitted he questioned his sanity, but his infatuation with her had not waned. Margot digested those words and played them to her advantage.

"I can't continue to live in limbo like this anymore. I need a firm commitment from you, or I'm moving back to Ohio permanently."

"So you're giving me an ultimatum?" asked Burt.

"I hate to put it in those words — but, yes."

Burt looked at her long and hard before acquiescing. "I'm willing to marry you on one condition. I'm going to have my attorney draw up a prenuptial agreement, and you have to agree to sign it."

Margot lunged on top of him, squeezing him tightly. "Of course, I'll sign it!"

"Notwithstanding the prenuptial agreement, there is one more caveat I want to make perfectly clear..."

Her eyes fixed upon him, Margot said nothing while she waited to hear his stipulation."No matter what the circumstance, if you ever try to dupe me again, there will be 'severe repercussions.'"

Margot's parents had known their daughter had been seeing someone, but that was the extent of it, so the news of her upcoming nuptials came as a complete surprise. They learned of it just three weeks before the scheduled wedding date when the official announcement came in the mail, along with two first-class tickets to Miami, Florida. Their daughter had waited as long as possible to spring the news on them, because she knew they wouldn't approve.

Now, as her mother was quietly adjusting her veil, she suddenly blurted out, "You know he is old enough to be your father."

"What does that matter?" Margot replied defensively. "Age is just a number — a preconceived notion of time."

"What about children? By the time you are ready to have a child, your husband will be too old."

"He already has two grown children. He doesn't want any more."

"But what about you, Margarita? Do you not want to have children of your own?"

Margot grew solemn and lashed out, "I'm still a child myself, Mama. I want someone to take care of *me*."

"So, I'll never be a *senelė*? (grandmother?)..."

Silence befell the room until her mother decided to continue with her lecture. "Perhaps you do not need a child. As long as you love each other. When I first met your father, he had nothing, but I loved him with my whole heart and soul. Big houses, fancy cars, and beautiful clothes mean nothing if you do not have love... Do you love him, Margarita?"

"Of course I do, Mama."

"No, I mean, *really* love *him*. Not the possessions he has to offer."

Margot did not respond, her eyes dropping to the floor.

Her mother clenched her jaw. "This could end badly for you, dear daughter. I hope you have weighed all of the consequences of your choices."

Margot swept her veil to the side and turned around to face her mother. "Trust me, Mama, I have never done *anything* without weighing *all* the consequences."

CHAPTER 20

The sun had barely risen, and the limo was already waiting in the driveway. The wait staff was helping Margot with her luggage when, halfway to the car, she realized she had forgotten her purse. She thought she had left it on the bed, so she hurried back into the bedroom. When she got there, it wasn't there, so she frantically began searching every perimeter of the suite. Still, it was nowhere to be found. "Jacques!" she yelled out, stepping out into the hallway. She apparently hadn't noticed that he was standing right next to the bedroom door, because she almost ran into him. "Oh my God, Jacques, you scared me half to death!" she exclaimed, raising her hand to her chest.

"Are you looking for this?" he asked, holding the purse by its thin straps and dangling it in front of her with his index finger.

"Yes! Where did you find it?"

"It was sitting on the hallway table."

Margot cocked her head and gave him a questioning look. "I could have sworn I left it in the bedroom."

"Maybe you carried it out with your luggage and just don't remember."

Margot ripped the purse from his hand and rushed toward the front door.

"I'm ready," she said exhaustively, slipping into the back of the limousine next to her husband, who was immersed in a business call on his cell. Once she was all settled in, he ended his phone conversation and instructed the chauffeur to drive.

"Thank you for being so patient," said Margot, stretching her neck to give him a peck on the cheek. While doing so, she couldn't help but notice Jacques through the vehicle's tinted glass. He was standing on the front landing as erect and focused as a periscope on a submarine, watching intently as the limo began to make its way around the circular drive.

Margot reached into her purse to take out her phone, which she always kept in the outer pocket. It wasn't there. *Oh, no. I hope I didn't forget that, too,* she fretted, rummaging through her bag. She was relieved when she discovered it tucked away in the special cell phone pouch located in the inner compartment of her purse. The odd thing was, she *never* kept it in there. A strange feeling descended into her gut. Immediately, she took the phone out to scroll through her most recent texts, and that instinct suddenly turned to paranoia. She raised her head, only to gaze through the front windshield. "Why do I get the impression that Jacques doesn't like me?" she said aloud.

Burt smiled furtively and patted her on the knee. "Of course he likes you; he's just looking out for me."

"But we're married now. Shouldn't he also be looking out for me?"

"Don't worry, my dear — he is."

When the limo pulled up to the marina where Burt's yacht was docked, his private captain and deck crew were standing at the ready to launch the newlyweds off on their honeymoon.

This was the first time Margot had been made privy to Burt's prized possession. He was very protective of his floating enterprise, and only a select group of people were allowed on its sacred planks. Her pupils brimmed when she laid eyes on the magnificent vessel, which Burt aptly named, *Magnuson's Millions*.

She had never been on a watercraft of this magnitude before. Upon stepping foot onto the impressive multi-tiered yacht, she was given a private tour by one of the deckhands while Burt settled comfortably in his leather serpentine sofa on the lower level with his cell phone glued to his ear.

After meeting Captain Overland on the fly bridge, the tour descended to the Promenade Deck, which had an outdoor dining area, a small bar, and plenty of room for sunning and lounging. Below that was the Main Deck, where Burt was situated. It comprised an expansive living area, a full kitchen, and an even larger bar with half a dozen barstools. The deck hand informed Mrs. Magnuson that there would be a personal chef, a bartender, a maid, as well as a housekeeper on staff throughout the duration of their voyage.

A mahogany paneled stairwell led to a lower floor where Margot was delighted to find an enormous master bedroom with a luxurious ensuite and sunken Jacuzzi tub. A separate door off the master suite led to a private office where, apparently, Burt conducted much of his business. Several guestrooms with their own private baths were on the opposite end of the boat.

The lowest level or "Stern" had additional sleeping quarters, lavatory facilities, and a separate kitchen area specifically for the crew.

When the tour ended, Margot settled into her master bedroom and began unpacking while *Magnuson's Millions* left the dock in Miami to begin a leisurely route to what would be its first stop, The Bahamas.

Burt, who was still on his phone in the living room when Margot joined him, ended his call and suggested they move up to the top deck to fully enjoy the scenery.

There, the two of them basked in the warm ocean breeze. Burt, with his favorite scotch and smoking one of his prized Arturo Fuente Cuban cigars, and Margot, sipping on her made-to-order Mai Tai. A complacent Mrs. Magnuson snuggled up close to her husband. As she nibbled off a chunk of the sweet, fresh pineapple from her spear, she couldn't help but look back on how she got here. She could not have envisioned a more perfect ending.

The only problem was that even perfect endings grow stale. She knew that she would never be satisfied with the status quo. She would always want more.

"I've got a surprise for you," said Burt.

"What? I love surprises!"

"I made a couple of hotel reservations. One for The Ocean Club in The Bahamas and the other at the Rosewood when we reach Bermuda."

"Who needs a fancy hotel when we've got this?" said Margot.

Burt grinned smugly. "I wouldn't want you to get cabin fever."

"You're too good to me," said Margot, expressing her gratitude with a smooch upon his weathered lips.

Midway into the cruise, all semblance of land had disappeared from sight. The wind felt like it had picked up a couple of knots, and the ocean grew exceedingly choppy, even for a boat of this size. Margot was starting to feel a little bit nervous. "I think I'd like to go below," she told Burt.

They made their way to the enclosed living area and sunk down into the serpentine couch. Margot set her drink on the coffee table and randomly began sorting through some magazines that were laying on top. There was one, in particular, that caught her eye. It had a picture of a swirling ocean vortex on the cover, and above it, in bold letters, was the heading: "*Bermuda Triangle*." She had heard of the Bermuda Triangle before, but really didn't know much about it. Curious, she picked up the magazine and started skimming through the article. The feature included a map of the area that the Triangle was thought to encompass. Margot studied the diagram and leaned over to her husband. "Look, Burt!" she said, holding the page up to his face. "Did you know we're going to be heading right through the middle of the Bermuda Triangle?"

Burt let out a chuckle. "Don't worry," he reassured her. "This is a sturdy vessel, and Captain Overland has years of experience. He and I have travelled this route many times, and nothing bad has ever happened to us."

"But, the waves are already getting rough..." Margot tarried, as if afraid to say anything more. Then she blurted out, "I don't know how to swim."

Burt looked at her in shock and broke into a hearty laugh. "Are you kidding?"

"No, I'm not." Margot bit her lower lip, as if she wasn't sure if she should add anything to her admission. Then she proceeded to tell him a story.

"When I was about the age of ten, I almost drowned. We were still living in Lithuania. I often accompanied my father when he would go fishing on the lake in the hopes of catching a fresh meal for dinner. One morning, I was standing next to him near the edge of a very long dock. He had just snagged a really big fish and was in the process of reeling it out of the water. That's when I noticed an older boy watching us from the shore. He looked cute, so I waved at him. He smiled and waved back. I liked the attention, so I spread my arms out and began to twirl around for his amusement. I guess I lost my balance, because the next thing I knew, my body went plunging into the murky lake. From what my father told me, he dove in after me, dropping his pole and losing his catch. The boy jumped into the lake too and swam over to help him. Together, they pulled me back up to the dock. My father said it took several attempts of chest compressions before the water came spewing out of my mouth. The next thing I remember is waking up to see the boy bent over me, staring at me with those dewy eyes and his mouth slightly open — like he wanted to kiss me. I realized then that I had almost drowned. But in that moment, it was worth it. I'll never forget what my father said to me on the way home that day, 'Margarita, if you are not careful, boys will be the death of you.'"

"Your father is a very wise man," said Burt, lending Margot a sympathetic smile. "I'll do my part to make sure that never happens again. When we get back to Miami, I'll see to it that you get professional swimming lessons." And on a stern note, added, "I trust you'll do your part not to become distracted by the roving eyes of salacious young men. In the meantime, this boat is equipped with life preservers."

Margot gave her husband a tight squeeze. "How did I get so lucky to have you, Burt?"

"I think we both know the answer to that question."

Margot let out a reckoning sigh. "I wish my friends shared my happiness."

"What makes you say that?"

"While I was getting ready for the wedding, I overheard them in the next room, whispering. They said the only reason I married you was for your money."

"They're just jealous."

Margot got down on her knees in front of her husband (fully aware of his reveling in this type of subservient gesture) and held his hands in hers. "You know that's not true, don't you, Burt? You know I love you."

"Love is a relative term."

"What do you mean?"

"It means we deserve each other. We're not all that different, you and I. We know what we want and we go after it."

Margot shimmied her way onto his lap and put her arms around his neck, smothering him in kisses from his face down to his neck, and she did not relent until they ended up on the lower deck.

As the sun began to set, the wind subsided and the waves applied a gentle rocking motion to the king-size nautical bed. Burt lay there pacified as a baby, while Margot's mind was still churning. "So, what do you think I should do?"

"About what?" asked a sedated Burt.

"About my 'so-called' friends."

Burt recouped his thoughts and turned to his wife. "I learned long ago that the green-eyed monster needs to be corralled so that you can keep a close eye on him and use him to your advantage."

Margot pondered those words for a moment, recalling the prophetic note she found wrapped in her fortune cookie. "So, in other words, I should 'keep my friends close and my enemies closer.'"

"Exactly, my dear."

She got out of bed and walked over to the window that extended all along the cabin's port side. Burt's eyes were fixed upon her naked body as she leaned against the coolness of the smooth, paneled bulkhead. With her arms crossed beneath her chin, she stared out at the dark, glistening ocean like a spider waiting for its prey to land in her intricate web. When all of a sudden, she pushed herself away from the window and lunged back onto the bed. "Thank you," she said, planting another seductive kiss on her husband's lips. "I know exactly what I need to do. How did you get to be so smart?"

"Experience begets wisdom."

Margot flipped over and looked up at the ceiling. *And wisdom begets power.*

CHAPTER 21

Jeffrey Holt had come highly recommended from the wife of one of Burt's wealthy acquaintances. He was a native Floridian, a high school dropout who used to spend most of his time surfing. He started out working as a lifeguard, learning everything from diving to rescue techniques and medical assistance. Sadly, for all the responsibilities that came with the job, there wasn't much money to be made. Eventually, he began supplementing his income by offering private swim lessons to the very rich — women in particular, using his bleached blond hair and muscular golden pecks to his advantage.

As much as Margot loved New York City, she hated its long, cold winters, opting to spend most of her time in Florida. If Burt wasn't in New York, he was travelling somewhere on business. She saw little of him in Florida, too. Much of their quality time was spent on his yacht. This allowed her to invest a great deal of hours in aquatic training.

Considering Margot had not ventured into any body of water over her head since her near-drowning experience in Lithuania, she took to the water like a mermaid. She was fearless, and she couldn't get enough of it. She loved the way it felt on her skin — the way it beaded up and sizzled from the heat and then evaporated into a taut coolness.

In addition, Holt's youthful vigor made him a good teacher. He had a way of making it fun, and so her lessons progressed fairly rapidly.

Three days a week, he provided personal instruction at her Miami Beach mansion. Never having had lessons before, she started out learning the basics like treading water and doing the dog paddle, then soon advanced to the backstroke, breaststroke, and sidestroke. Before long, she had mastered the more difficult techniques of both the butterfly and freestyle, too.

Since she would be spending a lot of time on her husband's yacht, Jeffrey thought it important for her to learn a few diving techniques as well. When it appeared that she was ready, he brought her to a three-tier diving pool just outside the city. It was where he had received his lifeguard training. Margot was a little nervous at first, but his gentle, easy-going manner prompted her to clear her head, admonish all fears, and just "take the plunge."

In time, she became bored with the limitations of man-made pools, no matter how deep they were. She wanted to experience the freedom of the ocean. One day, she insisted that Jeffrey take her to the seashore and teach her how to surf. He agreed to bring her to a beach that had a reputation for calm waves and set her up with a board and a wetsuit. Following a series of lessons in the sand and along the shoreline, she felt ready to go full in.

After conquering a succession of benign waves, Margot was feeling pretty confident. Her instructor was ready to call it a day, but she insisted on one more try. Holt paddled alongside her until they found the perfect spot, then propelled his board a safe distance away from her. As he bounced along the current waiting for her to take her last thrill ride of the day, Jeffrey caught sight of a large, fast approaching wave. It was twice as big as the previous ones, but before he could warn Margot of its magnitude, she was already up on her board.

"Kick out!" he shouted to her.

Margot could barely hear him over the roar of the surge. "What?" she yelled back.

"Kick out—like I taught you!"

"Why?"

"It's too big!" he yelled louder. "Sink the tail of your

surfboard into the water to slow it down and rotate your body away from the breaking face, not into the white water!"

"I've got this," she insisted, maintaining her form with fierce determination etched into her jaw. No sooner did she say that than a rogue wave came crashing down on her, engulfing her like a tiny pebble spiraling through a tunnel.

The swell had barely subsided when Holt dove off his board to try to locate her. Blocked by residual waves and the sun's bright reflection over the glistening blue ocean, his view was gravely diminished. He had reached full panic mode when, off in the distance, he spotted her head bobbing up and down like a buoy. Forcing his way through the current, his strength grew threefold as he tried to get to her as fast as he could.

Jeffrey dragged her to the shoreline and employed every life-saving technique he had learned as a lifeguard. Desperation was setting in after a series of chest compressions and mouth-to-mouth resuscitation appeared futile, until her entire torso heaved upward and a gush of water erupted from her throat. Gasping, she drew in her first breath.

When she opened her eyes, Jeffrey was leaning over her, his hand behind her neck. "I almost lost you," he choked out, holding back tears.

Margot glanced from side to side as if trying to figure out where she was, when she came to the realization. She had been in this situation before. It was almost like déjà vu. She grabbed Jeffrey's neck and pulled him down with all the strength her limp arms could muster. "I owe you," she whispered softly, then rendered a kiss upon his lips that he would never forget.

CHAPTER 22

It promised to be a good Friday in more ways than one. An unexpected April sun rose over the Manhattan skyline, casting an optimistic light throughout Burt and Margot's 35th-floor apartment. It had been the same apartment Burt had shared with his ex-wife prior to their divorce. Meredith allowed him to keep it in the settlement, preferring their Connecticut residence where she and her daughter could spend more time riding and taking care of their horses. That, and the fact that Meredith could not bear to face her peers after the incident at the art gallery, had significantly cut back her social activities.

Margot wanted to erase every memory of Meredith, so before she moved in, she had the whole apartment refurbished to her taste. The overflow of 18th-century French Baroque furnishings and draperies literally gave Margot claustrophobia. Her personal life was cluttered enough. She needed the clean lines a contemporary look had to offer, and had it decorated similar to the apartment she formerly shared with Burt.

Lucky for her, her husband had little interest in home decor. As long as his wife was happy, he was happy. Besides, his mind was too preoccupied with his business dealings to be bothered by domestic trivialities.

He and Margot had just finished eating a special brunch comprised of poached eggs and asparagus with Hollandaise sauce, croissants, fig jam, and Mimosas prepared by their multi-commissioned maid, Maria. Maria had stayed on to work for Mr. Magnuson after the divorce. She would much have preferred to go to Connecticut with Meredith, but could not leave her family in the city, and the commute would have been too arduous. Though she was not keen on Mr. Magnuson's aloofness, he always treated her with professional courtesy. Still, there was something about him that had always bothered her. Maybe it was a gut feeling, but from the moment she met him, she always suspected him of being an unfaithful husband.

When the new Mrs. Magnuson moved in, it became evident that she was not welcome. There was a tangible iciness to Maria's voice and demeanor. *What is it with servants?* thought Margot. *First Jacques, now Maria.* Not that she was going to let that bother her. She was never one to vie for the Miss Congeniality award. As far as she was concerned, Maria was there for one purpose, and that was to serve.

"Since it's Good Friday, when you're done with the dishes, you can take the rest of the day off," said Burt.

"Thank you, sir," answered Maria, bowing her head in appreciative servitude.

"Don't forget to take the garbage on your way out," inserted Margot. "The compactor is starting to smell and can't wait till Monday."

"Yes, Missus," said Maria, delivering an empty stare before retreating into the kitchen.

Margot stood up from the dining table and pushed her chair in. "It's now or never," she announced, bending over to give Burt a kiss. "Thank you for agreeing to let me do this."

"It's the least I could do. Did you make sure they'd all be present for the call?"

"Of course," said Margot, scooping her laptop up from the coffee table and plopping down on the couch. Taking a deep breath, she proceeded to initiate a five-way Skype call with her friends.

It had been five years ago, on her wedding day, since Margot and her bridesmaids had all gotten together. She had seen

Bethany, Doris, and Dana individually a couple of times, but this was going to be different. They had talked about the possibility of taking a cruise together, but nothing more had come of it. This time, Margot was determined to see it through.

Margot (initiating the call): "Bethany...Doris...Rachel...Dana...Can you hear me?"

One by one, their faces appeared on the screen.

Margot: "I've missed you guys. It's time to set up that reunion cruise we've been talking about."

Rachel: "I've thought about it and I really can't afford to go on a cruise."

Margot: "Don't worry, Rachel. I told you, the whole trip will be on me. All expenses paid."

Doris: "Why can't we just take a cruise on Burt's yacht? It would save you, I mean–Burt, a lot of money."

Margot glanced over at Burt, who was listening in on the discourse and shaking his head, no. "He considers his yacht his private business craft. He'd rather I didn't use it for personal extravaganzas."

Bethany: "A cruise is fine, as long as it's not one of those mega cruise ships. Too many people."

Margot: "Don't worry. I've looked into that, and it won't be."

Bethany: "Oh, good. Did you have a destination in mind?"

Margot: "I was thinking of Bermuda."

Rachel: "Why Bermuda?"

Margot: "Burt and I have sailed there several times on his yacht."

Doris: "If you've already been there, why do you want to go there again?"

Margot: "Because it's beautiful and I love it there. It's lush and tranquil, and the beaches are unlike any you've ever seen. The sand is actually pink."

Doris: "Pink?"

Margot: "Yeah, I read all about it. It's created by these tiny red organisms that grow under the coral reefs, and when they die, they mix with the crushed corals and shells on the ocean floor. Eventually, they get washed up on shore, creating this gorgeous pink hue."

Dana: "That's cool."

Margot: "Besides, the ship leaves from the New York Bay and goes directly to Bermuda."

Dana: "For how long?"

Margot: "Seven days."

Doris: "Seven days!"

Margot: "Yes, but half the cruise is spent on the water. That's what makes it so great, we'll have plenty of time to catch up. C'mon, you guys! We haven't been all together since the wedding."

Bethany (tapping her pencil and looking at her calendar): "What dates did you have in mind?"

Margot: "I was looking at the last week in August."

Bethany: "Isn't August supposed to be the hottest month in Bermuda?"

Margot: "It doesn't matter. We'll be spending most of the time relaxing and sunbathing on the deck while sipping on cool, refreshing cocktails. It doesn't get any better than that!"

Bethany: "Well, it certainly sounds like you've done your homework."

Margot: "Oh, believe me, I have."

Rachel: "It's easy for you, Doris and Bethany because you all live in New York, but Dana and I live in Ohio."

Margot: "I told you, it's *all expenses paid!* That includes your flights to New York. Look, don't look a gift horse in the mouth, Rachel."

Rachel: "Yeah, but I'm a little nervous about flying."

Margot: "There are drugs for that. You work in a hospital, don't you? Surely you can get one of your doctors to sign off on a few 'necessary' prescriptions."

Rachel: "I guess...but I don't know if I can take that much time off work."

Bethany: "Have you taken any time off since Lou's death?"

Rachel: "I couldn't—not with all the medical bills we incurred. In fact, I've had to put in extra shifts at the hospital just to stay afloat. The good news is, because of my nursing degree, I was able to care for him myself during those last few months before his pancreatic cancer did him in. If I had had to pay for hospice care, our bills would have skyrocketed even more. The bad news is, I'm still paying off my college debt for that nursing degree. I never even had time to properly grieve."

Margot: "All the more reason, Rachel. No one needs a vacation more than you!"

Rachel: "I guess...if it's all expenses paid..."

Dana: "I'm in."

Bethany: "I've been working on a major story for the magazine, which has to be out before the August edition. I'll be done by then, so August works for me."

Margot: "Doris?"

Doris: "I don't know. Who's going to take care of Shadow?"

Margot: "Doris, you've lived in the same apartment in Brooklyn for most of your adult life. Surely, you know some neighbor who can come in and feed your cat."

Doris: "Not really."

Margot: "What about your brother? Doesn't he live just a few blocks away from you?"

Doris: "Yeah, but we're not talking right now."

Margot (letting out an exasperated breath): "Oh my God, Doris, stop holding grudges!"

Doris (rolling her eyes): "I'll try and figure something out."

Margot: "So you're in?"

Doris: "Yeah, I'm in."

Margot (clapping her hands): "Yay! Then it's settled! I'll have Burt's secretary email each of you with all the details as soon as all the arrangements have been made. It'll be so much fun, you guys! I promise. It will be a cruise to remember!"

Margot turned off her laptop and closed the lid. "There," she said, looking over at her husband, who was still seated at the table reading the newspaper. "Nothing will bring me and my friends closer than spending *seven* days together on a cruise ship. Right, Burt?"

Burt lifted his eyes from his paper and lowered his reading glasses to peer over at his wife. "Are you sure that's what you want?"

"Wasn't it you who said, '*Keep your friends close and your enemies closer?*'"

CHAPTER 23

Margot was scavenging every perimeter of her bedroom-sized, walk-in closet, trying to decide what to pack for her cruise. She pulled a flowery chiffon dress off a hanger and held it up in front of her in the full-length mirror. Although it came down to her calves, it was light and sheer with a nice slit up the side. It should be perfect in Bermuda's balmy weather. As she stood there, still trying to decide if she should pack it, Maria walked in.

"Can I help you pack, Missus?"

"No thanks," said Margot.

Maria turned to walk out of the room.

"Wait a minute!" Margot shouted, tossing the dress in the maid's direction. "I'd like this washed. I haven't worn it for a while, and it could use a little 'freshening up.'"

"Of course," said Maria, picking it up off the floor.

"Make sure you hand-wash it and press it on the lowest setting. It's silk chiffon—very delicate and very expensive. Not that you'd know."

"Yes, Ma'am."

"Oh, by the way, I'm leaving in the morning, so I'll need it ready by tonight."

Without saying a word and her head held low, Maria shuffled out, closing the door firmly behind her.

Margot picked out a few more ensembles and threw them on the closet island. Then she reopened the door and headed to the bathroom to sort through the toiletries she'd need to bring. That's when she overheard Burt in the adjoining bedroom talking on his cell phone. He was speaking in a hushed tone, so she moved in closer with her ear against the wall to try to make out what he was saying.

"*Yes, Meredith, I know. I'll be there. You know I've never missed any of Kathryn's horse competitions...We can discuss that later...Okay, I've gotta go. Bye.*"

Margot made it a point to walk into the room. His back was toward her, and he was just hanging up. "Who was that?" she asked casually.

Startled at the sound of her voice, Burt turned around to face her. "Uh, just business. Nothing you need to be concerned with."

Margot studied the buried guilt on his face. "Does that mean you're going to be out of town while I'm on the cruise?"

"Yes. Yes I am."

"That's good. So, when I return from my trip, we'll have more time to spend together. Maybe we can have dinner with Kathryn and Robert."

"What?"

"Your children...when I get back from the cruise."

"I don't think that's a good idea."

"Why not?"

"You know how my kids feel about you."

Margot's eyes widened, and her demeanor took a hostile turn. "Why, Burt? Why do they feel that way about me? Is it because of what your ex-wife is feeding them? Or is it because of what they're hearing from you?"

"You know perfectly well I don't speak ill of you."

"Then why can't you stand up to Meredith, Burt? What does she have on you that makes you cow-tie to her the way you do?"

Burt's face reddened as he raised his voice. "Have you been listening in on my conversations? She has absolutely nothing on me, and I don't appreciate your accusatory language."

"I didn't mean to," said Margot, realizing she had overstepped her boundary. "I was just coming in to get something." She meandered over to Burt and wrapped her arms around his neck. "I'm sorry," she said, in a low, loving manner. "It doesn't matter what your kids think of me. All that matters is what *you* think of me."

CHAPTER 24

Dana and Rachel stood in line at Cleveland Hopkins International Airport, ready to board their plane for a direct flight to New York. Thanks to their good friend, Margot, they made themselves comfortable in their business-class seats. When the flight attendant asked if they wanted a pre-flight libation, Dana took advantage of it, but Rachel just asked for water.

"You're not getting a cocktail?" asked Dana. "It's free."

"I know," said Rachel, taking a prescription bottle of Xanax out of her purse. "I took Margot's advice and got some of these." She took out a pill and bit it in half. "I've never taken them before, and I'm not sure how they're going to affect me, so I don't want to take a whole tablet." Rachel popped it in her mouth and washed it down with water. "Do you want the other half?"

"No thanks," said Dana. "I'll stick to beer. When did you suddenly become afraid of flying?"

"Remember when we flew back from Margot's wedding, how rocky that flight was? I had a paper bag in my lap the whole time."

"Yeah, but that flight was to Miami. This trip's way shorter. We'll be there in less than an hour and a half. Besides, the chances of crashing are about one in five million. Your odds are better of dying from cancer."

"Like Lou," said Rachel, her voice dropping off.

"I didn't mean to go there," said Dana, taking a slug of her beer.

Rachel leaned from her window seat and stared out onto the tarmac. "Do you believe in fate, Dana?"

"No."

"Then what do you believe in?"

"I believe each person is in control of their own destiny."

"No wonder you're so cool and sure of yourself all the time."

"I wish," said Dana, taking another slug of beer and wiping the foam off her lips with the back of her hand. "It doesn't always go as planned, no matter how hard you try."

Once the plane took off and the Xanax started kicking in, Rachel laid her head against the pillow and closed her eyes, allowing her mind to wander back to Margot's wedding...

It couldn't have been a more perfect day for a Spring wedding. The weather was warm, but a gentle easterly wind kept the humidity at bay while an explosion of early blooms of chromatic Azaleas and Shasta daisies sweetened the air and brightened the grounds.

The wedding took place at Burt's magnificent ocean villa in Miami Beach. It was a grand affair, filled with a who's-who of Burt's most influential friends. At the rear of the sprawling, white concrete estate, a series of French doors opened up to an expansive outdoor patio area. A smattering of open bars and pedestal cocktail tables were set up to overlook an Olympic-sized pool where pink, purple, and white Lily pads floated above its crystal clear water.

To the left of the pool, sequestered beneath a white canopy, was the banquet area where a dozen or so tables, each accommodating six to eight guests, faced an elevated stage and wood-planked dance floor.

To the right of the pool was where the ceremony was to take place. Two sections of white folding chairs were positioned atop a carpet of lush green grass and separated by a satin runner, which led to the altar: a white latticed archway overflowing with pink and lavender fresh-cut flowers with a commanding view of the sparkling blue ocean behind it.

Margot had chosen Rachel, Dana, and Doris to be her bridesmaids and Bethany to be her matron of honor. This was the first time the women had all become acquainted with one another. Doris and Bethany had actually met before, meeting up with Margot after work for drinks and sometimes dinner. But it wasn't until today that Doris and Bethany got to meet Margot's school friends, Rachel and Dana.

In a large sitting room off the master suite, a flurry of conversation ensued between the four bridesmaids as they were getting ready.

Rachel: "Bethany, you and Margot worked together, right? When did you first find out that she was getting married?"

Bethany: "Not until two months before the wedding, when she asked me to be her maid of honor." Bethany let out a chuckle. "The funny thing is, I thought she was having an affair with my husband, when all along, she was secretly shacked up with Dillon, McCain & Dermot's top client."

Doris: "I knew she was secretly dating someone from work, but she never said anything more than that. She told me she wanted to keep it quiet, because she didn't want to risk losing her job."

Bethany: "Both she and Burt did a good job of hiding it because no one in the whole firm had a clue about their relationship."

Rachel: "I didn't find out about it until she asked me to be a bridesmaid. What about you, Dana? Did you know anything about it?"

Dana, who had been quiet up until now, was positioned in front of a full-length mirror, attempting to tie her satin sash into a bow. "Nope," she answered with a scowl on her face while scrutinizing her reflection. "I look ridiculous."

The string quartet began to play, and the bridesmaids

lined up to begin their walk down the silken aisle to the altar. Jacques, who was Burt's head butler and long-time confidant, took time out of his ordinary routine of supervising the staff to be Burt's best man. As Jacques took Bethany's arm to escort her down the aisle, Rachel looked around and whispered in Doris's ear. "Where are *our* escorts?"

Doris partially covered her mouth and sniggered, "I guess Burt didn't have any friends our age to accompany us."

The guests looked on from their seats as the shortest bridesmaid, Dana, was the last to reach the altar. At that point, the chamber musicians laid down their instruments, and the French doors opened up to reveal an angelically radiant bride with her father at her side, proclaiming her innocence in a dazzling white designer gown, carrying a cascading bouquet of the themed white roses and pink and purple orchids.

In that moment, the Baby Grand piano in the veranda overtook the outdoor speakers and began to pipe out a sonorous Wedding March as Margot and her father took their first steps toward what Margot had previously described to her friends as "*the finish line.*"

Margot's father held on tightly to his daughter's arm as if he were not yet willing to let her go. As they promenaded down the aisle, Mr. Kazlauskas could be seen whispering something into his daughter's ear, which Margot would later admit only to Rachel, "It is not too late to back out, Margarita. It is never too late."

Beneath the floral-infused trellis, at the minister's side, stood Margot's husband-to-be. A man twice her age, boasting the grin of a wide-eyed teenager. And next to him was his comparably-aged best man, Jacques, looking as staid and stern as an embalmed corpse.

Burt raised his glazed eyes to meet those of his lovely young bride, who hovered a full head-length taller than him, as they stood face-to-face exchanging their vows.

As soon as the ceremony ended, the festivities kicked off with music, hors d'oeuvres, and an open bar while the kitchen staff prepared for the distribution of a five-course banquet.

The bridesmaids had gathered at one of the small tables near the bar when someone snuck up behind Bethany and kissed her on the neck. Bethany jerked around, nearly spilling her drink on her pale lilac dress. "Oh my God, Charles, you startled me!" she shrieked. "Did you just get here?"

"My flight was delayed. Didn't you get my text?"

"No, but I haven't really had a chance to check my phone. You missed a beautiful ceremony," she said, glancing at the drink in his hand. "I see you had time to make a stop at the bar."

Charles flushed a little as he peered into his near-empty glass.

"Oh, let me introduce you to my new friends. This is Dana, Rachel, and Doris."

The group exchanged pleasantries, then turned their eyes toward the bride and groom, who had begun making their rounds. "She looks beautiful, doesn't she?" exclaimed Bethany to her husband, who couldn't seem to take his dark eyes off her.

"Yeah...beautiful," he said resignedly.

"So, you had no clue, either, that she was seeing Burt?" asked Bethany.

"None," said Charles, shaking the ice cubes around in his glass before taking a hard gulp of what was left of his whiskey.

"I need to go to the ladies' room," announced Doris.

"I'll join you," said Rachel.

While the two of them maneuvered their way through the crowd, Doris moved in closer to Rachel's ear, "It's no wonder Bethany suspected her husband of having an affair with Margot from the way he was staring at her."

As crystal flutes brimming with sparkling Champagne

were being distributed, dinner was announced, and attendees were asked to find their way to their assigned seats. The bride and groom sat at the centermost table facing the stage between her parents, the minister, and the best man. Also seated with them were Burt's two adult children, Robert and Kathryn, whose lack of enthusiasm was on display for everyone to see.

The reception was officiated when silver knives began to clang louder and louder against the fine porcelain dishes, prompting a heartfelt kiss between the two newlyweds. This was followed by a toast from Burt's best man. Jacques delivered his brief tribute in an almost business-like manner and ended by raising his glass, wherein he wished the couple a "lifetime" of happiness.

That was the cue for the waiters in black tie and white gloves to begin serving an exquisite meal as well as bottomless libations. By the time dessert arrived, the alcohol was in full swing, and the gossip flowed as easily as the Champagne.

Charles had gone back to the bar for a third refill of his whiskey on the rocks when the band began to play a slow music set.

Rachel (looking in the bride's direction): "How much do you think that dress cost?"

Bethany: "Probably more than my yearly income."

Doris: "How did she get so lucky?"

Bethany: "I think there was more than mere luck involved. I think she worked hard to get him once she found out how much he was worth."

Doris: "I wouldn't call lying on your back and spreading your legs hard work."

Dana: "I would, considering he's twice her age."

Rachel (lowering her voice and giggling): "Shshsh, you guys. That's not nice!"

Bethany: "She did convince him to leave his wife."

Dana: "I don't think it took too much convincing. His wife left *him*, remember?"

Rachel: "Are those his two kids sitting at the table with them?"

Doris: "Yeah. They look about as happy to be here as we are."

Rachel: "Speak for yourself, Doris! I'm very happy to be here."

Doris: "I wonder what Margot's parents think about her marrying a guy whose kids are almost the same age as her."

The gossip abruptly came to an end when the bride and groom stopped by their table. Margot bent down to give each of them a hug before introducing them to her new husband. Except for Bethany, that is, who needed no introduction since she had known him longer than Margot.

Rachel wiped a teardrop from her eye: "You look beautiful, Margot."

Bethany: "And the food was delicious."

Dana: "I appreciate the fact that you had a vegetarian option."

Margot: "I wouldn't forget about you, Dana. You know that."

Bethany stood up to give Burt an embrace: "Congratulations, Burt."

Just then, Charles returned to the table, extending his hand to Burt for a handshake. "Congratulations, Burt."

"Thank you, Charles."

"May I kiss the bride?"

"Of course," said Burt, paying close attention to the expression on Margot's face while Charles gave her a delicate peck on the cheek.

Before long, partner Bill McCain walked up behind the groom. He was holding a drink in one hand and patted him on the back with the other. "Burt, you sly dog, how could you keep this from everyone at Dillon, McCain for so long?"

Burt turned a bright shade of red and smiled sheepishly.

Bill bent over to give Margot a quick kiss on the lips. "You look ravishing, Margot! Now, if you'll excuse me, I'm going to steal your husband away from you for just a moment. Charles, would you mind joining us, too? Bethany, I'll speak to you later."

"Oh, you're not going to talk business, are you?" exclaimed Margot, as they began to shuffle off. "This is my wedding day!"

Bill, who had his arm around Burt's shoulders, cocked his head back at the bride. "I promise I'll bring him back real soon."

Margot gave her friends a flabbergasted look, then went in for a group hug. "I'm so happy you could all come and get to know each other because you are my closest friends in the whole world!" She broke free to grab someone's half-drank cocktail from the table and raised it up in the air. "Here's to old friendships and to new."

"Here, here," reciprocated the ladies.

Dana: "Does this mean you're going to be moving here — to Florida — permanently?"

Margot: "Oh no, this is our winter getaway. Our primary residence will still be our apartment in Manhattan.

Rachel: "So, where are you going for your honeymoon?"

Margot: "We're leaving here Monday on Burt's yacht and sailing to The Bahamas for a few days. Then we're going to Bermuda, where we'll be docked for a couple more days..."

Margot's response was cut short when the band announced that the customary matrimonial dance was about to begin, so she excused herself to go find Burt. After the initial bride and groom dance, everyone else joined in.

Bethany was on the floor with her husband, Charles, when he asked her if she wouldn't mind him breaking away for one dance with the bride. Charles crept up behind Burt, tapping him on the shoulder. "May I butt-in?"

"Of course," said Burt, strolling off to the bar to get another drink, then positioning himself where he could watch the two of them dance.

Bethany left the floor to join Dana, who was sitting all alone at the dinner table.

Rachel and Doris were on the dance floor, shimmying to the lively music in front of one another, and observed Charles slow-stepping to the beat with Margot. He was holding her pretty close and whispering in her ear. Rachel sidled up to Doris while continuing to rock her hips back and forth. "What do you think he's saying to her?" she asked, after which the two of them shared a hushed word and a foolhardy laugh before trotting back to the table.

As the reception was coming to a close, the wedding planner instructed all the single ladies to congregate on the veranda where the bride was going to be tossing her bouquet for one lucky bachelorette to catch. Margot sized up the small group of females as she approached. Bethany was off in a corner to witness the spectacle with Dana, who refused to participate in what she referred to as "a manic display of spinster phobia." The bride positioned herself accordingly, then turned to face the opposite direction just before throwing the bouquet over her shoulder. Rachel, her chosen target, had reluctantly joined the cluster; then, at the last minute, she changed her mind and stepped away, causing it to land in the hands of the dumbfounded female who had been struggling to get to the front of the line: Doris.

CHAPTER 25

Standing at the edge of a busy sidewalk on the Village's south side was a stylish young woman in high-heeled sandals, a linen jacket, and matching capris with her face buried in her smart phone. A few minutes later, a yellow cab pulled up to the curb, and the driver lowered his passenger window to get her attention. "Hey!" he yelled out. "You, Bethany?"

Glancing up from her phone, she swept her shoulder-length blond hair to the side and answered, "Yes."

"Sorry I'm late," said the burly driver in a heavy Bronx accent, jumping out to help her with her bags. "Traffic's busier than usual for a Saturday. By the way, I'm Tony."

"I'm kind of in a hurry — Tony," said Bethany, stepping into the back seat.

"Where're we goin' again?"

"Manhattan Cruise Terminal."

"Don't worry. I'll get you there in time."

As soon as Bethany sat down, she was inundated with the scent of artificial pine and had to roll her window down halfway. Poking her nose out, she took in a breath of fresh air, then grabbed up her cell phone, which was laying on the seat to type in a message:

Just got in a cab. should be there in twenty min. beth

After pushing **send**, she opened her inbox to find the most recent email from her managing editor: Great job on the article. Let's plan on a celebratory lunch at Hugo's when you get back. Grace

Bethany shot back a quick reply: Sounds great, Thanks.

Tucking her phone into her purse, she laid her head back against the headrest and closed her eyes while her mind drifted back to that initial job interview at *The Architectural Investigator*...

It had been three years ago, shortly after Charles was sentenced to prison when she walked into the no-frills office building in Greenwich Village. It was the complete opposite of the elite architectural headquarters of Dillon, McCain & Dermot, which she had haughtily grown accustomed to. When she walked through the door of *The Architectural Investigator*, she was immediately met by a short, middle-aged woman donning a budget haircut and red polyester pantsuit. Clearly less threatening than the uptown stiffs she had interviewed with for the previous position of architect.

"Hi, I'm Grace Barrows, the managing editor," she said, offering a hearty handshake.

"Bethany Langford. Nice to meet you."

"Come on over and have a seat," she said, leading Bethany into a back office. While Ms. Barrows settled into her worn-out desk chair, Bethany sat down in a seat in front of her. Ms. Barrows picked up Bethany's resume from a short stack of other applications and did a quick, top-to-bottom glance-over. "So, Bethany, you're an architect — and with an impressive list of credentials, I might add. What brings you here?"

"I need a job," said Bethany, who endeavored to explain her situation as candidly as possible. She began by referencing that pivotal meeting two years ago, which took place on the top floor in the boardroom of Dillon, McCain & Dermot when she was about to be confronted by the board members. Alan Dermot had apparently been given the task of doing the dirty work because he was pacing nervously at the head of the sixteen-seat conference table. Bethany, who was perched at the opposite end, remembered sitting on the edge of her chair while tiny beads of perspiration accumulated on her forehead, exposing her dread of what she was expecting to hear.

"Bethany," Mr. Dermot started out. "When you and Charles first arrived here eight years ago, the Board had its trepidations about bringing a married couple into the firm, but we chose to make an exception because of your unparalleled qualifications. Our presumption was that any possible conflict of interest would likely be avoided since you and your husband would be working in different capacities—you, as an architect, and Charles, as counselor." Dermot paused to take a drink from his water glass and then continued.

"As you know, Charles was entrusted with some of the firm's most prominent clients' accounts. We coupled him with Burton Magnuson because we trusted Charles to represent him with the highest integrity. When it came to choosing an architect for his latest enterprise, *Magnuson Towers*, there were plenty of long-standing and well-qualified candidates in the firm that we tried to sway Mr. Magnuson towards, citing the potential for a conflict of interest. Irregardless of that fact, Burton was so impressed with your style and vision that he insisted he wanted you to handle the project."

Then came the clincher:

"Bethany, we understand that you were exonerated of any wrongdoing, including conspiracy or having any knowledge of your husband's illegal transactions. Be that as it may, we have an obligation to our shareholders to uphold the company's reputation. The Board, therefore, has unanimously come to the decision that you should no longer be associated with Dillon, McCain & Dermot. It was agreed that you be let go under the best possible condition, insofar as you will receive our recommendation for any future endeavor you might wish to pursue."

To that end, Alan Dermot walked over to Bethany and laid out a stack of documents in front of her and handed her a pen. "We have drawn up your termination papers—which we *urge* you to sign."

Beneath the shadow of Dermot's uncompromising stealth, Bethany considered the papers in front of her with downcast eyes. Reluctantly, she picked up the pen and proceeded to sign and initial, one by one, each and every page.

"Which Pier?" yelled the cab driver, followed by a few expletives and a resounding blast of his horn. The distraction forced Bethany to reemerge from her thoughts. "I'm sorry," she said, leaning forward, "What?"

"Did you see that? That bleeping guy cut me off!"

"No, before that."

"I said, 'Which pier?'"

"Oh—Pier 92."

Bethany leaned back into her seat, beleaguered by another flashback...

This time, she was sitting in a molded plastic chair opposite her husband, Charles, who was cupping his hands over hers on the laminate table between them. The room in the Federal Prison was large but otherwise barren, except for two rectangular tables and a couple of chairs. The only other person in the room was a security officer standing guard next to the heavy metal door.

"How are you, Charles?"

"I'm alright. I'm more worried about you, Bethany. How are you doing?"

"I'm okay. I found another job—as a writer for a magazine." Bethany forced out a terse laugh. "Ironically, it's for *The Architectural Investigator*. It's not as prestigious as being an architect by any means, and barely pays half as much, but it appears I've been blackballed all over town. So much for the high recommendations I was promised. So, I had to take what I could get. I had to downsize to a smaller apartment in the South Village to make ends meet. The good news is, it's a straight shot on the subway to my office in East Greenwich."

Charles squeezed her hands tightly. "We're still working on my appeal, and my attorney says they've hired another investigator."

"What happened to the last one?"

"They think he might have been bought off."

"By whom? The firm?"

"I don't know, maybe," shrugged Charles.

"Why would they pay someone to keep them from uncovering the truth?"

"I don't know, but I'm telling you, someone had me framed. You believe that I'm innocent, don't you, Beth?"

"Of course I do, Charles...I *want* to believe you."

Charles squeezed her hands again. Tighter, this time. "You're my rock, Bethany. I promise when I get out of here, I'll make it up to you. We can leave New York, maybe go back to Boston, where we can start all over. I love you, Bethany... Please tell me you'll wait for me..."

Bethany was jarred back into the present once again by the familiar buzz of her instant messenger:

No worries. Doris and I are at pier entrance, about to check in. Will be in waiting area. Margot

CHAPTER 26

Doris and Margot arrived at the *Dream Voyager* cruise terminal at the same time, dragging their luggage over to the conveyor belt where an attendant was ready to help them load it.

"Good grief, Margot, how many suitcases do you need?" exclaimed Doris. "We're only on the ship for a week!"

"A girl's got to be prepared for any occasion," said Margot, unabashedly.

Doris shook her head and gave her a cockeyed glance while she proceeded to go through the security line.

Once the check-in process was complete, the two of them found a couple of open seats in the cruise line's waiting area.

"So, what have you been up to?" asked Margot, tucking away her passport. "It's been a while since I've seen you."

"Not much... I started seeing a therapist."

"What for?"

"Anxiety issues."

"Hmm," said Margot, looking around as though she had little interest in the conversation.

"You know how I tend to overthink everything."

"Is it helping?"

"I don't know."

"Maybe you could try looking at the bright side every once in a while."

"You know I really didn't want to come on this cruise," said Doris, obviously offended by Margot's lack of empathy. "The only reason I came was because my therapist thought it would do me good to get away."

"What do you mean, you didn't want to come on this cruise?" exclaimed Margot in an incensed tone. "After I paid for the whole trip?"

Doris let out a deep sigh before revealing her true feelings. "I know... It's just that...here you are happily married and living this great life, and here I am, living in the same crappy apartment, working in the same boring job—and still single."

"Why must you always compare yourself to me, Doris? Bethany's husband is in jail for embezzlement, Rachel's husband is dead from pancreatic cancer, and Dana, well, she's got her own issues."

"I guess, but..."

"You've got to get over it and quit feeling sorry for yourself."

Before Doris could respond, Margot spotted Rachel and Dana entering the terminal and jumped up to wave them down and let them know where they were sitting.

"Sorry," said Margot, dropping back into her seat. "Were you going to say something?"

"Never mind," said Doris, turning her head the other way while looking both annoyed and defeated at the same time.

The conversation fell flat until Rachel and Dana joined them and exchanged hugs. "We saved these seats," said Margot, pointing to the empty chairs. "But we're still waiting on Beth. I'm surprised she's not here yet; she's usually 'Miss Punctuality.' So, how was your flight, you guys?"

"Not as bad as I expected," said Rachel, lifting her palm to the side of her mouth and whispering, "The Xanax helped. I slept the whole way. I still feel a little groggy."

Margot cackled loudly, "Always works for me."

"I had to shake her a couple of times to wake her up. I think the fresh air helped once we got out of the airport," said Dana.

"So, how've you been, Dana? Have you met anyone since the last time I saw you?"

"No, but I haven't really been looking."

"How far do you have to look?" butt in Doris. "I wish I worked in the tech industry. Isn't it mostly all men?"

"Yeah, but a lot of them are programmers like me who mostly work from home."

"What about online dating?" asked Margot. "Have you tried that?"

"I don't like the sites that are currently out there. People are never who they say they are."

"Well, we're going to find you someone on this cruise. I'm going to make it my mission!" spouted off Margot, pinching her friend's cheek and generating an immediate flush over Dana's sun-deprived skin.

Minutes before boarding was about to commence, Bethany finally showed up. She had just completed the check-in process when Margot ran up to the counter to greet her, locking her in a big bear hug. "I've missed you, Bethany," she said, as she led her to where the other women were sitting. "...Our lunches and our after-work talks."

"Me too," replied Bethany, half-heartedly, just before approaching the others.

"What took you so long?" asked Doris. "Did you get tied up in traffic?"

"I don't know. I think I dozed off. I suspect my driver, 'Tony,' may have taken a longer route."

"Typical New York City cabbie," said Margot.

"Yeah. I probably should have gotten that new Uber service to pick me up."

"Still, that's not like you to doze off. You're always on top of your game."

Bethany moved in closer to Margot, lowering her voice.

"I've just had a lot on my mind lately... I saw Charles again last week."

Margot's demeanor suddenly tightened. "Oh? How's he doing?"

"He's alright, I guess."

"What did he have to say?" Margot asked nonchalantly, while nervously awaiting her friend's response.

"Not much. Just that he loves me and doesn't want to lose me. He said that when he gets out of prison, he wants to move away from New York. Maybe go back to Boston and start anew."

Margot released a steadied breath. "Did you tell him about our trip?"

"Yeah. He told me I should concentrate on having fun and not bring up his name while I'm on the cruise."

"Then you should take his advice. In fact, we should all take that advice." Margot announced loudly, turning to face the other women. "Did you hear that, ladies? From this moment forward and throughout the remainder of this trip, the name: 'Charles Langford,' shall not be brought up again!"

Everyone shook their heads in accord.

"Now come on, girls, they're boarding. Let's go have some fun!"

CHAPTER 27

Seeing *The Dream Voyager* for the first time caused Margot to get a lump in her throat. She had never been on a cruise ship before. It was much bigger than she had imagined, certainly bigger than her husband's yacht. She looked up at the sky. It was a beautiful azure except for a light smattering of downy cumulus clouds, which Burt had taught her would make for a perfect day for sailing.

In a display of camaraderie, Margot employed her friends to lock arms while they paraded up the ramp of the *Dream Voyager*. When they reached the top, they were stopped for a group photo to be taken before boarding. "I don't have to tell you pretty ladies to smile," remarked the photographer, hoping to evoke a reflection of the wide grin emitting from his own face. At first glance, the photo portrayed a cheerful image of five attractive women in their thirties about to embark on a care-free, seven-day cruise. But on closer inspection, every line, wrinkle, and slant offered a glimpse into the distorted reality lurking beneath each individual facade.

While Margot was busy taking up temporary residence in her Penthouse Suite, Bethany, Dana, Rachel, and Doris found their way to their individual cabins, which were situated side-by-side a couple of decks below. There was certainly no room for complaint. Their wealthy friend had taken good care of them, setting each of them up with a Veranda Stateroom complete with its own private balcony.

While the ladies were busy unpacking, the captain's voice came over the intercom to announce that a mandatory muster drill would soon be taking place. At exactly 3:00 o'clock post meridiem, eastern time, all passengers were required to assemble on the appropriate deck as indicated on their assigned ID cards.

Per protocol, Margot grabbed her life jacket, as well as a copy of the ship's bulletin, and made her way to deck three — the promenade level. She figured her friends would be meeting on a different floor since the deck assignments corresponded with the cabin room numbers.

When she reached the promenade level, she discovered that was where the work-out room was located, along with a sectioned-off area for yoga. Following the crowd, she made her way through the glass doors to the outdoor jogging track where the muster drill was going to take place. While the officers were waiting for everyone to show up, she thought she'd sneak off to do a little more investigating. As she meandered along the wood-plank track, she found that it circled almost the entirety of the deck. Most of it was fenced in with an open-air railing, but there were a few sections protected by a Plexiglas partition.

When she heard a loud voice on the speaker, she quickly made her way back to the assemblage. Positioning herself in front of the suspended lifeboats, she stood quietly in abeyance as the officers explained the emergency evacuation procedures, while continuing to take in her surroundings. The whole exercise lasted roughly, half-an-hour before the passengers were permitted to return to their cabins.

As soon as she returned to her room, she pulled off her life vest and picked up her phone, which she had left lying on the bed. She needed to send a quick message before the boat headed out to sea, figuring she wouldn't have cell service until they landed in Bermuda.

just had muster drill. no prob foreseen. see you soon. m

She threw her phone back on the bed, locked the door with her ID key card, and took the elevator to the upper deck, where the girls had previously agreed to meet for a celebratory toast before sailing off.

Dana, Doris, and Bethany had been the first to arrive, securing a table by the indoor pool. They had just sat down when Rachel walked up with a giddy smile on her face. "You guys, guess what I found sitting on my bed? There was the cutest elephant made out of towels!"

Doris: "I got one too."

Bethany: "All the cruise ships do that."

Margot stepped through the automatic glass doors, which opened up to the covered part of the lido deck, and immediately spotted her friends seated on the side nearest the bar.

Before she even got a chance to sit down, Doris opened her mouth. "What took you so long?"

Margot: "My drill station was on the same level as the workout room and the outdoor track, so I thought I'd check it out while I was there."

Bethany: "Which level was that?"

Margot: "The third deck, promenade level. Read the ship's bulletin. It says they have early morning yoga classes there, too."

Rachel: "I don't know if I'll be doing any yoga. I'm afraid I might get nauseous."

Margot: "You'll be fine."

Doris: "How do you know? Isn't this your first time on a cruise ship?"

Margot: "Yeah, but Burt told me that these big ships can counterbalance a great deal of motion—unless we run into some *really* bad weather."

Bethany: "I think we're about to enter hurricane season."

Rachel (gasping): "Oh no! Are you sure?"

Margot (crossing her fingers): "Burt's assistant, who made all the reservations, said that there were no hurricanes in the immediate forecast."

Dana (in a mocking tone): "If there are, you can mop up the mess with your little elephant friend." Dana turned her eyes toward Bethany. "Isn't that what those extra towels are really for?"

Rachel gave Dana a squeamish look: "Good thing I packed plenty of Dramamine."

Dana: "Well, you'd better start poppin' 'em because it takes a while for them to start working. Aren't you in the medical industry? You should know that."

Rachel: "That's right, I forgot! I'd better go back to my room and get some."

While the girls were chaffing back and forth, two male wait-staff members were behind the bar unloading their trays. "Hey, Jorge," said one of them, casting a wily grin. "Look who's sitting in your section."

The two men took turns casually throwing glances at the five attractive females seated at the table in the distance. The taller of the two slicked back his hair and straightened his bow tie. As he was about to head over to the table, he gave his friend a wink. "Don't be jealous, Raul. Maybe they will be in your section tomorrow. But for now, Jorge is going to show you how it's done."

Rachel had just stood up to leave when the handsome waiter in a white uniform with a black stripe down the sides of his pants came to take their orders.

"Hello, ladies. My name is Jorge. I'll be your server today. Can I get you anything to eat or drink?"

After eying him up and down, Margot was the first to speak up. "I think we'll start out with just drinks for now. Don't you agree, ladies?"

The women shook their heads in concurrence.

"I will need to see your drink cards first," said the waiter.

Rachel stopped short of leaving. "Drink cards?"

Margot pulled hers out from her pocket and showed it to Rachel. "Yeah, these came with your welcome package in the room. Didn't you read it? The silver sticker in the top right corner means we can have unlimited cocktails."

"I must have left mine in the room," said Rachel, turning to look at the waiter. "Can I order my drink and give it to you when I come back?"

"I am not supposed to do that. But, for you," he said, smiling, "I will make an exception."

Rachel, looking a bit embarrassed, sat back down. "Do you have a drink menu?"

The waiter pulled a couple of extra menus off a nearby empty table and handed them out. While the rest of the women were trying to decide what they wanted, Margot, whose eyes were still fixed on the young waiter, spoke up. "I love your British accent—JORGE. You must be from Bermuda."

"Yes. Born and raised," said Jorge, proudly eating up Margot's scrutinizing eyes. "So, uh...have you ladies decided what you would like to drink?"

Rachel (still poring over the menu): "I don't know. I can't make up my mind."

Margot (never having picked up her menu): "Well, I know what I want. I want a Dark 'N' Stormy."

Jorge: "Ahh, you have been to Bermuda before."

Margot: "Yes, several times."

Rachel: "What's a Dark 'N' Stormy?"

Jorge: "It is the National drink of Bermuda. It is made with *Gosling's Black Seal Rum*. It is darker and thicker than regular rum, with a little bit of a caramel flavor. It also contains Ginger Beer and a slice of lime for garnish. It is a favorite in Bermuda. You must be careful, though," he added, with a grin wide enough to expose all his teeth. "It is very potent."

Rachel: "If it's the National drink of Bermuda, I guess I

should try it. Maybe it'll help me stop worrying about getting sick."

Dana: "Yeah, by making you more sick."

Rachel (jumping out of her chair): "Okay, now I'm going. Be right back, you guys," she yelled as she scurried off.

Bethany (raising her eyes from her menu): "Well, I'm going to be safe and have something I know I can handle. I'll have a Rum Swizzle."

Doris: "What's that?"

Bethany: "It's sort of like a Mai Tai."

Jorge: "It contains pineapple juice, orange juice, Grenadine, and Rum."

Doris: "That sounds refreshing. I think I'll have the same."

Jorge looked over at Dana, who was still studying the beverage selection.

Dana finally dropped the laminated card on the table and looked up at Jorge: "I'll have a Heineken."

Rachel returned just as Jorge was coming back with their cocktails. Margot raised her glass for a toast. "To a cruise that will linger in our memories for as long as we live!"

One by one, the glasses chimed together as everyone echoed the sentiment.

Rachel took one sip of her Dark 'N' Stormy and immediately started coughing. "Woo, that's strong!"

Margot lifted her own tumbler to her mouth. "Strong to last long," she cooed, allowing the dark liquid to glide down her throat. "Mmm, smooth as silk."

Rachel giggled in between chokes and turned to Bethany. "How's your Rum Swizzle?"

"Good," said Bethany, taking a bite of her cherry from her fruit skewer.

Margot: "So, Bethany, what's this big story you just finished for *The Investigator*?"

Bethany: "It's an insider's view of how major companies illegally cut corners in order to meet their budget costs."

Margot raised an eyebrow: "Hmm, sounds interesting. So, what did you find out?"

Bethany: "A lot. You'd be surprised. I know I'm not supposed to bring *him* up, but I wish I'd known everything I've learned from my research before Charles got busted."

Rachel: "When will he get out?"

Bethany: "He's already served two years. He's got three more, so he'll be out by 2018. Sooner, if he wins his appeal."

Doris: "I heard those white collar crime prisons are more like country clubs than jails."

Bethany tilted her head in disdain. "You try being locked up for that long, regardless of the accommodations. See how you'd like it."

Doris lowered her eyes and removed the straw from her Rum Swizzle to take a gulp.

Margot: "Alright now. We weren't supposed to talk about *him*, remember?"

Bethany: "So, what about you, Dana? How's your job going?"

Dana: "Okay. Programming can get kinda boring. I've been thinking of maybe doing a startup."

Bethany: "Like what?"

Everyone moved in closer to hear what Dana was about to say. Everyone, that is, except for Doris, who was preoccupied surveying the bar for eligible prospects.

Dana: "It's an app linking...I don't know...I've just been tossing some ideas around in my head."

Margot turned to Doris, following her friend's gaze toward the bar. "Spot anything you like over there?"

Doris released a crooked smile without breaking her stare. "Yeah, except I can't tell from here if he's wearing a ring or not.

I guess I'm gonna have to mosey on over to the bar for my next drink."

The girls all laughed except for Rachel. "I'm never going to get married again. No one could ever replace Lou. He was my high school sweetheart, you know."

Doris, who never had empathy for anyone but herself, re-entered the conversation. "I thought you wanted kids. You should probably get married again if you wanna have kids. And you'd better hurry up 'cause you're not getting any younger."

Bethany: "You've still got time. Women are having kids well into their 40s nowadays."

Rachel (becoming teary-eyed): "I *do* want kids. I just don't think it's in the cards for me. You all know that I had a miscarriage when Lou and I were first married. What I never told you was that I suffered two more miscarriages after that."

A brief silence befell the table, and Bethany placed her palm over Rachel's hand. "I'm so sorry, Rachel."

Doris: "Maybe you can try that 'in vitro.'"

Rachel: "Do you know how expensive that is? Besides, even then, there's no guarantee it will work."

Doris: "Why don't you marry a guy who's already got kids? Like Margot." Doris turned her eyes to the other side of the table, where Margot was sitting. "What's it like, Margot—having a ready-made family?"

Margot (not ignorant of the implied insult): "First of all, they're adults now. Second of all, you know Burt's kids hate me. They blame me for breaking up their parents' marriage."

Doris (cracking a grin): "Well, you did, didn't you?"

Margot: "It takes two to break up a marriage, Doris."

Bethany: "At least they came to the wedding."

Doris: "It was pretty obvious they didn't want to be there."

Margot: "I think Burt threatened that if they didn't show up, they would lose their inheritance."

Dana returned to the subject at hand and looked back at Rachel: "You can always adopt. You don't need to be married anymore. I plan on adopting myself one day."

Margot gave Dana a stunned look.

Rachel: "I don't know. Between Lou's medical expenses and my student loans. I can barely afford to support myself, let alone another human being."

Doris (getting up from her chair): "Well, I'm tired of all this 'kid' talk. I'm ready for another drink, and I'm going to head over to the bar right now and get it."

All eyes were on Doris as she sashayed her way to the pub counter in a failed attempt to appear inconspicuous. Ten minutes later, she returned to the table with a full glass in her hand and a deflated look on her face. "He's married," she said, slumping back into her seat.

The *Dream Voyager* sounded a prolonged blast announcing it was about to leave the pier. Everyone, including the ladies, rushed to go stand along the open bow to fully experience the launch. The crowd watched as the ship maneuvered away from the dock and began to stream down the Hudson, past Ellis Island, and under the Verrazano-Narrows Bridge.

"Woo Hoo! We're off to Bermuda!" yelled Margot, balancing a second Dark 'N' Stormy in her hand while waving her long, slender arms in the air. The piped-in Calypso music playing in the background could barely be heard over the ship's roaring engines as they propelled their way through the ocean. That didn't stop Margot from shaking her hips back and forth and spurring her friends to do the same, ultimately precipitating a wave of passengers to join in the merriment.

In Margot's mind, *this party was just getting started.*

CHAPTER 28

The morning sun exploded onto the horizon, promising a sizzling day at sea. Bethany, Doris, Rachel, and Dana made a group effort to make it to the ship's upper deck by 9:00 a.m. in order to secure the best seats before the rest of the sun-worshiping mass set in. After aligning themselves at the front of the adults-only pool, they removed their swimsuit cover-ups and took turns applying suntan lotion on one another. Once all preliminaries were in order, they settled into their lounge chairs, ready to bask beneath those ultraviolet rays, made bearable by the cool ocean current.

Margot was the last to arrive, preferring to make a grand entrance when the opportunity afforded her the most exposure.

Doris: "'Bout time you got here."

Rachel: "We saved you a seat."

Margot: "Thanks. I had planned on going to yoga. My personal trainer highly recommends it, especially after a hard workout. Unfortunately, I didn't quite make it this morning." Margot lifted her sunglasses to reveal the dark circles under her eyes. "Oh well, I *am* on vacation."

Rachel: "You have a personal trainer? Is he hot?"

Margot: "*VERY.* Too bad he's got a boyfriend."

Bethany: "I was hoping to go to yoga too, but I was feeling a little hungover myself after all the dancing and drinking we did yesterday. We probably should have eaten a real meal instead of snacking on chips and salsa."

Rachel (concealing her own bloodshot eyes beneath her shades): "Yeah, I think I'll lay off the Dark 'N' Stormies for the rest of the trip. The tortilla chips might have helped soak up the alcohol if I hadn't launched them into the toilet when I got back to my room."

Bethany: "I'm going to be good today. I don't want to miss yoga again tomorrow. Seven a.m. on the promenade deck, right?"

Margot. "Right."

Rachel: "Maybe I'll meet you down there and just walk around the track."

Doris: "You girls go ahead and work out. I'd rather spend my vacation sleeping in."

Margot: "You should try it sometime, Doris. It might change your outlook."

Margot removed her embroidered, peek-a-boo cover-up and dropped it on the chaise. "Right now, I need to cool off." She walked over to the deep end of the pool, crouched down low, and with her arms pointing downward, plunged into the glistening blue water.

The rush of cool liquid against her warm skin tingled, precipitating an immediate flashback...

She was back at her Miami mansion, about to execute a forward dive off the board of their Olympic-size pool. Narrowly making a splash, she slowly resurfaced, alternating from back stroke to breast stroke, as if she were performing a choreographed water dance. After several laps, she glided toward her husband, who was in his swimming trunks, lounging on a chair at the far end of the pool, reading his newspaper. When she reached the pool's edge, she reared her head out of the crystal clear water, smoothing down her wet hair with her hands. "Come on in, Burt," she called out, treading in front of him flirtatiously. "The water is invigorating,"

Her deeply tanned husband lowered his paper, revealing a thicket of curly white chest hair, to observe his lovely wife. Her bright hazel eyes captured the reflection of the iridescent bubbles rising in her midst, creating the illusion of an elusive mermaid.

"Watching you is invigorating enough," he replied.

"If you come in, I can teach you some of the new strokes I learned."

Burt chuckled. "I'm sure you could. It's nice to see that all those hours of aquatic lessons have paid off. You know, for an immigrant girl who barely knew how to float, you've come a long way, Margarita Kazlauskas."

"Jeffrey says I'm a natural," said Margot, continuing to move her arms back and forth seductively in the water. "Can he come with us on our next trip to Bermuda? Oh, please, Burt! He wants to teach me how to snorkel. He says there's nothing better than snorkeling along Bermuda's beautiful coral reefs."

Burt surrendered a smile of acquiescence. In exchange, Margot lifted her palm to her lips to blow him a superficial kiss before plunging her torso back into the deep...

****

As she took her final lap in the *Dream Voyager's* deck-side pool, irrepressible thoughts of her swim instructor, Jeffrey, also came bubbling to the surface...

On their last trip to Bermuda aboard *Magnuson's Millions*, Burt spent much of his time on his cell phone, in his private office in the lower cabin. This was not unusual, as it was where he conducted most of his personal business transactions. None of which Margot was ever privy to, of course.

In the meantime, Jeffrey was teaching Burt's wife the best techniques for diving off his mega yacht. Margot was eager to show off her newfound skills and insisted on doing a more difficult backward dive from the upper platform into the water. Jeffrey stood near the boat's edge, anxiously awaiting her to rise back up through the undulating waves. When more than a few minutes went by, he became very concerned, thinking she might have hit the underside of the boat. Just as he was about to jump in after her, Margot's head slowly rose up, spewing out water from her mouth like a gushing whale.

"You scared me half to death," he yelled.

"I was just playing with you," she laughed, climbing up the boat ladder.

Jeffrey stretched out his hand to help boost her up. "You mean you did that on purpose?"

Margot responded with a wide, mischievous smile.

As soon as she was on deck, he grabbed a towel off the seat and wrapped it around her shoulders, pulling her in closely. "You siren, you can't be trusted," he murmured with a heavy breath.

Margot curled her lips and looked straight into her instructor's subaqueous blue eyes. "Sirens have been known to lure sailors to their death."

"Well, some say they bring good luck. Either way, I'm willing to take my chances," said Jeffrey, moving in for a full lip lock.

"Not now," whispered Margot, pushing him away. "He could come up at any moment..."

The memory faded as instantly as it appeared, and Margot was back on the *Dream Voyager*, lifting herself out of the pool. All eyes were on her while she lingered dripping wet, toward her lounge chair.

Doris lowered her sunglasses and remarked, "Could her bikini be any skimpier?"

Dana, who was lying in the chair next to her, set her book face down on her stomach to study Margot more discreetly beneath her aviators.

Doris: "She must have had work done. While we were living together, she'd strut around naked all the time, and I know for a fact that she wasn't *that* endowed."

Dana: "She showed them to me."

Doris shot Dana a bewildered look: "What?"

Dana (enunciating slowly): "...They're gorgeous."

Doris turned to give Dana a long, hard stare. "Geez, Dana, if I didn't know any better, I'd think you had a crush on her."

Dana turned an extra burnt shade of red before quickly lowering her head back into her book.

While Margot was toweling herself off, the pool waiter came by, trying not to look too obvious while he scanned her body from head to toe. "Would you ladies like something from the bar? Drinks or snacks?"

"Jorge — it's you again!" burst out Margot, while continuing to towel herself off (bending all the way down to dry her feet, in order to allot maximum exposure of her cleavage). When she stood back up, she couldn't help but take pleasure in seeing the whites of Jorge's frozen eyes swelling over his mocha-colored skin.

While he was busy taking the other women's orders, Margot conspicuously surveyed every inch of his young physique. He was, by far, the best-looking male staff member on the boat. He was tall and thin, probably in his mid-20s, with tendrils of inky black hair that framed his dimpled chin and protruding cheekbones.

When he was done taking her friends' orders, Margot approached him as closely as she could get away with, leaving barely an inch between his shirt buttons and her breasts. "So, Jorge," she posed, in her most seductive "Mae West" imitation. "What do you think I'm in the mood for right now?"

A wave of crimson tide washed over the waiter's face while he tried to play coy. "Hmm, let me guess. A Dark 'N' Stormy?"

"That's right," said Margot, stretching out the words. "Dark-and-Stormy, just like you."

One could almost hear the thud of Doris' jaw drop, as she and the other girls sat on the sidelines observing the tacky display before them.

Bethany leaned her mouth toward Rachel's ear and whispered, "Wow, this is a side of Margot I've never seen before. I mean, whenever we went to the bar after work, sure, she'd flirt a little, but she was never this...uh...obvious."

Rachel shrugged it off. "You haven't known her as long as Dana and I have. She's always been like this, even in high school." Then sighed, "I wish I had that much moxie."

Bethany laid her head back against the chaise and wondered. How had she not seen this side of Margot before?

CHAPTER 29

Neptune's Bounty was the ship's most prestigious restaurant. Margot had read that it filled up quickly, so she made sure to have Burt's assistant book it well in advance of their trip. It was located one level above the atrium, but in order to get there, you had to ascend a rounded staircase. The decor was reminiscent of a Vegas Casino. A large statue of Neptune guarded the waiting area, which led to a dining room canopied in thick brown fishing nets strewn with oversized replicas of marine creatures, such as blue marlins, golden starfish, red crabs, and gray clams, suspended beneath a pale blue and white ceiling.

While Margot, Bethany, Doris, and Rachel had all received their appetizers of shrimp cocktails and crab cakes, Dana was still waiting for her wedge salad, minus the bacon, and dressing on the side.

Rachel: "Do you want us to wait until you get your food, Dana?"

Doris (digging into her crab cake): "That may take forever."

Dana: "No. Just start without me. I'm used to this."

Margot (directing her comment at Dana): "If that's all you were planning on eating, I wouldn't have bothered to make reservations here."

Dana: "You knew I was a vegetarian."

Margot: "Don't vegetarians eat fish?"

Dana: "No. That would make me a *Pescatarian*."

Rachel: "Wait...Doesn't a wedge salad have blue cheese?"

Dana's annoyance was starting to show: "I'm a *Lacto-Vegetarian*. They can eat cheese and dairy products."

Rachel: "Oh, sorry. I didn't know there were so many varieties of 'arians.'"

Bethany: "Are you trying to lose weight, because you don't need to lose any weight, Dana."

Doris: "If anything, you should be trying to gain weight. You look a little sickly. You might wanna get back to eating meat."

Dana (losing her cool): "You could stand to lose a few pounds yourself, Doris."

Margot (raising her voice): "Whoa, truce, girls! Why don't we all kiss and make up?"

Dana and Doris both threw her a dirty look, but before anyone could say anything else, the women were silenced by a flurry of attendants parading over to the table next to them. The leader was carrying a small white cake topped with a single lit candle (which looked more like a sparkler) and placed it before the senior couple seated there.

As they yelled, "Happy Anniversary!" the short, stout woman stood up and leaned over the cake to blow out the blazing candle. It took her a few half-winded tries before she successfully extinguished the flame, after which she was rewarded with an exuberant applause from everyone in the vicinity.

After the wait staff had gone, Rachel leaned over the back of her chair to congratulate the couple, thus prompting her friends to do the same.

"Why, thank you," said the grandmotherly-looking woman. "I'm Agnes, and this is my husband, Harvey," she pointed out, giving her reticent companion a nudge. The nearly bald Harvey, with a trail of white fuzz encircling his skull, said nothing, but did manage to crack a smile.

"So, how many years have you been married?" inquired Rachel.

"Sixty years," Agnes said proudly.

"That's a long time."

"Tell me about it," grumbled Harvey, in a muffled voice.

"Oh, Harvey! He's just kidding," squawked Agnes, giving him a light whack on the shoulder (although he didn't look like he was kidding). "We were just eighteen when we got married. We wanted to do something special for our sixtieth, and since we had never been on a cruise before—here we are!"

Rachel raised her glass of Chardonnay toward the couple in a toast. "Well, here's to you and Harvey. May there be many more cruises to come!"

The other women followed suit, toasting the couple in unison.

"I can't imagine being married sixty years," murmured Margot, after turning back around to face her own table.

"I don't think you have to worry about that," said Doris. "Isn't Burt like, almost seventy?"

"Sixty-four actually," said Margot, taking a big gulp of her Prosecco.

Numerous glasses of libations later, and a shared Tiramisu, the five friends agreed to mosey on over to the piano bar for what promised to be a rousing round of sing-alongs. As they were high-heeling it through the dimly lit hallway, they happened to pass the on-board casino. Margot suddenly stopped in her tracks. "Hey, let's do some gambling, ladies. I'm feeling lucky!"

"How much luckier can you get?" remarked Doris, under her breath.

No one else was interested, so Margot promised she would go in "for just a few minutes" and meet up with them later in the lounge.

Taking advantage of the free-flowing drinks, Margot gambled a little longer than she'd planned and lost a little more money than she had expected at the craps table. A little over two hours had passed when she decided to start making her way toward the piano bar. Her drunken sea legs were about to give way when she noticed Jorge walking toward her in his white uniform and a tray in one hand.

"Jorge!" she blurted out, tripping over a seam in the carpet and almost falling into him, nearly causing him to drop his tray.

"Whoa," he said, grabbing her by the arm.

"I don't think I ever propperrllyy intrroduuced myself. I'm Maarrgot," she slurred.

The waiter tried to maintain a professional stance, holding back a smile. "I believe you did, actually."

"Soo, Jorrgge. You said you were from Bermuda."

"That is right."

Margot began poking her index finger against his chest. "Do you think that when we land in Georgetown tomorrow, you could be our perrssonnal tour guide?"

Jorge did his best not to laugh at her obvious drunkenness. "Unfortunately, I am not allowed to do that, Miss, uh...Margot."

"Why nottt?"

"I am not supposed to leave the boat."

Margot lowered her voice to a shush. "Are you sure? Maybe you can sneak out."

"I would lose my job."

"That's tooo baaad," she said, extending her vowels at great length. "Then maybe you could *draw* me a personal map of all the places I should see. You don't have to work all night, do you?" Margot's eyes were visibly fixed on Jorge's lips, while she waited for his reply.

"My shift ends at one o'clock."

Upon hearing those words, she moved her face right up to his and tapped his nose with her index finger. "Then I'll be waiting for you at *1:05 sharp*, in room...uh...I forgot the number — but it's on the sixth floor — the Penthouse suite at the very end of the hall. Do you think you can remember that, Jorge?"

"Yes. The Penthouse Suite, sixth floor. I will not forget."

CHAPTER 30

A warm beam of light filtered through the gap in the penthouse suite's drapes, nudging Margot awake. Her eyes still closed, she stretched her arm across the bed, hoping to encounter a warm body, but came up empty. She cracked her lids open and scanned the room. There was no sign of Jorge except for the essence of his cheap cologne still lingering in the sheets. Turning to look at the clock on the nightstand, it dawned on her that she had forgotten to set her alarm. It was already 9:30 a.m. She was supposed to meet her girlfriends in the lobby at 10:00. *I've got to get moving,* she said to herself, jerking herself upward. No sooner had she sat up than her head started pounding like a pair of cymbals. Slouched on the bed with her palms pressed against her temples, she tried to recall the events that led up to her late-night tryst. *I definitely over-imbibed,* she thought, while she mustered up the strength to get out of bed.

She staggered over to the bathroom and stood before the vanity mirror, inspecting the black skid marks beneath her eyes. Reaching into her toiletry bag, she pulled out a bottle of Tylenol and popped two tablets in her mouth. She washed them down with a half-empty bottle of water sitting on the counter, then pivoted around to turn on the shower.

While the shower was warming up, she thought she'd walk over to the patio door and let some air into the room. When she pushed the drapes aside, the whole room lit up like an explosive grenade, precipitating a brief sense of blindness followed by a residual trail of sunspots. Yanking open the glass slider, she stepped out onto the balcony and squinted at the picturesque setting materializing before her. She leaned against the banister to watch the *Dream Voyager* maneuver its way through the cluster of small islands surrounding Bermuda as it gradually approached the beautiful harbor of St. George.

The refreshing breeze blew through her tangled hair and brought her senses back to life, reminding Margot that she needed to hurry. She ran back to the bathroom, which was now engulfed in steam, and tiptoed into the shower. There, she dropped her neck back to allow the warm cascading liquid to wash over her face. With eyes closed and a locked smile, her recollection of the previous hours spent with Jorge started to bubble to the surface. Although the details leading up to the encounter were fuzzy, she distinctly remembered the stamina of his lovemaking, which caused a renewed tingling sensation.

In an instant, the water turned cold, dissolving all the passion vibrating from within and producing a Kaleidoscope of faces to appear before her. The apparitions circled in and out, growing bigger and bigger, and then receding to smaller and smaller. They were the faces of all the men in her life—both past and present: her father, her husband, her lovers. They were all there, except they all had sinister expressions on their faces. Some were laughing, some were screaming, and some looked like corpses...

Twisting the handle as hard as she could, she shut the water off and opened the door to grab a towel. For several minutes she stood, frozen, with her face buried in the security and warmth of the cotton cloth, trying to absorb the scorn that had obviously interloped her amoral psyche.

She threw on some clothes and hadn't even had time to dry her hair when she heard a persistent pounding on the door. Peering through the peephole, she observed Rachel and Dana standing there with a look of aggravation on their faces. "Just a minute," yelled Margot. As she scanned the room for her sunglasses, she saw an incriminating scene with empty wine bottles and layers of clothing from the night before scattered about the room. She found the sunglasses lying on the floor next to the bed and slipped them on before opening the door just a crack.

"Are you alright?" We've been downstairs waiting for you for at least twenty minutes," complained Rachel.

"Sorry, I overslept. I'll be out in a minute," said Margot, starting to push the door shut.

"Hurry up!" said Dana. "Bethany and Doris are downstairs waiting. The passengers have already started debarking."

"Let me just grab my purse and a bottled water," said Margot.

"Hey, wait!" burst in Rachel, pushing back against the partially-opened door and attempting to steer her neck through. "Is this a penthouse suite? Can we come in and see it?"

"Uh...not now. We're in a hurry, remember?" rambled Margot, stepping into the hallway and slamming the door behind her. "You can see it when we get back — It'll look better when the room's made up."

When they met up with Doris and Bethany, Doris needled Margot in her usual sardonic manner. "So, what happened to you last night? Did you get lost?"

Bethany chimed in. "We kept looking for you. You missed a really fun time."

"Sorry, guys. I gambled a little longer than I should have."

"What were you playing?" asked Rachel.

"Craps, mostly."

"Hopefully, you came out ahead," said Bethany.

Margot tried to maintain a poker face, but couldn't keep the corners of her lips from turning up slightly. "Oh, I came out 'a-head' alright."

After disembarking the ship, the five women took a ferry

to the Northern tip of St. George's Parish. Their first stop was at Fort St. Catherine. Built in the early 1600s, it was one of the oldest forts on the island. They spent a good deal of time exploring the fortress and its exhibits, and ended the tour standing atop its walls to take in a breathtaking view of the beach.

From there, they taxied over to St. George's "Olde Town" and hopped on a horse-drawn carriage (the preferred choice for easily navigating the narrow lanes and alleyways through town), which allowed them to leisurely view and make some quick stops at many of the historical churches, museums, and monuments of the old British colonial era. It worked out well for Margot, too, since her throbbing headache had barely subsided. In her favor, she had seen this all before with Burt, so she was able to rest her head against the back of the carriage and close her eyes beneath her dark sunglasses. She paid little attention to her friends, who were busy snapping photos while the driver/tour guide babbled on about the city and its founder, St. George. The carriage ride ended with a stop in front of a quaint little restaurant, which allowed them to grab a quick lunch before catching a cab to St. David's Lighthouse.

When they arrived at the lighthouse, the ladies agreed a personal guide wouldn't be necessary. Rachel grabbed an informational pamphlet at the entrance and took it upon herself to act as tour director by reading it aloud to her friends. "Listen, you guys, did you know that the lighthouse was not built on the coastline, but on a hilltop, to ensure the longest possible visibility? It was built in 1879 to provide signals to the ships so that they didn't come too close to the hidden reefs in the water. It's still in operation today as a lookout for ships that pass through the waters around Bermuda."

"Thanks, Rachel, we couldn't have read that ourselves," remarked Doris, as they began their eighty-five-step climb to the top of the watchtower. Margot, still jittery from the alcohol residuals, was last in line, keeping her hands firmly pressed against the narrow concrete walls to maintain her balance.

Once they reached the top, they spread out to take in the magnificent views. When it was decided that they had seen all that they could, they gathered together to get ready to make their descent back down the stairs.

Dana quickly huddled in the middle of the group with her head lowered. "Hey," she whispered, motioning with her shoulder. "Don't all look at once, but do you see that dude over there? I think he's following us."

Naturally, the women all turned their heads at the same time to take a look.

"I said, 'Don't all look at once!'"

Dropping their heads in unison, they began to take turns bobbing their eyeballs up and down in a flimsy attempt to not look conspicuous.

"Which one?" asked Rachel.

"That one over there," said Dana, pointing discreetly with her finger. "The one in the white baseball cap with a camera around his neck."

"I wouldn't mind if he *was* following us," quipped Doris. "He's kinda cute."

"What makes you think he's following us?" asked Margot, lowering her shades halfway.

"I noticed him in the old artillery store at Fort St. Catherine and out near the wall taking pictures. I could have sworn I saw him take our picture. I saw him again after the carriage dropped us off at St. Peter's Church."

"I don't remember seeing him," said Bethany.

"He was out by the graveyard next to the church."

"What's wrong with that?" asked Margot.

"He was pretending to look at the gravestones, but kept glancing over in our direction."

"Well, we are hot chicks," said Margot.

"I don't know, there's something suspicious about him."

"You're way too paranoid, Dana. I'm sure he's just a tourist like us."

"We'd better go," interrupted Bethany. "We need to catch the ferry back to the dock."

When they returned to the ship, the girls insisted on seeing Margot's suite, so they rode the elevator up to the sixth level and followed Margot to the very end of the hallway. Margot unlocked it with her key card and took a quick peek inside before fully opening the door. "Just wanted to make sure it was cleaned," she explained.

Finding that it was, her friends entered with mouths agape.

"I didn't know there were rooms this big on ships," exclaimed Rachel.

"How come we didn't all get a suite?" scoffed Doris.

Margot turned around to give her a dirty look, but before she could respond to her remark, Bethany spoke up. "Hey, beggars can't be choosers."

"Yeah, Doris," Rachel chimed in. "Our rooms are awesome too. Thank you, Margot. You deserve the best room. You set this all up, for Gosh sakes."

Doris bit her lip. "You know I was kidding."

By this time, the sun was about to set, and Margot's headache had lapsed from her memory, so she uncorked a couple of bottles of wine, and the five of them sat out on her large balcony watching the citrine sun splash a red haze over the vast Atlantic just before it disappeared into the horizon.

Margot initiated another one of her trademark toasts. "Here's to another fun-filled day in St. George tomorrow."

Rachel: "You know what they say, 'red sky at night, sailor's delight.'"

Doris (leaning back in her white chaise with a full glass in hand): "I could get used to this."

Rachel: "Me too. What about you, Dana, aren't you glad you came?"

Dana chugged the little bit of wine she allotted herself: "Sure."

Bethany: "Right now, I feel as though I'm getting a new lease on life."

Margot: "That was the whole point of this trip, wasn't it?"

The girls ended the evening early so they could rest up for another full day of pre-planned touristy excursions. While her friends returned to their individual cabins, an exhausted Margot dropped down on the bed and closed her eyes to dream of the excursion that lay ahead just for her.

CHAPTER 31

On their second day in St. George, Margot insisted her friends see the famous Crystal Cave in Hamilton Parish. "It's one of the largest caves on the island and is estimated to be millions of years old!" she touted. But since she had already seen it, she wouldn't be joining them. Instead, she told them she had booked a spa treatment at the famed Rosewood Bermuda Hotel.

"Why didn't you just schedule to have a spa treatment on the ship?" asked Doris.

"Because it wouldn't be nearly as good as the one I'm getting at the Rosewood. Burt and I stayed there while we were on our honeymoon, and the massages are amazing. It's only a mile from the cave, so I can meet up with you guys after my appointment."

From the dockyards, the women took a ferry, followed by a shuttle, to Hamilton Parish, where the Crystal Cave was located. That's where they parted ways. Margot could have made it to the Rosewood on foot, but she was wearing heels and she was in a hurry, so she hailed a cab. While waiting for her ride, her phone alerted her to an incoming text message:

Room 304 — I'll be waiting

Camouflaged beneath a wide-brimmed straw hat and sunglasses, Margot entered the lavish beachside hotel, casually bypassing the front desk, and made a beeline to the elevators. When the third-floor elevator button lit up, she got out and proceeded all the way to the end of the hall to the corner suite facing the bay. *Hmm, this looks familiar,* she thought, smiling to herself before landing a quick, double knock on the door. A minute later, the door opened to reveal a tall, shirtless man in straight black jeans. In that very moment, a stray breeze billowed through the sheer curtains of the open balcony into the provocative sunlit chamber and blew the hat right off Margot's head, obliging her to have no other option but to push him directly onto the bed.

Margot lay in bed dissecting this unconventional stranger who had come to be her lover. She didn't mind that his hair was almost as long as hers and that he had a perpetual five o'clock shadow extending below his jaw. She actually found it sexy. The sun cast a glow upon her lean companion's pale chest, accentuating a six-pack she hadn't initially expected to find. He told her he had wrestled during high school, picking it up only to help him ferret his way through the rough neighborhood he grew up in. Ultimately, it earned him a scholarship to college. That is, until he grew bored with academia. Gifted with an above-average IQ and satisfied that he had learned all he needed to know, he dropped out after only two years. It wasn't long afterwards that he got busted for hacking.

Inevitably, Margot's mind circled back to their first meeting in New York's Brookfield Place Mall and their subsequent lunch at the Steak & Ale when she first confronted him for stalking her. His initial reaction was to appear startled and deny the accusation. After realizing he couldn't lie his way out of it, he eventually admitted that he had been hired to follow her, although he did not divulge who hired him. At least, not right away.

Watching him now, as he lay next to her with his calm, resting facade, it appeared as though the world was his oyster. Because it was.

In the beginning, she figured him to be just another easily-manipulated male that she could utilize to her advantage. But as she got to know him, she learned that he was different from other men she had met in the past. He made it clear from the start of their relationship that he was not one who allowed himself to be controlled by emotion, but by logic.

Consequently, their alliance developed into a mutually surreptitious affair. Each of them using the other for their own personal gain. He had compiled enough evidence on her to know that she was unable to sustain a monogamous relationship. That didn't matter to him. He had told her quite candidly that he'd stick around for as long as it was beneficial and convenient for both of them.

For Margot, this did nothing more than create a challenge — and she always did love a challenge. The fact that he didn't care whether or not she stayed made her want to stick around that much longer. Plus, there was the fact that he had spent time in prison, which electrified her even more. The ironic part of all of this was that she had Burt to thank for it.

Margot leaned over her lover's muscular biceps, sweeping the long, black, loose-lying strands from his face, and kissed him gently along his shoulder. Gradually, he opened up his pale green eyes, and what she saw was the most revealing aspect of their relationship. What she saw was an exact reflection of herself.

"Get up," coaxed Margot. "We've got business to take care of."

"I thought we just did," he grinned.

She let out a wicked laugh and rolled out of bed, removed a robe from the closet, and wrapped it around herself. She then picked her purse up off the floor, pulled out a pack of cigarettes and a lighter, and headed toward the balcony.

In the meantime, he put his pants on and stepped out to join her. She was leaning against the waist-high, stucco balcony wall, staring out at the ocean while she puffed on her cigarette. "The view looks a lot different from the last time I was here," she said, without turning her head.

"How so?"

"Let's just say, my outlook is a lot better now — thanks to

you."

"You know you're not supposed to smoke in this hotel."

"So what?" said Margot, taking an extended puff. "We're outside."

"What if someone smells the smoke and complains?"

"You're just being paranoid. The wind will blow away the evidence. Besides, by then I'll have finished it."

Margot moved over to the lounge chair and sat down. "You mind getting me a drink from the minibar? White wine if they have it."

"Be right back," he said, walking back into the suite. He opened the mini fridge, pulled out a small twist-top bottle of wine, and delivered it to her. "Chardonnay, just like you requested."

"Thanks, sweetie. Would you mind throwing my butt out, too? I'd put it out with my foot, except that I'm barefoot."

Without saying a word, he took what was left of her cigarette and carried it into the bathroom, where he flushed it down the toilet. On the way back, he took a beer out for himself and sat down across from her. "The things I do for you."

"You mean the things *I do for you*," sneered Margot.

He lifted his bottle of beer, tilting the neck toward her, "Touché, you ravenous whore."

"I'll take that as a compliment," she responded, likewise pointing her wine bottle toward him. "So, have you been keeping him apprised of my whereabouts?"

He looked at her with those canny green eyes and let out a chuckle. "Yeah. He's obsessed with finding dirt on you and Holt."

Margot released an insidious laugh. "Old fool. He hasn't caught on to anything else, has he?"

"He hasn't let on, but you can be sure he will soon."

Margot's mood suddenly shifted as she stared back out over the ocean.

"Don't worry, Babe, everything will be fine," he promised, placing his hand on her exposed thigh.

"I know," said Margot, not sounding fully convinced. "By the way, how's that girlfriend of yours?"

"I told you, she's not really my girlfriend. When I got out of prison, I needed a place to stay, so I looked her up."

Crow's feet formed in the corners of Margot's eyes while she studied his expression. "So you're saying that all the time you've been living together, you never...?"

"I never said that."

"So, you're 'friends with benefits.'"

"Yeah," he grinned. "Kinda' like you and me."

Margot got up and swatted him in the arm, then drained the rest of the Chardonnay in her bottle. "Let's go back inside. We've got some plans that need shoring up."

He followed her back into the room and grabbed her by the waist. "How 'bout we take care of that after," he said, pushing her back on the bed.

After everything that needed tending to was finalized, Margot got up and got dressed. "I've got to get going," she said, adjusting her large straw hat on her head. On her way out, she noticed his white baseball cap sitting on the chair and picked it up and threw it at him. "Don't forget this."

As she opened the door, he yelled out, "Make sure you act surprised when you see him."

"Oh, don't worry," she replied. "I'm fully adept at 'faking it.'"

While Margot was "getting her massage," her friends were 120 feet below ground level in the Crystal Cave, walking along a floating bridge above the *Cahow Lake*, which rose and waned with the tides from the sea, while marveling at the shimmering stalactites and stalagmites reflecting in its crystal clear water.

After the tour, Bethany, Doris, Rachel, and Dana waited

outside the cave's entrance for Margot. After ten minutes and still no sign of her, they tried texting her, but received no response. Since they had all worn comfortable shoes for the outing, they opted to make their way on foot toward the hotel, figuring they might run into her along the way.

Upon their arrival at the Rosewood Bermuda Hotel, they stopped by the front desk to inquire where the spa facilities were located. While they were waiting in line to speak to the desk attendant, Rachel spotted Margot stepping out of one of the elevators. "There she is! I recognize the hat," she shouted, waving her arm in the air to flag her down.

Margot appeared to be caught by surprise, looking both ways before scurrying toward her friends. "I thought we were going to meet in front of the caves," sounded Margot, rather agitated. "I was just about to call you to let you know I was on my way."

"We tried texting, but you didn't answer," said Rachel. "Maybe you were still in the spa?"

"Uh, yeah. I was probably in the shower. So, how did you like the Crystal Cave?" she asked, changing the subject.

Everyone agreed it was a sight worth seeing. "It was so incredible, it gave me goose bumps," said Rachel. "How was your spa treatment?"

"It gave me goose bumps, too," said Margot, trying to keep a straight face.

"You smell like wine," said Doris.

"Oh, uh, wine is included in the package."

"They usually are in the better establishments," stated Bethany.

In that moment, another elevator door opened up, and Dana happened to notice someone familiar coming out. Once again, Dana turned inward to face her friends. "Don't look now," she said in a lowered voice, "but there he is again." The girls all looked up to see that same "tourist" in the white baseball cap heading toward the front entrance.

Margot quickly lowered her gaze to the marble floor.

"What a weird coincidence," said Bethany.

"Maybe this is where he's staying," Doris remarked excitedly. "He must make pretty good money if he can afford to stay in this hotel."

"Or, maybe he knows someone who's staying here," said Bethany.

"Hey, maybe we should follow him!" giggled Rachel.

"Yeah!" agreed Doris.

"No! I need to use the restroom," halted Margot. "Come with me. It'll be a while before we get back to the boat. I think there's one down the hall in the lobby."

"Didn't you just come from the spa? Why didn't you use the bathroom there?" questioned Doris.

"I did! But I have to go again...Must be the wine."

CHAPTER 32

Early the next morning, the *Dream Voyager* left St. George floating eastward. As it entered the Great Sound, what unfolded was a picturesque setting of hundreds of boats lining the Hamilton Harbor. By 8:00 a.m., the ship had arrived at its port at King's Wharf, where it would remain docked for a day and a half.

On their first day in Hamilton, the women took a bus to the National Museum of Bermuda (formerly known as the Bermuda Maritime Museum). Among the exhibits were gold bars, jewelry, and other treasures recovered by scuba diving archeologists from centuries-old shipwrecks. Afterwards, they walked over to the Dolphin Center to watch a dolphin show, where they got the opportunity to pet the friendly sea mammals and learned how they are trained.

From there, they made their way to the Royal Naval Dockyard and strolled around the Bermuda Art Center, where they found a wide variety of artwork for sale by resident artists. There was also an adjoining craft market displaying a wide assortment of handcrafted souvenirs. Bethany bought a beaded, peach coral necklace which complemented her strawberry blond hair. Rachel purchased a pendant necklace with a glass charm containing Bermuda's famous pink sand, and Doris bought a jar of Bermuda's famous pepper jam and a trio of mini black rum cakes. Despite the hot and humid weather, Dana bought a burnt-orange-colored knit cap, which she wore folded over her head for the rest of the day. The girls thought it was out of character for Margot not to buy anything, but she summed it up to say that she had already bought more than enough souvenirs on her previous trips to the island.

Eventually, they made their way back to the tour bus, which was scheduled to return to port by dinner hour. When they arrived there, however, they decided not to board the ship; instead, they opted to take a taxi into town to find a place where they could better savor Bermuda's authentic local fare.

The cab driver recommended a new upscale, yet casual, open-air restaurant that Margot had not yet been to. While she, Bethany, Rachel, and Doris feasted on fish chowder, codfish, and yellowfin tuna, Dana found a number of lacto-vegetarian options to her liking. Their meal could not have been more complete without a slice of the island's famous black rum cake while they sat out on the deck witnessing yet another glorious sunset.

Since the girls needed to work off the huge meal they had just eaten and didn't have to return to the boat until late, Margot insisted they remain in the city and do a little bar-hopping at some of the local nightclubs.

After hitting a couple of taverns, the women were getting tired, but Margot prodded them to make one final stop at her favorite watering hole: Gilby's. Gilby's was a popular saloon for both locals and tourists. They featured a band every Thursday through Sunday and played a nice mix of old and new music. Margot said she had been there on more than one occasion and highly recommended it because of the higher ratio of men to women.

The place was already packed when they walked in, forcing them to zigzag their way through the crowd to get to the horseshoe-shaped bar at the opposite end of the room. The girls stood by silently while their leader, Margot, squeezed in between two patrons to catch the bartender's attention. The minute he noticed her, the bartender with the shaved head and tattooed neck and forearms fast approached.

"Hey Margot, what's shakin'?"

"I'm ready to party," said Margot, shimmying her shoulders. "How ya doin', Jake?"

"Great—now that you're here," he commented with a big grin. "You soloing it tonight?"

"Actually, I'm here with my very good friends: Beth, Rachel, Doris, and Dana," replied Margot, pointing over people's heads in order to identify them one by one. "I thought I'd show them where the *real* party's at."

"Well, you've come to the right place," said Jake, watching her friends inch in closer to the bar, prompting him to lay five cocktail napkins out on the counter. "So, what'll you ladies have?"

"The usual for me," said Margot. "Drinks on me, girls," she shouted to her friends, handing Jake her credit card. "Here, I wanna start a tab."

Two barstools opened up, which Dana and Bethany were quick to claim, while Rachel and Doris sidled up between them and Margot. Even though the band had gone on break, the place was so loud and raucous that it was difficult to carry on a conversation.

As the drinks showed up, one by one, Margot reached over to grab her Dark 'N' Stormy, then twisted back around to face the mob. With her eyes on the prowl, it didn't take her long to spot someone sitting at the far corner of the bar. Right away, she turned to her girlfriends. "Be right back," she said, leaving with her drink in hand.

Bethany, Dana, Rachel, and Doris kept watch while their friend moseyed on over toward the curved end of the bar where a good-looking blond guy sat nursing his beer. Positioning herself right next to him, she stood with her back against the counter and quietly sipped her drink.

"Do you think she knows him?" asked Rachel.

"I doubt it," said Doris. "She was always doing stuff like this when we went out."

When the young man looked up, his solemn demeanor suddenly brightened. He set his bottle down and jumped up from his stool, throwing his arms around her.

"I was wondering how long it would take you to realize I was standing here," said Margot.

"I thought you weren't gonna show."

"Why wouldn't I show?"

"I don't know. I thought you might have chickened out or changed your mind or something."

"Well, I'm here, aren't I?"

"Are you alone?"

Margot inconspicuously pointed over to her friends, who still had their eyes keenly set on her. "My girlfriends are over there."

The guy placed his arms around Margot's waist and whispered in her ear. "I was thinking, when all this is over, maybe you and me can get together and..."

"I told you, Jeffrey. You and I—that was just a fling."

Suddenly, the band started up again and began playing that song by Gotye: *"Just somebody that I used to know."*

"I love this song!" exclaimed Margot, plunking her drink down on the counter and grabbing him by the arms. "Come on," she said, forcing him off the barstool. "Let's dance!"

"You can't dance to this song. It's too slow."

"Yes, we can. C'mon!"

They were the first couple to arrive on the dance floor. Margot pressed her body up against his and wrapped her arms around his neck. As they swayed back and forth, she sang the lyrics in his ear, just loud enough for him to hear. "You know we can still be friends," she whispered.

Dana and Bethany were still planted in their seats at the bar while Rachel and Doris stood by their side, still focused on Margot and her partner while they canoodled on the dance floor.

"She acts like she knows him," said Rachel.

"She must," said Bethany. "Even so, I can't imagine why she'd dance with him like that, given that she's married."

"I can," said Doris.

Dana, keeping a steady and silent vigil, took a slug of her beer.

At the end of the Gotye song, the band began playing a much livelier tune, and the dance floor instantly got crowded. "Come on," shouted Rachel, attempting to pull Dana out onto the dance floor. But Dana wouldn't budge.

Doris polished off the remainder of her tropical drink and slammed her empty glass on the bar. "I'll join you. I'm getting tired of standing here watching everyone else have fun."

Dana continued to sit on her revolving stool facing the dance floor, while nursing her amber ale. Bethany swiveled her seat around as well and saw that a couple of young men had joined their friends.

"Why don't you go out there?" asked Bethany.

"Not my scene," said Dana, taking another sip. "What's stopping you?"

"It wouldn't feel right—like I was cheating on Charles."

"Dancing's not cheating."

"I know, but I feel guilty just going out when he's stuck back there in a jail cell."

Dana's eyes were still fixed on Margot. She was clearly in command of the whole floor. No one could swing those hips like her. All the while, laughing and carrying on like she didn't have a care in the world. And why would she? She had everything she wanted—and more. *Why can't I get the one thing I want?* thought Dana, taking one last slug of her beer and motioning to the bartender for another.

A good deal of time had passed when Bethany looked at the large lasso-shaped clock on the wall. "It's late, we need to go," said Bethany, moving her eyes to the dance floor. Rachel and Doris were still rockin' and a-rollin', but Margot and her partner were gone. "Do you see Margot anywhere?" she asked Dana while scanning the room.

"I lost sight of her when I ordered my last drink."

"I need to go to the ladies' room. Maybe I'll find her in there," said Bethany. Bethany slid off her barstool and made her way to the restroom. When she was coming back out, the band had gone on a break, and Rachel and Doris were on their way in. "We have to get going soon," said Bethany. "Have you seen Margot?"

Doris and Rachel both shook their head, "No."

"I'll meet you guys back at the bar," said Bethany. "She can't leave without her credit card."

While the four friends were congregated at the bar surveying every perimeter of the club, Dana was the first to spot Margot as she was walking through the front entrance, straightening her dress and fluffing her hair.

The four women all scampered toward the door to confront her before she disappeared again. "What happened to you?" they exclaimed.

"I just went out for a cigarette," said Margot, wiping her smeared lipstick with her fingers and glancing back toward the entrance.

"We have to go," Bethany said forcefully. "It's late."

"Wait! I have to get my credit card from the bartender."

"I already got it," said Bethany. "And I went ahead and paid the tab. I told your bartender friend, Jake, I'd return your card to you — Here."

"Thanks, Bethany. You didn't have to do that."

"Yeah, well, we were getting tired of waiting for you. Besides, it was the least I could do. After all, you did pay for this trip."

Margot glanced at her wrist watch. "We've got time for another drink. Come on! This time, I'm paying."

"No, we don't," said Bethany, growing impatient and grabbing her by the arm. "We have to get back to the ship."

"Fine!" said Margot, begrudgingly.

As the five women headed into the parking lot to wait for a cab, a beat-up old car drove by in front of them. The driver's window was rolled all the way down, and the young, shaggy-haired blond guy, who Margot had been dancing with earlier, was at the wheel. As he was passing, he rendered a stony glare, then lifted his palm and gave her an admiral's salute.

"Who was that guy?" asked Rachel.

Margot took a minute to respond, then, wistfully, she replied, "Oh...he's just somebody that I used to know."

CHAPTER 33

The *Dream Voyager* was scheduled to leave port at 2:00 p.m., so the women thought they'd spend their last day in Hamilton leisurely strolling around the capital city and ending with a quick lunch before returning to the ship.

From the time of their arrival, the city had been bustling with tourists, but since many of the cruise ships had already left, they were lucky enough to secure an outdoor table at a popular beachy cafe with a birds-eye view of the pier.

The ladies were busy studying their menus when Dana happened to peer out over her signature aviators. "You're never going to believe this, but there he is again."

In that moment, the cruise liner, *Blue Gables,* which was docked nearby, sounded its powerful horn signaling its imminent departure and drowned out Dana's words.

"What did you say?" bellowed her friends.

"I said, 'There's that dude again!'"

"Where?" asked Rachel, twisting her head back and forth.

"Over there," said Dana, lowering her eyeshot toward a nearby building. "Leaning against the brick wall, talking into his cell phone."

The girls lifted their eyes from their menus and veered them toward the stranger.

"So what?" said Margot. "He's probably from one of the other cruise lines." "Then he missed his boat," replied Dana. "The Blue Gables is the only other ship left here besides ours, and it's about to leave."

"Maybe he's on our ship, but we just hadn't noticed him,"

Rachel jumped in excitedly.

Doris lowered her oversized sunglasses for a better look. "If he was, I think I would have noticed him by now."

The girls all giggled and returned to their laminated luncheon menu. Margot lifted hers in front of her face while discreetly watching the pony-tailed stranger in the white baseball cap from the side. As she was doing so, her mind couldn't help but slip back to that all-important day six months ago, in that dingy little office in East Harlem...

There he was, slumped over his computer in full-on nerd mode, with his long hair pulled up into a bun, submerged in a black screen filled with white numbers. Margot was standing next to him, flipping through photos from a folder she had picked up off his desk. One particularly revealing photograph caught her eye. She lifted it out to study it more closely. "I still don't get how you were able to get a picture of me and Charles this close up in my apartment."

"I told you, Burt gave me keycards to the building. When I knew you wouldn't be home, I planted a hidden camera in your bedroom."

"Yeah, but where was it? I never even noticed it."

"That's the point. You're not supposed to. It was hidden behind the drapes, jutting out just enough to catch 'all the action.'"

"But how does that work without someone there to snap it?"

"It has a motion sensor. Don't worry about it. It's just one of the many tricks of the trade."

Margot squelched her lips and squinted her eyes. She tilted the photograph from right to left and then again, from left to right, examining it from different angles. "Well, it didn't capture my best side."

James adjusted his glasses and delivered a self-serving chuckle. "Next time I'll give you a 'heads-up.'"

Margot slugged him on the shoulder and shoved it back into a Manila envelope with the rest of the photos and stuck it back in the folder. "Want me to put this away?"

James, whose fingers were vigorously tapping away on the keyboard, clearly did not want to be interrupted. "Sure."

"Where do they go?"

"In the back room," he answered without looking up. "The metal file cabinet."

Margot strolled over to the door at the far end of the office and turned the knob. "It's so dark in here! Where's the light switch?" she yelled out.

"There's a bulb hanging from the ceiling. Just pull the chain."

She yanked on the metal chain, and the room lit to a mellow yellow. "You should turn this into a darkroom. Just switch out the white bulb for a red one."

A burst of laughter echoed through to the back room from the front office. "A darkroom! No one uses those anymore. Everything's gone digital. I can just print pictures off my computer."

Margot spun around, looking for a file cabinet. "I don't see it."

"Behind the curtain," hollered back James.

In the rear corner of the room was a doorless entryway camouflaged by a floor-length curtain hanging from a spring rod. Margot pushed the dusty curtain aside to find a metal cabinet with a rusty key still stuck in the keyhole. Bending over, it took her two hard yanks before she was able to open the sticking drawer. The file folders didn't appear to be in any particular order, so she dropped her file in with others, locked it back up, and slid the key into the back pocket of her jeans.

As she was heading back to the front office, she stopped by a small table butting up against the wall. Sitting on the top was a near-empty Mr. Coffee machine that had been left on for who knows how long. Right next to it was a short stack of Styrofoam cups, as well as a random selection of sugar packets, powdered coffee creamers, and stir-sticks collected from various fast-food restaurants and coffee shops.

She poured herself what was left of the condensed brew and turned it off, then she ripped open a packet of the instant coffee creamer and poured it into her cup. "How come you don't have any Sweet'N Low or Splenda?" She yelled out as she was stirring in her Coffee Mate.

"Because I don't use 'em. Stop asking questions, I'm busy!"

Margot threw her stir stick in the adjacent wastebasket and returned to James's desk. "Where do you want this key?" she asked, pulling it out of her back pocket.

"What?" said James, once again distracted.

"I said, 'Where do you want me to put this?'" (holding it up from its thin metal ring and dangling it in front of his face).

"Oh, uh, just throw it in my backpack."

Margot threw it into his open backpack, which was sitting on the floor, then leaned her right hip against his desk, intermittently taking sips from her Styrofoam cup. Silently, she watched as rows upon rows of numbers moved up and down his screen at incredible rates of speed.

"Almost done," said James, breaking his concentration for just a moment. "I can't believe you were able to get his password. I may have to hire you as my permanent assistant."

Margot swiped the tips of her lacquer-painted nails across her shoulder and blew on them proudly. "What can I say? I'm a natural when it comes to getting what I want."

As those words trickled out of her mouth, she recalled having to seduce Burt while in his Manhattan office and then scouring through his bureau drawers while he was in the bathroom, freshening up for his next appointment.

"When I didn't find it in his office, I figured it had to be somewhere on his yacht because he conducted a large part of his business from there. I knew all those trips to Bermuda and the Bahamas weren't just for his amusement. He didn't name his boat *Magnuson's Millions* for nothing."

"So where was the password?"

"In his office next to our bedroom, in the middle desk drawer. It was written on a piece of paper — underneath his gun."

"I thought you said he kept that drawer locked?"

"Minor obstacle. The desk key was hidden exactly where I would have expected him to hide it."

"Which was?"

"In his humidor, lying beneath four layers of cigars. All I had to do was wait for him to fall asleep."

James clicked the final button on his computer, threw up his hands, and then smacked them back down on the desk. "It's done!" he gloated with a glimmer in his eyes. "The dirty laundry has left the building, and there's nothing left to wash."

Margot gave him a delirious smile and jumped onto his lap, smothering him with kisses. "You did it, baby!"

"*We* did it. Now, let's hurry up and get outta here."

She shot up from his lap, taking one last swig of coffee before slapping the Styrofoam cup back down on the desk. "I can't finish this," she blurted out, crinkling her nose with revulsion and wiping the muddy residue from her lips. "It's disgusting!"

As Margot waited for her lunch to be served, she could still taste the pungency of that rank coffee in her throat while imagining what the "mysterious tourist," whose face was shadowed beneath a white baseball cap, was saying into his lowered mouthpiece.

"*I'm just outside of Parrot Grove. No, no sign of Holt. It's just her and her friends having lunch. You'd better hurry, the cruise ship leaves at two.*"

CHAPTER 34

Burt sat in his high-back leather chair, staring blindly through the floor-to-ceiling windows of his Manhattan office, when his secretary tapped lightly against his open door.

"Mr. Magnuson," she announced, "Your next appointment, Mr. McAvee, is here."

"Show him in," he said in a subdued tone, while slowly spinning his chair around to face her.

A minute later, James McAvee entered, and his secretary left the room, closing the door behind him.

"Have a seat, Mr. McAvee."

James sat down and glanced around the richly appointed room, noting the fine mahogany furniture and thick Persian rug, while Burt was eyeing him with equal discernment. "I must say, you're not what I expected."

"What did you expect?" answered McAvee.

"The long hair is a surprise."

"Let's just say, it helps me keep a low profile."

"Yes, well, you might want to work on that."

"What do you mean?"

"I know that you're a computer whiz who hails from Queens. I know that you went to Penn State on a wrestling scholarship and dropped out in your second year. Two years later, you got busted for computer hacking and spent time in Federal Prison. After your release, that's when you went undercover as a private eye."

"You've done your research. So, how did you find me?"

"I've got connections—even in the Federal prison," said

Burt, allowing a crooked smile to show through. "Now, let's get down to business, shall we?"

McAvee pulled out one of the chairs facing Magnuson's desk and sat down. "So what can I do for you?"

"I suspect my wife is having an affair."

The private eye leaned over to pick up a full-face photo of a woman positioned at the edge of Magnuson's desk. "Is this her?"

"Yes."

"I can see why you'd be worried. What's her name?"

"Her maiden name is Kazlauskas—Margarita Kazlauskas, but she goes by 'Margot.'"

"If you don't mind my asking, how long have the two of you been married?"

"Two years."

McAvee set the picture back down. "So what exactly do you want me to do?"

"I want you to follow her, take pictures. You know, the usual. I want to know everything. When, where, and with whom."

"Where do you live?"

"What difference does that make?"

"You both still live together, right?"

"Yes, of course."

"Then, I'm going to need access to your building."

"What for?"

"So I can plant a hidden camera in your bedroom. You did say you wanted to know everything."

"I'm not sure I want to observe it that closely."

"The truth is always hard to face."

Burt gave the private eye a long, hard glance, then pulled open his top drawer. He took out two key cards and slid them over to the P.I. "1400 Winfield Towers on West 57th. One card gives you access to the building, the other is for the apartment."

McAvee took out his phone to punch in the information. "I'm going to need a rundown of your wife's schedule."

"I'm gone a lot, so you're going to have to figure that out. All I know is she supposedly goes to the gym every morning, Monday through Thursday. We also have a maid, Maria, who works Monday through Friday until 3:00 p.m., unless Margot requests otherwise. I'm leaving for a business trip tomorrow and I'll be gone all week. You can install it then. The sooner the better."

McAvee took one last look around the room before standing up to leave. "I want half my fee up front. The rest, when I turn in all the evidence."

CHAPTER 35

The prior evening's drizzle had all but evaporated, and the mid-morning sun glimmered through the sheer curtains of his fourth-floor apartment window, serving as a wake-up call. Margot squinted at the light and rolled out of bed. She snatched up her jeans that were lying on the floor and quickly shimmied into them.

On the other side of the bed, wedged between crumpled sheets, lay the vainglorious male she had grown accustomed to. Hearing the rustling of clothes, he gradually forced his eyes open. "What time is it?" he asked, groggily.

"It doesn't matter, I've gotta go," said Margot, buttoning up her blouse.

"Why? My wife won't be back till three."

"I know, but Burt will be home around two, and I've got some errands to take care of before he gets back."

"What's so important that it can't wait until tomorrow? Come, back here," he said, patting the bed with a big, boyish grin and lifting the sheet to expose his eagerness.

"None of your business," she said, gathering up her things.

"Don't I at least get a goodbye kiss?"

Giving in to those dark, wanting eyes, Margot stooped down to give him a quick smack on the lips, offering him the perfect opportunity to pull her back down on the bed.

"I told you, I have to go!" she protested adamantly, pushing herself back up into a standing position.

"When can I see you again?"

As she walked out the door, her voice trailed simply with,

"...I'll be in touch."

The stunning, long-haired brunette in a cropped metallic jacket and jeans so tight you'd have to peel them like a banana to get them off, descended the concrete stairs of the mature brownstone on New York's Upper East Side. She did a quick scan of the street, paying particular note of the wall of automobiles parked bumper-to-bumper along the curb, then walked over to the edge of the sidewalk and raised her arm to hail a cab.

A few buildings down, sandwiched in between the line of cars across the street, was a rusted-out and dented black Honda Civic. Behind the wheel sat a guy in a baseball cap concealed beneath a dark hoodie, with a camera in his hands. Slouched down in his seat and lying low, he watched her, snapping photos, until a cab pulled up to let her in. As the taxi pulled out, so did the guy in the dark hoodie, following it all the way to lower Manhattan until it stopped at the front entrance of the Brookfield Place Mall.

At that point, the black Honda Civic passed the cab and continued toward the nearest parking garage. There, the man got out of his vehicle, let down his hood, and made his way to the elevator, which would lead him into the giant indoor shopping center. Once inside, he wandered around from floor to floor, scouring each corner of the mall. He feared he had lost her when, suddenly, he spotted her walking into one of those expensive designer men's shops.

Casually, he lowered the visor of his cap and headed toward the specialty store. When he walked in, he noticed her standing in the tie section. Gradually, he started to move in closer while making sure to keep a safe distance. In the meantime, he pretended to be shopping, nonchalantly lifting and inspecting items, until a sales clerk approached him. "Can I help you find anything?" asked the sales associate, eying him up and down suspiciously.

"Uh, no thanks," said the guy in the baseball cap, glancing

upward to catch Margot looking at him.

"Well, let me know if you need anything," said the clerk, appearing hesitant to leave.

As the stranger continued to idle about the store, he noticed that Margot was no longer in the same section. He turned around to see where she had gone, when all of a sudden, there she was standing directly in front of him with a tie in her hand. "What do you think of this one?" she asked, holding it up to his face.

Startled, his initial reaction was to say, "What?"

"I said, 'What do you think of this one?'" she repeated.

"Uh...it depends. Who is it for?"

"It's for my brother. His birthday's coming up."

The stranger studied the tie for a moment. "It's a little loud for me."

Margot looked at the tie, then back at him. "You're right," she said, tossing it on the nearest counter. "I guess you wouldn't want to *stand out* now, would you? What's your name?"

"Uh...James."

She turned her eyes toward the display table again and grabbed another tie. Then she held it up over her chest. "How about this one — *JAMES*?"

James reached his hand up to turn over the price tag. "You've got good taste, but isn't that a little pricey for 'your brother?'"

Margot busted out a smile while she sized "James" up and down. She guessed him to be in his mid-thirties, at least 6'2" (she liked that), with a lanky, yet sturdy build. He also had a "macho" look about him, boasting a five o'clock shadow even though it was only noon. Maybe that's what impressed her the most, the fact that he seemed like he didn't give a shit. "You're right, she said, giving the necktie a second look. "He's not worth it. But I'm going to buy it for him anyway."

In that moment, the store clerk came over and asked,

"Have you made up your mind, Mrs. Magnuson?"

"Yes, Justin. Wrap this up for me, will you? I'll be back to pick it up in about an hour. She then turned to James. "I'm hungry. Do you think you can afford lunch?"

"It depends, what did you have in mind?"

"There's a place here in the mall. It's upstairs — follow me."

Together, they traversed the concourse of the shopping plaza and rode up the escalator until they came to an informal bistro called the *Steak and Ale*. After a short ten-minute wait, the two were escorted to a booth. "Is this all right?" asked the hostess.

Margot looked at James, who appeared a little uneasy. "Sure," he said, waiting for her to sit down before sitting himself across from her.

She sat there quietly for a moment studying his face, then broke out with, "Are you going to leave that hat on while we're eating?"

"Oh, no — sorry," he said. As he removed his cap, a ponytail that had been tucked under it came falling down well past his shoulders.

Margot was surprised by the long hair, but found that she was not put off by it. In fact, she kind of liked it. It made him look like a rock star. Without the cap, she was better able to appraise his face, which revealed a chiseled jaw to die for and the palest green eyes she had ever seen.

As he set the cap down on the table and lifted his head back up, it became obvious that he noticed she was staring at him. "I take it you've been here before," he said, in an apparent attempt to break her concentration.

"I have."

"So, what do you recommend?"

Margot pursed her lips and looked him straight in the eyes. "I recommend you tell me why you're following me, 'James.' If that's your real name?"

The abruptness of the question took him aback. "What?"

"I'm not blind. I've noticed you shadowing me on the street on more than one occasion. I've also seen you sitting in your little black car with your zoom lens pointed at my window. So, who are you, *James* – really?"

****

Trish Dearden was curled up on the futon with a pillow on her lap, watching the late show when James walked through the door of the narrow Queens rowhouse. "You musta' had a productive day, it's almost midnight," she said, looking up in his direction, but not bothering to get up.

James threw his white baseball cap on the chair and walked into the kitchen to get a beer from the fridge.

"You missed a really good documentary on the Beatles," Trish yelled from the other room.

"Oh yeah?" he said, cracking open the flip top of a Corona while walking back into the front room. "Did you record it for me?"

"Yeah."

"Thanks," he said, plopping down next to her.

"Don't I at least get a kiss?" she asked, moving in closer.

"Sorry," said James, leaning over to give her a quick peck on the lips.

"That's it?"

"I'm sorry, I'm just tired. This new case I'm on has got me running all over town."

Trish stared at him for a minute, trying to read his face, when she noticed what looked like a smudged red lipstick mark on his neck. It obviously wasn't from her. She never wore lipstick, let alone red.

"I can imagine," she said, her words trailing. "So, who is this person you're tracking?"

James took a gulp of his beer before answering. "Just

another broad whose husband thinks she's cheating on him."

"Is she?"

"Rest assured, by the time a husband becomes suspicious, it's always too late."

Trish cozied up to him even closer. "I'd love to hear all the *sordid* details."

"You know I can't tell you anything else. It's classified between me and my client. It would ruin my reputation if word got out that I was a snitch."

"Reputation! I think that ship has sailed," she laughed, trying to make it sound like a joke.

James guzzled the rest of his beer, crushing the can with his fist. "I'm tired. I think I'll go to bed."

CHAPTER 36

The *Dream Voyager* left port in Hamilton late Friday afternoon to begin its journey back to the States. It would continue to sail throughout the day and all night on Saturday before arriving in New York early Sunday morning.

Margot was getting ready to meet her gal pals for dinner. She had just gotten out of the shower and was in the process of toweling off her hair when there was a knock on her door. Before answering, she slipped on her robe and walked over to the entryway to take a peek through the peephole. There he was, just as she had expected, standing ever so stoic, with a bottle of Champagne in one hand and two flutes in the other.

With her mouth agape and her eyes appropriately swelling in size, she pulled open the door. "What are you doing here?" she exclaimed, throwing her arms around his neck.

"I wanted to surprise you," he said, withholding all trace of emotion.

"But how? When?"

"After my secretary had finalized all the plans for your reunion cruise, I had Jacques check my schedule to see if there was any way I could meet you there at some point. It just so happened I was available to spend this final day with you. So Jacques booked me a flight and here I am."

"But..."

"I flew into Hamilton this morning. Are you surprised?"

"Yes—very! My romantic husband," swooned Margot, going in for a smooch.

The door slammed behind Burt as he walked toward the

table in the middle of the room to set down the glasses and the bottle of Champagne. "I missed you," he said, untying her robe.

"I've missed you too," repeated Margot, wiggling out of it, eventually pulling him down onto the bed.

BUZZ...BUZZ...BUZZ! The room phone wouldn't stop ringing. Margot rolled over to look at the clock on the nightstand. "Shit! I must have fallen asleep." It was already quarter of six. She had forgotten all about dinner. When she finally picked up the receiver, it was Bethany (as she suspected) letting her know that she and the other girls were upstairs, ready to be seated for their dinner reservation and were waiting on her.

"You'll never guess," Margot started out. "Burt is here... Yeah, Burt! He wanted to surprise me. Sorry, but I don't think I'll be joining you guys tonight. I'll meet up with you tomorrow after breakfast and tell you all about it then." When she hung up the phone, Burt had risen from the bed to find another white robe in her closet and was in the process of uncorking the bottle of Champagne. Margot went into the bath to freshen up while he poured two glasses and carried them out to the balcony.

In her matching robe, she stepped out to join him. As she sat down, Burt lifted his glass to initiate a toast. "Here's to surprises," he said.

"And to many more," replied Margot, her eyes fixed on him while she slowly tilted her glass to her lips.

"Who was that?" asked Burt, with a hint of suspicion in his voice.

"It was Bethany."

"Oh... How is Bethany these days?"

"She's alright, all things considered. I was supposed to meet her and the other girls for dinner. Of course, I'd much rather spend the evening here with you."

Burt made an attempt at a meager smile.

"Are you hungry?"

Burt laid his hand over her exposed leg. "I'm feasting off your beauty, my Dear."

"No, really, Burt..."

"I suppose if I'm to keep up with you, I'm going to need to replenish my strength."

Margot teased him with her seductive eyes. "Then let's order room service and eat in the room tonight."

"You read my mind."

"So, what are you in the mood for?" she asked, standing up to get the à la carte menu.

"I think I'd like the surf 'n' turf."

"How appropriate," said Margot. "Land and sea."

"Rare on the fillet...and let me see the wine list."

"Oooh," drooled Margot, handing him the list of options. "Can we have chocolate-dipped strawberries for dessert?"

"Whatever you want, my Dear."

"But I want *you* to want it too."

"I want what makes *you* happy," said Burt, opening the deck screen to go in and place the order on the in-house phone. When he came back, he poured the last of the Champagne into their flutes and sat down. He took a long swig before turning his eyes on his wife. "Are you happy, Margot?"

"Why would you ask that?"

"Wouldn't you say that I've given you everything you could ever possibly want?"

Margot reached over to place her hand over his. "You've given me more than any woman could ever possibly want or need, Burt."

"Then why would you cheat on me?"

At first, Margot appeared startled by the accusation, but then she calmly rose from her chair to go sit on his lap. "I would never cheat on you, Burt, I love you," she proclaimed, squeezing his face between her palms in order to initiate a long, drawn-out kiss. Which he did not reciprocate.

Slowly, she drew her mouth away while he maintained a steely demeanor. Then, he took in a long, deliberate breath and exhaled. "Don't take me for a fool, Margot. I've got proof."

"What do you mean?" asked Margot, playing coy. "What kind of proof?"

"I hired a private investigator to have you followed."

Easing up from his lap, she walked back to her seat to drain the rest of her Champagne and regroup before facing him again. Just as she was about to say something, the conversation was cut short by a knock on the door, followed by an announcement, "Room service."

A flustered Margot rushed over to let the attendant in. With one arm, she held the door while a man in a white jacket and black trousers rolled in a stainless steel cart. Burt and Margot both watched quietly as he removed an array of silver-covered platters and placed them on the table. He then arranged two porcelain place settings with cloth napkins and silverware across from one another. When he was done, he pulled out the bottle of vintage red wine that Burt had ordered and said, "I'm sorry, Sir, but I need to see your drink card before I can uncork it." "Margot, would you mind getting my card?" said Burt. "It's in my wallet over there."

Grabbing it off the nightstand, Margot rifled through the billfold until she found the card, presented it to the steward, then stuck it in her robe pocket.

Much of the meal was eaten in silence until Margot determined it was time for her to speak up. In her most theatrical voice, she began to establish her defense. "I don't know what I was thinking, Burt. It's just that...(pause)...you're out of town so much. I miss you when you're not around. You know how I am. I need constant affection to keep me going..."

Burt appeared unmoved by her paltry excuse and

remained quiet until they were almost done with their entrees. He set his fork down and polished off the last of his Bordeaux. Then he lifted the white linen napkin from his lap and dabbed his mouth. "I'm getting too old for this, Margot. A relationship has to be built on trust. I feel like I can no longer trust you."

Margot summoned a bed of tears to cushion themselves between the corners of her eyes and leaned across the table to grab her husband's hands. "Whatever I did to hurt you, Burt, I'm truly sorry." The droplets broke loose and trickled down her blushed cheeks. "What can I do to make it up to you, Burt? I'll do *anything* if you'll please just give me one more chance."

The look on her face was so sincere, all Burt could do was to take a deep breath and steadily release it until it was completely exhausted. "I don't know how many more chances I can give you, Margot. I should know better." He looked down at his nearly empty plate, shaking his head back and forth. "With that said, I'm willing to allow you one final opportunity to prove your commitment to me."

Margot squeezed his hands tightly into hers. "I promise you, Burt. For as long as I'm alive, you'll never have to worry about me being unfaithful again."

Burt's eyes rendered a look that Margot had never seen before. "I'm going to hold you to your word, my Darling; otherwise...you may live to regret it."

The following morning, Margot didn't resurface until just before noon, when she joined her friends on the lido deck, where they were sunning themselves by the pool.

Rachel was the first to spot her, raising her arm to wave her down. "Margot!" she yelled. "We didn't see you at breakfast. Where's Burt?"

"We had breakfast in bed. He's in the workout room now."

"I can't believe he just showed up on the ship like that," broke in Bethany.

"Yeah. He wanted to surprise me."

"Isn't that romantic?" Doris drawled out, mockingly.

"Will he be joining us for lunch or dinner?" asked Bethany. "I haven't seen him since the wedding. It would be nice to see him again."

"Probably not," Margot went on to explain. "He booked a sauna after his workout. After that, he was planning on going up to the observatory to do some reading. He said he didn't want to 'spoil' our girls' reunion, and insisted I spend the whole day with you. Isn't that sweet of him?"

"Aw," droned Rachel.

"However, since this will be our last night on the open sea, he made it clear I had to spend the night with him. So I promised to give him 'a night he'd never forget.'"

"Whew," said Rachel, fanning herself with her hand. "Is he staying in your room?"

"No, he's got his own stateroom—although he hasn't seen much of it so far," chuckled Margot.

"OK," cut in Dana, "I think I've heard enough. Can we please move on to another subject?"

"I want to hear more!" blurted out Rachel. "I may need to take notes—it's been a while."

Margot rippled in laughter. "Dana's right. I think I'll stop there. Although let's just say, given his age, he might not make it out alive. But, at least...he'll go out with a smile."

CHAPTER 37

On the final evening of their trip, the five friends had a celebratory dinner followed by a night of dancing in the ship's lounge. There, they grooved to the beat of the 80s music, dancing and singing along to such songs as *Girls Just Wanna Have Fun, I Wanna Dance With Somebody,* and *Wake Me Up Before You Go-Go.* After sweating it out on the dance floor, they rode the elevator to the top deck—the observation deck—to cool off. With cocktails in hand, they gathered side by side along the ship's rail, bathing in the brisk ocean air while admiring the incandescent moonbeams deflected off the shifting waves.

As midnight drew near, the impact of a supermoon combined with the repercussions from the consumption of alcohol began to go into full swing.

All of a sudden, Rachel set her drink on one of the side tables and decided to start climbing up the railing. When she reached the top rung, she raised her arms (mimicking the famous scene in the movie, *Titanic*) and spread them up toward the sky. "Look at me," she shouted. "I'm on top of the world!"

"Whoa," yelled Dana and Bethany, who were standing nearby, clamoring to get a hold of her. "That's dangerous, you could fall!"

Rachel held their arms, getting teary-eyed, while they slowly helped her down. "You guys, I can't believe this is our last evening on the boat. This has been so much fun, I don't want it to end. Tomorrow I'll be home, back to my hum-drum routine, with nothing to look forward to, except work and sleep..."

Doris, having witnessed the event, sashayed over to the

railing. "Don't be so dramatic, Rachel."

"Can't you see she's hurting?" jumped in Dana, somewhat out of character. "If anyone's overly dramatic, it's you."

"Oh, really, Miss Ice Princess. Since when did you ever care about anybody's feelings?" retorted Doris.

"Just because I don't wear my emotions on my sleeve doesn't mean they're not there."

Rachel stepped away from them and started looking for her glass. "Where's my drink?" she stammered.

Dana stepped in front of her. "I think you've had enough, Rachel. You never could hold your liquor."

Margot looked around and recognized the tall, narrow glass that Rachel had been nursing on one of the patio tables and carried it over to her. "Relax, Dana. It's nothing but melted ice, anyway." She handed it to Rachel, taking a final swallow from her own tumbler. "There's nothing left in mine either," she said, shaking the cubes around. "I need another drink."

Doris: "Me too."

Bethany: "There's a waiter over there. I'll call him over."

Margot: "No, I want Jorge!"

Doris echoed Margot's charge: "Yeah, we want Jorge."

Bethany lifted her hand to motion to the attendant to come over. When he arrived, she and Dana both ordered another drink, but when he went to take Margot's order, she strode up to his face. "What's your name?" she sputtered.

"Uh...Raul."

"So, *Raul*, where's Jorge?"

"Jorge? Do you mean, Albuoy?"

"Albuoy? Is that his last name? Sure, where is he?"

"He is working the promenade deck tonight."

"Well, go fetch him, Raul," she commanded. "And tell him MARGOT (emphasizing her name) sent for him." Just as he was about to leave, she grabbed him by the arm. "Wait! In the meantime, get me another Dark 'N' Stormy, will you?"

"And I'll have another...uh... What was I drinking?" cut in Doris. "Oh yeah—a rum swizzle—I like those."

At this point, Rachel was slouching over and holding her stomach. "I think I'm going to throw up."

Dana put her arms up around her shoulders, doing her best to hold her taller friend upright. "Come on, Rachel. There's a public restroom on the lower level."

After they left, a brief period of silence went by before Bethany spoke up. "Margot, I want to thank you for setting up this trip. It helped me get my mind off of Charles. At least for a while."

Margot raised her finger to her lips. "Shush...you're not supposed to talk about him, remember?"

"I know...I just worry about him."

"What are you worried about?"

"I don't know, all alone in that cell, day in and day out, with nothing to do but think. He's afraid I'll cheat on him and leave him for someone else."

"So what? Wasn't he cheating on you?"

Bethany cocked an inquisitive eye on Margot. "How do you know he was cheating on me?"

Margot attempted to gloss over her remark. "You told me that you suspected him of cheating. Don't you remember?"

"Yes, but he never admitted it. When I confronted him, he adamantly denied it, telling me how much he loved me and that he'd never hurt me..."

While Bethany jabbered on about her husband's virtues, Margot's mind reverted back to that pivotal Thursday evening just before Charles' 37th birthday. To celebrate, Bethany had talked him into going away for a long weekend. They were going to be staying at her childhood home in Maine. After her parents' death, she couldn't bear to sell it, so she hung on to it to use as a summer retreat or as a peaceful escape whenever she felt the need to get away.

Burt was going to be away on another business trip, so before Charles left for his birthday weekend, Margot invited him over so she could give him an early Birthday present.

She started out the evening by giving him a special lap dance, which included handing him a rectangular box wrapped in a red bow. While she was still on his lap, he unwrapped the box to find a very expensive silk tie inside. When he looked at the tag, his eyes bugged out, "This is a Brioni! What's my wife going to think when she sees me wearing it?"

"I don't know, Charles," huffed Margot, winding the tie around his neck and pulling his face toward her mouth. "An important New York City lawyer such as yourself deserves to have nice ties, doesn't he?"

"Well, yeah...but she might get suspicious."

"You're a big boy, Charles. I'm sure you can come up with a good story. You should be an expert liar by now. You've been lying to her this long."

Charles got a sullen look on his face, so Margot planted her tongue deep within his throat in an effort to mitigate his anxiety. Before he could come up for air, Charles pushed her off his lap, causing her to land with a hard thud on the floor. For a moment, she just sat there frozen, propped up on her elbows, staring at him in disbelief.

"I need a drink," he said, getting up to go to the bar.

Margot rushed up behind him. "What's the matter? Don't tell me all of a sudden you're feeling guilty."

Charles poured himself half a tumbler of Burt's favorite scotch and took a hard slug.

Margot got up in his face. "So, what made you do it?"

"Do what?"

"Cheat, Charles. Why would you cheat on her if you were

going to feel guilty about it later?"

Margot's lover stared soberly into his glass. "I don't know," he said, remorse trailing in his voice, then doused it with another ounce of amber liquid. "After Bethany's parents died, I became her whole world. At first, I was flattered, but as time went on, it became unbearable. She was smothering me. I had no room to breathe. I felt suffocated. We were *always* together. Hell, we even worked together.

"And then *you* came along. From the first moment I saw you, you were all I could think of. To the point of obsession. You became this fantasy that I could never have. The throbbing fascination overwhelmed me. I tried to extinguish it by avoiding you and denying that it even existed. I wanted to remain faithful because I couldn't imagine hurting her, but I had to take a chance. The first night you and I had dinner together, and then afterward, when we made love. It felt almost surreal. I had taken up residence in my fantasy world — a world that had no room for guilt..."

As his repenting face faded, all Margot could see was her own shadow clouding Bethany's blue eyes. "So, you believe him, right?"

Bethany: "What else can I do? He's always been my one and only."

Margot shrugged: "Well, he'll be out before you know it."

Bethany: "That's easy for you to say, you've got Burt."

Margot (laughing): "Right — Burt."

Bethany: "So, how are you and Burt getting along?"

Margot: "Just smashingly, Daaarling."

Doris, who had been off to the side listening, moved in closer and chimed in: "Where is Burt anyway?"

Margot: "I told him I'd meet him in his room later this evening."

Doris: "And he trusts you to show up?"

Margot: "What's that supposed to mean?"

Just then, Raul came back with their drinks, and Dana and Rachel returned from the ladies' room.

"Whew! I feel way better!" said Rachel. "Let's rally!"

Following her cue, the women gave a rousing round of toasts and continued drinking well into the night.

CHAPTER 38

It was in the wee hours of the morning on Sunday, August 30, 2015, that a passenger by the name of Agnes Haggerby reported seeing what looked like a body falling overboard on the *Dream Voyager's* starboard side. Not wanting to wake the rest of the passengers, which could lead to an unnecessary panic, a preliminary on-board investigation began with ship personnel questioning only those witnesses who were awake or on duty at the time. Other than the senior, Mrs. Haggerby, no one admitted to hearing or seeing anything out of the ordinary.

At 6:00 a.m., the *Dream Voyager* had reached the New York City Harbor. Since it had not been verified that anyone actually had gone overboard, the captain ordered a concise passenger-verified head count to be taken as each person disembarked the ship.

By 8:00 a.m., the hallways were filled with passengers lined up in front of the gangway, ready to debark. Standing together in that procession was that same group of attractive gal pals who had put on a happy facade for the camera when boarding the ship eight days ago. However, this time around, the women's personas appeared to be very different. They were all slumped over, dragging their wheeled suitcases behind them, while they hid beneath their hats and dark sunglasses to conceal their bloodshot eyes. All of them, that is—except one.

After all the passengers had been accounted for, the captain's headcount revealed that there was still one person who had not yet disembarked: Mrs. Margarita Magnuson.

An immediate search of her suite followed, where it was

found that all her clothing and belongings remained in the room. The only thing that appeared to be missing was her cell phone. The hunt for Margarita Magnuson was officially underway.

Burton Magnuson had already left Pier 92 and was in the back of a cab on his way to his Manhattan office when he felt the phone in his suit pocket vibrating frantically. He pulled it out to read the name of the sender flashing before him: JACQUES.

"Yes, Jacques. What is it?"

"Sir, we have a problem. There's been a data breach. I've booked a flight for you to Miami this afternoon. *Magnuson's Millions* is being prepped, and Captain Overland and the staff are on stand-by for your arrival."

****

Even though the cruise ship officials found no other witnesses, besides the old lady with poor vision, to corroborate that Mrs. Magnuson (or anyone else, for that matter) had gone overboard, the Coast Guard was immediately sent out. The divers did a thorough search in and around the waters surrounding the area where Mrs. Haggerby had alleged to have seen a person go overboard. After the search and rescue was exhausted with no trace of a body having been found, it subsequently turned into a recovery mission—meaning that if someone had indeed fallen into the water, there was no likelihood that they would be found alive. Though they did not find a body, they did find one "key" piece of evidence floating in the area. It was a plastic key card for Room 620, the Dream Voyager's Penthouse Suite, which was later identified as belonging to Margarita Magnuson.

On board, the cruise line's investigation team gathered whatever evidence they could, beginning with witness statements taken from ship personnel and a DNA sample retrieved from a hairbrush taken from a toiletry bag in Mrs. Magnuson's cabin. The only relevant camera footage captured (which was substantiated by a passing night steward) was that of a female fitting the missing person's description walking down the hallway on the sixth floor approximately ten to fifteen minutes prior to the time the incident was reported. In addition, several potentially-significant items were found on the observation deck where the "so-called" victim was purported to have last been seen prior to her disappearance. They were: a magnetic name card, a drink card, and a black, satin and lace thong, with nearly ripped elastic.

The cruise line was obligated to notify Margarita Magnuson's next of kin of her disappearance, but when her husband could not immediately be reached, they contacted her parents, who Margarita had listed in her emergency contacts. Following tears of shock and disbelief, the only thing her parents could muster, in broken English, was to say, "Please find her body, so we can give her a proper burial."

It wasn't long before the headline was all over the news:

"Margarita Magnuson, Wife of Multi-Millionaire Land Developer, Burton Magnuson, Goes Missing From Cruise Ship."

With no body having been found, the recovery mission was ultimately abandoned, and the matter would have to remain a missing person's case until suicide or foul play could be determined. At this point, the cruise line was relieved from all further investigation, and the matter of the disappearance of Margarita Magnuson would be reassigned to the Federal Bureau of Investigation.

Only the most qualified of agents could be selected to take over a case such as this. Someone with years of experience and a naval background to back it up. The case was assigned to Special Agent Richard Heller.

CHAPTER 39

Special Agent Richard Heller was a 24-year veteran with the FBI. He was divorced with no children and never remarried. His imposing 6'4" stature and square brush cut, which he'd worn since his Navy days, rendered him intimidating to most, including his colleagues. The lines etched into his forehead were derived from his lack of any semblance of humor, earning him the nickname: "No-Nonsense Dick."

Except how could he have a sense of humor? He was an only child who grew up in a small town in Minnesota. His mother left when he was barely a teen (according to his father — for another man). "Dickie," as his mom used to like to call him, never saw much of his dad. He spent six days a week working at the local mill, and after hours, he'd go to the local bar and drink alongside his work buddies until well into the night. The only time he saw him was on Sundays, when his dad spent much of the time arguing with his mother to the point where it often became physical. Young Dickie did his best to try to intervene, often putting himself in harm's way. Then one afternoon, Dickie came home from school to find his mother gone. For many years, he believed she would come back for him, but eventually, he gave up hope.

When he should have been out having fun with friends his own age, Richard was forced to grow up fast. While his father's alcoholism grew progressively worse, Richard continued to go to school, keeping up with his studies, while at the same time doing the cooking, the laundry, and other household chores. His father was missing so much time from work, he eventually got fired from his job at the mill. In his senior year, at the age of sixteen, Richard dropped out of school to work full-time at a local gas station in order to pay the bills.

Late one night, his father stumbled home from the bar in one of his usual drunken stupors. Richard was asleep in his bed and never heard him come in. When he woke up the next morning, he found his father lying on the uneven wooden porch steps, unconscious. It was later determined that his father had tripped and passed out, subsequently drowning in his own vomit.

By then, Richard was seventeen. That's when he left to join the Navy, promising himself to never look back.

While stationed in Norfolk, Richard thought he had found happiness when he met his future wife, Stacy. She was serving as a medical assistant on the same naval ship. They married when their tours of duty were over, and both remained on active reserve for four more years. During that time, Richard went back to school for a bachelor's degree in criminal justice, which would eventually lead him to join the FBI.

Stacy filled the void in his heart. The love he felt for her took the place of the love he'd had for his mother. Sadly, it didn't last, and his heart was broken once again. Their brief four-year marriage ended when he found her cheating with his best friend, Chuck, his Navy buddy since boot camp. He felt betrayed, just as he had felt betrayed when his mom left. Richard swore he'd never trust another woman again.

Since joining the FBI, Heller had conducted hundreds of missing person cases, but his first missing person case came just after he had completed his 20-week training in Quantico, Virginia. In his mind, it was the case that marked his career: the case of his own mother's disappearance.

CHAPTER 40

The *Dream Voyager* was preparing to set sail again when Jorge Albuoy was escorted to a back office on the ship's lower level by two security officers. When Mr. Albuoy walked into the room, a man in a gray suit was seated at a table waiting for him. The man stood up and extended his arm in a handshake.

"Hello, Jorge. I'm Special Agent Richard Heller from the FBI. Have a seat," he said, motioning to the wooden chair across from him.

Mr. Albuoy said nothing as he sat down and folded his arms in front of his chest. The two security attendants positioned themselves on each side of the door, and Agent Heller was about to begin his interrogation when Albuoy spoke up. "Why am I here? I have done nothing wrong."

"We're not accusing you of anything, Mr. Albuoy. Just some routine preliminary questioning. May I call you Jorge?"

"Sure," said Albuoy, his shoulders relaxing a bit.

Heller paced back and forth as he began his line of inquiry." How long have you been working for the cruise line, Jorge?"

"I began as a deckhand when I was eighteen years old and moved my way up."

"How old are you now?"

"I am twenty-three."

"How long have you been a waiter on the *Dream Voyager*?"

"Two years. I had to wait until I was 21 so that I could serve alcohol."

"I've taken over the investigation relating to the disappearance of a female passenger on board this ship." Agent

Heller pulled out an enlarged photograph from his inner pocket and set it in front of Albuoy. "This was taken on August 22, 2015, just before the *Dream Voyager*'s departure to Bermuda. The five women in this picture boarded the boat together that day." Heller pointed to the tall, slender female in the middle of the group. "Do you recognize this woman?"

Jorge glanced at the photo with an indifferent look on his face and leaned back into his seat. "I meet a lot of people in my job."

"According to numerous ship attendants that were interviewed, she and her four friends were often seen sitting together in your assigned serving area."

Jorge remained silent.

"Surely, you remember them."

"Oh, yes... Now I remember. They were always together."

"Do you recall anything specific about these women, besides the fact that they were 'always together?' Was there anything else about *any* of them that stood out?"

Jorge Albuoy stared at the picture for a moment, as if contemplating what he was going to say next. "They drank a lot. Especially that one in the middle," he said, tapping Margot's image with his finger. "She liked to drink the Dark 'N' Stormies. They are very strong," he added with a smirk.

"Her name is Margarita Magnuson," said the agent.

Jorge hesitated again. "Yes—Margarita. That was the name on her drink card, but she told me to call her Margot."

"So you were on a first name basis?"

"That is my job. I am supposed to be friendly with all the passengers."

"You must have been pretty friendly with them if they kept coming back to your station." Heller waited for a reaction, but got none, and continued. "Do you remember how the women acted when they were together? Did they appear to get along?"

"I believe so. But Margot, she was definitely the leader of the group."

"How so?

"She was the most loud."

"As I'm sure you've heard, around 3:00 a.m., Sunday, August 30th, a body was alleged to have been seen going overboard. Did you observe the women together or have any interaction with them about that time or prior thereto?"

"No."

"Are you sure, Mr. Albuoy? Because a server by the name of Raul Ramos reported serving the women on the observation deck the night of the 29th. Raul stated that 'the beautiful tall one with the long, black hair' specifically asked for you by name."

Albuoy cocked his head and squinted. "I do not remember."

Heller threw a magnetic I.D. badge engraved with the name: JORGE ALBUOY down on the table.

The attendant's eyes widened. "Where did you get that?"

"One of the ship's investigators found it stuck to one of the tables on the top deck the morning after Mrs. Magnuson's disappearance. Think very hard, Jorge. Are you *sure* you didn't see her on the evening of August 29th or later, in the early hours of August 30th?"

Beads of sweat started to form on Jorge's brow as he attempted to fill in the blanks. "Yes, on Saturday — August 29. But only for a very short time. I was working at a different station that night."

"Apparently, you were there long enough to remove your badge."

"It must have fallen off."

"Do you lose your badge often, Mr. Albuoy?"

Albuoy didn't reply.

"When you saw her — Margot — that evening, was she with her girlfriends?"

"No."

"You stated that she was 'always with her girlfriends.' So, this time she was alone?"

"No. She was with an older gentleman. I believe it was her husband."

The special agent was caught off guard by this statement and raised his eyebrows in surprise. As Heller was about to resume his questioning, Jorge's mind drifted back to that night on August 29th...

Jorge was on the promenade deck refilling drinks when he was told he had an in-house call from his fellow coworker, Raul. Raul told him he was working the top deck and that one of the patrons had specifically asked for him by name. When Jorge asked who it was, Raul told him it was the beautiful woman with long black hair, who referred to herself as 'Margot,' and that she said she would be waiting for him on the observation deck.

Jorge waited approximately fifteen minutes before asking another attendant to cover for him while he took a quick break. As the elevator opened up to the lookout level, Jorge spotted Margot on the ship's starboard side. She was by herself, leaning against the railing and looking out at the ocean.

When she heard him approaching, she quickly turned around and shouted, "There you are!" She stumbled over to him and threw her arms around his neck. "I've been waiting for you."

As she drawled on, it became clear to Jorge that she was well over her alcohol limit. "My friends just left, but I waited because I needed to see you," she said, tightening her grip around his neck.

"I'll be off my shift soon," Jorge replied.

"Do you promise to come back?"

"Yes, I promise."

Just as he was turning to leave, she grabbed him by the collar and pulled him up to her face. "Hurry up," she slurred, planting a wet, steamy kiss on his full lips. But just before releasing him, she plucked off his name tag, which was adhered to his shirt pocket by a magnet, and clutched it tightly behind her back.

"Hey, I need that!" he exclaimed, trying to grab it away from her.

"Insurance. You'll get it back when you return," said Margot, tucking it into her cleavage..."I'll be waiting."

"You are a devil," replied Jorge, boomeranging her nefarious grin. Then he promptly left.

Half an hour later, he anxiously returned to the observation deck. When he got there, however, she wasn't alone. She and an older gentleman were standing near the railing, face-to-face, in what appeared to be a heated argument. Aided by the shadow of the moonlight, Jorge sheltered himself behind a partition while he did his best to eavesdrop on the conversation. He could not make out exactly what they were saying, but the man's tone was becoming significantly more and more incensed, and Margot was visibly crying. The white-haired gentleman finally threw up his hands in a fit of exasperation and left, leaving Margot bent over the side of the boat with her hands cupped over her face.

When the old guy was clear out of sight, Jorge ran up to Margot, grabbing her by the shoulders. "Are you all right?"

"No, I'm not alright," she said.

"Who was that?"

"That was my husband. We just had a fight."

Jorge put his arms around her to try to comfort her. As her tears subsided, he began to kiss her. First, slowly, then steadily more aggressively as she responded more willingly to his advances. As things were heating up, he pressed his tongue forcefully down her throat while lifting her skirt. He started to pull down her panties when suddenly, she went cold and pushed him away.

"What's the matter with you?" he said angrily.

"Get away from me, you creep!" she shouted, throwing out her arms.

Albuoy, who was past the point of arousal, was beyond miffed and thrust his body into hers. "First, you're hot, and then you are cold!" he seethed.

Margot let down her guard and broke down again. "My husband knows I've been cheating on him."

Jorge held her firmly against the railing. "If he knows, then what difference does that make now?" he said in a calmer tone, while driving his hand back up beneath her chiffon skirt.

"You don't understand. He's threatened to leave me – or worse!"

At this point, Albuoy unzipped his pants while yanking at her panties to the point of nearly ripping them. Margot continued to fight him off, finally kneeing him as hard as she could in the groin. This enraged Jorge all the more...to the point of...

"How do you know it was her husband?" asked the agent.

"What?" said Jorge, gradually waning from his inner thoughts.

"I said, 'How did you know the older gentleman was Margarita's husband?'"

"He was yelling at her, and she was crying. I heard her say she still loved him, but he just kept calling her names like 'slut' and 'whore.'"

"Was that the last time you saw her?"

"Yes."

Heller paused for a minute. "Are you a single man, Mr. Albuoy?"

"No. I am married."

"Do you have any children?"

"Yes."

The agent pulled something else out of his inner lapel pocket. It was a plastic zip-lock bag containing what looked like a black thong whose waistband had been stretched to near rippage. "Does this look familiar to you?"

Jorge's eyes grew wide, visibly unnerved. "I don't know. What is that?"

"It's a pair of women's underwear found on the observation deck where you said you last saw Margot."

"I have never seen those. They could belong to anyone."

Heller placed the bag back in his pocket. "Do you know what the penalty is for perjury, Mr. Albuoy?"

"I did not do anything wrong. If anyone is to blame for her disappearance, you should look to her husband."

CHAPTER 41

FBI Agent Richard Heller stood in the glass-encased elevator, somberly watching the Manhattan skyline shrink smaller and smaller as it carried him up to the 25th floor of the luxurious condominium complex. He had yet to meet Burton Magnuson, but from his experience, he found that when people reach this level of success, so does their level of omnipotence.

He had arrived in the lobby without an appointment, hoping, by chance, to catch the multi-millionaire at home. When the concierge rang the unit, the maid answered to say that Mr. Magnuson was not in. After announcing himself as an FBI agent, he was allowed to go up and talk to the housekeeper despite the owner's absence. Heller waited for several minutes outside the unit's grandiose double entryway before a timid-looking, middle-aged woman, wearing a uniform black dress and white apron, creaked the door open only slightly.

Agent Heller pulled out his badge and held it up for the sable-haired woman to see.

"Mr. Magnuson, he not here," she said softly with a heavy accent.

"When do you expect him?"

"I not know."

Heller thought he'd take a shot and asked, "What about *Mrs.* Magnuson? Is she in?"

"Margarita?"

"Yes."

"She go on trip."

"Have you seen her since she came back?"

The maid stared blankly at the agent. "I not know."

"When was the last time you saw her?"

"Before she leave for trip."

"How long have you known Mrs. Magnuson?"

"Margarita? Only since she marry Mr. Magnuson and she move in here."

"How would you say she and her husband got along? Specifically, just before she left for her trip?"

The maid pursed her lips together tightly, as if wanting to say something, but held back.

"What I mean is, did you witness any fighting between them — verbally or physically?"

The maid gulped hard. "They seem good."

"Look, uh...what is your name?"

"Maria," she replied nervously.

"Your last name?"

Pausing for a moment, as if fearful of revealing her full identity, she answered, "...Alvarez."

"Look, Ms. Alvarez, it's important that I speak with Mr. Magnuson. I promise it has nothing to do with you, and you won't get into any kind of trouble. Do you know where I can find him?"

Again, she was reluctant to speak. "Maybe you ask the ex-Missus Magnuson. They still talk."

"Oh, really? Where does she live?"

"She live in Connecticut."

"Thank you, Ms. Alvarez," said Heller, as he was about to leave.

Ms. Alvarez started closing the door against him when he turned around and handed her his card. "When you do see him, make sure you tell him I'm looking for him."

CHAPTER 42

It only took an hour to get from Manhattan to Greenwich, Connecticut. Heller didn't mind the drive. It was an especially bright and sunny day for mid-September. Once he got off the freeway and was out of the city, the route turned scenic and quite calming. It gave him time to think. If you could afford to live out here, you had it all. You could be near the ocean and enjoy the beauty of country living while still being close enough to the city if you needed to commute.

He hated urban living—everything about it: the noise, the traffic, the smells, and the feeling of claustrophobia he got from the massive structures casting their shadow over every inch of the concrete pavement. He looked forward to the day when he could retire and live wherever he wanted—somewhere like the small town where he grew up in Minnesota, surrounded by clear lakes and green forests. On second thought, he could never go back home—too many bad memories. He'd have to retire somewhere else. It would have to be someplace peaceful, though. Somewhere where he could write. When he was a boy, if nothing else, his mom did instill in him a love of reading. After she left, it was the one thing that kept his mind off her. Every night after supper, he'd wash the dishes, do his homework, and escape into a novel. It's no surprise that mysteries were his favorite. While in the Navy, he began to dabble in writing, as well, and continued to do so whenever he had spare time. His dream was to one day write his own mystery novel, and the years he'd spent with the FBI would certainly provide him with plenty of fodder.

After rambling along rural country roads and passing

several country clubs and a nature reserve along the way, he had finally arrived at his destination.

Parking his car along the long gravel driveway, he got out, scoping the grounds while he made his way to the grand wrap-around porch of the grand equestrian estate. It was hard to fathom the size of the immense property encompassing the homestead. Adjacent to the home on the right, and visible through a white slatted fence, was a large built-in pool with a curving water slide and expansive patio area. And to the left of the property, sectioned off by white horse fencing, was a large-scale riding arena with a big red barn and stables in the far rear.

Heller squinted to watch the ranch hands move horse jumps and dressage boards beneath the glinting rays of the afternoon sun, while he waited patiently in the shade of the portico for someone to answer the door. Eventually, a young lady dressed in riding breeches and her hair tied up in a ponytail appeared on the other side of the screen. She was chewing a wad of gum and looked like she might have been in her late teens or early 20s. He couldn't tell anymore. It seemed that the older he got, the younger the women looked.

"I'm Special Agent Richard Heller here to see Meredith Magnuson." (A search of her public records showed that she had not changed her name.)

"Is she expecting you?"

Heller had contacted her in advance. "Yes."

"C'mon in," the young woman said flippantly, opening the door and leaving him in the entryway. "Wait here, I'll go get her."

While standing in the vestibule of the vintage-style home, he felt as though he had stepped into one of those fancy old hotels you see in magazines. He was besieged by flowery wallpaper as far as the eye could see. He expected a Maitre d' to walk in any minute. Instead, an older woman, also in riding pants, entered the room.

"Hello, Mr. Heller. You'll have to excuse the way I look. My daughter, Kathryn, and I just came in from riding. Follow me into the sitting room, won't you?"

Heller followed her to an enormous living area with a wall of windows delineated with white, vertical and horizontal muntins.

"I appreciate you meeting with me on such short notice, Mrs. Magnuson."

"Please, call me Meredith."

Mrs. Magnuson was an attractive, slim, and trim woman with grayish blond hair pulled tightly into a bun. She had a very refined look about her. From the way she talked to the way she carried herself. Heller figured her to be probably in her 50s; although, just as it was hard for him to tell younger women's ages, it was also hard for him to determine older women's ages. Especially rich women who could afford plastic surgery and all that.

"Beautiful place you have here."

"Why, thank you—part of my divorce settlement. Burt was happy to give it up. He never did like horses. I acquiesced the Miami property to him. He doesn't mind the heat. Me, I tend to avoid the sun. Causes premature aging of the skin," she added, patting the sides of her cheeks.

Meredith spread her arm out over the overstuffed sofa. "Please, sit down. Would you like something to drink?"

"No, thank you," said Heller, picking out a spot across from his hostess. For some reason, he had not expected her to be this amiable.

"So, what can I do for you, Mr. Heller?'

"I'd like to ask you a few questions about your ex-husband."

"We've been divorced for six years now. I don't know

what I can offer that isn't already of public record."

"As it relates to his wife — Margarita Magnuson."

Meredith's cheerful comportment quickly took a downward slide, the hostility in her voice palpable. "I really don't know anything about her, except that it was she who broke up my marriage." It appeared that the ex-Mrs. Magnuson's true colors were starting to show.

"Did you ever have the opportunity to meet her?"

"Of course not. How on earth would I ever have had the opportunity to meet her?"

"I don't know, maybe a chance encounter somewhere?"

"No."

"I take it your marriage did not end under amicable terms."

"That is the understatement of the year."

"Mr. Magnuson's maid, Ms. Alvarez, mentioned that you and your ex-husband continue to keep in touch. Is that true?"

"We stay in touch for the sole reason that we have two children together. Granted, they are no longer minors, but they will always be an important part of our lives. Burton's young bride wants nothing to do with them. She'll stop at nothing to keep him from seeing them. She wants all the attention on her. Sometimes he is forced to extend his 'out of town' business just so he can see Kathryn and Robert without her knowing."

"Do they both live here with you?"

"Our son has his own place in the city, but our daughter, who you've already met, still lives here with me."

"Did Mr. Magnuson ever confide in you regarding his relationship with Margarita?"

"On occasion."

"Would you care to share any of that information with me?"

"What exactly do you want to know?"

"How were they getting along?"

"A while back, he did tell me he suspected her of having an affair. Of course, I wasn't surprised. A woman like that cannot be trusted for long."

"When was the last time you heard from your ex-husband?"

"Let me think," said Meredith. "I believe it was mid-July. It was particularly hot and humid that day. He stopped by to watch Kathryn practice her dressage training for an upcoming equestrian event. Afterwards, he and I were sitting out on the veranda drinking lemonade."

"And?"

"That's when he told me he suspected his beloved Margarita of having an affair. He said he had hired an investigator to follow her."

"Did he happen to mention who he suspected her of having an affair with?"

Meredith released a curdling laugh. "My husband was extremely jealous of that harlot; in his eyes, everyone was a suspect."

"Have you ever known your husband to have a temper?"

"Not with me. Of course, I never gave him any cause to."

"Did you know that Margarita has gone missing? She was last seen on August 29th, on a cruise ship over the Atlantic Ocean."

"How could I not? It's the talk of the town."

"We believe your husband may have been on the ship when she went missing."

"You're not insinuating he had anything to do with her disappearance?"

"We would just like to talk to him. We've yet to establish whether or not foul play was involved. It could have been accidental or a suicide. Perhaps he can shed some light on her state of mind at the time. You mentioned Mr. Magnuson got the

Miami property. Do you think I might find him there?"

"Perhaps...although he does travel a great deal for his business. It would not be unusual for him to be out of the country."

"I'll take my chances."

"You might want to call ahead and make arrangements with his head butler, Jacques Gagnon. He handles all of my husband...ex-husband's affairs."

"I'll do that," said Heller, standing up to leave.

"You can be sure of one thing, Agent Heller. She got what she deserved. Women like that always do."

"Thank you for your time, Mrs. Magnuson." Heller handed her his business card. "If you do hear from Mr. Magnuson, make sure you tell him I'd like to talk to him, won't you?"

CHAPTER 43

As the plane prepared for its descent at Miami-Dade International Airport, Richard Heller shifted his seat to the upright position. He laid his head back and closed his eyes in anticipation of what this trip might uncover because Burton Magnuson was looking more and more suspicious.

Even though it was early morning, it was already hot and humid. This was typical for Florida, even in September. Beads of sweat formed over Richard's brow while he waited for an operative from the FBI's Miramar field office to arrive with his car. Luckily, he didn't have to wait too long before two black sedans pulled up in front of him. The agent in the first automobile got out, leaving it for Heller, then jumped into the one behind it with the other driver and took off. Settling comfortably in his air-conditioned vehicle, Heller began his trek through the slow-moving traffic to one of the most expensive residential streets in the county.

Prior to flying to Miami, Heller's team had done its due diligence in accessing copies of Magnuson's divorce records. According to the settlement, Meredith was awarded the equestrian estate in Connecticut, a ski chalet in Breckenridge, and more than her share of monetary assets. Burton retained full possession of the condo in New York, the Miami residence, and a mega yacht aptly named, *Magnuson's Millions*, which was docked near his home in Florida.

After a preliminary screening via speakers and security cameras, the agent was allowed entry through the ornate wrought iron gates of the grand estate. From there, he followed an extensive driveway that ended up looping around an elaborate fountain commanding the ostentatious mansion. Heller parked his vehicle in front of the enormous marble structure from which the Greek God, Neptune, rose up from the center, brandishing his trident, while nose-diving dolphins spewing water from their beaks encircled him.

No sooner had the agent stepped from his vehicle than he was met outside the entryway by a stately-looking gentleman in a black coat and tie who introduced himself as Monsieur Jacques Gagnon, head butler. Mr. Gagnon was a slight man with grayish-white sideburns and just enough of an accent as to pass himself off as French.

In addition to Magnuson's ex-wife, Meredith, Heller had done his homework on Mr. Gagnon, too. Not only was the "head butler" charged with hiring and overseeing the complete staff of the Miami estate, but he was also the estate manager entrusted with the management and financial concerns of all of Mr. Magnuson's properties.

It appeared that Jacques was very loyal to Burt. He'd been with him since they'd met in Bermuda twenty years prior. Jacques was working as the head butler and estate manager for a wealthy local banker at the time. During that period, Monsieur Gagnon came into contact with a lot of brokers and financiers and became privy to a great deal of inside information. When the wealthy banker suffered a sudden heart attack, Burton Magnuson wasted no time recruiting Mr. Gagnon to come work for him.

"Thank you for agreeing to meet with me," said Richard.

"As I explained to you over the telephone, Mr. Magnuson is out of the country on company business. I don't see how I could be of help to you."

"I just have a few questions, which I prefer to ask you in person rather than over the phone."

"Very well," said Mr. Gagnon.

Heller followed him through the massive entryway into an opulent foyer, then through an enormous salon centered around an ivory grand piano illuminated by the wall of white, French doors, which opened up to an alfresco patio and pool area.

Once outside, the agent sank into one of the many overstuffed rattan chairs with tropically designed pillows. A light breeze fluttered through the multitude of palms scattered about the private grounds, but it did little to curb the sweat forming over Richard's upper lip.

"You look like you could use a drink," announced Jacques.

"A lemonade would be great," replied Heller, as his host called for an attendant. He would have liked to remove his jacket, but thought it more important to demonstrate as professional an appearance as that of the head butler. He was impressed at how Monsieur Gagnon was able to maintain such a glacial countenance in his otherwise stuffy attire.

When the server returned, Jacques watched while Agent Heller drank a good portion of the ice-cube infused citrusy beverage in one single gulp, and so ordered another one to be brought out for his guest.

"So, what exactly would you like to know, Agent Heller?"

"I'm sure you're well aware that Margarita Magnuson disappeared from the *Dream Voyager* cruise ship on August 30th."

"I am."

"When was the last time you saw her?"

Jacques squeezed his lips together and tilted his head toward the sky. "Hmm...let me think...it's been some time. I believe it was early Spring. She spent half her time in New York and the other half here."

"Had you spoken to her since then? Say, by telephone?"

"No. She would have no reason to contact me."

Heller looked puzzled. "She's your employer's wife. Didn't she ask you to do things for her?"

"I take my orders strictly from *Mr. Magnuson.*"

"Didn't Mr. Magnuson trust his wife?"

"Mr. Magnuson trusts me."

"Did he ever confide in you as to any marital problems they might have been having?"

"Agent Heller, any conversation between me and Mr. Magnuson is held in strictest confidence."

"Did you know that he was on the *Dream Voyager* the night that Mrs. Magnuson went missing?"

"Yes, I am aware. I made his reservations myself."

"Do you think he might have had something to do with her disappearance?"

Gagnon took in a deep breath before huffing out a steady reply. "Mr. Magnuson is a highly respected businessman who values his reputation. The mere fact that you would suggest such a thing is highly offensive."

"Do you think she could have committed suicide?"

Before Jacques could answer, the waiter came back with another cooling beverage, enticing the agent to take several more gulps before concluding his questioning. "Let me backtrack. Did Mrs. Magnuson have any close friends here in Florida? Someone who she might have confided in? I'm just trying to determine her state of mind before she left on her cruise."

Gagnon allowed a grimace to surface on his stone face. "Mrs. Magnuson had no female acquaintances in Florida that I know of. However, there is someone—a male—you might be interested in speaking with. Jacques stood up from his seat. "If you'll excuse me for a moment," he said, as he strode back into the house. A few minutes later, he returned with a business card in his hand and dropped it on the table in front of the agent.

Heller looked at the card, which read:

JEFFREY HOLT, Certified Swimming Instructor
swimming, surfing, snorkeling, diving

"He was Mrs. Magnuson's aquatics instructor. They spent a good deal of time together. Perhaps he can provide you with the insight you need."

The simple fact was that Jacques never liked Margot. He saw through her kitten act and tried to warn his employer on more than one occasion that she was a gold digger. Unfortunately, Burt had been blinded by desire and refused to listen to reason. He told Jacques he was willing to risk it. While Jacques secretly continued to keep a watchful eye on her, he came to suspect she might be having an affair with her swim instructor, and eventually divulged his suspicions to his employer.

Heller put Holt's card in his pocket, swallowed the rest of his lemonade, and lifted himself out of the chair. "When do you expect Mr. Magnuson to return from his 'business trip?'"

"It's hard to say."

Heller dropped his own card on the table. "I'd appreciate it if you could let Mr. Magnuson know I'm looking for him. I'm sure there's a way you can get in touch with him— and I suggest you do that as soon as possible."

CHAPTER 44

Heller removed his jacket, cranked up the air, and entered Holt's address into his GPS. The map eventually led him to 32915 Palmetto Drive, which was located in a tacky seaside community on Miami's south side. Because of its close proximity to the beach, Heller was hard-pressed to find an empty spot along the aptly-named, overgrown palm-lined neighborhood, and ended up having to park a few streets away from the intended address.

Throwing his coat back on, he sweltered along until he came to a tiny, run-down bungalow with a chipped and weather-faded, baby-blue 1960s Volkswagen Beetle, parked in the short gravel driveway. Akin to most of the other homes on the street, surfboards and a faded kayak leaned up against a side wall, with paddles and snorkeling gear lying on the ground beside them. As Heller followed the cobbled path overrun with crab grass toward the front entrance, he couldn't help but form an opinion of who lived inside.

When he stepped onto the porch stoop, he saw that all the shades were drawn, even though it was almost noon. It took several hard knocks before a tanned and shirtless dude with disheveled blond hair answered the door. *Just as I had imagined,* thought Richard, holding back a grin.

"Special Agent Richard Heller, FBI," he said, flashing his badge. "Are you Jeffrey Holt?"

"Yeah, why?" asked the young man, rubbing his eyes.

"Sorry to bother you. Were you sleeping?"

"It's okay. Rough night, ya know?"

Heller didn't know. His whole life had been based on

discipline. "I have a couple of questions concerning Margarita Magnuson. I understand she was a client of yours."

"Yeah, so? What about her?"

"You haven't heard? It's been all over the news."

"Man, I don't even own a TV. Heard what?"

"She's been missing since August 30th."

Holt squinted his aqua marine eyes into his crinkled forehead. "What do you mean—*missing*?"

"She disappeared off a cruise ship returning from Bermuda just before it reached New York."

"Do you think something bad happened to her?"

"We don't know. A passenger reported seeing someone falling overboard on the date she went missing."

Holt covered his face with his hands. "Aw, no, man! You're kidding," he exclaimed, scraping his bangs up over his forehead.

Heller gave him a moment before continuing with his questioning. "How long have you known Mrs. Magnuson?"

"I met her a few years ago. Her old man hired me to teach her to swim."

"You mean, her husband?"

"Yeah," chuckled Holt. "Her husband. Except he looks more like her father."

"When did these lessons begin?"

"Like, right after they got married, man. Maybe a month after."

"Where did you conduct these lessons?"

"Sometimes at her Miami mansion. They had an Olympic-sized pool in their backyard with a diving board and all. Other times, I'd take her to the beach. She loved the ocean. She became obsessed. She wanted to try it all: surfing, snorkeling, diving. She was a fast learner, too. It was like she was born for it. For someone who didn't even know how to tread water, in less than a year she was tacklin' the waves like a pro."

"So, when was the last time you saw her?"

Holt lowered his head, rubbing his fingers against his temples. "About two summers ago, in Bermuda. They invited me out on their yacht."

"They?"

"Yeah. I guess her husband goes there a lot, for one reason or another. So while he'd be below deck conducting business and shit, I'd take her out snorkeling."

"And Mr. Magnuson was alright with that?"

Holt broke into a wide grin. "I guess she talked him into it. She could be pretty persuasive, ya know?"

"Had you ever seen or heard the two of them argue?"

"Nope. She made him think he was in control, but believe me, she always had the upper hand."

"Did you ever witness Mr. Magnuson lay a hand on his wife?"

"You mean like hit her? Not that I ever saw."

"Did she ever complain to you about her marriage?"

"What would she have to complain about? I mean, she was livin' the life."

"When was the last time you saw her?"

"Holt thought for a minute. "It had to be the last time I went out on the boat with them. That was last summer."

"Have you talked to her since then?"

"Just once. When she called me to tell me she was quitting our lessons—said she learned everything she needed to know. I didn't doubt it. Those long legs could propel her wherever she wanted to go."

"And where did she want to go?"

"Jeffrey let out a chuckle, "As high up the fish ladder as she could climb."

Richard handed him his card. "Thank you, Mr. Holt. If you remember anything else, give me a call."

As he was heading for the door, Jeffrey yelled out, "One thing's for sure. She didn't love him. She's a Barracuda."

Heller turned back around and noticed a melancholy expression had taken over the young man's face.

"Do you know about Barracudas, Agent? A Barracuda is an opportunistic, competitive predator. It's long and sleek and attracted to reflective, metallic objects like gold and silver. That was Margot."

Holt followed the agent out and pushed the door shut behind him. Resting his forehead against the cracked, wooden surface, his mind drew him back to Bermuda. Before he met Margot, he had spent a good deal of time on the island. He knew the surrounding waters like the back of his hand. When he was a guest on Burt's yacht, he would sometimes take Margot snorkeling along its coral reefs to some of the most isolated spots away from the mob of tourists. Jeffrey stood against the door wallowing over that last serendipitous day he had spent with her there...

He had rented a small boat and had taken her to an offshore island on Bermuda's south side. They went snorkeling through the beautiful coral reefs and had a picnic lunch on the secluded beach. Afterwards, they made love on the warm pink sand. He specifically remembered how the reflection from the sand in the midday sun radiated in her crystal-clear eyes, transforming her pupils into dancing flames, and how they burned through him like a torch. He couldn't stop staring at her.

"What's the matter?" she asked, while twisting the cap off a small bottle of sparkling Rosé and pouring it into a plastic cup.

He recalled looking up into the horizon and shaking his head back and forth, trying to suppress his feelings. "I'm falling for you, Mrs. Magnuson," he announced, dropping his gaze back upon her.

"Do you fall in love with all your students?" she responded sarcastically.

"No...I mean, I've had my fair share of flings with clients before,

but this is different. You're different."

"And how so?" she asked, knowing full well what his answer would be, but wanting to hear it anyway.

"You're beautiful, you're smart...you're everything a man could ever want."

She replied almost automatically. "You're only attracted to me because I'm unavailable."

He scooted closer and looked directly into her eyes. "That's not true. I want to share my life with you. I want you to have my baby."

Wine spewed out of Margot's mouth as she broke out into a gurgling laugh. "Your baby!" she cracked, wiping the splattered droplets from her bikini top. That's NEVER going to happen, so you'd better get over it."

CHAPTER 45

Maria allowed FBI Agent Heller entry into the Manhattan residence before excusing herself to notify her employer of his arrival. While waiting in the foyer for Mr. Magnuson, his eyes had a direct shot into the open living space. There, amidst all of the opulence, was something that stood out above all else. Taking up a large portion of the wall, it was a stunningly provocative picture of a nude woman lying atop a bed of shimmering satin sheets. The image was mostly black and white with shades of natural beige and appropriately laden rose petals in the deepest shade of crimson. Beyond beholden, Richard could not take his eyes off it.

In that moment, a distinguished-looking gentleman entered the room. He was wearing a pale yellow dress shirt and black pleated trousers, seemingly formal for a weekend afternoon.

Deliberately breaking the agent's gaze, he extended his arm out in a handshake. "I'm Burton Magnuson. Agent Heller, is it?"

"Actually, it's Special Agent."

"Why don't we go and have a seat, *Special* Agent Heller?" said Mr. Magnuson, leading him into the living room."

Heller found a spot on one of the white Italian leather sofas facing the conspicuous portrait. "Nice place you've got here."

"Thank you," said Burton, sitting on the duplicate couch to his left. "Would you like something to drink?"

"No thanks," said Heller.

"You don't mind if I have one, do you?"

"Of course not."

"Maria!" yelled Burt from his seat.

Promptly, the maid appeared. "Yes, Mr. Magnuson."

"Bring me a Scotch on the rocks, please."

"Yes, Sir," she replied subserviently, conferring a slight bow.

Magnuson turned his focus back on Heller to find him once again staring at the portrait on the wall. "Beautiful, isn't she?"

Heller dropped his eyes and cleared his throat. "Uh...yes," he said, shifting back over to Burton. "Is that Mrs. Magnuson?"

"Yes," he replied with a lingering sigh.

Just then, Maria walked into the room and set his drink on the glass table in front of him.

Burton waited for her to leave the room before speaking. "I understand you've been looking for me."

"You're a hard man to pin down, Mr. Magnuson."

"It's true, I am a very busy man, Mr. Heller. So, how can I be of help to you?"

"You know I'm investigating your wife's disappearance, and it's believed you may have been one of the last persons to have seen her."

"What would cause you to come to that conclusion?" asked Burt, leaning over to pick up his drink. In doing so, something caught the agent's eye.

"What happened to your ear?"

Burton lifted his hand and lightly brushed the side of his head. "Oh, that? It's nothing—just a small nick. I was shaving and became distracted."

Heller cocked an eyebrow, appearing unconvinced. "Records show that on the afternoon of August 28th, you boarded the *Dream Voyager* while it was docked in the port of Hamilton in Bermuda. Why would you get on a cruise ship just before it was scheduled to return to New York?"

Burton Magnuson stood up and began pacing behind the sofa as if he were formulating an explanation. "I work a lot of hours, Special Agent Heller. Sometimes I'm gone for days, even weeks at a time." He paused to examine the portrait on the wall. "My wife is a very needy woman and requires a lot of attention, as you can see by the portrait she had made for me." Magnuson returned his focus to the agent. "I knew she had planned this cruise with her friends. It so happened that I had a couple of free days at the end of her tour, so I decided to surprise her. I thought I could spend some 'quality' moments with her without taking too much time away from her and her friends."

As Burton Magnuson was considering the agent's next line of questioning, his concentration reverted back to the last time he saw his beloved Margarita...

On the evening of August 29th, Burt had been in his room patiently waiting for Margot, where she promised to meet him after her dinner with the girls. When nine o'clock rolled around, he tried calling her suite, but there was no answer. He tried again at ten and then again at eleven. Still, there was no answer. By the time it was well past midnight, he was so angry that he decided to go looking for her. After searching every possible venue that she could have gone to, he finally found her on the uppermost deck. Stupefied beyond shock, there she was, off in a corner, making out with one of the ship attendants. When just the night before, she had begged him for one more chance to prove that she could be faithful to him!

Burt snuck up behind them, and in a fit of rage, grabbed his wife's arm. A startled Margot wiped her lips with the back of her hand and pushed the young man in the white uniform off to the side. "Burt, what are you doing here?" she exclaimed in a ridiculously innocent voice. "I thought you were going to wait for me in your suite?"

"What am I doing here? The better question is what are YOU doing here!" he roared back.

"Really, Burt, it's not what you think," blubbered Margot, while

attempting to flatten her billowing skirt.

"Don't take me for a fool, Margot," said Burt, getting right up in her face. "Then again, I must be a fool for ever thinking you could be anything but the wretched immigrant whore that you are. I guess I wouldn't have been so surprised if I found you with Jeffrey Holt. But really, Margot, a boat hand? I had no idea how low you were willing to debase yourself in order to satisfy your salacity."

At that point, the attendant stepped in, extending his hands between them in an attempt to break them apart. "Look, sir, you do not wish to do something you will regret."

Fueled by adrenaline, the old man grabbed the much younger man tightly by the collar, pulling him up to his face. "What's your name, boy?"

"Um, Jorge, Sir."

"Do you value your job, Jorge? I'm sure you've got a family out there somewhere you're having to support — most of 'you' people do. Apparently, you don't know who you're dealing with. I can easily report you to your captain and make sure you never set foot on this or any other cruise ship again."

Jorge threw up his hands. "You will not see me near your wife again, Sir. You have my word."

Burt released his collar, and Jorge pulled away. As Jorge was leaving, Burt turned back to Margot. "Jacques was right from the very beginning when he said you were not to be trusted. He warned me that you weren't a typical gold digger like my former mistresses. He sensed something else lurking in those cold, crystal eyes of yours — something more conniving, more deviant. I should have listened to him, but I was bewitched by your feminine wiles. No more! As soon as I get back to New York, I'm going to file for divorce. And I'll see to it that you don't see a dime, not even the pittance allowed in the Prenup."

As Burt turned to leave, Margot grabbed him by the arm and tried to yank him back, crying for forgiveness. He pushed her away, causing her to fall against a small deck-side table, knocking it over along *with all the empty beer bottles that were sitting on top.*

Margot pulled herself up from the floor, her eyes widening to the point of a crazed lunatic. "What did you expect?" she screamed back at him. "Did you really think I would be turned on by a wrinkled old man like you? You're as guilty of your lust for me as I'm guilty of my lust for your money!" She bent over and picked up a broken bottle from the floor and flung it at his head, side-swiping him in the head. Burt lifted his hand to his ear and felt that it was wet with blood. From the expression on her face, it was clear that she could feel the rage racing through his veins. As Burt rushed toward her, she pulled herself up and tried to get away, but before she could, he grabbed her by the neck and began pushing her closer and closer toward the railing until she was pinned against it...

"Was she surprised to see you?" asked Heller.

"What?"

"When you showed up on the boat, was your wife surprised to see you?"

Burt attempted to gather his thoughts. "Oh, uh...yes. I told her I wanted to rekindle our romance."

"So, did you — rekindle your romance?"

"It didn't quite go as planned. I found her later that evening on the top deck of the ship, lip-locked in the arms of a ship hand." Burt stopped to force out a chuckle. "I guess I wasn't that shocked. I knew she had been cheating on me."

"How did you know she was cheating on you?"

"I hired a private eye to follow her."

Heller remembered his ex-wife, Meredith, mentioning that he had hired a private eye. "Who's the private eye?"

"It doesn't matter. His work is done."

"For the record," said Heller.

"James McAvee."

Heller took out a small notebook and wrote down the name before continuing with his questioning. "So what happened when you caught your wife with the ship attendant?"

"She insisted it wasn't what it looked like. I told her I knew she had been cheating on me and that I would be filing for divorce. She grabbed my arm, begging me for forgiveness, to give her one more chance. I pushed her away and went back to my room. And that's the last I saw of her."

"You know a passenger reported seeing a body go overboard that evening."

"Of course I know, it was in all the papers. What makes you think it was Margot? Her body was never found."

"There was a tipped-over table and a broken bottle found on the top deck where she was last seen, and her clothes were all still in her room. Are you sure your anger didn't get the best of you, Mr. Magnuson?"

"I did not kill my wife, Agent, if that's what you're insinuating."

"I just find it odd that you don't seem the least bit concerned."

"Look, Agent Heller, I told you I had planned on filing for divorce. Now, you can consider this conversation over, and if you have any further questions, you can contact my lawyer." Burt took a breath. "You know, she was on that cruise with her four so-called 'best' friends. Maybe you should pay them a visit."

"I plan on it," said Heller, getting up to leave.

On his way out, he noticed a small framed headshot of Margarita on a sideboard and picked it up to have a closer look. Those hypnotizing eyes and translucent smile made her look as though she were holding a secret. "Mind if I take this? The only picture I have of her is a group shot with her friends. It will help identify her — should we ever find her."

"Sure, take it," scoffed Burt.

"Thanks," said Heller, about to open the door. But then he

stopped and pivoted back around. "Oh, you might want to get that cut on your ear checked. It looks pretty deep."

CHAPTER 46

It was time to pay Magnuson's private eye a visit. James McAvee's office was sandwiched between a tobacco shop and a dry cleaner in East Harlem, with no official signage, except for an address number stenciled over the door. When the outer buzzer prompted no response, Heller discreetly unlocked the deadbolt with the use of a bump key he kept stashed in his pocket. Upon entering the pitch-black, windowless room, he was able to locate a wall switch with the help of the daylight shining through the open door. A quick flick of the switch, and two fluorescent tubes suspended from the ceiling were ignited, lighting up the whole space.

Heller took a quick look around. The place had been pretty much cleaned out, with the exception of a few large pieces of furniture. Commanding the center of the room was a particleboard desk and an office chair. Behind the desk was a wooden file cabinet butting up against the wall with a set of shelves hanging over it. The shelves were empty except for the dusty imprints of whatever had previously occupied them. A power cord lay strewn on the floor beneath the desk, but the computer, screen, and keyboard were all gone. All that was left on its surface was a permanently etched and soiled plastic mat and a Styrofoam cup in the corner, still harboring the pungent odor of cold coffee. As he lifted the half-drank cup of coffee to his nose, he noticed what appeared to be a smudge of red lipstick along the rim. He set it back down to walk around and survey the room further. There were two other doors in the roughly eleven-by-twelve-foot space. The nearest door opened up to a small lavatory with a toilet and a stand-alone sink with a small faded mirror hanging above it. He strode over to the back of the room, where the other door was situated, and opened it. While his eyes adjusted to the added darkness, he noticed a single bulb hanging from a wooden beam in the unfinished ceiling. As he pulled the dangling metal chain beside it, he discovered that it was merely a storage room. It contained nothing more than a fan, an electric space heater, a mop and bucket with a yellow rubber glove hanging over the edge, and a cardboard box filled with miscellaneous wires and small, outdated electronic equipment. In the far corner of the room, there was an additional open closet space camouflaged by a chintzy lace curtain whose border had turned black from dragging on the gritty cement floor. Pushing the curtain aside, there appeared to be nothing of major significance. Just a rusted-out, two-drawer, gray file cabinet with its noticeably empty top drawer hanging open. Sitting atop the cabinet was a small cardboard box with some nails, a pair of pliers, a hammer, and a single rubber glove matching the one on the bucket. The only other thing in there was a sooty black plunger fenced in between cobwebs.

Allowing the curtain to fall back into place, he headed back out toward the front desk. Heller sank into the ratty chair and pulled open each of the two desk drawers on the right side. They were both empty except for a couple of paperclips, a pencil with a broken tip, and a single plastic camera lens cap. He spun around to check the contents of the long wooden file cabinet behind him and found that it, too, had been cleaned out. He sat there for a moment, looking around the room to see if there was anything he might have missed. It struck him to go check out the storage area one more time. Walking back over to the closet, he shoved the curtain aside and yanked on the handle of the bottom drawer of the file cabinet. It wouldn't budge. It must have been locked. Maybe the key fell out. He combed the floor with his eyes. Nothing. He searched the surrounding walls to see if it was perhaps hanging somewhere. Still no luck. This wasn't the type of lock in which he could use his bump key, so he returned to the front desk. He opened the drawer and took out one of the paperclips. After reconfiguring it, he walked back to the metal cabinet. He stuck the clip through the corroded aluminum keyhole, and after a couple of twists and turns — *presto!* The drawer creaked open to reveal a dozen or so file folders. They were each labeled in black magic marker by what appeared to be a surname. *Either they were very old files and no longer important, or Mr. McAvee split in a really big hurry to have left them behind*, thought Heller.

The files didn't appear to be in any apparent order. Some were empty, and some had either notes or photographs in them, or both. One by one, Heller began filtering through them, hoping to find something: *Williams, Bergman, Federline, Arden*...and lo and behold: *Magnuson*.

When he lifted out the file, he uncovered a large assortment of black and white proofs of Margarita with a variety of male counterparts. Carrying the folder back to the front desk, he set it down to get a closer look at the contents beneath the fluorescent lights. Some of the initial pictures were taken at random restaurants and bars or other public places, and though there were hints of flirtation, such as Margarita whispering in a man's ear or some guy with his arm around her waist, they were fairly non-incriminating. But as Richard thumbed further, he came upon the mother lode. There were some very racy and compromising photos involving Mrs. Magnuson with two men in particular. One of the subjects was a clean-cut, dark-haired male. Some of the photos with him were taken via close range in a bedroom setting. A few others displayed what looked like the couple's silhouettes through the window of a brick Brownstone, most likely taken by a long-range lens from across the street.

The other subject was a younger-looking male with blond

hair. Most of the images were of the two of them lying naked on a beach. These photos were snapped from far away, so Heller could not get a good close-up view of the guy. In another photo, you could see Margarita with what might have been the same guy in the back seat of an automobile, but again, his face wasn't clear due to the fact that the windows were steamed up. The car was an older model, one that you normally didn't see on the road anymore. It was, however, one that Heller distinctly remembered seeing—quite recently. It was a baby-blue Volkswagen Beetle.

Agent Heller gathered up the file and was about to turn off the lights and leave when he spotted the Styrofoam cup on the top, right-hand corner of the desk. He walked back to the desk, set the file down, and carried the cup into the bathroom to dump out the remaining coffee into the sink. He shoved the cup into his jacket pocket, went back to grab the file, and left the building.

CHAPTER 47

When Heller returned to his office, he directed his assistant Barney to get the proofs blown up and send the Styrofoam cup over to the forensics lab. In the meantime, he had a few more interviews to conduct. With the information he had obtained from the cruise ship records, including passport information and a variety of other sources, he had compiled a fair amount of data on the backgrounds of the five women pictured in the photograph taken on that first day they boarded the *Dream Voyager*.

Heller thought he'd begin with Ms. Bethany Langford. She lived in Greenwich's South Village, which was less than a ten-minute drive from the Federal Plaza. He opted to take the subway because he knew parking would be nearly impossible to find. Plus, he had calculated that his destination was just a short walk from the subway exit.

The deteriorating brick structure fronted by a crisscrossing metal fire escape wasn't the type of place Heller had imagined a person with an architectural degree to be living. He located a rusty call plate held up by a single loose screw next to the street-level entrance and pored over the template until he came to #403. He pressed the button below the untagged number several times while he waited for a response. He had not called ahead, but because it was early in the morning on a Saturday, he figured there'd be a good chance she was home. Of course, there was the chance she could still be in bed, so he waited a while longer. Eventually, he pulled out his cell to retrieve her number when a remote-sounding voice siphoned through the intercom. "Who's there?"

Heller drew his mouth in closer to the transmitter. "I'm looking for Bethany Langford."

"And who are you?"

"Special Agent Richard Heller — FBI. If you don't mind, I'd like to ask you a few questions."

"If this is regarding my husband, I've already answered everything there is to answer."

"No, ma'am, this is concerning Margarita Magnuson."

A second later, a buzzer sounded, unlocking the paint-splintered door in front of him. When Heller walked in, there was no elevator, forcing him to hike up a narrow set of stairs to get to the fourth floor. Although FBI agents are required to take yearly fitness tests, he wasn't in as great a shape as when he first joined the bureau. He tried to eat right, but it's hard when you're on the road all the time, so he couldn't help but gain some weight. And the fact that he was in his fifties didn't help either. By the time he reached the fourth floor, he had to take a short breather before rapping on the entryway.

An attractive strawberry blond, wearing gold-emblemed designer eyeglasses, cracked the door open just enough to inspect the flash of his badge.

Upon entering the apartment, he was immediately enticed by a unique aroma of freshly-brewed coffee. He was struck by the interior of the apartment as well. It was quite a contrast from what you'd expect to find after seeing the outside of the building. This was where Mrs. Langford's inner architect and interior design background were allowed to shine through. The room looked like a picture taken right out of a *House Beautiful* magazine. The sofa and loveseat were covered in flowers and stripes with matching drapes sweeping the floor from tall, narrow window frames. Still-life prints of fruit and trellised outdoor scenes were hung along the wall in perfect symmetry, and everything was strategically placed — from the beveled glass coffee table that was centered in front of the couch to the pink throw folded into a perfect triangle and draped over the backside of an armchair.

Ms. Langford walked over to her laptop that was sitting on the coffee table and closed the lid, then she removed her eyeglasses and placed them on top.

With her glasses off, she looked a lot younger than her almost 40 years.

"Have a seat," she said, repositioning the row of decorative couch pillows so he'd have room to sit. "I was just about to have some coffee. Would you like some?"

"Sure," said Richard. "Black, please."

In her fuzzy sock slippers, Ms. Langford padded over to the counter separating the living area from the kitchen. "Have you ever had French Press before?"

"Uh, no, I haven't."

"It's an acquired taste. I hope you like it. It's stronger than regular coffee." The polite hostess filled two mugs with the mahogany-colored liquid and added a douse of almond milk into hers. She set them down on the glass table, then sank into the flowery cushions of the side armchair with the pink throw.

Heller took a large sip from his coffee mug and winced. "It's definitely different," he commented, trying his best not to be rude.

"You said you wanted to talk about Margot?"

"Uh...yes," said Heller, setting the cup back down. "How long have you known Marga...Margot?"

Bethany took an extended breath. "Geez, we met when she joined the firm at Dillon, McCain & Dermot. So, about eight years?"

"And you've remained friends all this time?"

Ms. Langford didn't answer, but took a sip from her mug.

"Do you still work at Dillon, McCain & Dermot?" asked Heller (fully knowing what the answer would be).

"No. I'm currently working for *The Architectural Investigator*."

"Why did you leave Dillon, McCain & Dermot?"

"It's a long story, which I don't care to go into. Besides, you said you were here to inquire about Margot."

"Then I'll cut right to the chase. I'm conducting a missing person investigation. A body was alleged to have gone overboard on the *Dream Voyager* in the early hours of August 30th."

"I know the media speculates that it was Margot, but it couldn't have been her, responded Bethany."

"What makes you think it couldn't have been her? Did you see her on the morning that you de-boarded the ship?"

"No, not when I was de-boarding."

"You and your friends didn't all leave at the same time?"

"Well, sort of. Me, Dana, Doris, and Rachel did, but Margot wasn't with us. None of us thought anything of it because it wasn't unlike her to be late."

"So when was the last time you saw her?"

"We all had dinner together the night before to celebrate the end of our trip."

"At dinner, did Margot appear to be acting any differently than normal? I mean, was she in good spirits?"

"No different than usual. Her husband surprised her by coming on board in Hamilton. She seemed happy about that."

"Did he join you ladies at dinner?"

"No. Margot said she was going to meet up with him later."

"What did you do after dinner? Did you each go back to your cabins?"

"No. We decided to extend the celebration and had drinks on the top deck."

"All of you?"

"Yeah. Me, Doris, Rachel, Dana, and Margot."

"Do you remember what time you returned to your rooms?"

"Gosh. I don't know for sure. We kind of left at different times. I know it was after midnight when I got back to my room."

"When did you find out someone had fallen off your cruise ship?"

"Probably the day after I got back home."

"When you heard the news, did you try to get in touch with Margot to make sure it wasn't her — since you didn't see her when you got off the ship?"

"No."

Heller lowered his gaze on his subject and wrinkled his brow. "It was my impression that the two of you were good friends."

Bethany took a breath. "We were good friends. But since she got married, we sort of grew apart. That's why we all went on that trip together. It was supposed to have been a sort of 'reunion' cruise.'" Then she lowered her head to study the design on her decorative rug before redirecting her pupils toward the agent. "To be honest with you, we had a bit of a 'falling out.'"

"What do you mean, 'falling out?'"

"Things were said...things we probably both regret."

"What 'things' exactly, Ms. Langford?"

Bethany lifted her cup toward her lips as though she were going to take another sip of her coffee, but then brought it back down to her lap. "I accused her of having an affair with my husband."

Richard tried to keep his expression detached. "Did she *admit* to having an affair with your husband?"

"No."

"Did your husband tell you he was having an affair with your friend?"

"...No."

As Heller asked that last question, he noticed a framed, black and white photograph on top of a small bookcase against the wall. It was a picture of Bethany, arm-in-arm, with an attractive dark-haired man. Even at that distance, the man looked very familiar. Heller got up from the couch to get a closer look. "Is this your husband?" he asked, holding the frame in his hands.

"Yes."

"How do you know he was cheating on you with your friend?"

Bethany stared at the photo in Heller's grasp for several seconds without batting an eye before answering, "Woman's intuition."

Heller set the picture back down and headed back over to the couch. As he was doing so, Bethany's mind trailed off to her last encounter with Margot...

The five friends were on the top deck of the Dream Voyager imbibing late into the night. Bethany and Margot had separated from the others and were off in a corner, immersed in deep conversation. As she leaned against the railing, gazing out into the deep, dark sea, the liquor began to take control, and Bethany started to cry. "I miss Charles. He doesn't deserve to be in jail. He's innocent, you know. He believes someone set him up, but he can't prove it."

It was apparent Bethany was seeking solace, but, instead, what she got was a remarkably cold and callous response from her friend. "Face it, Bethany, he got what was coming to him."

Upon hearing that, Bethany became inflamed and couldn't hold it in any longer. "The only thing he's paying for is having an affair with you!"

"What are you talking about?" said Margot, pretending to be stunned by the accusation.

"I knew Charles was having an affair. When I finally confronted him, he vehemently denied it. I so desperately wanted to believe him that I gave him the benefit of the doubt. I guess I wasn't ready to face the

truth, but deep down, I always suspected it was you, Margot. I refused to believe that you could be capable of such betrayal. That is, until I saw how you acted on the ship with Jorge. That's when I knew for sure. If you could act like that with a random waiter, even though you're a married woman... You're nothing more than a two-faced, lying cunt who doesn't care about anyone but herself." At this point, tears were streaming down Bethany's cheeks. "Why Margot? Why would you do that to me? I thought you were my friend!"

Margot lifted her glass containing the rest of her Dark 'N' Stormy antidote and chugged it. "Charles is the one who pursued me," she countered. "Like a dog in heat. Why on earth would you stay with a man who's not only a lying cheat, but worse than that, a convicted thief?"

"Because I love him!" screamed Bethany.

Margot looked Bethany straight in the eyes with no iota of remorse and flatly stated, "Let him go, Beth. He's not that good of a lay anyway." Then she turned to walk away.

Before she could go, Bethany, whose eyes had grown as big as saucers, pointedly placed her glass on the floor just before lunging herself at Margot and pushing her into the railing...

"So, why did you agree to go on a cruise with Margot if you suspected her of having an affair with your husband?" asked the agent.

Bethany drifted back from her subconscious rumination and tried to focus on the agent's questioning. "Because... (pausing)...I wanted the opportunity to confront her with it."

"Did you?"

Ms. Langford stared blankly across the room. "Did I what?"

"Did you confront her?"

Bethany reverted her focus back on Heller. "She denied it. I told her I wanted to believe her. She wrapped her arms around me and swore to me that she was telling the truth. Then we both started crying. I said I was sorry for accusing her, and we hugged and made up. At that point, we agreed we'd both had too much to drink, so we said goodnight and went back to our separate cabins."

"Was anyone else around who might have heard your conversation?"

"No."

Heller stood up from his seat. "Thank you, Ms. Langford, you've been very helpful. I'm sorry I couldn't finish my coffee."

CHAPTER 48

Heller pulled up to a contemporary concrete building that housed a number of different corporate offices and parked his unmarked vehicle in the designated visitors' area. There, he found an elevator that carried him to his intended destination on the 15th floor.

This company's doing pretty well, he thought, when he walked into the atrium of the architectural firm, taking in its modern facade with steel beams and shiny metal artwork hanging high above. In addition, there was an expansive curving staircase off to the right with a black metal railing that led up to an open hallway with what looked like three additional elevators at the top. The focal point, however, had to be the elevated reception area in the middle of the room, which stood before a backdrop of rich mahogany with the name Dillon, McCain & Dermot regaled in golden cursive.

Heller approached the desk where a very attractive receptionist, who identified herself as Dahlia, asked him to have a seat while she announced his arrival. Meandering over to the cowhide sofa, he sat down and picked up one of several architectural design magazines fanned out on the table in front of him, and began flipping through it. A short while later, one of the elevators opened up at the top of the stairway, and a sharp-looking, middle-aged man in a gray wool suit stepped out and descended the staircase. The gentleman walked up to him, shook his hand, and introduced himself as Alan Dermot. "Hold my calls," he voiced formally to Dahlia, while instructing the agent to follow him.

Heller followed him around the reception desk and down an endless hall of glass-partitioned offices until they came to a large conference room. When they entered the room, Mr. Dermot shut the door behind him. Although a stream of windows overlooking the main avenue lined the opposite wall, it was so quiet in there that you could hear a pin drop.

Dermot waved his hand over the first of a dozen or so leather chairs lining each side of the oblong table and asked the agent to have a seat. "So," began Mr. Dermot, as he positioned himself at the head of the table. "You've come to inquire about Margarita Magnuson?"

"On August 30th, a passenger aboard the cruise ship, *Dream Voyager*, was alleged to have fallen overboard, and we have every reason to believe it was Margarita Magnuson."

"Yes, yes, the company grieves for her loss. What a shame. Notwithstanding her beautiful facade, she was an extremely smart young woman. Do you have any clue as to how such a terrible accident could have happened?"

"We have not yet established that it was an accident. It could have been suicide or possibly, something else."

Mr. Dermot raised his eyebrows. "You mean, a homicide? What makes you think that?"

"I'm not here to speculate," said Heller. "I'm here to gather the facts."

"Well, I don't see how we can be of help to you. Margarita hasn't worked here since her marriage to Burton Magnuson. That was five years ago."

"He was one of your clients, is that correct?"

"He was more than one of our clients; he was one of our principal patrons. His business is what allowed this company to flourish."

Heller paused to take a look at his surroundings, paying particular attention to the signature artwork on the walls and the life-size marble statue in the corner of the room. "Flourish indeed," he commented, pointing to the statue. "That looks like it belongs in a museum."

Dermot's eyes lit up. "We're very proud of that piece. She's *Hestia*, the Greek Goddess of hearth, home, and architecture."

Heller returned to his previous line of thought. "So — Burton Magnuson — I take it Margot met him here?"

"That's correct," said Mr. Dermot. "We frown on our staff having anything other than a professional relationship with our clients, but Burt and Margot successfully kept it a secret for over a year, until they officially announced their wedding plans.

"Did anyone from your firm attend the wedding?"

"Bill McCain was there to represent the firm. Theodore Dillon was out of the country, and I was not able to go because it was on the same day as my daughter's graduation."

"Did anyone else from the company attend?"

"Yes, Bethany Langford. In fact, Bethany was Margot's maid of honor. They became quite close while working here."

"What about Mr. Langford? Was he there?"

"Oh, yes. Although, as I recall, he arrived late."

"Is there any way I can speak to Mr. Langford?"

"Unfortunately, he and his wife are no longer employed here."

"Why is that?"

Alan Dermot cleared his throat as if he really didn't want to answer that particular question, but proceeded nonetheless, paraphrasing carefully. "Charles Langford was our in-house counsel. He was the sole lawyer strictly assigned to handle all of Mr. Magnuson's affairs. We were completely stunned when we discovered that he was embezzling money from Mr. Magnuson's account."

"Was Mrs. Langford also involved?

"No, she was cleared of any involvement or wrongdoing.

She was one of our best architects and Mr. Magnuson's favorite. Sadly, we had no recourse but to let her go. As you can well appreciate, keeping her would have been bad 'PR' for the firm."

CHAPTER 49

Subsequent to his interview with Alan Dermot, Richard Heller returned to his office to do a little research on Mr. Charles Langford. What he found was that approximately two years after Margot's marriage to Burton Magnuson, Langford was accused of embezzling funds from his client's account. Langford was subsequently tried and, in addition to monetary restitution, was sentenced to five years in federal prison. His attorney has filed an appeal, which is still pending.

Before he was allowed entry into the New York Federal Correctional Institution, the special agent was forced to remove his Glock from its concealed holster, as well as his jacket, phone, watch, badge, wallet, belt, and keys, laying them all down on the conveyor belt before going through the scanner. After passing checkpoint security, he was led to a private room on the main floor where he was granted access to the witness.

When he walked in the door, Charles Langford was already seated at an empty table near the front of the room. An officer remained inside, standing guard by the door while Heller identified himself and flashed the inmate his badge. The inmate casually leaned back in his seat with his arms crossed behind his head when Heller pulled a chair out and sat down across the table from him.

"So why are you here?" Langford asked brusquely. "I've already been convicted."

The agent maintained a poker face. "How well did you know Margarita Magnuson?"

Charles looked surprised, as if that were the last question

he expected to hear. "You mean, Margot?" He vacillated. "...Uh, not very well... She used to be a receptionist at Dillon, McCain & Dermot. Why?"

Heller pulled out a Manila envelope from inside his coat pocket and slid it across the table toward him. "Open it," he said.

Charles dropped his arms to his sides and shot the agent a dubious glance. Hesitating, he opened it up and began sifting through the photos inside. His shoulders slumped forward, and his insolent demeanor suddenly turned sober. There were pictures of him and Margot holding hands in a dark restaurant, Margot smoking a cigarette on the front steps of his Brownstone townhome, zoomed-in photos of their naked silhouettes kissing through the sheer curtains of his upstairs window, and provocative photos of the two of them in bed inside the married Mrs. Magnuson's condominium.

"Where did you get these?"

"Mr. Magnuson hired a private investigator to follow his wife because he suspected her of having an affair."

A flushed Langford shoved the pictures back in the envelope and slid it back across the table. "Has my wife seen these?"

Heller gave Charles a hard stare. "I don't know."

Langford squirmed nervously in his seat. "I thought it would be a quick fling and then it'd be over. But you've *seen* the pictures. It's pretty hard to resist a woman like that."

"How long did the affair last?"

"Well-beyond her marriage to Burt. I kept telling myself it would fizzle out after she got married, but she still made time for me whenever he was out of town—which was a lot. She was insatiable. You see why it was so hard to let her go."

"Apparently, someone let her go," Heller commented sarcastically.

"What do you mean?"

"Margarita Magnuson went missing on August 30th off a cruise ship somewhere in the Atlantic while it was making a return trip from Bermuda. We suspect there could have been foul play."

Langford took on a defensive tone. "Well, there's no way you can implicate me; I was right here in my cell."

Heller stood up. "You'd be surprised," he said, picking up the envelope and pushing his chair in beneath the table.

Langford's voice grew louder. "Yeah, well, don't bother coming to see me again — unless my lawyer is right here next to me."

Heller was halfway to the door when Charles called back out to him, "You're not going to tell my wife, are you? It would ruin our marriage."

Slowly, the special agent turned back around and looked him square in the eye. "It might be a little late for that."

CHAPTER 50

Next on Heller's list was Doris Mulvaney. According to cruise ship records, she too resided in the New York area. Her current address led him to a hackneyed apartment building on Brooklyn's west side.

After announcing himself on the outside speaker, a 30-something, auburn-haired woman with a sturdy build was quick to come to the door. "I know why you're here," she said, eying him up and down. "I read about the incident on our cruise ship."

"Yes, about that. I'd like to ask you a few questions. Mind if I sit down?"

"Sure," she said, opening the door wide to let him in.

Ms. Mulvaney's eyes were permanently fixed on the agent while he walked over to the couch. "Mind if I sit down?" he asked.

"Sure. Make yourself comfortable." Before he could say another word, he was caught by surprise when she came right out and asked, "You really think it was Margot who fell off the ship?"

"We don't know that for sure. Right now, I'm conducting a missing person investigation."

"You can ask me anything you want," said Ms. Mulvaney, perched on the edge of the loveseat across from him. "I've got nothing to hide," she added, twisting a lock of hair between her fingers.

"Uh...thank you...Ms. Mulvaney," said the agent, clearing his throat.

"It's *Miss* Mulvaney. I'm not married. Oh—and you can

call me Doris."

Unlike the other witnesses Heller had interrogated thus far, Doris was more than amenable to answering his questions. Not so amenable, though, was the gray, short-haired feline that hovered around the room, hissing at him from the moment he walked in.

"So how long have you known Margarita Magnuson?" began the agent.

Doris took in a deep breath and exhaled. "I think it was about twelve years ago when she started working for the credit union where I worked. She needed an apartment, and I needed a roommate, so I let her move in."

"And how long did you two live together?"

"About four years — until her rich boyfriend set her up in her own apartment."

"You mean, Burton Magnuson?"

"Yeah. Although she kept it a secret because he was married at the time."

Doris was eyeing Richard's bare ring finger. "I would never *knowingly* date a married man."

Heller was rarely flustered, but this woman was succeeding in making him feel a little less than comfortable. "So, during the time you and Margarita...or um...Margot lived together, how would you say the two of you got along?"

"Alright at first, but then her true colors began to show. Let's just say, we were complete opposites."

"You must have remained friends because you went on a cruise together."

"Well, it *was* 'all expenses paid.'"

"Who paid for it?"

"Margot, of course. Or should I say, 'her rich husband, Burton.' She paid for all of us — me, Bethany, Rachel, and Dana."

"That was generous."

"I don't know about generous. She liked to flaunt her money."

It was becoming increasingly clear that Ms. Mulvaney harbored some resentment toward Margot. But how much? As he continued his questioning, he came to ask her about the last conversation she had with her friend on the evening of the 29th aboard the *Dream Voyager*.

"We were on the top deck drinking for quite a while. I'm not sure what time it was, but it was well after midnight. I had only had a few Rum Swizzles, but Margot was getting pretty hammered. She was pounding those Dark N' Stormies like there was no tomorrow. I don't know if you know what those are, but they're really strong. A waiter came up and asked if we wanted anything else to drink. Of course, she did. She never knew when to quit. Then she asked him where Jorge was, because she wanted to be served by him."

"Jorge?"

"Yeah. He was our usual waiter. Margot had made it pretty clear that she liked him. A little while later, he showed up and told her he'd been assigned to another section that evening. Margot grabbed him by the shirt collar and started flirting with him. He told her he had to get back to work and broke away. But before he left, I heard him say that he'd be getting off his shift soon and that he'd come back."

"Did he come back?"

"Yeah, he came back alright. That's when he and Margot started making out in the corner like a couple of high schoolers. It was disgusting. Especially for the fact that she was married. Though it wasn't that surprising, that's how she was."

"What happened after that?"

Before Doris was asked that question, her mind had already drifted back to that moment when Jorge told Margot he'd return when his shift was over.......

No sooner had he left than Doris remembered getting really angry at Margot and crying out, "Why can't I ever get the guy? I'm never going to get married! You — you're already married. Why couldn't you let me have him?" Having said that, Doris took her drink and splashed it in her friend's face, screaming, "You're nothing but a selfish whore!"

Margot's eyes burgeoned, and she began to lash back. "'LET you have him? Really? As if he'd ever want the likes of you. You're never going to get married because you can't see past your own morose, pathetic existence!"

Those words were all Doris needed to prompt her to become so furious that she charged at Margot, railroading her into the ship's metal rails, and wrapped her fists around her neck and began choking her. Gagging, Margot tried to release Doris's grip, but could barely combat her strength as her back bent farther and farther over the edge...

In that instant, Doris' cat jumped up on the couch behind Heller, growling and batting his neck with its paw.

Richard jumped to his feet, raising his voice toward Ms. Mulvaney. "Do you mind getting this cat away from me?"

Doris suddenly snapped out of her head zone and realized what was happening. Jumping up from her chair, she shooed the animal away into the bedroom and shut the door. "Sorry about that," she said, making her way back to the loveseat. "Shadow's just overly protective of me. She's not used to people, especially now that I have no more roommate."

Heller sat back down and continued where he left off. "So, what happened after that?"

"After what?"

"After you saw Margot making out with the waiter?"

Doris regrouped and resumed her narrative. "I got really angry. Margot knew I had my eyes on Jorge. It was like she was throwing it in my face."

"Did you tell her how you felt?"

"No...I just left."

Heller gave her a scrutinizing glare.

"I admit I would have liked to push Margot off that boat, if that's what you're thinking. But I didn't—even though she's a cheating, selfish whore. Jorge is the one you should really be investigating. It's probably a good thing I didn't hook up with him."

Heller stood up and thanked Ms. Mulvaney for her time.

"Wait," she said, jumping up from her seat. "Let me give you my phone number—in case you have any more questions. "You can call me anytime. I'm *always* available."

CHAPTER 51

The least favorite part of his job was flying. Richard hated navigating those ever-expanding international airports, waiting for his flight to arrive, and sitting in an airplane for hours. Luckily, it was a short jaunt from New York's LaGuardia Airport to Cleveland Hopkins International, and he was able to get an early flight.

The Cleveland field office was no more than 20 minutes from the airport, and when he arrived, his counterpart was already waiting for him. After dropping the agent back at his office, Heller proceeded to drive to the first of two interviews in the area where Margot grew up. Records showed that the two women pictured boarding the cruise ship with Margot attended the same middle and high school as her. Preferring to catch his interrogees off guard, he hadn't let them know he was coming.

Three weeks after returning from the reunion cruise, Dana had settled back into her stationary routine. She was caught off guard when she heard the doorbell ring. She rarely had visitors and wasn't expecting anyone, especially this early in the morning. Tiptoeing to the front window, she pushed back the curtain just enough to catch a peek of who it could be. From her upper-level duplex, she looked down to see a dark sedan parked against the curb, and standing on the porch landing was a tall man with a brush cut, in a brown suit coat. She waited until the third ring to slowly pad lightly down the stairs, hoping for a chance that he might leave. With the chain lock still in place, she cracked the door open just enough to hear what he had to say.

"Are you Dana Sherer?" he asked

"Maybe. Who's asking?"

"I'm FBI Special Agent Richard Heller," he said, removing his badge from inside his suit pocket and flashing it in her face through the break in the door.

"What makes you so 'special,' Agent Heller?" she responded in a denigrating tone.

Richard remained staunch-faced. "I'm conducting a missing person investigation."

"What's that got to do with me?"

"It's regarding Margarita Magnuson."

Quietly, Ms. Sherer unlatched the chain from the door. "Come on up."

Agent Heller followed the stringy-haired, undernourished-looking female up the steps to her tiny apartment and took a quick glance at the surroundings. The dimly lit, no-frills studio appeared to fit her personality to a tee. A gray loveseat sat near the middle of the room, and across from that, pushed up against the wall, was a rectangular folding table with a chair at each end. On one side sat an open box of cereal, an empty bowl with a spoon in it, and what looked like half a glass of orange juice. The opposite end of the table was apparently being used as a desk because a hard drive sat beneath it, and a computer screen, keyboard, and small desk lamp sat on top.

"Have a seat," said Dana, positioning herself on the folding chair next to the bowl.

Heller sat down on the worn sofa. "As you no doubt have heard by now, Margarita Magnuson went missing on the *Dream Voyager* cruise ship on August 30, 2015, during a return trip from Bermuda."

Dana stared rigidly at the agent.

"She was never seen nor accounted for at disembarkment, and a follow-up inspection of her suite revealed that her clothing and luggage were all still in the room."

Dana continued to display no emotion and took a sip from her juice glass.

Heller pulled out a photo of the five friends posing together when they initially boarded the ship and walked over to Ms. Sherer. "That's you, isn't it?" he said, pointing to the petite girl on the far left, with the same dirty ash-blond hair and straight pixie cut that she currently sported.

"Yeah, so? We were on a 'reunion' cruise."

Heller walked back to the couch and sat down. "You ladies apparently boarded together. Was there a plan to leave together, as well?"

"Sort of...but Margot never showed."

"Didn't you find it odd that you all left at the same time except for Margot?"

"No. We just figured she left with her husband. He came on board when we were docked in Hamilton."

"Did she have any idea that he might show up?"

"I don't think so. She said he told her he wanted to 'surprise' her."

"So, when was the last time you saw her?"

"The night before we docked in New York."

"Where exactly were you when you last saw her?"

"On the top deck."

"What were you doing up there?"

"Drinking."

"Did Margarita appear to be in good spirits at the time?"

"I don't know. Sure."

Dana was a tough nut to crack. She didn't appear to want to give away any more information than she had to. "Did you try getting in touch with her when you got back from your trip?"

"No, why?"

"It seems that if she were your friend, you would have tried calling her to see if she had made it home all right since you didn't see her when you disembarked."

"I told you, I just assumed she left with her husband." Dana paused to finish off the rest of her juice. "...Besides, we didn't exactly part on the best of terms."

Heller creased his forehead. He was beginning to see a pattern among Margot's 'so-called' friends.

"Would you like to tell me what happened between you and Margot that might have caused a rift between the two of you?"

"Once again, Dana wasn't quick to respond, but complied with the request nonetheless. "Like I said, we were all on the upper deck drinking late into the night."

"Who's 'we?'"

"Me, Bethany, Rachel, Doris, and Margot."

"Go on."

"Margot and I were off in one corner, leaning against the railing, looking out at the ocean."

"Where were the other girls?"

"I don't know. Somewhere on the other end, I think."

Heller waited for her to expand on that.

"Anyway, we were standing there, talking."

"What were you talking about?"

"Nothing important, at first. But, I guess I'd had one too many beers, because the alcohol made me say things I would never have had the nerve to say before. I couldn't help it. I just started spilling my guts out."

Unable to hide her anguish, Dana lifted her eyes to the ceiling, tears welling up in them, as her mind took her back to that last night on the ship...

During dinner, the captain of the ship had announced that there was a full sturgeon moon out that night, which would favor everyone with a brightly lit skyline. Not ready to end the evening and eager to experience a commanding view of the majestic ocean in full rage, after their meal, the five friends decided to climb to the uppermost deck and continue their celebration.

While Bethany, Rachel, and Doris were somewhere on the other side of the ship, she and Margot were huddled in a corner trying to shield themselves from the harshness of the ripping wind. Dana had already polished off several beers, but at Margot's insistence, she decided to try a Dark 'N' Stormy – which ultimately put her over the edge. By the time she had swallowed the last drop, her liquid courage came bubbling to the surface. She was ready. There would never be a more perfect time than this to divulge her long-buried secret to her very best friend.

Dana remembered looking straight into Margot's eyes and confessing, "It's time you know, Margot. I'm a closet lesbian, and I've been in love with you ever since the 7th grade when you first walked into the gym at Ellison Junior High and sat down next to me."

Initially, Margot said nothing, casting a thoughtful, seemingly tender gaze upon her friend that appeared to invoke compassion and love, thus prompting Dana to move in closer and spontaneously bury her lips into Margot's for a long, drawn-out, passionate kiss. For a moment, it seemed as though Margot were enjoying it. Until suddenly, she broke out into a guttural laugh, spewing out remnants of saliva before the kiss was even over. Immediately, Dana backed away in mortification, wiping her wet mouth with the top of her hand.

"Should I be surprised?" Margot blurted out. "Of course, I've known all along that you were in love with me. The way you defended me in front of anyone who maligned me, the way you kept tabs on everything I did, the way you blushed whenever I complimented you, the way you watched me with those repressed, puppy dog eyes..."

"Then why did you lead me on?" Dana interrupted, tears now streaming down her cheeks. "Flaunting your naked body in front of me, the flirtatious kisses, the locked embraces!"

"Sorry if you took it the wrong way, but that's how I am with everybody. You, of all people, should know that by now."

Dana tried to justify her reaction. "I just thought..."

"'You just thought what?'" said Margot. "Did you really think I would ever reciprocate your feelings? I'll admit, I thought about it once or twice, maybe try it just for fun. But I love men, remember? And what they have to offer. Unfortunately, I wouldn't be able to get that kind of satisfaction from you. You should try having sex with a man sometime – see how it feels. Maybe then you'd understand. Hell, you might even like it."

Angry and humiliated, Dana smoothed away her tears. "It's not all about sex, Margot. It's about **love**. Something you know nothing about!"

Margot burst out laughing again. "Love!" she shouted. "Is that what you want?" She moved in closer and started kissing Dana again. This time with more fervor. First on the lips, moving down to her neck, and cupping her hand over Dana's tiny breast. That's when Dana exploded. With both fists, she began punching Margot as hard as she could, pushing her into the rail, screaming, "You're nothing but a tease!" All the while, Margot kept on laughing, so hard, she had to hold her stomach to keep from doubling over, not realizing the power of a small girl's adrenaline..."

"What exactly did you say to her?" asked Heller.

Dana looked down from the ceiling, shaking her head back and forth. "Excuse me?"

"When you were 'spilling your guts out.' What exactly did you tell Margot?"

Dana swept her hair behind her ears, looking a little embarrassed. "I told her I was in love with her."

Heller's mouth squeezed shut, but he didn't appear to be overly surprised. "And what was her reaction?"

Dana smudged away a renegade tear. "She told me she didn't reciprocate my feelings. I mean, what did I expect? As if a woman like that could ever fall for someone like me."

Heller lowered his eyes in a sympathetic manner. "Was that the end of the conversation?"

"Yeah, that was it. Then, I told her I was going back to my cabin."

"Did Margot leave at the same time?"

"No. She just turned back around and stared out into the ocean."

"Do you have any idea what happened to Margot after that, Ms. Sherer?"

Dana drove a dagger into the agent's eyes. "Do you think I killed her?"

"Did you?"

Dana lowered her eyes to her feet.

A minute of silence went by, and Heller got up from his seat. "Thank you for your time, Ms. Sherer," then added, "I'll be in touch."

As he was walking out the door, Dana yelled out. "Hey, Dick! I was in *love* with Margot. I would never have killed her."

Heller pulled away from the curb and headed off to his next interview. As he drove, he did his best to concentrate on the road, but his mind was consumed with this woman. Margot. What was it about her that provoked such an intense range of emotion from everyone in her circle? As cool as he was on the outside, he was burning on the inside. Maybe he'd been without a woman for too long, but he felt his own self falling in love with her — or rather, the illusion of her. As his list of suspects grew, he told himself he had to keep a cool head. He could not allow his own growing obsession to cloud his reasoning.

CHAPTER 52

Less than ten miles away on a quiet suburban street lived Margot's other childhood friend, Rachel Knowles. Heller had checked Ms. Knowles' hospital schedule before flying out. She was on the early-morning shift and clocked out about 2:00 in the afternoon. This gave him enough time to stop and grab lunch, which was a good thing because all he'd had for breakfast was a cup of coffee on the plane. He stopped at a McDonald's drive-through and ate in his car in the parking lot. By the time he was done, it was 2:30 p.m. The hospital wasn't far away, so she had to be home by now. After driving along endless rows of identical, single-story bungalows, he found the address he was looking for. It had no driveway, but he noticed an old Ford Focus parked in front of the house, so he assumed she was home. Parking his vehicle a few doors down, he sucked down the last of his Diet Coke and made his way to the front door.

Rachel had just ignited the top burner of the gas stove to heat a small aluminum tea kettle when she heard a knock at her front entrance. Thinking it was her neighbor, Lillian, having come to borrow eggs or butter or milk, as she often did, she hurried to answer the door. Rachel was taken aback to find that it was not Lillian at all, but an intimidating-looking stranger instead. Once the agent identified himself and told her why he was there, she reluctantly let him in.

Richard's first impression of Ms. Knowles was that she was very different from Margot's other friends, who he had interrogated thus far. Wearing a thick blue knitted sweater over her white uniform and a red headband holding her shoulder-length brown hair in place, she could have been the poster girl for wholesomeness. Unlike the other women, she also appeared to be inherently nervous.

"Um...would you like some tea?" she asked, her voice cracking. "I just put a pot on."

"Thank you," said the agent, seating himself against a colorful crocheted afghan on the colonial-style sofa. Ms. Knowles' small, but comfy home, fit her motherly demeanor to a tee. The space was overflowing with country flair, from the kitchen chairs padded with frilly cushions to the human-like rabbits in farm-style attire carefully positioned on the shelves.

Almost every cabinet and accent table had a picture of her and a gaunt-looking, fair-skinned male. Heller scooted across the couch to pick up one of the photographs on the side table. "Is this your husband?" he asked.

"Yes," Rachel replied with downcast eyes. "He died in 2008 of pancreatic cancer."

"I'm sorry," said Richard, setting the photo back down.

Rachel sniffled. "How can I help you, Mr. Heller?"

As he began his series of questions, Ms. Knowles relayed that the last time she saw Margot was on the evening of August 29th. She explained that they had had a pleasant farewell dinner, and being that it was the last day of their cruise, afterwards she and her friends went up to the top deck for a nightcap.

"It was such a fun trip. Me and the girls had gotten to know one another really well, and none of us wanted it to end. We chatted and drank, and chatted and drank some more, sometimes splitting up in groups of two or three, making plans to keep in touch after the trip. By the time Margot and I met up, we had had quite a lot to drink. We were both hunched over the railing and staring down into the water. There was a full moon shining down on the waves, which magnified them all the more." Rachel stopped for a moment of contemplation. "I have to admit, I never could handle my liquor very well. Taking in the sheer strength of the ocean, I felt so...so insignificant. Like my life didn't matter. I know I had gone over the limit because I broke out into a pity party. I couldn't help it. I told Margot I felt like I'd been cheated out of life—with my husband dying and being left childless. I told her I had nothing left to live for. I wanted to commit suicide."

Heller continued to listen, curious as to how this would play out, when the tea kettle began to whistle.

Distracted from her narrative, Rachel jumped up from her seat. "I'll be right back," she said, running into the kitchen. "Sugar or cream?"

"Plain," said Heller.

Ms. Knowles hurried back into the front room, balancing two mugs filled with hot water and tea bag strings hanging over the side. Richard couldn't help but notice that her hands were shaking when she placed them on the coffee table.

"Thank you," said Richard, waiting for the tea to cool before attempting to drink it. "But you didn't..."

"Didn't what?"

"Try to commit suicide."

With her hands still trembling, Rachel lifted her cup to her lips before answering. "It still upsets me to think about it...and I'm very embarrassed to admit it, but I actually did. I tried to jump over the railing."

As Rachel uttered those words, her mind drew her back to that moment...

She had broken down crying, "I've got nothing left to live for but a lifetime of medical bills," she bellowed into the wind, while proceeding to mount the railing. "I'm coming Lou — we'll be together soon!"

"No!" yelled Margot, climbing up the metal rungs after her and grabbing her by the shoulder. "You think my life is perfect? I've never told this to anyone — not my parents, not even Remy. But before I moved to New York, I got an abortion."

Rachel halted her climb midway and turned to look at Margot, as her friend went on.

"I can't expect to have kids with Burt because after his two were born, he didn't want any more, so he got a vasectomy. Not that that matters anyway, because the abortion left me pretty scarred up. Years later, a gynecologist told me that because of the tissue damage, I'd probably never be able to bear children again. So, where does that leave me? In the same predicament as you, Rachel."

Rachel's sorrow shifted toward her friend and started to calm down. With Margot balancing on the metal rail beside her, Rachel began descending the railing until the heel of her sandal caught on a bolt and she lost her footing. Margot climbed to the same rung and leaned forward with her arms out to keep Rachel from falling, when all of a sudden, she lost her balance...

Heller was thrown off guard by Rachel's response. "You tried to jump from the railing?"

"Yes, but Margot stopped me. She pulled me back down. She told me she had had an abortion and probably would never be able to have children either. I settled down, and we stood there and hugged for several minutes. We were both crying, and I thanked her for stopping me from jumping. I wiped the tears from my face and told her I was going back to my room. I needed to sleep off the booze. By that time, the other girls had left, and I told Margot she should call it a night, too, but she said she wanted to hang out alone a while longer — to think. So I hugged her one more time and said 'goodnight.' I was a little hesitant about leaving her alone because she still looked distraught over the whole situation, but Margot's always been strong. I figured she would be okay. And that's the last time I saw her."

Tears began to saturate Rachel's cheeks. "I tried calling her after I got home to see if she made it back alright. I even left several messages. But I never heard back. I thought maybe she was busy or just didn't want to talk about it. Then, when

I heard that someone had fallen off the ship that same night, I feared the worst. What if it really was Margot? What if, after I left her all alone, she decided to commit suicide — because of me? I've anguished over the possibility ever since, but I couldn't tell anyone."

"Why not? Don't you think you should have come forward with this information?"

"I didn't want to know. Because I'd never forgive myself."

****

Richard had some time to kill before heading to the airport, so he parked at a rest area alongside a riverbank and sat down on a bench to think. He observed a group of ducks huddled together along the water's edge. They appeared to get along fine until one began to ruffle its feathers, forcing the rest to drift off one by one.

He compared Margot and her friends to the ducks in the water, their feathers ruffling until all that jealousy and resentment floated to the surface. He wondered what brought these women together in the first place They seemed to have so little in common.

Other than work acquaintances, Richard didn't really have any close friends. But then, what did he need friends for anyway? He used to have a best friend once — his Navy buddy, Chuck. They had plenty in common — especially his wife.

CHAPTER 53

Heller was back in his office again when his phone lit up. It was the forensics unit. The results were back from the lipstick marks on the Styrofoam cup found in James McAvee's office. It was a long shot, but there was a chance it could be linked to someone in the system, hopefully, some girlfriend who might know of the private eye's whereabouts.

Much to Heller's amazement, the DNA extracted from the cup did link to someone in the system. Except it was someone that he never would have suspected: *Margarita Magnuson*. It was a perfect match to the DNA samples taken from the lip balm and mascara found in her cosmetic bag that was left in her suite on the *Dream Voyager*. Now, why would Mrs. Magnuson be in the office of the private investigator that her husband had hired to follow her? Richard was mad at himself for not having dusted for fingerprints while he was in McAvee's office. So the first thing he did was to employ one of the rookie agents from the bureau to go back there and do it. Hopefully, the office hadn't been rented out to a new tenant yet.

In the meantime, he had his assistant, Barney, conduct a thorough online search of nationwide directories to try to come up with a current address for McAvee. No luck there. However, with the help of McAvee's landlord, Barney was able to obtain the address that was provided in the lease agreement for the rental of the office space.

The address listed on the agreement led Heller to a modest rowhouse in Queens with a six-cement-step climb to the entrance. Not surprisingly, the doorbell had been replaced with an intercom button. Richard pressed it and waited a few minutes before a female voice answered. After he identified himself as FBI, a slender young woman with wire-rimmed glasses and straight brown hair parted in the middle, partially opened the door.

"Special Agent Richard Heller," he announced more specifically, flashing his badge. "I'm looking for a Mr. James McAvee."

"He's not here," she replied.

"May I have your name, Ma'am?"

"Trish."

"Your full name."

"Dearden—Trish Dearden."

"Do you know where I can find him, Ms. Dearden?"

"No idea," she said flatly. "Is he in trouble?"

"No. He might have some information relevant to a case we're working on. If you don't mind, I'd like to ask you a few questions. May I come in?"

Wavering a little, she agreed. "Sure..."

As soon as Heller stepped into the house, he felt as though he had been transported back to the 60s. The walls were covered with Beatles posters, from *A Hard Day's Night* to *Sgt. Pepper's Lonely Hearts Club Band*, including their famous *Abby Road* album cover and a reproduction of *The Fab Four* by Andy Warhol.

The blinds were partially drawn, so there was little illumination in the room except for the two large, side-by-side computer screens that were perched atop a modular desk in one corner. The liquefying shapes on the screen savers bounced along the walls, morphing from black and white to yellow and purple and green and red, bringing the posters to life in a way that made them appear as though they were trying to reveal a secret.

"Let me open the blinds and get some light in here," said Ms. Dearden, stumbling over a trail of newspapers and magazines stacked along the floor. "Sorry about the mess," she said. "I've been in a bit of a funk lately."

"That's quite alright," said the agent, noticing the mound of unwashed dishes on the counter as well as empty beer bottles and carry-out containers through the open kitchen door.

"Have a seat," said Ms. Dearden, rushing to gather up a pile of clothes lying on the futon and tossing them onto the floor, before plopping herself down on a side recliner with her legs crisscrossed in front of her.

As Heller made his way to the center of the room, his attention was drawn to the outdated television set and Marantz turntable on the fiberboard stand against the wall. Leaning against it on one side was an old, wooden Fender guitar, and on the other side was a row of plywood crates filled with vinyl records.

Richard strode over to the crates. "May I?" he asked, pointing to the albums.

Ms. Dearden nodded, watching him while he kneeled over and started sifting through the lot.

Though not a collector himself, he appreciated the smell and feel of vintage vinyl in his hands. Judging from the wall art, he was not surprised that most of the albums were by The Beatles. "Someone likes the Beatles," he said, glancing up at Ms. Dearden and grinning. "I'm a big Beatles fan myself."

"Yeah," she replied, a wistful smile breaking through.

Heller stood back up and walked over to the futon.

"Does Mr. McAvee live here?" he asked, as he sat down.

"Some of the time."

"Are the two of you married?"

"No."

"Are you boyfriend and girlfriend?"

The young woman belted out a sarcastic laugh. "Some of the time."

Though outwardly amenable, Ms. Dearden did not appear

overly eager to give out any more information than she had to.

"How long have you known each other?"

"We met in college—music appreciation class. You know, one of those classes you take when you need extra credit. As you can see," she said glancing up at the walls, "we bonded over our mutual love for the Beatles. Jim especially liked John Lennon for his simple, abstract lyrics. His favorite song was *"Everybody's Got Something to Hide Except Me and My Monkey,"* she chuckled.

"I don't think I know that one."

"It's from their White Album. Actually, John and Paul both wrote the lyrics."

"Heller cracked an unlikely smile and nodded.

"After he dropped out, I didn't hear from him for a long time. Then years later, out of the blue, he calls me—said he needed a place to stay. So I let him move in."

"When was the last time you saw him?"

"A couple of weeks ago."

"Has he been in contact with you via telephone?"

"Nope."

"When you last saw him, did he tell you he was planning on moving out?"

"No. One day, I was running errands, and when I came home, his backpack and all of his clothes were gone. He kept most everything else, like camera equipment and stuff like that, in his office in Harlem. You might want to check there."

"I did," said the agent. "His office was empty."

"I figured. Right after he left, I tried calling his work phone, but it was disconnected."

"Have you ever been in his office, Ms. Dearden?"

"No. He didn't want me going there. He said he liked to keep his work private."

"Did he ever talk about work? You know, like the cases he was working on?"

"Not really."

"Did he ever mention a *Margarita or Margot Magnuson*?"

That name must have triggered something because the minute he said it, Ms. Dearden's expression and tone turned chafed. "He mentioned her name once and the fact that he was tailing her because her husband suspected her of cheating. That's all I know."

Agent Heller stood up. "Well, thank you for your help, Ms. Dearden," he said, handing her his card. If you do hear from Mr. McAvee, I'd appreciate you letting me know right away."

Trish's voice began to crack. "Most of those albums and posters are his. He wouldn't just leave them unless he was planning on coming back. He's got a habit of strolling in and out of my life whenever it's convenient for him." She lowered her gaze to the floor. "I guess I've got no one to blame for that but myself."

Ms. Dearden followed the agent to the door to let him out. As she was about to shut the door behind him, he said, "I'm glad I caught you. I was afraid you might be working."

"I was. I work from home — for an online auction company. That's where most of the posters came from." Ms. Dearden shut the door behind him, walked over to her desk, and sat down in front of her keyboard. Punching down a key, she pulled up one of the screens, which opened up to *The New York Times* front page headline: **"Margarita Magnuson, Wife of Multi-Millionaire Land Developer, Burton Magnuson, Goes Missing From Cruise Ship."**

Trish glared at it with vengeance in her eyes. *'Everybody's got something to hide,' don't they, Mrs. Magnuson? Who's the monkey now?*

CHAPTER 54

Richard Heller stared out of his 24th-floor window in frustration. The overcast sky made everything look bleak. Two months had passed since the alleged incident, with no body having been recovered and no explanation as to how Margarita Magnuson went overboard. He returned to his desk, sat down in his chair, and began tapping the end of his pencil against his temple. Bending over, he slid the Magnuson evidence box, which he kept on the floor near his desk, closer. He took out the picture that Burton had given him and held it up to his eyes. God, she was beautiful! A woman like that — what a waste.

He had to assume that it was Margarita Magnuson who had gone overboard, given the fact that she was never accounted for at the time of disembarkment and that her clothes were found to still be in her suite. In addition, her key card was found floating in an area not too far from where the body had purportedly fallen. The problem was that the only "eyewitness" was an elderly woman who wasn't wearing her glasses at the time.

There was the remote possibility that she could have survived the fall, although it was highly unlikely. Mainly because her body was never found.

The big question was: if it was indeed Margot who fell into the water, why?

Was it an accident? By all accounts, she was definitely over the limit in her consumption of alcohol. She may have climbed up the railing for whatever reason and just slipped. But if that was the case, why didn't any of her friends report it? Unless it happened after they had all gone back to their cabins.

Could it have been suicide? According to Rachel, Margot appeared to be distraught after their conversation. Maybe she did, in fact, decide to end it all. With everything Heller had learned thus far, it was hard for him to conceive that this type of woman would purposely kill herself. This woman who had it all—beauty and money. Although one never knows, vanity can be a fickle foe. Burt had allegedly told Margot he would be filing for divorce, thus leaving her penniless. Having grown accustomed to a life of luxury, perhaps she couldn't deal with the prospect of having to lower her standards.

Or was it something more sinister? Like murder. In Heller's mind, this was the most likely scenario. It had become more than just a missing person's investigation; it had turned into a criminal investigation. From the interviews conducted, there were plenty of suspects, but no concrete evidence. At least, not yet.

Because Margot was one of those "women you love to hate," as portrayed so many times in the movies, it was hard to tell who her friends were and who her enemies were.

First, there was Bethany. She believed Margot was having an affair with her husband.

Then there was Doris, who was insanely jealous of her more attractive friend.

Finally, there was Dana, who was in love with Margot but was ultimately spurned by her.

Any one of them could have had the incentive to push her off the boat.

Rachel seemed to be the only one of Margot's friends with no axe to grind—at least, not so far as Heller knew.

The other persons of interest on his list were, of course, Jorge Albuoy and Burton Magnuson. Richard lifted the plastic zip-lock bags of evidence from the box and laid them across his desk. One bag contained Jorge Albuoy's magnetic name badge. That, in itself, didn't prove anything except to place him at the alleged scene of the crime. Another bag contained Margot's black thong. Fingerprints lifted from the front satin portion confirmed that Albuoy had indeed placed his hands on them. But that didn't necessarily mean he killed her. Everyone attested to Margot's promiscuity. All it really proved was that she had had an inappropriate relationship with him. Could it have escalated to murder? Perhaps.

Then there was her husband, Burton Magnuson. He was at the top of Heller's radar. He had every reason to want to kill his wife. The photos found in McAvee's office confirmed that she had cheated on him more than once, and when he caught her "red-handed" on the ship with Mr. Albuoy, that could have been the last straw. Whether it was accidental or intentional remained to be determined. A crucial piece of evidence was Mr. Magnuson's drink card, also found where the alleged incident took place. That alone was insufficient evidence to make an arrest, but it was that cut on Burton's ear that lingered at the forefront of Heller's mind.

It was hard to believe that a man of Burton Magnuson's caliber would risk being caught in the act of killing his wife. Unless he hired someone else to kill her. And if he did, could it have been James McAvee?

After Heller's team went to his office and dusted for fingerprints, it was revealed that the private investigator had a past criminal record for cybercrime and had served time in jail. Margot's husband had hired him to trail his wife. When Burton Magnuson boarded the ship while it was docked in Hamilton, McAvee could have boarded as well — perhaps under an assumed name. Heller made a mental note. *I'd better have Barney get me a list of anyone else who might have boarded the Dream Voyage that same day.*

But what about the Styrofoam cup he found in McAvee's office that had Margot's DNA on it? Why would she be drinking coffee in his office? Heller had more than a gut feeling that the private investigator was involved in her disappearance. The only problem was that McAvee had also disappeared without a trace. When he got the results of the fingerprints, Heller immediately put him into the FBI's National Data Exchange to try to locate him. Unfortunately, nothing had yet transpired from that.

In the meantime, he was going to concentrate his efforts on Burton Magnuson. The last time he spoke to Mr. Gagnon, the butler stated that "Mr. Magnuson was out of the country." Heller thought he'd call him back to see if he had returned. When he picked up his phone and dialed the number, Mr. Gagnon answered, stating that his employer, Mr. Magnuson, was currently on his way back to his New York office.

Heller hung up and was just about to call Burt's office when his assistant, Barney, barged into the room. "Sorry to bother you, Boss, but I thought you'd want to know right away... "

Heller set down the receiver.

"Burton Magnuson was just involved in a really bad automobile accident..."

Not wasting a minute, Heller grabbed his jacket hanging on the back of his chair and sped off to the hospital. When he got there, the waiting room was full of reporters and photographers biding their time until they could get more information. The wealthy patient had already been admitted and was being prepped for emergency surgery, with no one allowed to see him except for his immediate family. The special agent did manage to get a partial eye-witness account from the police officers who had arrived at the scene and were still there completing their report.

Apparently, Mr. Magnuson was on his way from JFK International Airport to his Manhattan office when the limo he was a passenger in was sideswiped by a garbage collection truck, causing his vehicle to hit the freeway embankment and roll over. The limo driver was pronounced dead at the scene, and Mr. Magnuson was immediately transported to Mount Sinai

Hospital in critical condition.

A few days later, Agent Heller returned to the hospital for an update on the mega millionaire's health, but when he got there, he received word that Burton Magnuson had just expired "from complications due to internal injuries."

So what did this mean? To Heller's knowledge and according to public records, Margarita Magnuson had not yet been legally served with divorce papers; so, if Margarita Magnuson were still alive, she would stand to inherit whatever Burton provided for her in their prenuptial agreement.

Now that Burton was deceased, if he was responsible for her death, the case might never be solved. All Heller could do now was to keep searching for McAvee for answers.

At the end of the week, Barney walked into Richard's office with a newspaper obituary detailing arrangements for an upcoming Memorial Service where Burton Magnuson's ashes would be entombed.

"Thanks, Barney," said Heller. "I think I'll go and pay my respects. You'd be surprised what you can uncover at a funeral."

The largely attended service was held in one of New York's most prominent cemeteries. Leading the procession was Burton's ex-wife, Meredith, accompanied by Burt's head butler, Jacques Gagnon, and her two grown children, Robert and Kathryn. Also in attendance were Messrs. Theodore Dillon, William McCain, and Alan Dermot, as well as Bethany Langford.

When Agent Heller got a chance to offer his private condolences to the ex-Mrs. Magnuson, her somber comportment imploded, and all shrapnel broke loose. "It's *her* fault, you know! I don't know how, but she *definitely* had something to do with it!"

CHAPTER 55

It was another cloud-covered September morning when Richard Heller made his way through the parking lot to the Jacob K. Javits Center. The trees planted in and around Foley Square were already beginning to change their leaves. A year had gone by since Margarita Magnuson went missing, and the case had turned as cold as the unseasonable autumn chill that had taken over New York City.

The circumstantial evidence Heller thought he had in order to build a case against Burton Magnuson died along with him. Barney's search for anyone else who may have boarded the Dream Voyager in Hamilton brought up no one, short of two additional boat attendants with clearance. McAvee had yet to be found, and as far as Margot's friends and lovers were concerned, no further concrete evidence had surfaced pointing to foul play.

As new cases began to take precedence, Richard suffered through months of sleepless nights over the only case he cared about. He had this recurring dream: It's nightfall, and he's sitting on a dock in the middle of a secluded wood staring out at the moonlit lake. All of a sudden, *she* rises out of the water, extending her arms and beckoning him to come in—like a siren luring a sailor to his death. Transfixed by the beautiful apparition, he steps off the dock and reaches out to her. As he falls deeper and deeper into the lake, he is unable to see through the murkiness, until he finally hits rock bottom, and there she is, sitting in front of him, her body aglow from a single break of piercing moonlight, glaring at him with a mocking grin that is as tantalizing as it is insidious...

That's when he wakes up. Was this some sort of sign? Or would this case just continue to haunt him forever?

No sooner did Agent Heller step into his office in the Federal Plaza building than his eager assistant, Barney, strode in directly behind him with a large cup of coffee in his hand and a *New York Times* and a *Wall Street Journal* under his arm. For the two years Barney had been working for Heller, he had been steadfast in his efforts to gain favor with his reticent superior. "Strong and black, Boss, just the way you like it."

"Thanks," said Richard, taking a sip from the cup and then sitting down.

Barney dropped the newspapers on his desk and pulled out the *Mansion* section from the *Journal*, holding it up for his boss to see. "I thought you might be interested in this," he said, pointing to the picture featured on the front page. "Burton Magnuson's Miami mansion is in escrow for $34 million."

Heller raised an eyebrow, although he wasn't surprised. Burt's ex-wife, Meredith, had told him she wasn't interested in the place in Florida. "Let me see that," he said, taking the paper from him. As Barney left, Heller did a quick perusal of the article. It stated that the mansion was being contracted through the estate's trustee, but the buyer remained anonymous. Continuing onto the next page, there was an aerial photograph of the grounds surrounding the house, including the huge, Olympic-sized pool.

Richard leaned back in his chair, allowing his mind to wander while he focused on the photo. He envisioned Margot swimming in the pool, gliding through the water, graceful as a swan...but then, his thoughts shifted. This time, her body was floating in the vast blue sea, her flesh being devoured by sharks, leaving the remnants to decompose. He imagined her lovely bones settling deeper and deeper into the ocean floor until the seagrasses surrounding them took root and slowly began to flower, infusing life back into her spirit. Her watery grave required no marker because she was not one to be easily forgotten — least not by him.

"Ahem, hem...excuse me," said Barney, entering Heller's office again, this time with a handful of mail. "Looks like you've got a lot of fan mail today," he grinned, trying to get a smile out of his boss while placing the bundle on his desk.

Heller shot Barney a curious look, then waited for his assistant to leave before sifting through the pile. Most of his correspondence was done on his computer via email, but he still received a fair amount through the post. There were a couple of reports he had been waiting for, various seminar brochures, and other pieces of miscellaneous correspondence. When he came to the bottom of the stack, there was an oversized Manila envelope. It had no return address, but was postmarked: *Miami, Florida.*

Carefully, he inserted his letter opener into the top corner of the envelope and ran it across the fold. When he pulled out the contents, he couldn't believe his eyes. Out spilled three enlarged photographs that appeared to have been zoomed in from a distance. They all had one thing in common, the focal point being the same woman in her mid-to-late thirties. The more Richard examined the photos, the more familiar she became.

He swiveled his chair around to the box he kept close to his desk and pulled out the file folder containing all the photographs he had of Margarita Magnuson. These included the headshot he got from Burt, the group picture taken aboard the Dream Voyager, and all the ones taken by the private investigator. He took them all out and placed them, one by one, next to the photos he had removed from the Manila envelope. Holding them up at close range, he examined them from left to right and right to left, then grabbed a magnifying glass from his desk drawer to scrutinize them more carefully.

The woman in the zoomed-in photos he had just received looked an awful lot like Margarita Magnuson. The only difference was that the female had short, cropped hair, dyed to a brassy platinum which, in the sun's glare, permeated a lilac sheen. There was something else. The woman was pushing a stroller with an infant in it.

Heller dug into the Manila envelope and held it upside down, shaking it in search of some kind of note or explanation, but found nothing. Could it be? Could this actually be the illusive Margarita Magnuson? Or was he being played, and this was just some random person who happened to look like her?

All this time, Heller had treated the case as if she were dead. What if somehow she did survive the fall? But then, why had her body not been found?

Then, again, what if it was not her body that fell over that night? What if it were someone else who went overboard? Just because she wasn't accounted for at the time of debarkation didn't necessarily mean she didn't get off. Maybe human error was to blame, allowing her to slip through the checkpoint undetected. So, why were all her belongings left in the room? Unless she wanted to leave undetected. Heller learned early on in his career that there are many ways people can avoid detection—which brought forth the possibility that someone else was involved.

The sheer thought of finding Margarita Magnuson alive and well caused the veins in his body to percolate with excitement.

He picked up one of the photos where the woman was bending over the stroller, tending to the baby. From everything he had learned about Margot, he would never have guessed her to be the motherly type. But then, you never know. When he was first married, he would have loved to have been a dad one day. It's funny how time has a way of settling things.

Heller continued to dissect each and every photograph. The scenery clearly depicted a beach town. The cement walkway where the woman was pushing the buggy was fronted by sand, and aligned in the background was a nondescript row of small retail businesses, including a beach apparel store, a surf shop, and a small bar-type restaurant. Zoning in with his magnifying glass, he scoured for additional details that might help him decipher where, exactly, in Florida they had been taken. The signage above the restaurant was partially obstructed by palm trees. He was, however, able to make out part of the letters: *OT GROVE*

Immediately, Heller got on his computer to search for any and all bars or restaurants in Florida whose names ended with those letters. After expending a good amount of time, he came up with several possibilities that needed to be checked out. Then it occurred to him. Just because the envelope was postmarked "Florida," it didn't necessarily mean that the photos were taken in Florida. There was the possibility that they had been taken somewhere else. But where? This was going to entail much more digging. This was a job for Barney.

In the meantime, Heller needed to find out who sent the photographs.

Was it possible that McAvee had taken the photos? Being that he was a private eye, he would easily have had access to a zoom lens. It was a long shot, but Heller decided to give the private eye's one-time girlfriend, Ms. Trish Dearden, a call to see if she had heard from him.

She had not. At least, she said she hadn't.

Richard hung up the phone and began tapping his pencil against his desk, wondering what to do next, when his eyes fell on the Mansion section of the Journal still laying on his desk. Right away, he picked up his handset and buzzed his assistant. "Barney, book me the next flight out to Miami."

CHAPTER 56

Heller arrived at the Miami mansion to find the security gates open and a convoy of moving trucks lined up all along the driveway. After finding an open spot to park his vehicle, he began walking toward the front entrance, where a team of movers was removing furniture. Filtering in between them, he proceeded to make his way through the open doors when he was suddenly met by the sole individual who was directing the movers along.

At his initial sight of the agent, the late owner's head butler took a step backward. "Why, Agent Heller, this is a surprise. What, may I ask, brings you here?"

"Is there somewhere we can talk?"

Mr. Gagnon did not appear readily inclined to do so. "As you can see, I am quite busy."

"This won't take long."

Gagnon straightened out his stiff lapels. "This way," he said, before leading the agent into a corner office and shutting the door.

Heller took a quick glance around. Unlike the rest of the house, everything in this room was in place. Nothing appeared to have been packed yet.

"This is my office," said Jacques, seating himself behind the desk. "I need to be here until all matters are finalized."

"*You* need to be here?" asked Heller.

"Yes. I am the trustee."

"Oh, I assumed the bank..."

"Mr. Magnuson's Will named me Executor and Trustee in

all matters concerning his estate."

That's interesting, thought Heller.

"So, how may I be of help to you?"

"I have something to show you." Heller pulled the Manila envelope out from the inside of his jacket and handed it over to Jacques.

Jacques eyed the envelope suspiciously. With a little hesitancy, he pulled out the contents and, one by one, proceeded to examine each and every photo with careful scrutiny. A lump formed in his throat. "Where did you get these?"

"I thought you'd be able to answer that question."

"I've never seen them before."

"They look a lot like Margarita Magnuson, wouldn't you say?"

"Yes, I would. The likeness is remarkable," said Mr. Gagnon, appearing rather dumbfounded.

"So, you didn't send them to me?"

"What? No."

"The envelope is postmarked Miami, Florida. Do you have any idea who might have sent them?"

Jacques lowered his head, placing his hands in a prayer-like position, and began tapping his fingertips together. Slowly, he raised his eyes and fixed them upon the agent as if he'd had a breakthrough moment. "You might want to check out Mr. Jeffrey Holt, Mrs. Magnuson's former aquatics instructor. Perhaps he might have some insight into them."

Agent Heller gathered the photos from the desk and pushed them back into the envelope. "I'll do just that."

Mr. Gagnon pushed his chair back and was about to stand.

"Don't bother getting up," said Heller, "I'll see my way out."

The head butler waited for Heller to leave, and when the agent was clear out of sight, he picked up his desk phone and dialed out. "Gagnon here. An interesting development has emerged..."

CHAPTER 57

On the advice of Mr. Gagnon, Heller found his way back to Holt's south side bungalow. After knocking and waiting on the front porch for several minutes, Heller thought he'd walk around back to see if he might be there. He wasn't, but there was a rear door, so he tried giving a quick rap before covertly making his way in. Just as he was about to, a woman who apparently had been stooped over in the garden next door stood up. (That was the nice thing about Florida, you could still harvest in September.) She must have heard him rustling through the overgrown weeds because she glanced up in his direction. "Lookin' for Jeff?" she called out.

Heller quickly dropped his hands from the knob. "Yeah. Do you know if he's home?" he yelled back.

The slim young female with long golden hair and a bandana wrapped around her forehead stood up, revealing her short, cut-off jeans and tie-dyed T-shirt. To Heller, she looked like a hippie straight out of the '60s. "He won't be back for a few hours. Who's asking?"

"Uh...his uncle," responded Heller. "I haven't seen him for a while, and I wanted to surprise him."

The girl lifted her hand over her eyes to shield them from the sun's glare, then squinted with uncertainty while she sized him up and down. "He's at the boat rental," she shouted.

"The boat rental?"

"Yeah, he's got a boat rental business down by the docks. You *must not* have seen him in a while—he's had it for almost a year now."

"Thanks," said Heller. "I'll head down there right now." The girl kept watch on him until he turned the corner, then ducked back into her jungly vegetation.

Heller drove directly to the marina and parked his car in a lot beside the boat docks. When he exited from his vehicle, he spotted a huge carrier off in the distance, causing him to reminisce about his younger days in the Navy. He actually missed those days. Sure, it wasn't easy. The rigorous training and the extensive months at sea. But he loved it nonetheless. After all those years of "serving" his father, it gave him a new purpose: serving his country. He would have made a career out of it, too, if it hadn't been for Stacy. She wanted out, and she wanted him out, as well. Then she betrayed him. That's what led him to law enforcement; he wanted to make sure people paid for their misdoings.

Heller meandered along the pier toward his destination, admiring all the boats resting in their berths. There were all different sizes, makes, and models, the smaller ones gently bobbing up and down from the rebounding waves. Until one boat, in particular, caught his eye, and he stopped to take a moment and check it out. It was a sleek 37-foot white cruiser with dark blue trim. The Navy had taught him just about everything there was to know about watercraft. This vessel wasn't as big as some, but it was powerful enough to handle even the toughest waves. But what struck him most about the boat was the name painted over the stern: *Barracuda.*

He continued on his way until he came to a row of small, shanty-like buildings along the pier. There was a snack shack, advertising fried clams and homemade fries; a weathered bait and tackle shop that looked like it had been around for half a century; and finally, there was a residential home which had been converted into an office. It had a gray-shingled roof and a frame that appeared to have been newly painted in a pale shade of blue. Out front, pounded into the sand, was a post with a hanging white plank that had a picture of an anchor on one side and bold black letters that read: **Holt's Boat Rentals.**

When Richard walked in, there were two people already in line to speak to the middle-aged woman behind the counter who was handling the charter agreements, so he patiently waited for his turn. When he reached the front, he asked her if Mr. Holt was in.

"Jeffrey!" she yelled, turning her neck toward an open office door behind her. Two minutes later, out came the same young man Heller remembered interviewing almost ten months ago. This time, however, he was wearing a shirt, and his former shaggy mane was cut almost to Navy standards. It was apparent the young man remembered the agent, too, because he gave a startled look as soon as he stepped out.

"Can we speak in your office?" asked Heller.

"Uh...sure," said Jeffrey, his voice teetering, then led the way while Agent Heller followed him into the back room. "Have a seat," said Holt, shutting the door behind him.

Heller started out by asking Mr. Holt if he had seen or heard from Margot since her disappearance.

"How could I have?" replied Holt. "The last time I talked to you, you said she fell off a cruise ship."

"I never said she *fell* off the cruise ship," said Heller, making a mental note of that comment. "I only told you she went missing. Her body was never found."

Holt's shoulders tensed up with his voice taking on a defensive tone. "So what do you want from me?"

That's when the agent took out the envelope from his inner pocket and laid it on Mr. Holt's desk.

A gulp slithered down the young man's throat as he opened the envelope and pulled out the pictures. "What are these?"

"You knew Mrs. Magnuson pretty well. Wouldn't you say

that's her?"

Jeffrey took his time to examine the photos. "I don't think so."

"Are you sure?" asked Heller, his eyes fixed on his subject.

"Margot...I mean...Mrs. Magnuson told me she couldn't have kids. This woman's pushing a baby buggy."

"It might not be hers," said Heller. "It could be someone else's kid."

Jeffrey appeared flustered. "Besides, Margot had long dark hair. This chick's hair is short and platinum blond."

"She could have cut it, dyed it."

"She would never do that. Her hair was her trademark."

"She would if she were trying to hide."

"Why would she be trying to hide?"

"You tell me."

"I have no idea. She had the perfect life."

"This envelope came postmarked from Florida. Did you take these photos, Mr. Holt? "

"Of course not. Why would I take pictures of some random lady pushing a baby buggy?"

"Do you have any idea who could have taken these photos?"

"How would I know?" answered Jeffrey, his anger growing in his reddening cheeks.

Heller grabbed the envelope, placed the photographs back inside, and stood up. "If you happen to hear from her, you'll let me know, won't you?"

Jeffrey forced himself to look up at the agent. "Yeah, sure."

Just as Heller was about to leave, he turned to Jeffrey and said, "By the way, nice little business you got here. How were you able to pay for it on a swimming instructor's salary?"

Holt stared blankly at him for a moment before answering. "Inheritance."

"...Hmm, lucky you."

When the agent was out of sight, Jeffrey picked up his cell phone that was laying on top of his desk and began scrolling through a string of unanswered texts. His eyes welled up with tears while a mix of emotions pelted him...love...anguish...rage.

By the time Heller returned to his vehicle, he noticed he'd gotten a message from his assistant. Barney had come up with a couple of names from his internet search for any and all restaurants in the U.S. and abroad that were located in beachside locations, and whose name ended in "−ROT GROVE." Heller listened carefully to the recording left on his cell:

"Hey Boss, Barney here. I was able to find three restaurants that fit the description of a beachside bistro and could possibly be the one pictured in your photos. One is a vegan restaurant, called 'Carrot Grove,' in Hawaii. Then, there's 'Tarot Grove,' a restaurant-bar in Jamaica. Finally, there's the 'Parrot Grove.' That one's in Bermuda. Let me know how you want me to proceed from here."

Heller dropped his phone on the empty seat next to him, his eyes glazed against the windshield. *Of course. How did I not figure it out from the start?*

CHAPTER 58

The departure board at Miami-Dade Airport showed Flight 487 to L.F. Wade International Airport in St. George Parish, Bermuda to be — ON TIME. Heller normally wasn't nervous about flying — except when he had to fly over one of the deepest parts of the ocean on earth: *The Bermuda Triangle*.

In his Navy days, he was equally as nervous crossing that same area by boat. He had heard plenty of stories of ships and planes that had gone missing over "The Triangle." He was not one to fall prey to supernatural ideology like UFOs, but he did believe in extraordinary natural phenomena. He had read all about these abnormally large and unexpected waves called *rogue tidal waves* and *hexagonal clouds* that cause 170mph winds or "air bombs" powerful enough to generate waves over 45ft high. Then there's *methane gas*. Research proved that there is more methane gas in some ocean spots than others, and if that gas is released into the water, it could quickly sink ships and even bring down planes. If that wasn't enough, there was also this thing called *electronic fog*, which is a meteorological phenomenon that sticks to aircraft or ships. It's said that the fog can cause equipment on aircrafts and ships to malfunction — which would explain compasses spinning out of control.

Lucky for him, he had never experienced any of the above, but on one of his deployments taking him through the "Devil's Triangle" (as the Navy men liked to call it), he did witness something which really freaked him out. It happened during a particularly rough thunderstorm. It looked like blue lightning, but apparently, it's caused by electrons shooting through the air to create these bright pointy objects in what is known as *"Saint Elmo's Fire."* It was named after *Erasmus of Formia* or *Saint Elmo*. He was a Christian saint and martyr, venerated as the patron saint of sailors because it was said that he continued to preach even after a thunderbolt struck the ground beside him. Sailors who were in danger from sudden storms and lightning would pray to him for safety and guidance. When these electrical discharges appeared before their ship's mast, it was read as a sign of his protection, and so it came to be called "Saint Elmo's Fire."

In any case, Heller needed a drink to calm his nerves.

After coming out of his bout of depression over Stacy, he had curbed his drinking of hard alcohol, but for occasions like this, he'd make an exception. Once the plane had reached maximum cruising altitude, he ordered a nice stiff Bourbon on the rocks. It not only eased his anxiety, but he slept the full two-and-a-half hours to his destination. When he woke up, he was relieved to find that his plane had landed safely.

Tourists are not allowed to rent cars in Bermuda, so from the airport, the agent grabbed a cab, which took him approximately seven miles through Hamilton to his ultimate destination. That was the restaurant all right. Same as in the picture. Except now, all the letters were visible: **PARROT GROVE**. The thing he found most ironic was its close approximation to the pier and its excellent view of the cruise ships docked there.

Heller paid the cabbie and headed straight toward the entrance. Like Florida in late September, even though the weather is still hot and humid, the heavy crowds of tourists had subsided, and there was no wait line to get in. Looking like he meant business in his trademark brown suit coat, without cracking a smile, Heller walked past the hostess and headed straight for the bar. The sole bartender on the floor, busy drying some glasses, caught sight of him and eyed him suspiciously while he sat down on one of the barstools. Heller motioned his hand toward him.

"Can I get a beer over here?"

"Sure, what'll you have?" asked the bartender, cautiously approaching.

Richard ordered a beer on tap and attempted to make small talk with the bartender in an effort to catch him off guard. The problem was that Heller was never good at small talk. After two sips, he pulled out the photo of the woman pushing the stroller from inside his pocket. "Do you recognize this woman?"

The bartender glanced at the picture for a brief second, keeping his concentration on a drink he was mixing in a cocktail shaker. "A lot of people come in here," he said, pouring the beverage into a glass.

Heller took out his badge and slapped it down on the counter.

The bartender didn't bat an eye while he inserted a toothpick into a cherry and citrus rind and slid the fruity drink over to the patron seated nearby. "She looks vaguely familiar."

"I'd appreciate it if you could be a little more specific. I'd hate to have to bring you in for questioning."

The bartender grabbed the photo from the agent's hand and pretended to take a closer look. "Oh, yeah. That's Alex."

"Alex? Do you have a last name?"

"I think it's Johnson."

"Does she live around here?"

"Don't know. She used to come in pretty regularly, but I haven't seen her for a while."

Heller stood up, stowed the photo back in his inner pocket, and slapped a few bucks down on the bar. "Thanks," he said, and walked out of the restaurant.

Outside, he took out his cell phone to call his assistant. It was almost 8:00 p.m. and there was an hour difference between New York and Bermuda, so it was only 7:00 p.m. in New York. There was a good chance Barney might still be in the office. When he didn't answer, Richard left a message: "Barney, this is Heller. I'm at the Parrot Grove in Hamilton. See if you can come up with an address for an 'Alex Johnson.' It's obviously an alias."

Before hailing another cab, Heller checked the map on his phone to see where the hotel was that Barney booked for him. It was a little way out, in Flatts Village, but cheaper than anything you'd find in Hamilton or St. George, even in the off-season.

By the time he arrived at his hotel and checked in, his stomach was growling. Other than a coffee at the airport, a bourbon on the plane, and a quarter of a beer at the bar, he hadn't eaten anything all day. He should have grabbed a bite while he was at the Parrot Grove. It was pretty late now, but hopefully, there was something still open. He had noticed a little taqueria within walking distance of the hotel. It probably wasn't the healthiest option, but he decided to give it a try.

When he got there, there was only one car parked out front. It didn't look like anyone was in there, but the lights were still on inside. A chime rang when he walked in, but no one came out to greet him. As he waited for someone to appear, he had time to read the whole menu scrawled out on a chalkboard against the wall. Finally, someone stepped out of the back room. "You come just in time," said the short, stocky man with a heavy Latino accent. "I was just about to close up."

He was so hungry, he ordered three *Supreme Machos Tacos* and an extra-large Diet Coke. Then he sat down at one of the three small tables and proceeded to devour every bit of the greasy, beef, bean, and cheese-filled tortillas before walking back to his hotel room with the remainder of his Coke in hand. When he got there, he set his Coke on the nightstand, along with his phone, stacked a few pillows on one side of the bed, and laid down. Suddenly, he felt a sharp, burning sensation in his chest — followed by another. *Great, the heartburn is already setting in. Why didn't I just get a salad?* he thought to himself while rubbing his hand over his chest. *Good thing I packed those Rolaids.* Getting up, he searched his overnight bag until he found a roll and popped a couple of the antacids in his mouth. Then he took one last swig of his drink, grabbed the TV remote, and plopped himself back down on the bed.

After streaming through an endless list of channels, he came upon one of those reality-based crime mysteries and started watching it. Those Machos Tacos had set in pretty heavy. That, coupled with all the traveling he'd done today, he could feel himself fading. Eventually, his mind began to drift from the made-for-TV dramatization to his own real-life drama...

He had sworn to himself he would never become like his father, but when his marriage to Stacy ended, he took to drinking away his sorrows on a nightly basis. During those bouts, he would mull over all the possible reasons why both his mother and his wife had left him. He began to wonder if he had been part of the problem. Was it his fault that the women he loved left? The more he drank, the more consumed he became. He had confronted Stacy when he caught her in bed with Chuck, but all she could say was, "I'm sorry, Richard. I never loved you." That was a hard pill to swallow. Had his mother felt the same way? He understood why she would want out of a bad marriage, but what woman would leave her child behind like that?

When it became clear that she was never coming back, he was so angry that he didn't care if he ever saw her again, so for a long time, he made no attempt to find her. He had no idea of where to even start looking.

Then, when he joined the FBI, it changed his whole outlook. He sobered up and decided to quit feeling sorry for himself. By the time he had graduated from the FBI Academy in Quantico, not only did he learn the skills he needed for the job, but he also acquired the confidence and courage required of such a position. In addition, it gave him the determination to seek out his mother. He viewed the abandonment in a whole new light.

As far as he knew, she had never tried to get in touch with him.

Unless his father had purposely hidden the truth from him. What if she had every intention of coming back, but then something terrible happened to her? If nothing else, after all these years, he needed to find out whether she was dead or alive. If she were still alive, he felt that he was emotionally ready to confront her and give her the chance to explain her side of the story, and hopefully, lead him to forgiveness.

In addition, he now had the resources to help him in his investigation. A thorough search through years of obituaries found no one deceased under the name of Darlene Heller. As it turned out, she was living under the assumed name of: Alice Perkins. What he hadn't expected was that she had been living, right under his nose, in their own home state all along. Unfortunately, Richard did not get the results he had hoped for.

He found her living on a farm in rural Minnesota. She was cohabitating with, but not legally married to, a fellow, and they had four children together — two of which still lived with them and helped run the farm. Richard was devastated. He had four half-siblings he never even knew about.

When he showed up at her doorstep, she recognized him right away. "Hello Dickie," she said with complete calm, observing him through the screen.

She, too, appeared just as he remembered. Still thin and fragile-looking, although her dark hair had faded to an ashen gray and her blue eyes had dulled to an exact match.

"Hello, Mother. You don't seem that surprised to see me."

"I'm surprised it took you this long to find me," she answered, stepping out, allowing the screen door to slam behind her.

"I figured you would have wanted to move as far away as possible," said Richard.

"People often hide in plain sight because, deep down, they secretly want to be found," she said, descending the porch steps and heading toward the gravel driveway.

Dickie followed behind her, allowing himself to become emotional.

"If you secretly wanted to be found, then why didn't you come back for me?"

He hoped for some kind of appeasing explanation, but sadly, she showed little, if any remorse.

"I never loved your father. The only reason I married him was to escape an abusive relationship at the hands of my own father. What ended up happening is I traded one abusive relationship for another. I had no recourse but to leave again and start my life over. I'm a weak woman, Dickie. I couldn't take you with me because every time I looked at you, I saw your father's face." She ended by saying, "I wasn't worried, Dickie. You were always such a serious child. You were my little man. You were much stronger than I could ever be. I knew you'd be able to handle the situation even if I couldn't."

*This was more than Richard could take. He was about to turn and leave when, instead, he reached into his coat pocket and pulled out a handgun. "You **KNEW** I would be able to handle the situation? This is how I've handled it." He pointed the revolver at his right temple and looked his mother straight in the eyes. "This is what I've wanted to do every day since you left."*

His mother bit her lip, the hard lines on her face softening, as she took a guarded step closer toward him.

"Stop!" shouted Richard. "It's too late. You've made your bed, now you're going to sleep in it." He then turned the gun toward her and...

Heller jerked awake. He must have dozed off. He leaned toward the nightstand to check the time on his cell. It was almost 1:00 o'clock and the late-night show was about to go off the air. He pressed the OFF button on the television remote, removed his clothes, and crawled under the covers. It had been a long day, and he needed to get some sleep. Hopefully, Barney and his team would have an address for him by morning.

CHAPTER 59

Just as Heller expected, his trusty assistant came through again with flying colors. *I need to recommend Barney for a raise*, he thought, while he waited at the front entrance of his hotel for local backup to show. In conjunction with Bermuda's government, the Chief Inspector of the Bermuda Police pulled up in his service vehicle, and Heller jumped in. The address Barney provided them was located in Paget Parish's Grape Bay. "You may not know this," said the chief inspector, "but Grape Bay is considered one of the island's most premier real estate. Considering the type of woman this Margarita Magnuson is purported to be, it doesn't surprise me that she chose to live here."

Alex sat on the sofa rocking her baby to sleep while the sound of waves crashing against the jetted rocks vibrated through the glass door wall. Her initial plans hadn't prepared her for this, but it couldn't have turned out better. Motherhood suited her. She was happier than she ever imagined she could be.

Her daughter was four months old now, so there was no doubt that it happened during the cruise. She studied the features on her child's innocent face, contemplating all the possibilities of who the father might be. It couldn't be Burt. After his two children were born, he got a vasectomy. Although she did hear of rare cases where the vasectomy failed. First, she had that fling on the ship with Jorge. Afterwards, she met up with James at the Rosewood Hotel. And finally, there was that unintended hook-up with Jeffrey in Gilby's parking lot. As she caressed her daughter's wispy locks and gazed into her eyes, there was no doubt in her mind who the father was.

She wasn't a religious person, but she couldn't help wonder about the baby whose precious life she had chosen to terminate in what now seemed like a lifetime ago. It probably would have had thick, dark hair and penetrating brown eyes like its father. Thinking about it caused a tear to trickle down her cheek. What if she had told Remy she was pregnant? He likely would have married her. But then, she wouldn't be here today. Was it worth it? Other than the fact that she was now blessed with this gorgeous child, she questioned her decision. She wiped away the droplets that had reached the curvature of her full lips. Of course, she married Burt for his money. For a while, she even believed she could learn to love him. But who was she kidding? There was no repressing her appetite for young blood. The problem was that she couldn't decide what she liked best — blood or money.

The baby was fast asleep now, so she got up and carried her to her crib. Gently, she laid her down and gave her a light peck on her sun-kissed cheek. Quietly, she shut the door and jumped slightly. She thought she'd heard a noise. She couldn't help but be on edge, always conscious of her surroundings whenever she went into town, studying every passerby, trusting no one. Maybe it was the wind. The gusts get pretty loud when they propel along the shore.

Even though she believed her plan was foolproof, she still had that nagging voice in the back of her mind. What if she were discovered? Initially, she worried about Burt finding her. But when she got the news of his "accidental" death, she felt even less safe. There was always the chance that whoever did him in for "stealing" the money would one day figure out who the real facilitators were. She never trusted Jacques. She knew from the start he was much more than a butler to Burt. He was Burt's liaison to the underworld. As long as he was around, she would never feel completely free.

Gently, she tiptoed out of the baby's room and shut the door behind her. She overheard Maya, her live-in housekeeper, and nanny, speaking into the security speaker, and walked into the den where the surveillance monitor was.

Officer Smith had just arrived at the iron gates sequestering the beautiful seaside villa overlooking the bay. As soon as he pulled his vehicle up to the intercom, a female voice with a deep British accent requested that they identify themselves.

"Chief Officer Smith, Bermuda Police, and Special Agent Richard Heller of the FBI here to see Alex Johnson."

Maya, who was sitting behind the computer screen, looked up at Alex apprehensively.

Alex bent over Maya's shoulder to get a better look at the video. She could clearly see two men, one wearing a policeman's uniform and the other in plain clothes, sitting in a marked car.

Of course, the FBI, thought Alex. Strangely enough, those words were almost reassuring. She was so concerned with being found out by Jacques' henchmen, she had put the possibility of being discovered by the FBI on the back burner.

"We have a warrant," said Officer Smith. "I suggest you let us in."

A moment went by with no response until Alex gave Maya a nod. "It's alright. Let them through."

The gates opened up, and Officer Smith and Agent Heller followed the lengthy drive until they reached a modern, one-story compound. Together, they got out of their vehicle, walked up to the door, and rang the doorbell. While they stood rigidly behind the transparent glass and wrought-iron entrance, a matronly Bermudian woman, dressed in a navy blue cotton dress, slowly approached. As she opened the door, the stern-looking man in the sedentary brown suit pulled out his badge and held it up. No sooner than he uttered, "I'm Special Agent Richard Heller from the FBI," a tall specimen of a model, in an ankle-length tunic dress, slit up on one side, appeared in the hallway. Maya threw her a concerned glance and left the room.

Heller looked at her with the intensity of a man who had stared at her photo on a daily basis for over a year. There was no doubt in his mind. This was Margot. Alive and well and as striking in her short, platinum blond hair as she was in her pictures, with sleek raven hair that draped down to her breasts. He could barely contain his excitement. What a pity it had to end this way.

"Are you Alex Johnson?"

"Yes," she said calmly.

"You're under arrest. You have the right to remain silent..."

CHAPTER 60

Maya ran into the room just as the chief inspector was handcuffing Ms. Johnson. "Miss...!" she shouted, with a shocked look on her face.

"It's okay, Maya," said Alex, looking back at the agent. "On what grounds?"

"False impersonation and conspiracy to commit fraud, for starters..."

"I choose to remain silent, and I demand to speak to my attorney." Alex was no fool. Even though she had not expected to be found, she did have a personal lawyer with expertise in these matters on hand—just in case.

"You'll get that chance as soon as we bring you in."

"But, I have a baby," she said forcefully.

"If you don't have anyone to stay with her, we'll appoint a temporary custodian."

Alex turned to her nanny. "Maya, can you take care of her until I get this matter handled?"

"Sure, of course, Miss. I will be here as long as you need me."

"I'll be in touch as soon as I can," said Alex, as she was led out the front door.

After Alex's fingerprints were taken and the case was being processed, she was moved to a cold, sparse waiting room. As she sat there quietly waiting for her lawyer to arrive, her mind took her back to that last night aboard the *Dream Voyager* and the events that led up to this moment...

Everyone had left, and she was all alone on the top deck,

leaning against the metal railing, mentally surveying the distance to the ocean's surface. The full moon had reached its peak, transforming the black water into a reflective mirror, promising a divine resurrection from an otherwise inky grave.

She slid her palm against her burnished cheek that was still stinging from the slap she had incurred from Burt. Her neck was sore, too. She cupped her hands around it, trying to loosen it up. As she was twisting it back and forth, she noticed a ripped piece of Rachel's shirt stuck on one of the protruding bolts on the metal bar. She picked off the small piece of fabric and held it up to the wind, then released it from her fingers, where she watched it funnel its way into the brisk night air, turning into a mere speck before disappearing completely.

As she attempted to smooth down her billowing chiffon dress, she felt the lacy waistband of her thong dangling by a thread. She lifted her hand up under her dress to remove it, then wrapped it tightly around the protruding bolt where Rachel's shirt had ripped, making sure the elastic was secure so it wouldn't fly away.

Turning around, she looked to see what other incriminating evidence had been left behind. She couldn't help but crack a smile at all the empty Heineken bottles scattered about. For such a tiny girl, Dana could really put it away.

There were probably a dozen empty wine and cocktail glasses, their edges smeared with various shades of lipstick. Adjacent to the railing, Bethany's glass was still standing upright with a spear of saturated fruit resting at the bottom, while farther inward, an empty tumbler from Doris's Rum Swizzle rolled back and forth on the deck with a soggy umbrella and chewed-up citrus rinds laying in close proximity.

Margot reached into her right pocket and pulled out a badge, confirming Jorge's name in dark letters printed on its surface. Being careful not to step on any broken glass or slip on the melted ice cubes, she tiptoed over to one of the Plexiglas-top tables and secured the magnetic badge against its side metal rim.

Next, she walked over to another cocktail table and reached into her left pocket. From there, she pulled out two cards. One was her key card, which she held onto, and the other one was Burt's drink card (The one she had made sure to keep when they had dinner in the room earlier that evening). Since the drink card was plastic and not magnetic, she placed it underneath the table leg so it wouldn't blow away, but made sure it noticeably stuck out. She took another quick look around and glanced at her waterproof Rolex Oyster watch. Ironically, Burt had given it to her as a gift for having successfully completed her swimming lessons. It was almost time.

She proceeded to the doorway leading to the ship's inner hallway and took the elevator down to the sixth level, where she got off and speed-walked back to her suite. After unlocking the door with her key card, she went in and pulled out one of her suitcases from the under-bed storage — the one that contained her wetsuit. Quickly, she removed her clothes and changed into it, making sure to put everything else she had been wearing that evening into the bag. Afterwards, she zipped it up and stowed it back under the bed. Next, she covered herself in one of the ankle-length robes provided by the cruise line, rolling up the bottoms of her wetsuit from her ankles to her shins, so they couldn't be detected beneath the robe. Finally, she opened her entryway door and took a peek up and down the hall to make sure there was no one in sight before locking it. Then she stuck the key card in her robe pocket and started to make her way through the hallway.

Halfway down the hall, she noticed an attendant walking toward her. Quickly, she lowered her head, pretending to check the time on her watch. "Can I help you, ma'am?" he asked as he got closer.

"No, thank you...uh, can't sleep," she replied in a hushed

voice, while keeping her head to the ground and shaking her hair in her face. Passing him as quickly as she could, she made her way to the outer glass facing elevator and pressed the button, which brought her to the third-floor promenade level. Before stepping out, she stuck her head out to make sure the coast was clear before entering the yoga and workout room. The whole area was empty and dark. She ran over to the used towel bin and removed her robe. She removed the key card from inside the pocket, dropped her robe into the bin, and made a fast exit through the door leading to the outdoor jogging track. From there, she jogged along the stretch of Plexiglas and wooden barrier walls until she came to the open-air railing.

At that point, she stopped, kissed her key card, and hurled it off into the ocean. As she watched it tumble and drift over the open sea, she leaned over the rail and rubbernecked to her left. A motor boat travelling from the opposite direction was fast approaching. She glanced at her watch once more to confirm the time. It was exactly 2:50 a.m. As the speedboat was closing in, the cruise ship sounded two short blasts of its horn, indicating that the two boats would be passing each other on their starboard side.

Margot knew that a head-first dive from this distance could be deadly, so she climbed to the top rung of the barrier just as she had practiced many times before on the edge of her husband's yacht. There, she carefully positioned herself and stared into the mouth of the ravenous ocean, which she was about to challenge head-on. Then she took one deep, long breath and closed her eyes in absolute concentration, before proceeding to dive, feet-first, into the rippling white foam. Her perfect form barely creating a wake.

In what could easily have resulted in instant death, her head eventually bobbed back up to the surface, where she continued to tread water until the 37-foot cruiser idled its engine and the dark shadow of a man leaned over the side to toss her a lifebuoy. In an instant, he pulled her out of the water just before the captain put it in full throttle and jetted off southbound.

CHAPTER 61

The FBI could not initially charge Margarita Magnuson for anything other than committing fraud by using a false identity (which is subject to incarceration and/or fines) because staging your own death or "pseudocide" in and of itself is not inherently illegal. However, when you resurface with a new identity, you are defrauding every government agency that processes your new and old identities. For example, you're defrauding new lenders if you buy a house or car under your new identity, not to mention tax evasion and insurance fraud.

There would be no problem in extraditing her. Heller had enough experience to know there had to be some other fraudulent or illicit activity that Margot was involved in, given the great lengths she took to fake her death by risking her life when she jumped off that ship.

In order to lessen her sentence, she was obliged to name her accomplices, namely, the person or persons who had rescued her on the boat the evening she went missing. At first, she refused to cooperate, but eventually, at the advice of her counsel, she named Jeffrey Holt as the driver of the 37-foot cruiser and James McAvee as the man who pulled her out. She did not offer any information as to where either of them could be found.

Heller had already found Holt, but as far as McAvee was concerned, he could be anywhere. Luckily, the fingerprints lifted from McAvee's office were on file from his past criminal record; however, tracking him down could still be a problem, since he was probably using a fake passport and ID.

As soon as Heller returned to New York, he thought he'd

pay Ms. Dearden another visit on the off-chance she might have heard from McAvee. He didn't know if she would freely divulge any knowledge of his whereabouts, but it was worth a try.

The agent's perseverance paid off. It just so happened that Ms. Dearden had heard from James in a rather roundabout way. Just about a month previous, the auction company that Ms. Dearden worked for listed a hand-written copy of the lyrics to "*Everybody's Got Something to Hide Except Me and My Monkey*," by John Lennon and Paul McCartney, as well as the original guitar pick inscribed with both their signatures. James had desperately wanted to add these to his collection. The identity of buyers and sellers on the site is secretive, so he contacted Trish through the site's online portal, providing clues as to his identity and asking if she could see to it that he got it. He also reassured her that "one day" he'd be back for the memorabilia he had left behind. Hoping to see him again, she made sure his offer was accepted. When it came time to ship the scored property to its winning bidder, a P.O. box number was provided in lieu of an address. Dearden had access to the box number and, to her amusement, found that it was located in, of all places — the birthplace of the Beatles: Liverpool, England.

Over threats that she could be named as an accomplice to McAvee's disappearance, Ms. Dearden gave in to Agent Heller's demands.

In coordination with the United Kingdom's NCA (National Crime Agency) and the SFO (Serious Fraud Office), Heller and his team were able to track down McAvee and obtain an arrest warrant, as well as a search warrant. As it turned out, he was operating a small computer repair shop in a less-than-desirable part of town along the A562 motorway under the name of "Gordon Kingsley."

It was a typical, rainy, but mild 9.4 °C (or 49 °F) day in February in the port city when Heller, along with a fellow FBI agent, arrived at Liverpool Airport. After meeting up with their counterparts, the officers wasted no time homing in on their destination. The team arrived at a grungy little storefront with the words "computer repair" stenciled on the window. A bell chimed when they walked through the door, alerting the operator to their entry. Heller knew immediately that he was in the right place when he saw all the Beatles paraphernalia hanging on the walls.

Except for an old mug shot he had seen in the police files, Heller wasn't sure what McAvee would look like now. He knew he had his guy when a tall, thin man in straight-legged jeans and a V-neck T-shirt, whistling *Band on the Run*, walked in from the back room. With his bushy beard and moustache and his long, dark hair, tied into a ponytail, he could have been one of the Beatles himself. When the guy saw the three men in dark suits, his carefree demeanor quickly disappeared, and he greeted them with trepid reservation.

"What can I do for you gentlemen?" he asked nervously.

"Are you the owner—Gordon Kingsley?"

"Uh, yeah."

"You forgot your guitar," Heller said with a sneer.

"What?"

"And all your other Beatles albums and posters..."

"Hey, uh...if you don't mind," he interrupted. "I was just about to go to lunch. Can you come back later?"

Heller pulled out his badge. "If *you* don't mind, we'd like to take you in for questioning *right now*. You're under arrest. The agents handcuffed him, read him his rights, and led him to the back of their vehicle.

While James McAvee a/ka Gordon Kingsley was being detained at the SFO headquarters, a thorough search of his repair shop and his apartment above it was conducted. The agents confiscated his computer and other pertinent evidence and brought it back to the Federal Bureau of Investigation in New York. For starters, McAvee was booked for aiding and abetting a fugitive and passport fraud (which is a felony offense) and subsequently extradited to the U.S. to stand trial in New York.

He, as well as Jeffrey Holt and Margarita Magnuson, retained their own lawyer and would be tried separately.

CHAPTER 62

A comprehensive probe of McAvee's hard drive brought the case against Margot and her accomplice far beyond what the FBI had ever imagined.

In an attempt to cut a plea deal, McAvee explained from the very beginning how his initial involvement in the case evolved to the extent that it had.

He started out by telling them that he was initially hired by Burton Magnuson to prove that his wife was cheating on him. When the private eye supplied Burt with proof in the way of photos that Margot was having an affair with Charles Langford, Burt was furious and wanted revenge against his former trusted lawyer. He offered to pay McAvee, who had served time in jail for computer hacking, an extra twenty thousand dollars to help him frame Langford for embezzlement.

At Magnuson's direction, McAvee hacked into Langford's office computer and removed funds in Magnuson's business account held in trust by Dillon, McCain & Dermot, then transferred the monies into Langford's personal account, thereby making it look like the attorney was stealing from his client. The expectation was to get Langford fired and subsequently sent to jail. The plan worked without a hitch.

As far as Margot was concerned, Burt was still in love with her and continued to hold out hope that she would come clean and repent for her adulterous transgressions. But if that didn't happen, he was also ready to file for divorce.

Prior to their marriage, Burt had compelled Margot to sign a prenuptial agreement that left her a fair amount of money on which to live comfortably if he should ever divorce her. *However*, there was a clause that specified that if the reason for the divorce was *her cheating on him*, she would relinquish all rights to any and all spousal benefits that she would otherwise incur. In other words, she would be left with nothing.

While Burton was busy framing Langford, Margot had already seduced the private eye whom he had hired to follow her. McAvee told Margot that when he presented her husband with the photos of her and Charles, Burt mentioned that he had growing suspicions that she was sleeping with her swim instructor, too, and wanted proof of that as well.

The reality was that McAvee had already obtained compromising pictures of his wife with her swim instructor, but had not yet relinquished them. At Margot's request, McAvee agreed not to hand those photos over to Burt. "Holt means nothing to me," she insisted. "He was just a brief fling. Please don't give Burt the photos. I promise I'll make it worth your while." But then added, "Besides, I would hate to have to tell my husband that his own private investigator screwed his wife." So, when Burt pressed McAvee for proof that Margot was sleeping with Holt, the private eye maintained he had found nothing to substantiate his concerns.

During the interrogation, McAvee just shrugged his shoulders. "What could I do?"

From there, the plan began to proliferate.

While McAvee was in the process of transferring money from the Magnuson account into Langford's account, he became suspicious that most of the funds originated from bogus contributors. So, he decided to do some additional probing on his own. That's when he discovered a treasure trove of illegal activity orchestrated by the mega-millionaire.

During this time, the relationship between James and Margot was heating up. He confessed to her that her husband had him frame Charles Langford, and in the process, he became aware of what looked like fraudulent accounts. She could have cared less about Charles Langford, but she did care a great deal about her husband — or more precisely — his money.

"The moment I told her that, her eyes lit up like fireworks, and her mouth fell agape like she had just discovered buried treasure. She had always suspected Burt of being involved in some sort of illegal money dealings because of his frequent visits to The Bahamas and Bermuda, but until now, she had not known to what extent. She became silent and started pacing back and forth. I could tell that her brain was spinning into overdrive."

McAvee took a sip of his water and continued. "She was the master mind behind it all."

"She was able to sneak into Burt's office and find the secret passwords to his computer. Once I had those, I was able to hack into his personal files. That's when I discovered that most of the private lenders funding Magnuson's projects were under bogus entities. Further, that he was laundering those monies and transferring them to fake offshore accounts in foreign depositories in The Bahamas and Bermuda."

"The next step was to get Burt's money and make our escape."

"I retrieved the list of offshore accounts and the names of foreign banks holding the laundered money. Then I diverted the funds into a joint bank account, which Margot and I had secretly opened together with the intent of ultimately dividing the proceeds between us.

"We figured it wouldn't take long for her husband to discover that his money had been diverted, so we needed to come up with a scheme to lead him off track. I've got to hand it to her, she is one crafty little vixen. 'What if I died?' she asked me.

"With that idea in mind, she conjured up this impromptu 'reunion cruise' with her four 'best friends.' Not only would it allow her the opportunity to fake her own death, but it would also provide her with a convenient line-up of suspects.

"I thought her plan was *way* too dangerous, but she was adamant that she could pull it off. The idea was for her to dive off the cruise ship at a pre-planned hour, at which time I would come by in another boat and pick her up. The only problem, other than the fact that she could actually die from the jump, was that we needed two people to retrieve her. I had no experience with watercrafts, so we needed another person to drive the boat.

"Margot insisted we call her former swimming instructor, Jeffrey Holt, because she knew that with his connections, he'd have access to a boat and was more than capable of operating it. We had a bit of a disagreement on this, too. I wasn't sure we could trust him. She contended she was sure she could convince Jeffrey because he was as opportunistic as she was when it came to making easy cash. She also believed he still had feelings for her and would likely do whatever she asked. Proof of that was in the text messages she continued to receive from him long after she had cut off her swim lessons. We finally came to an agreement to offer Jeffrey a cut of the proceeds from our net gain.

"When it was all over, we went our separate ways."

CHAPTER 63

There was still one question harping on Richard Heller's mind. Who sent the pictures?

It could not have been James McAvee or Jeffrey Holt because they were in on the scheme.

It could not have been Charles Langford; he was still incarcerated at the time. Unless he employed a jail connection to look into her disappearance for him.

It couldn't have been Burt. The photographs showed up long after his demise.

Could it have been Meredith Magnuson, the bitter ex-wife? She certainly had cause. She had always suspected Margot of somehow being responsible for Burt's death.

It might have been Burt's grown children, Robert or Kathryn. The few times they showed up during Margot's trial, their facial expressions made it clear that they never approved of their father's young bride.

It could have been Jacques Gagnon. He never trusted Margot from the start. But why would he have denied sending the photographs? Why wouldn't he just have presented them to the FBI? Unless he was trying to hide something of his own. After the trial, the FBI continued its investigation into Mr. Gagnon, including all his past and present business dealings.

There was the possibility that it might have been Jorge Albuoy. He was a native resident of Bermuda. Maybe he had gone back home and happened to stumble upon Margot on the street. By outing her, it would have cleared him of being a potential murder suspect. Heller could understand why he would want to remain incognito; he had a family to protect.

Then there was Trish Dearden—McAvee's wannabe girlfriend. It was obvious she still had feelings for him. Each day at McAvee's trial, she sat in the third row offering support. Maybe she had found out that he was seeing Margot, and her jealousy got the better of her. But how did she figure out where Margot was? It's possible that James accidentally left some evidence of her intended whereabouts at her home.

Finally, there was the matter of Margot's so-called girlfriends: Dana, Doris, Rachel, and Bethany. Each of them (except maybe for Rachel) had their own reason for wanting to expose their friend if they somehow discovered that she was alive and well and living it up in Bermuda.

It wasn't until the middle of her trial that Agent Heller finally became privy to the one glitch in Margot's scheme that she had failed to foresee:

It was late August of 2016, and enough time had elapsed since Margot's disappearance to cause him any further dissuasion. *He* hadn't heard from the FBI since his initial interview with Agent Heller after she'd gone missing. It appeared as though they had stopped looking for her, perhaps chalking it up as an apparent suicide.

As the young man arrived at the fortified gate of the obscure seaside villa, he nervously took a deep breath before announcing himself on the intercom. "I'm here to see Margot."

"I am sorry, but there is no one here by that name," answered a female voice with a typical Bermudian British accent.

"Oh...right...um, tell her..."

Margot had heard the buzzer and had already entered the room where the surveillance monitor was located and immediately recognized the face on the camera screen. "It's okay, Maya, you can let him in."

A few minutes later, the doorbell rang, and a mochacomplected woman answered to see a ruggedly handsome young male standing in the doorway with a single red rose in his hand.

In that moment, Margot walked into the room to approach her guest. She was wearing a form-fitting, ankle-length, beige knit dress, and accentuating her plunging neckline was a necklace made of turquoise shells.

The man appeared awestruck. "You...you...look incredible. Were you going somewhere?"

"No. This is what I normally wear around the house," she replied flippantly, then turned to the Bermudian woman, "You can go now, Maya."

Maya ceded an inquisitive eye and left the room.

"You cut your hair," said Margot, extending her arm to brush the top of his head.

"Yeah...uh...so did you."

"Do you like it?" she asked, lifting one side of her platinum mini bob with her palm.

"You'd look beautiful if you were bald."

Margot looked at the single red rose in his hand. "Is that for me?" she asked, grabbing it out of his hand and bending over to sniff it.

"Yeah," he said sheepishly.

Margot took his hand. "Come on, let's go sit down."

He followed her into a glamorous, sunny room with white furniture, surrounded by huge windows that faced the ocean. Just as he expected, that was her taste—bright and showy, just like her personality. She sat herself down on the sleek white leather sofa, and motioned for him to come sit next to her.

"Nice place you've got here," he said, leaving a clear empty spot between them.

"Thanks," said Margot, laying the rose on the black and white lacquer coffee table. "So how did you find me?" she asked, suddenly taking on a serious tone.

"You know I have a lot of friends in Bermuda."

"No one is supposed to know I'm here," she said, lowering her voice and looking sideways to see if Maya was in the vicinity.

"Don't worry. I didn't tell anybody anything—really, Margot."

"It's not a good idea for you to come here," she said angrily. "By the way, my name is Alex Johnson now."

"I just wanted to see you, that's all. I figured enough time had passed..."

"It doesn't matter how much time has passed. We had an agreement, remember?"

Just then, Maya walked in. "Excuse me, Miss Johnson, but the baby, she refuses to sleep."

Margot stood up. "It's alright, Maya, I'll go get her."

"You have a baby?" exclaimed the young man as she was leaving the room.

Margot came back into the living room with a baby in her arms and a proud smile on her face. "It's a girl."

"How old is she?" asked the young man, looking stunned.

"She's three months old."

He gazed upon the child's soft, pale face and bright blue eyes and stroked her fine golden locks. "She's beautiful," he said, mesmerized. "Just like you. What's her name?"

"I thought I'd name her after me—Margaret."

Her blond hair, blue-eyed suitor gazed down at the floor, in a brief moment of contemplation. "If she's three months old... then...that means you must have gotten pregnant right about the time of the cruise."

"Maybe."

"I thought you said Burt had gotten a vasectomy?"

"He did."

An expression of dumbfoundedness spread across his face. "Is it mine? That night at Gilby's, in my car..."

"Don't be ridiculous!" cracked Margot. "You know I've always been on the pill." (The truth was that Margot had stopped taking the pill ever since her gynecologist told her she would probably never be able to conceive.)

"Well, obviously, they're not foolproof," said the young man. "How do you know it's not mine? She looks just like me."

"Trust me, she's not yours," said Margot, getting up and calling for Maya.

"Yes, Miss Johnson," said Maya, scurrying into the room.

Margot handed the baby over to her. "Here, why don't you try to put her back down to sleep. Maybe you can sing her a lullaby or something."

"The young man waited until Maya was out of the room, then leaned over toward Margot and whispered, "Have you had a paternity test?"

Margot released another curdling laugh. "Well, that would be a stupid thing to do, wouldn't it? It would lead the cops right to me."

A short pause went by before he spoke again. "So, if it's not Burt's...and it's not mine... then who is it? Who's the father, Margot?"

"That's none of your business!"

The young man grew quiet again. "You know, I have my own business now—boat rentals mostly. Remember the one I picked you up in? I use that one for special excursions."

Margot looked at him. "Is that wise, Captain? It can be traced, you know."

"Don't worry. I gave it a new paint job, and I renamed it—after you."

Margot shot him a concerned glance.

"I named it, '*Barracuda.*'"

Margot let out a hearty laugh. "So what do you want, Mr. Holt? You've already received your cut."

Jeffrey tried to maintain his composure as he stared into Margot's impenetrable eyes. "I've never gotten over you, Margot," he said, his voice breaking up.

Margot did her best to sound empathetic. "I thought I had made myself perfectly clear, Jeffrey. You and I will never be."

Jeffrey got up and stood before her with a profound sense of sadness. "I loved you, Margot. More than Burt or anyone else ever could." And then he turned and walked out.

Three weeks later, he was sitting in the back office of his boat rental shop. As he sealed the large Manila envelope, that song kept playing in his head. It was the one where he and Margot danced, cheek-to-cheek to, at Gilby's.

"Now you're just somebody that I used to know..."

Jeffrey Holt stood up and carried the unmarked parcel to the front desk. "Sandy, can you make sure and give this to the postman when he comes in to deliver the mail..."

CHAPTER 64

Heller was present during all three trials: Margarita Magnuson, James McAvee, and Jeffrey Holt. When Margot's trial came to an end and she was being escorted out of the courtroom in handcuffs, the agent siphoned his way through the crowd of lawyers and reporters to ask her something that was weighing on his mind.

"Of all the places you could have escaped to, why on earth would you pick Bermuda?"

The moment she heard that, her eyes rose to meet his, and a smile formed across her face. Then, she uttered something the agent remembered hearing long ago. They were the exact same words his mother had said to him the day he found her.

"People often hide in plain sight because, deep down, they secretly want to be found."

EPILOGUE

Margarita Magnuson and James McAvee were found guilty of embezzlement, money fraud, and conspiracy to commit fraud, as well as some lesser offenses, and sentenced to serve a combined total of thirty-five years in prison in addition to some pretty hefty fines.

Margarita's parents were awarded temporary custody of her baby pending the outcome of the trial.

Jeffrey Holt was the last to be tried. He eventually confessed to having sent the photos and supplying the evidence that led the FBI to make their arrests. Therefore, he got off the easiest, with only three years' probation for his part in acting as an accomplice to the hoax.

Pending the outcome of the trial, Holt filed a civil lawsuit of his own, requesting that the court allow a paternity test to be taken to determine the father of Margarita's child. As a result, Jeffrey was indeed proven to be the father and was subsequently awarded full custody of his little daughter, Margaret, who, except for the blond hair and blue eyes, was the spitting image of her mother.

Since virtually all of Magnuson's funds had gone missing, as Executor and Trustee of Magnuson's estate, Jacques Gagnon was forced to liquidate most of Magnuson's assets, including the yacht, the Miami mansion, and his New York penthouse, in order to compensate his "creditors." This left very little for Burt's family.

Mr. Gagnon was later captured while attempting to flee the country and was arrested for being involved in Burt Magnuson's money laundering scheme, and was sentenced to jail for a very long time. Consequently, this also led to an investigation into Burton Magnuson's "accidental" demise.

Meredith Magnuson had no recourse but to sell her Connecticut ranch and face her peers by moving back to New York into a significantly smaller apartment. Her daughter, Kathryn, became engaged to the son of a wealthy racehorse owner and breeder. Her son, Robert's, "business venture" fizzled out after he snorted all the money his father had given him, and he is currently living somewhere on the streets of New York.

All charges were dropped against Charles Langford when he was proven innocent of embezzlement and was immediately released from prison. Upon his release, his wife, Bethany, filed for divorce. He moved back to Boston without her, and she stayed in New York, where she was awarded a Pulitzer Prize in the category of Investigative Reporting for her article in *The Architectural Investigator*, entitled "The Whitewashed World of Crime Design." Subsequent to that, she moved up the ladder to become Editor in Chief.

Dana made a lot of money on a new dating app she started strictly for lesbians, called *The Girls' Locker Room*. She moved into a large condo in the Columbus area and is living happily with her partner, whom she met on her own website. Ironically, the person she met was someone who had attended Ellison High School the same year she did, but who Dana had overlooked because she was too busy obsessing over Margot.

Doris has since adopted two more cats and continues to be miserable and single.

Rachel remarried, and with the help of in vitro fertilization, eventually gave birth to triplets. A year later, she was surprised to hear she was pregnant again, this time, without the help of in vitro fertilization.

Jorge quit working for the cruise line and returned to

his wife and four kids in his homeland of Bermuda. He is now employed as a waiter for the Spa & Poolside Dining at the Rosewood Bermuda Hotel.

Trish Dearden contacted James McAvee in prison and has offered him a place to stay when he gets out.

As for Special Agent Richard Heller, he has since retired to a peaceful lakeside retreat in upstate New York and is on his way to publishing his first mystery novel, which involves an FBI agent pursuing an elusive femme fatale. For the sake of authenticity, he has had to maintain weekly visitations with Margarita Kazlauskas (who filed to reinstate her maiden name) to provide him insight into the deviously genius mind of his beautiful protagonist.

ACKNOWLEDGEMENTS

I want to extend a special thank you to my good friend and avid reader, Elizabeth Buchler, for spending much of the winter months going through each and every chapter with me.

I'd like to thank my husband, Bill, whose intellectual critique saw things that no one else would notice.

Finally, to Karen Fuller of World Castle Publishing, thank you for everything that you do and for producing a standout copy of my book.

ABOUT THE AUTHOR

Maria was born in the Republic of San Marino, an enclave in the Apennine Mountains of northern Italy. It is one of the smallest independent states in Europe. At the age of five, she immigrated to the United States with her family and settled in the Midwest. After raising three children and living on the East Coast as well as the West Coast, she and her husband retired to the state of Nevada. There she joined the High Sierra Writers, leading her to publish her first novel, *Chapter Thirteen*, which earned her the Silver Literary Titan award.

Reunion Cruise is her second novel.

www.ingramcontent.com/pod-product-compliance
Lightning Source LLC
Chambersburg PA
CBHW050546260626
47157CB00002B/463